STRAY DOGS

IMAGE COMICS PRESENTS

STRAY DOGS

Writer .... TONY FLEECS
Artist .... TRISH FORSTNER
Colorist .... BRAD SIMPSON
Layouts .... TONE RODRIGUEZ
Flatter .... LAUREN PERRY
Logo/Design .... LAUREN HERDA
Pre-Press .... GABRIELA DOWNIE

COVER BY
TRISH FORSTNER and TONY FLEECS

Stray Dogs Created by
TONY FLEECS and TRISH FORSTNER

STRAYDOGSCOMIC.COM

Chapter 1:
GOOD GIRL

ISBN, Standard Edition: 978-1-5343-1983-7 • ISBN, Izzy's Comics Exclusive: 978-1-5343-2154-0 • ISBN, Bry's Comics Exclusive: 978-1-5343-2155-7 • ISBN, Mutant Beaver/Trinity Comics Exclusive: 978-1-5343-2156-4 • ISBN, Bird City Comics Exclusive: 978-1-5343-2157-1 • ISBN, Kowabunga Comics Exclusive Variant A: 978-1-5343-2158-8 • ISBN, Kowabunga Comics Exclusive Variant B: 978-1-5343-2159-5 • ISBN, Collector's Paradise Exclusive: 978-1-5343-2160-1 • ISBN, Nerd Store Exclusive: 978-1-5343-2161-8 • ISBN, Third Eye Comics Exclusive Variant A: 978-1-5343-2162-5 • ISBN, Third Eye Comics Exclusive Variant B: 978-1-5343-2163-2 ISBN, Rainbow Comics Exclusive: 978-1-5343-2164-9 • ISBN, JJ's Comics Exclusive: 978-1-5343-2165-6 • ISBN, Rabbit Comics Exclusive: 978-1-5343-2166-3 ISBN, Black Cape Exclusive: 978-1-5343-2167-0 • ISBN, Indigo Exclusive: 978-1-5343-2151-9

IMAGE COMICS, INC. • Todd McFarlane: President • Jim Valentino: Vice President • Marc Silvestri: Chief Executive Officer • Erik Larsen: Chief Financial Officer • Robert Kirkman: Chief Operating Officer • Eric Stephenson: Publisher / Chief Creative Officer • Nicole Lapalme: Controller • Leanna Caunter: Accounting Analyst • Sue Korpela: Accounting & HR Manager • Marla Eizik: Talent Liaison • Jeff Boison: Director of Sales & Publishing Planning • Dirk Wood: Director of International Sales & Licensing • Alex Cox: Director of Direct Market Sales • Chloe Ramos: Book Market & Library Sales Manager • Emilio Bautista: Digital Sales Coordinator • Jon Schlaffman: Specialty Sales Coordinator • Kat Salazar: Director of PR & Marketing • Drew Fitzgerald: Marketing Content Associate • Heather Doornink: Production Director • Drew Gill: Art Director • Hilary DiLoreto: Print Manager • Tricia Ramos: Traffic Manager • Melissa Gifford: Content Manager • Erika Schnatz: Senior Production Artist • Ryan Brewer: Production Artist • Deanna Phelps: Production Artist • IMAGECOMICS.COM

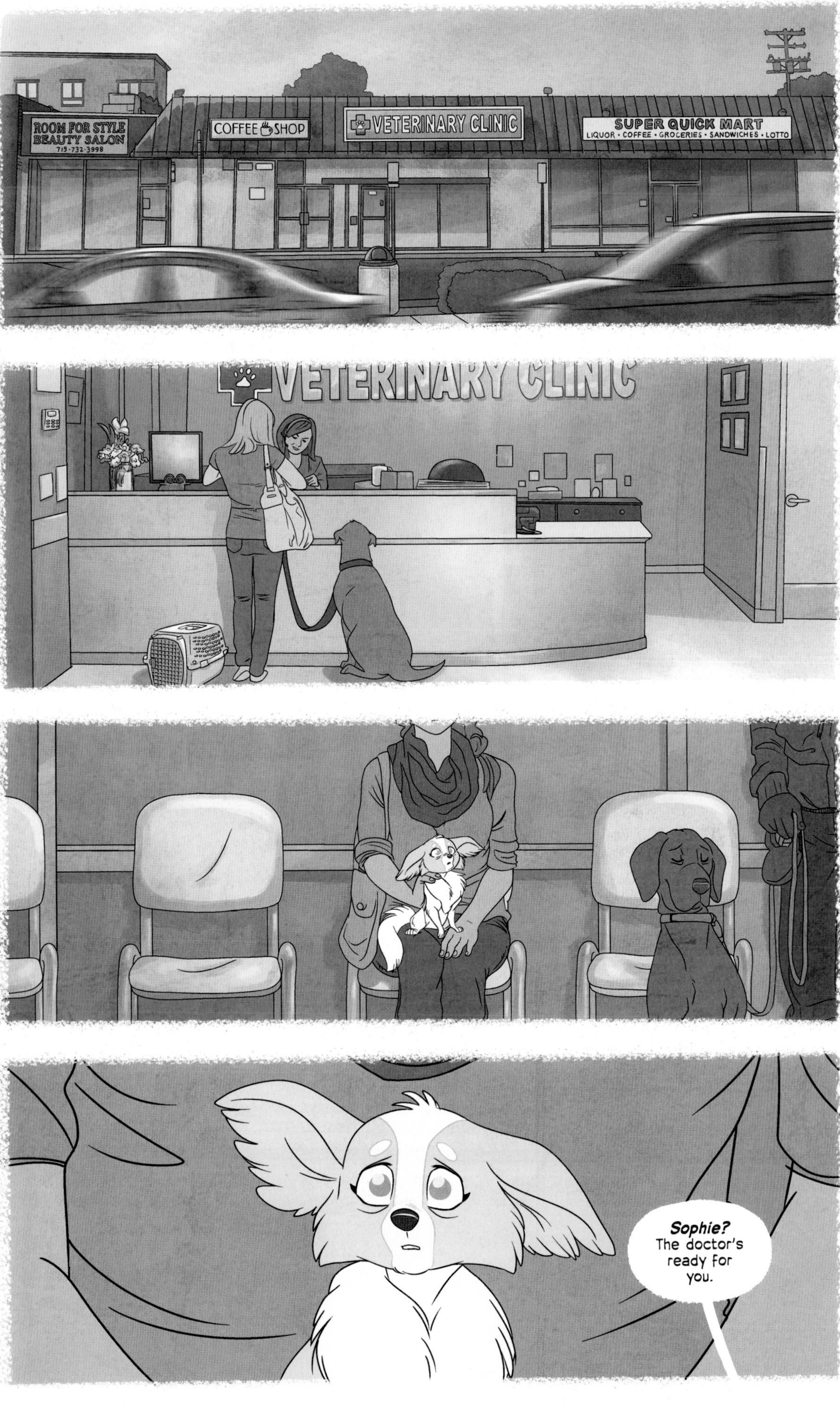
ROOM FOR STYLE
BEAUTY SALON
719-732-3998
COFFEE SHOP
VETERINARY CLINIC
SUPER QUICK MART
LIQUOR • COFFEE • GROCERIES • SANDWICHES • LOTTO
VETERINARY CLINIC
Sophie? The doctor's ready for you.

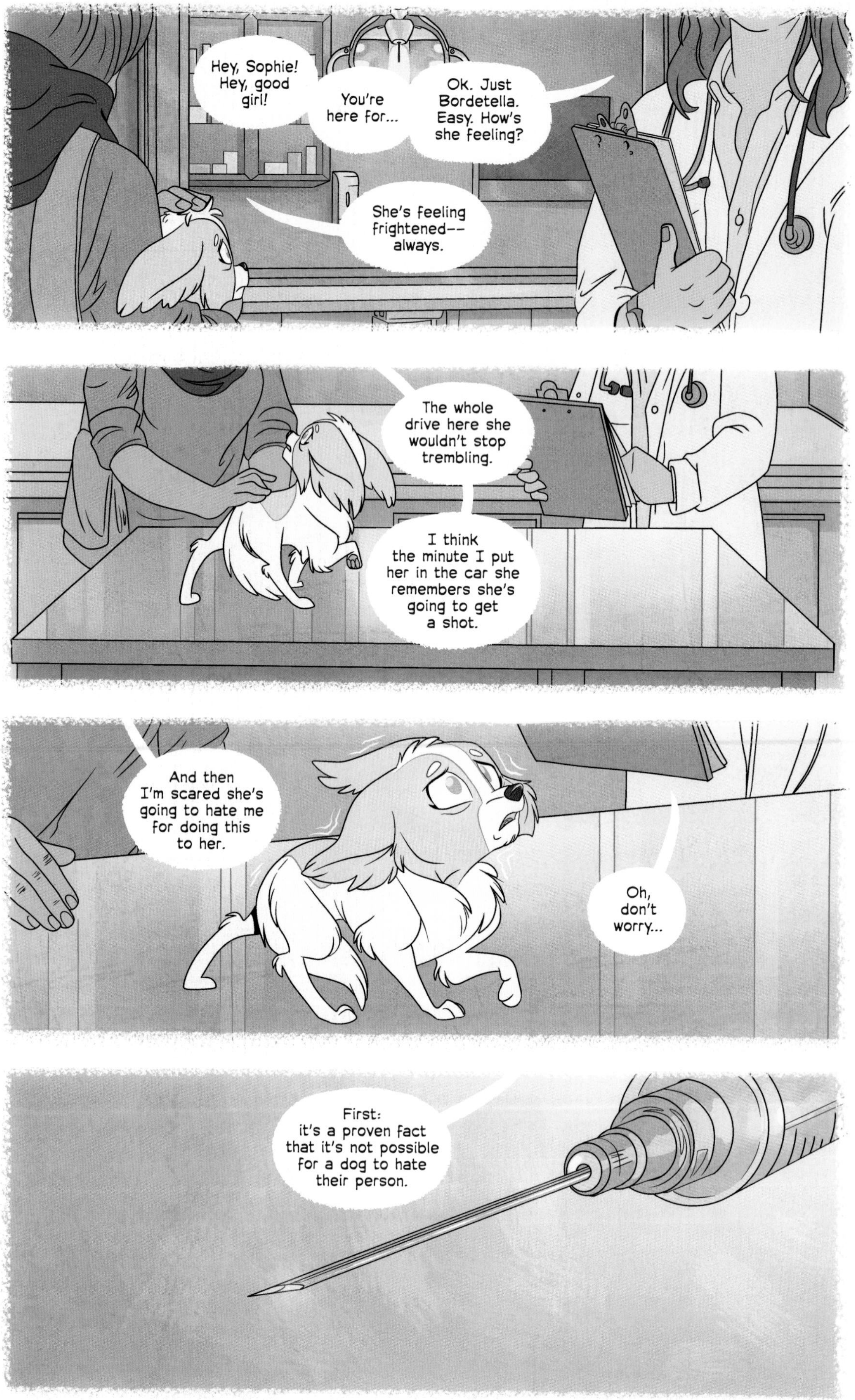
Hey, Sophie! Hey, good girl!
You're here for...
Ok. Just Bordetella. Easy. How's she feeling?
She's feeling frightened-- always.
The whole drive here she wouldn't stop trembling.
I think the minute I put her in the car she remembers she's going to get a shot.
And then I'm scared she's going to hate me for doing this to her.
Oh, don't worry...
First: it's a proven fact that it's not possible for a dog to hate their person.

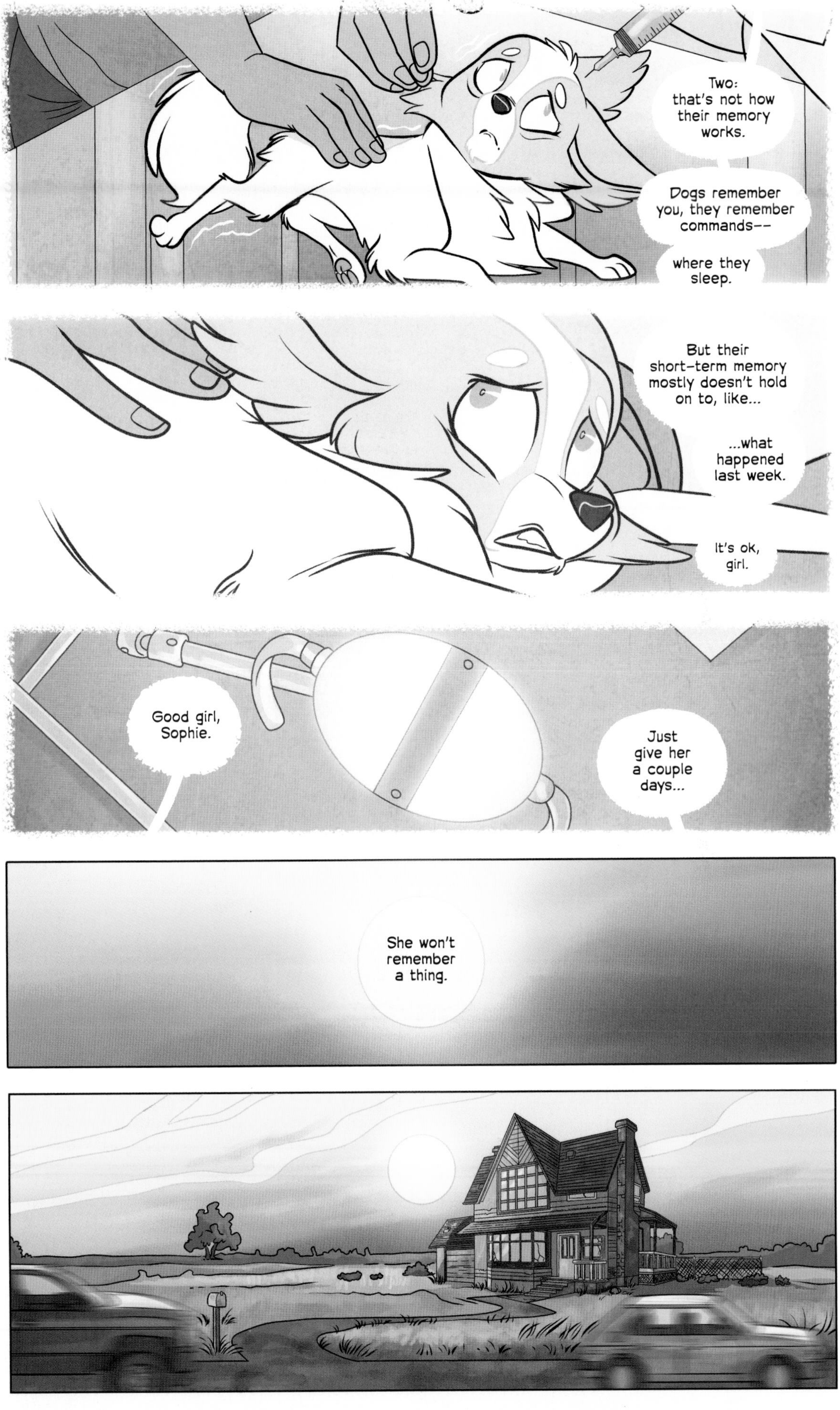
Two:
that's not how
their memory
works.
Dogs remember
you, they remember
commands--
where they
sleep.
But their
short-term memory
mostly doesn't hold
on to, like...
...what
happened
last week.
It's ok,
girl.
Good girl,
Sophie.
Just
give her
a couple
days...
She won't
remember
a thing.

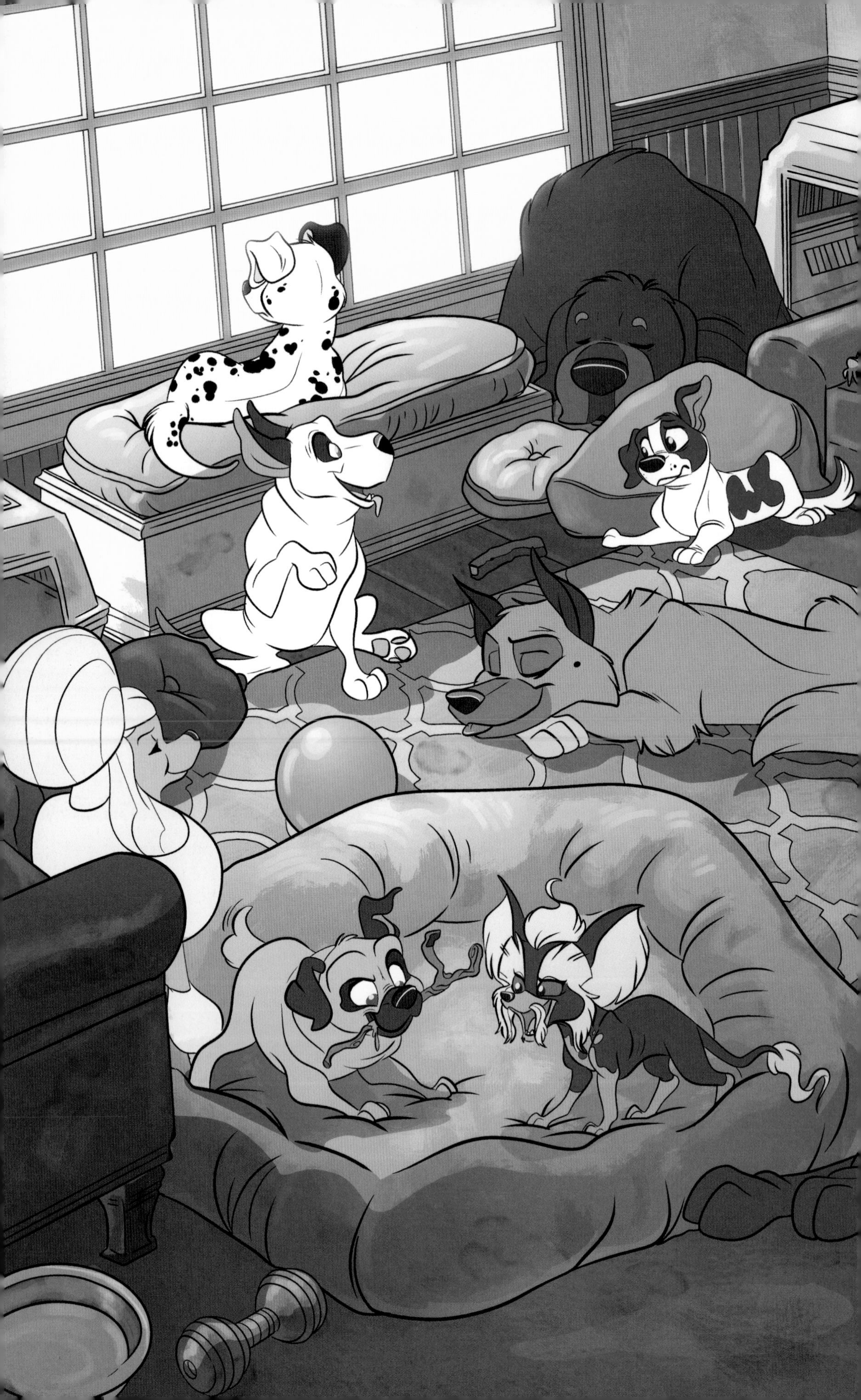

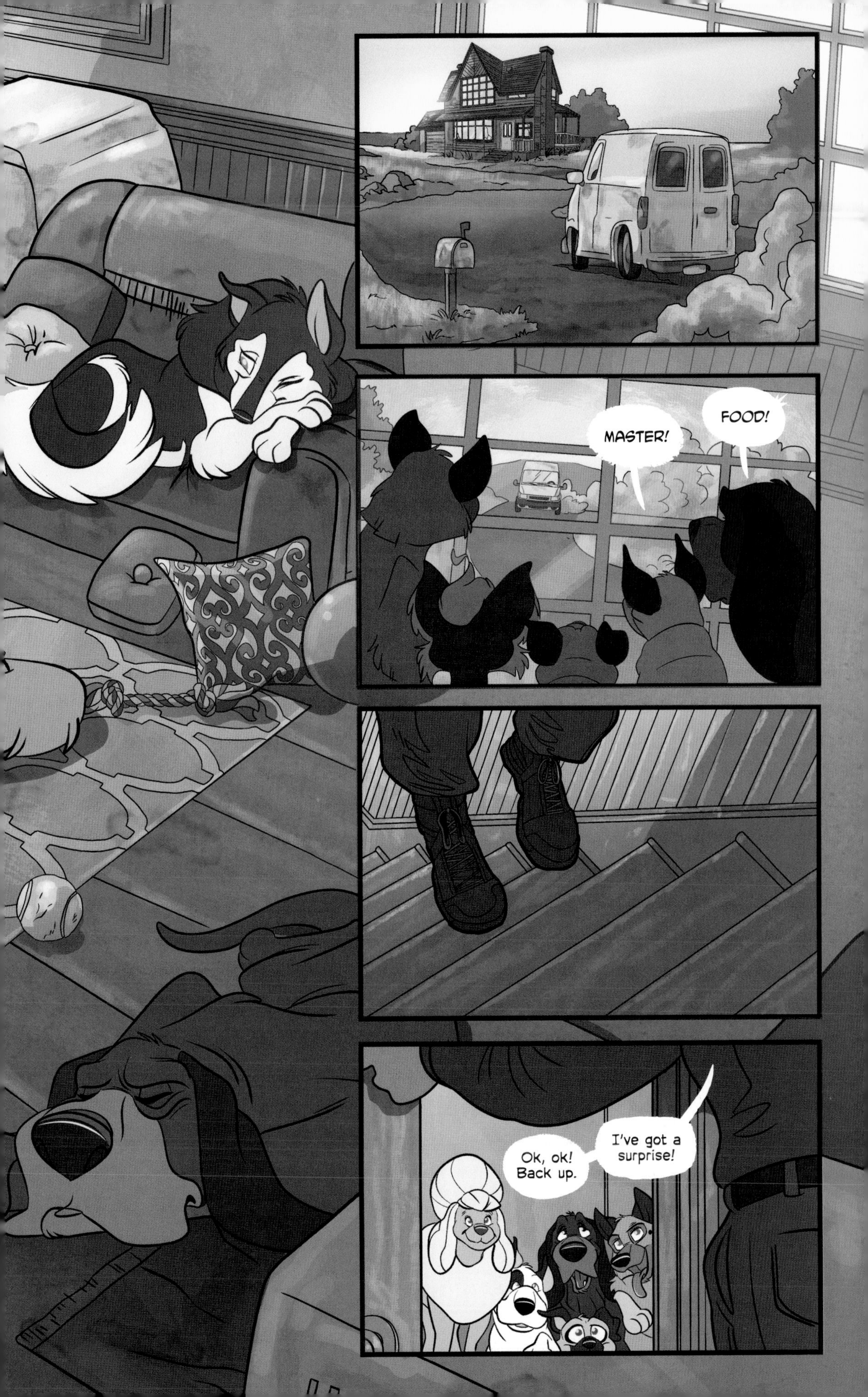
MASTER!
FOOD!
Ok, ok! Back up.
I've got a surprise!

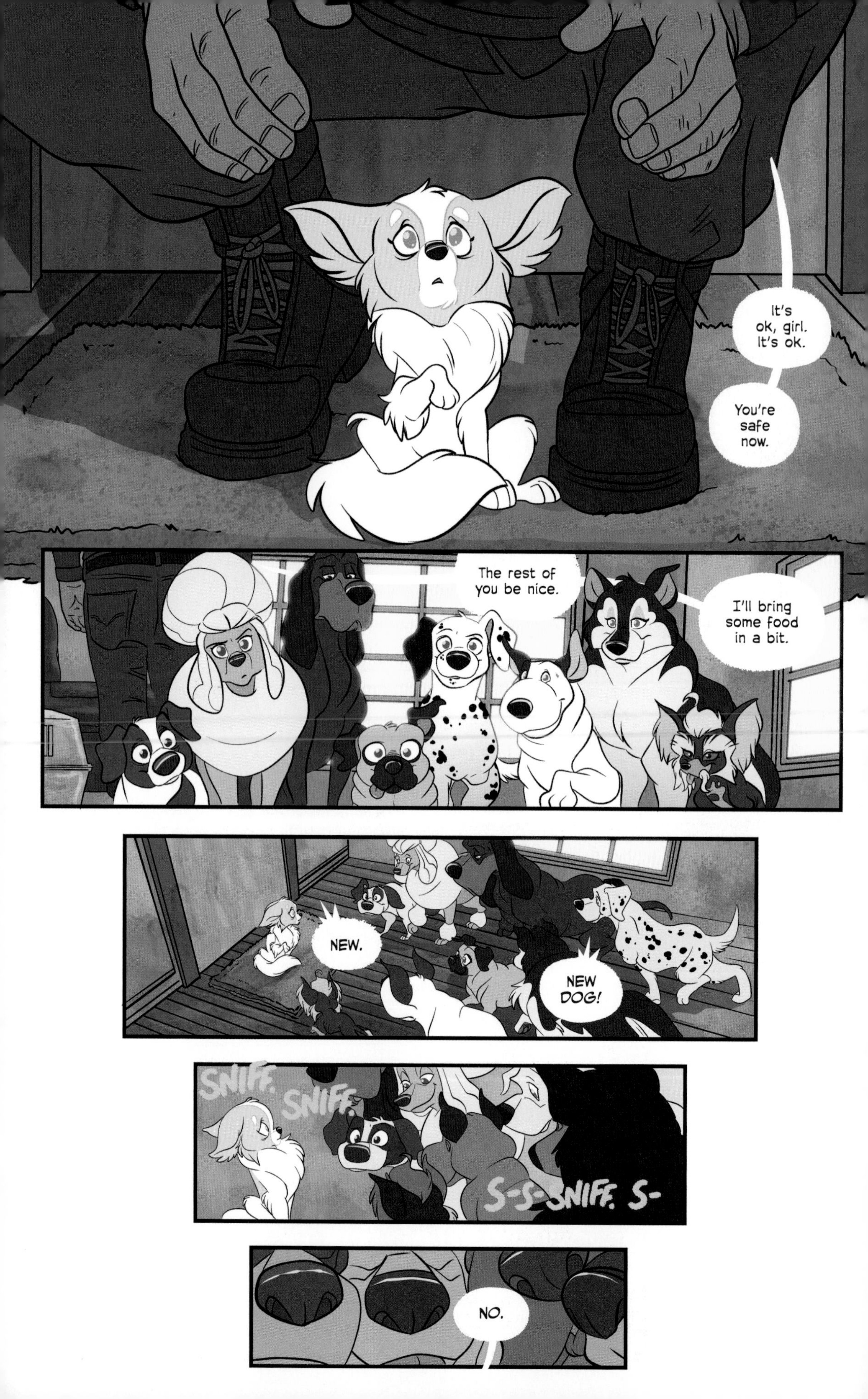
It's ok, girl. It's ok.
You're safe now.
The rest of you be nice.
I'll bring some food in a bit.
NEW.
NEW DOG!
SNIFF. SNIFF.
S-S-SNIFF. S-
NO.

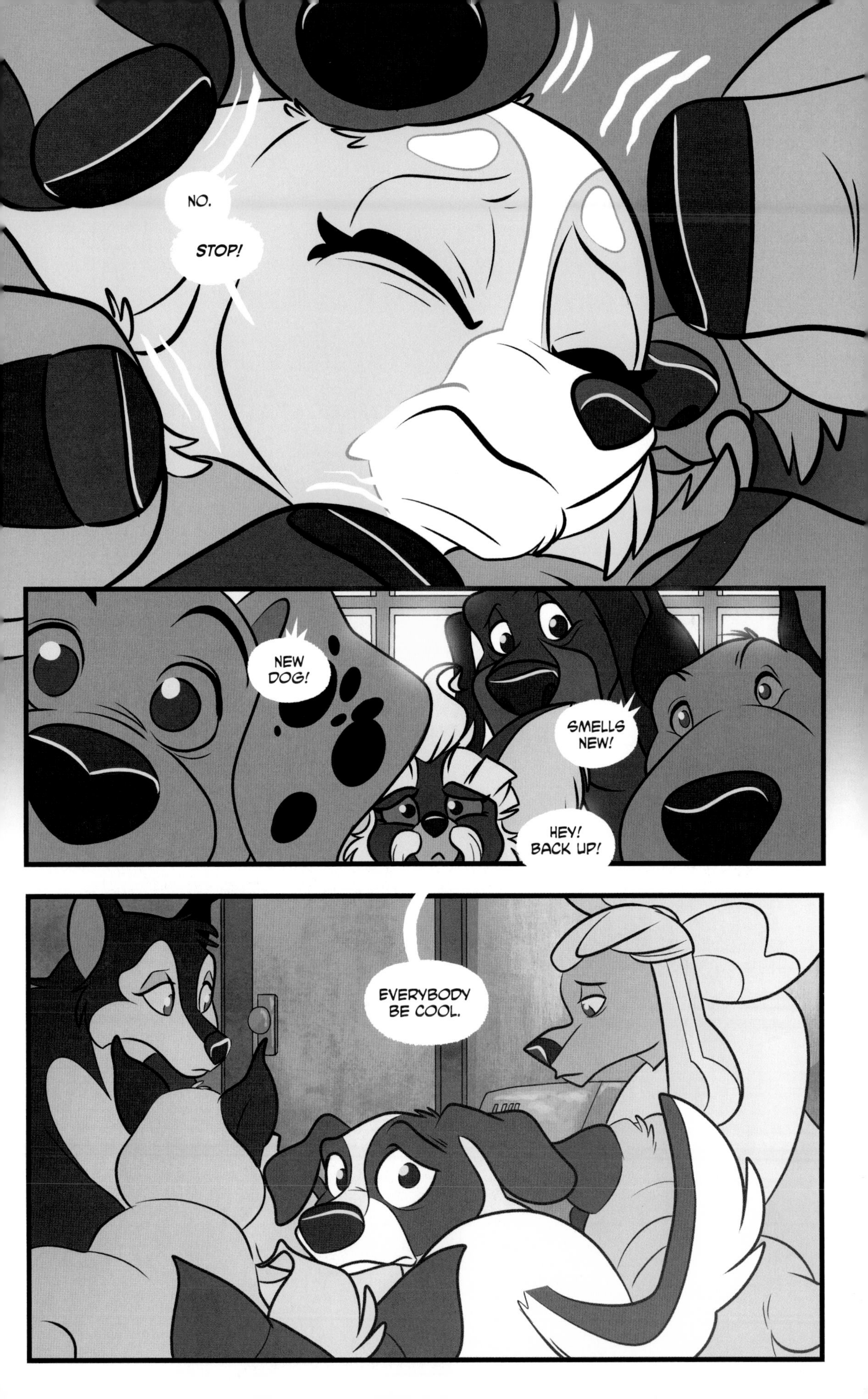
NO.
STOP!
NEW DOG!
SMELLS NEW!
HEY! BACK UP!
EVERYBODY BE COOL.

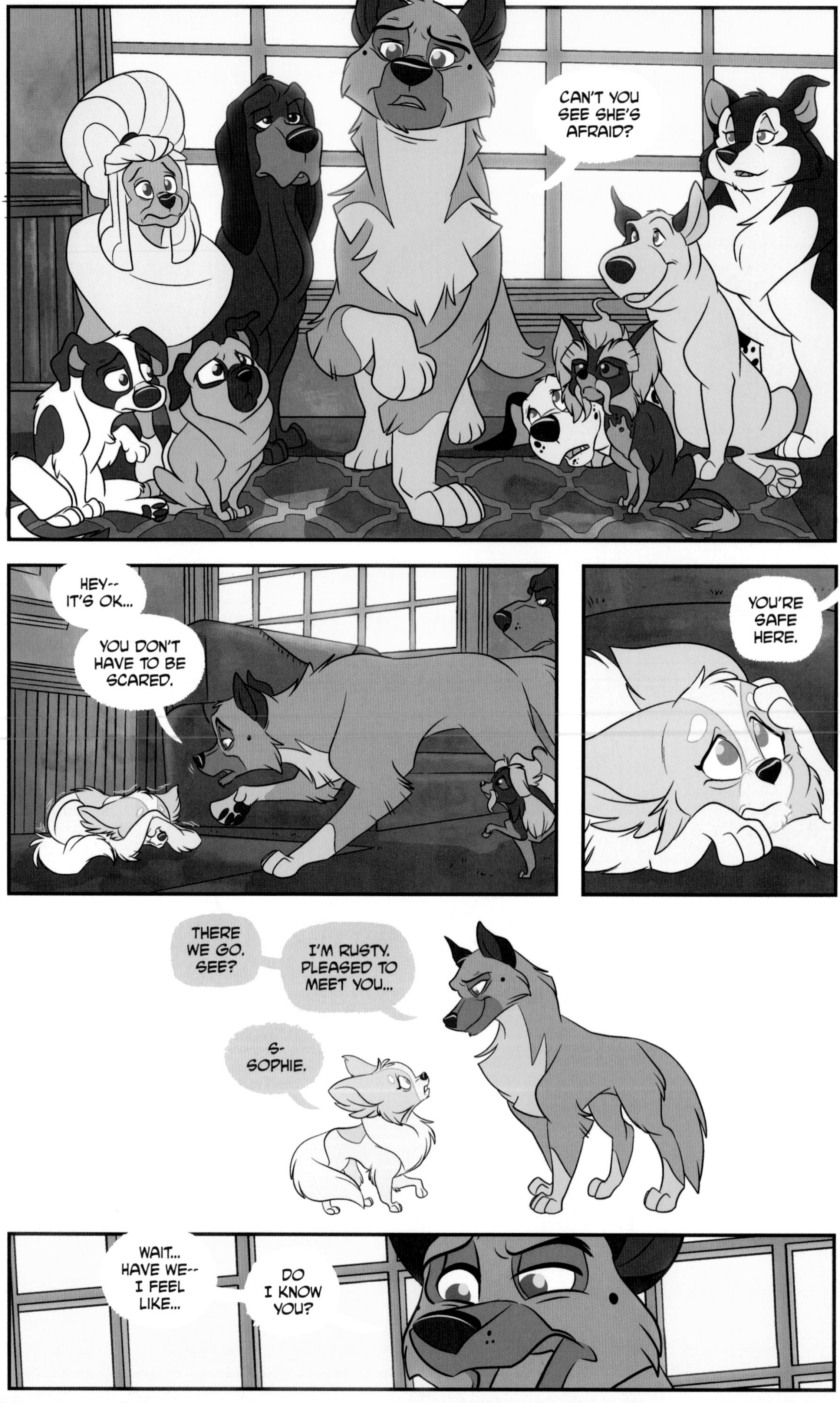
CAN'T YOU SEE SHE'S AFRAID?
HEY-- IT'S OK...
YOU DON'T HAVE TO BE SCARED.
YOU'RE SAFE HERE.
THERE WE GO. SEE?
I'M RUSTY. PLEASED TO MEET YOU...
S- SOPHIE.
WAIT... HAVE WE-- I FEEL LIKE...
DO I KNOW YOU?

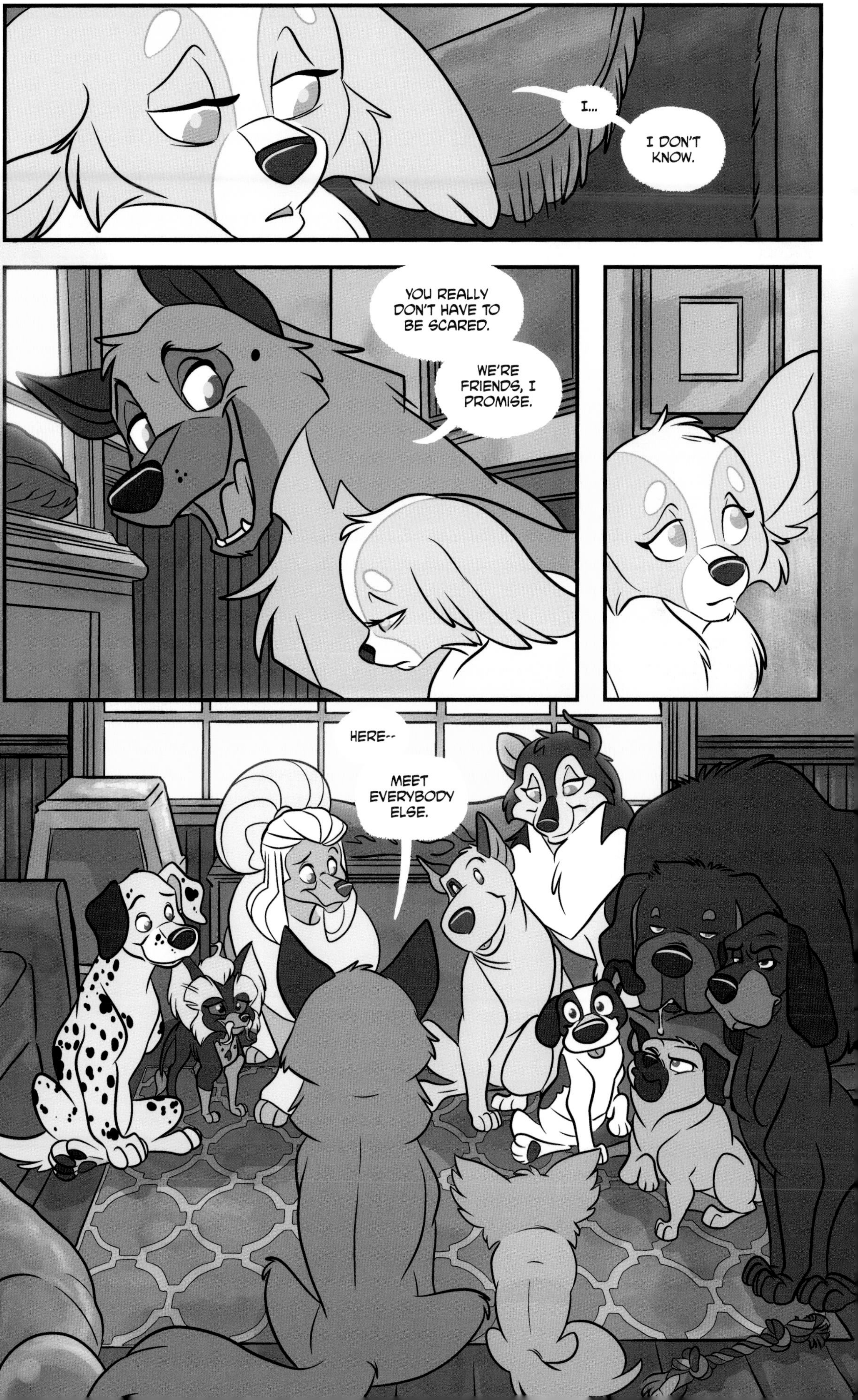
I...
I DON'T KNOW.
YOU REALLY DON'T HAVE TO BE SCARED.
WE'RE FRIENDS, I PROMISE.
HERE--
MEET EVERYBODY ELSE.

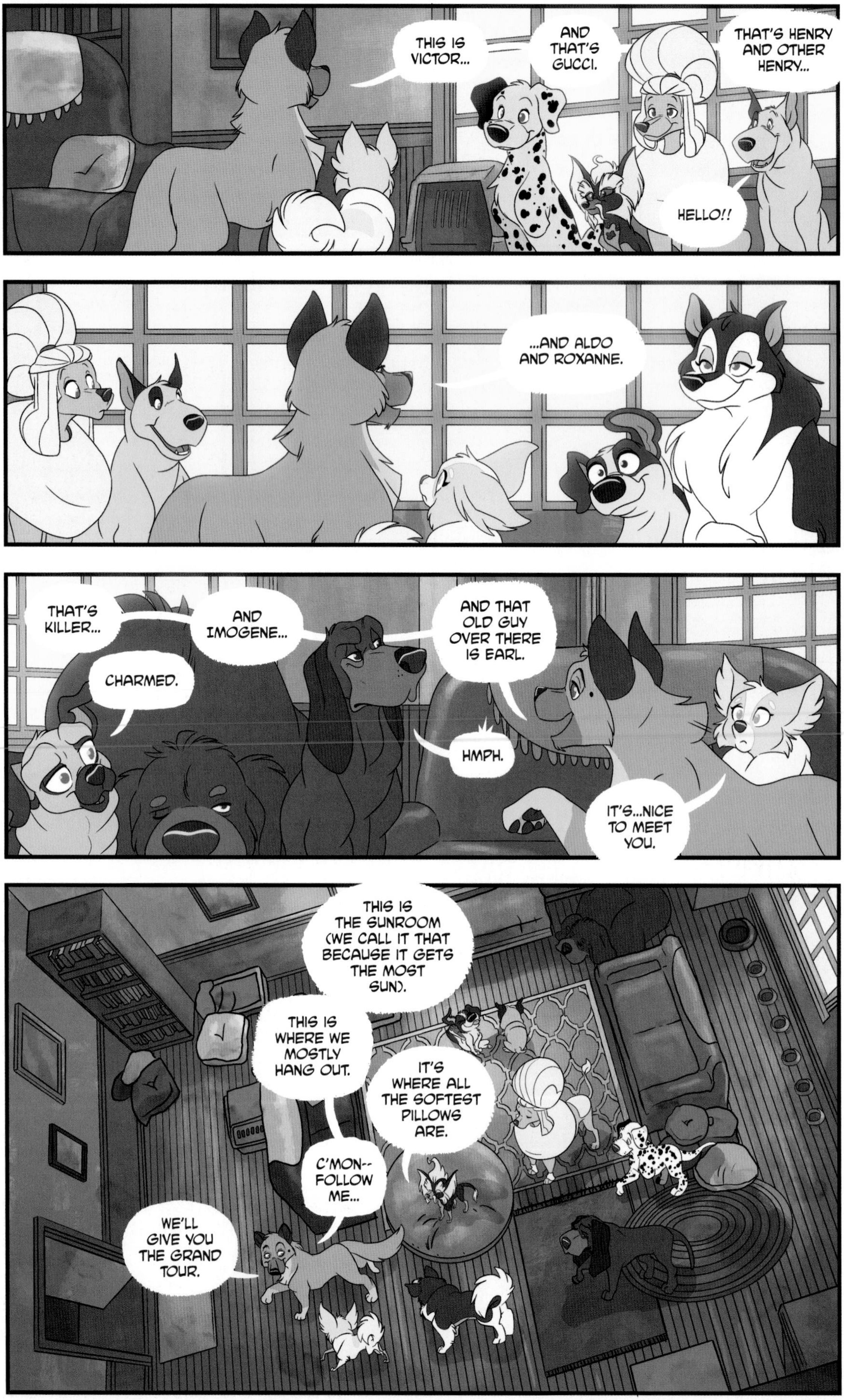
THIS IS VICTOR...
AND THAT'S GUCCI.
THAT'S HENRY AND OTHER HENRY...
HELLO!!
...AND ALDO AND ROXANNE.
THAT'S KILLER...
AND IMOGENE...
AND THAT OLD GUY OVER THERE IS EARL.
CHARMED.
HMPH.
IT'S...NICE TO MEET YOU.
THIS IS THE SUNROOM (WE CALL IT THAT BECAUSE IT GETS THE MOST SUN).
THIS IS WHERE WE MOSTLY HANG OUT.
IT'S WHERE ALL THE SOFTEST PILLOWS ARE.
C'MON--FOLLOW ME...
WE'LL GIVE YOU THE GRAND TOUR.

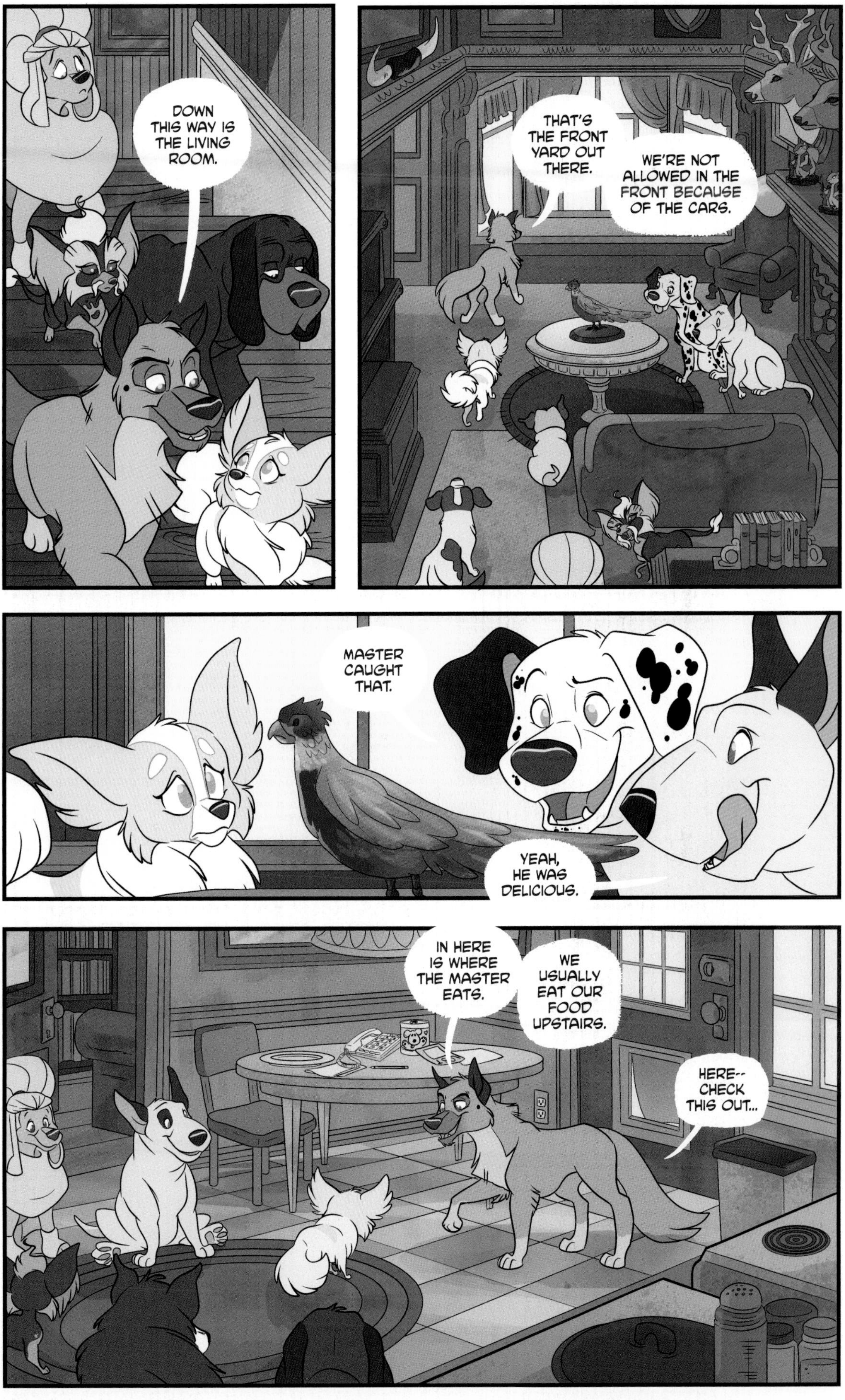
DOWN THIS WAY IS THE LIVING ROOM.
THAT'S THE FRONT YARD OUT THERE.
WE'RE NOT ALLOWED IN THE FRONT BECAUSE OF THE CARS.
MASTER CAUGHT THAT.
YEAH, HE WAS DELICIOUS.
IN HERE IS WHERE THE MASTER EATS.
WE USUALLY EAT OUR FOOD UPSTAIRS.
HERE-- CHECK THIS OUT...

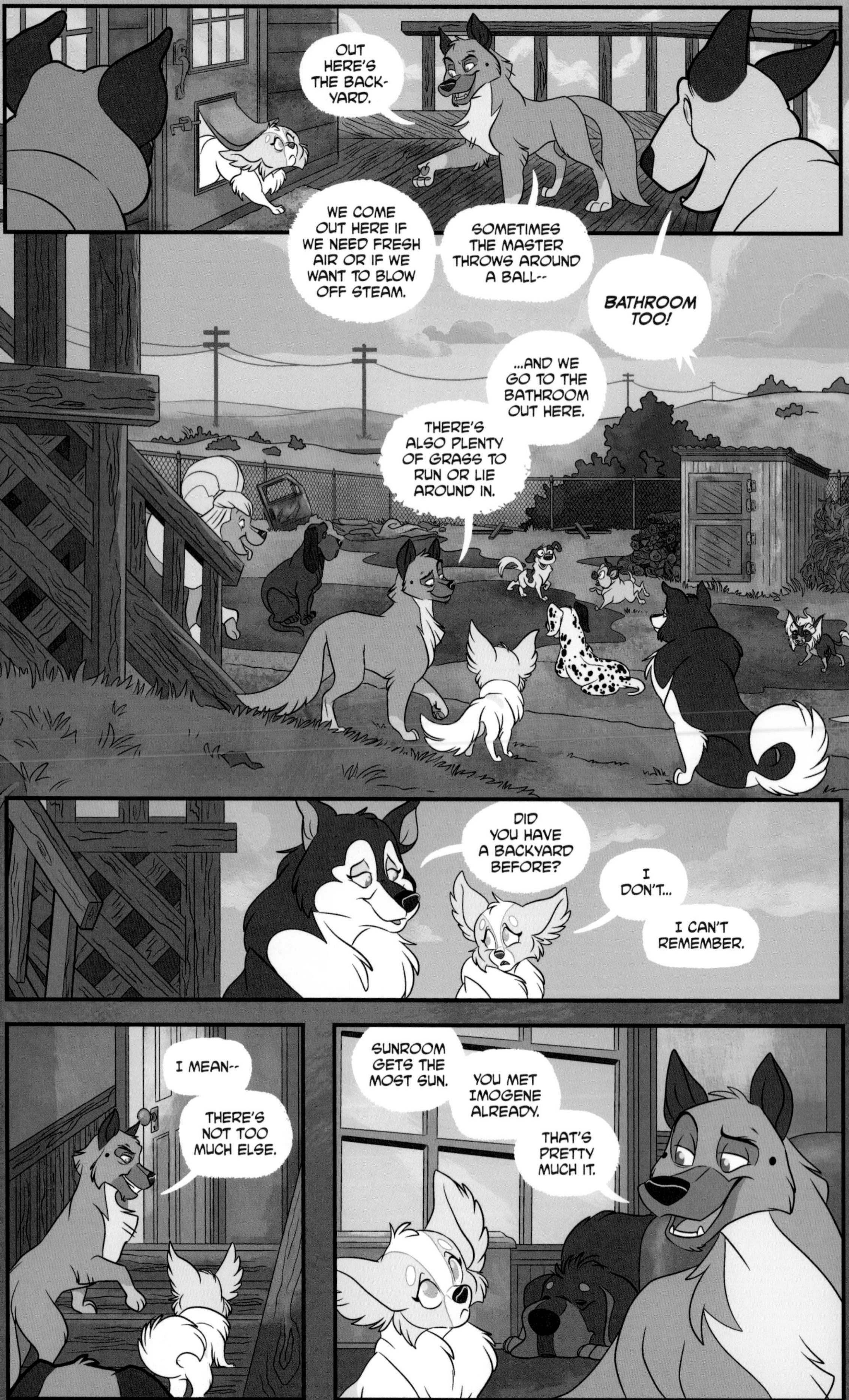
OUT HERE'S THE BACK-YARD.
WE COME OUT HERE IF WE NEED FRESH AIR OR IF WE WANT TO BLOW OFF STEAM.
SOMETIMES THE MASTER THROWS AROUND A BALL--
BATHROOM TOO!
...AND WE GO TO THE BATHROOM OUT HERE.
THERE'S ALSO PLENTY OF GRASS TO RUN OR LIE AROUND IN.
DID YOU HAVE A BACKYARD BEFORE?
I DON'T...
I CAN'T REMEMBER.
I MEAN--
THERE'S NOT TOO MUCH ELSE.
SUNROOM GETS THE MOST SUN.
YOU MET IMOGENE ALREADY.
THAT'S PRETTY MUCH IT.

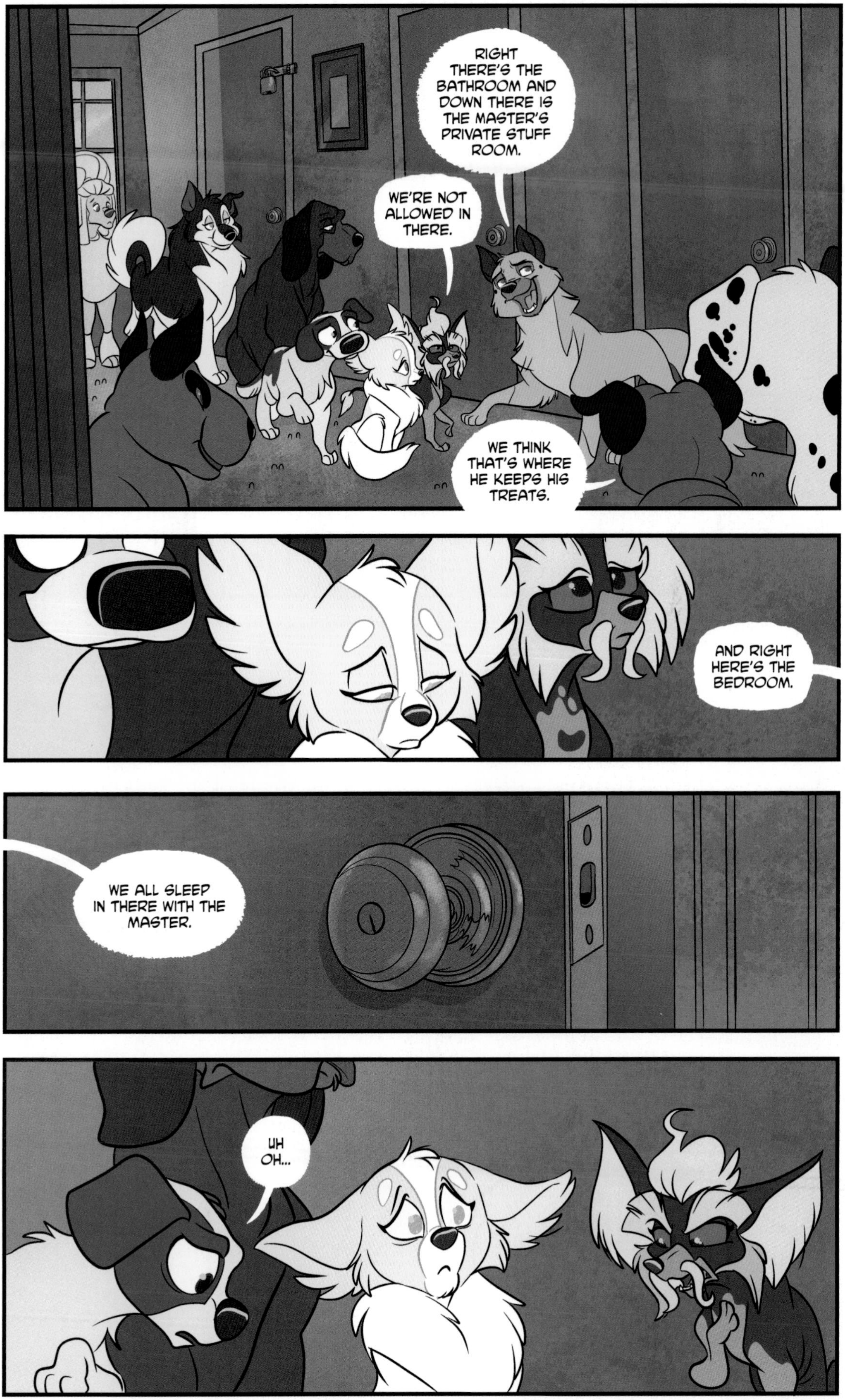
RIGHT THERE'S THE BATHROOM AND DOWN THERE IS THE MASTER'S PRIVATE STUFF ROOM.
WE'RE NOT ALLOWED IN THERE.
WE THINK THAT'S WHERE HE KEEPS HIS TREATS.
AND RIGHT HERE'S THE BEDROOM.
WE ALL SLEEP IN THERE WITH THE MASTER.
UH OH...

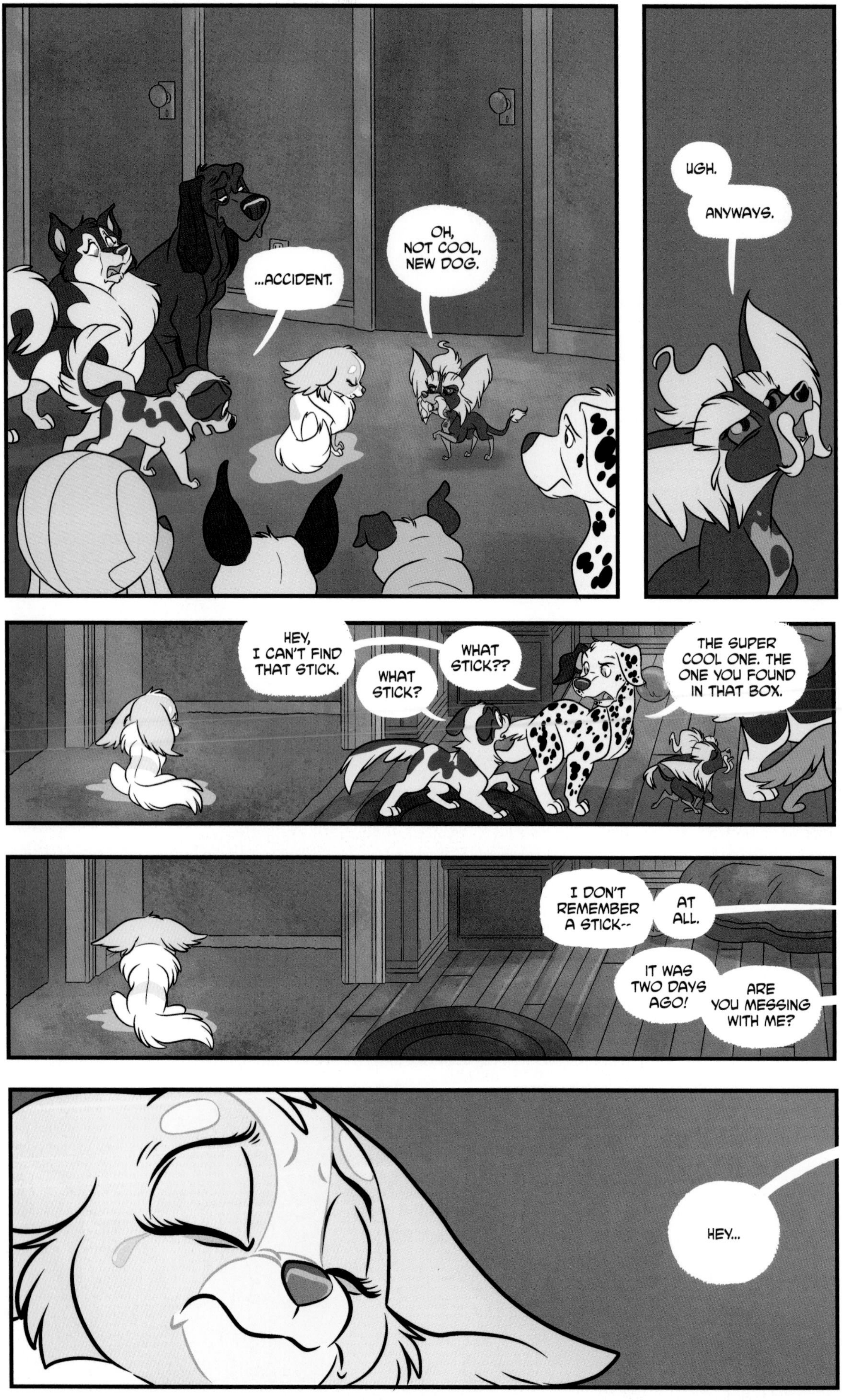
...ACCIDENT.
OH, NOT COOL, NEW DOG.
UGH.
ANYWAYS.
HEY, I CAN'T FIND THAT STICK.
WHAT STICK?
WHAT STICK??
THE SUPER COOL ONE. THE ONE YOU FOUND IN THAT BOX.
I DON'T REMEMBER A STICK--
AT ALL.
IT WAS TWO DAYS AGO!
ARE YOU MESSING WITH ME?
HEY...

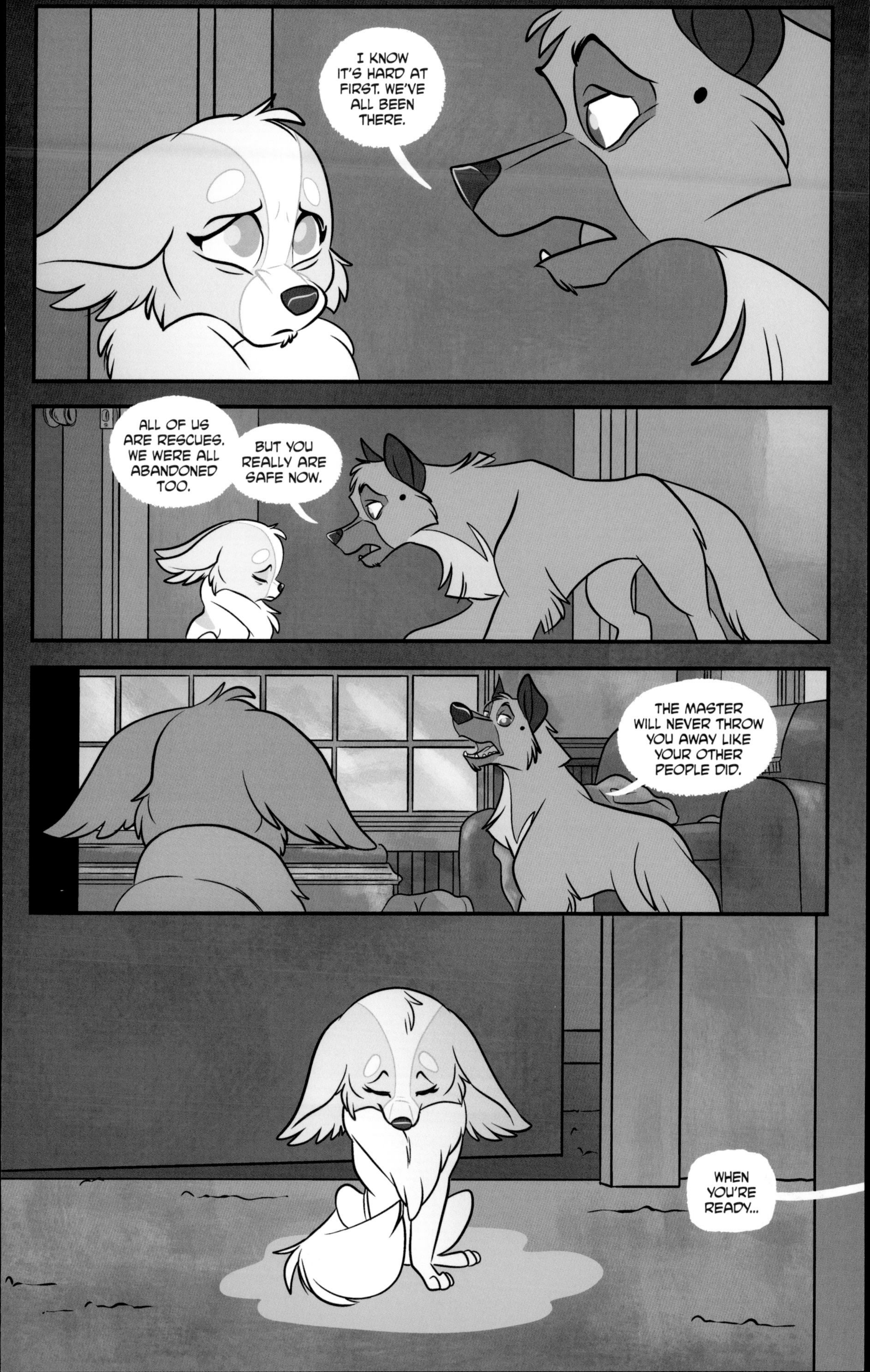
I KNOW IT'S HARD AT FIRST. WE'VE ALL BEEN THERE.
ALL OF US ARE RESCUES. WE WERE ALL ABANDONED TOO.
BUT YOU REALLY ARE SAFE NOW.
THE MASTER WILL NEVER THROW YOU AWAY LIKE YOUR OTHER PEOPLE DID.
WHEN YOU'RE READY...

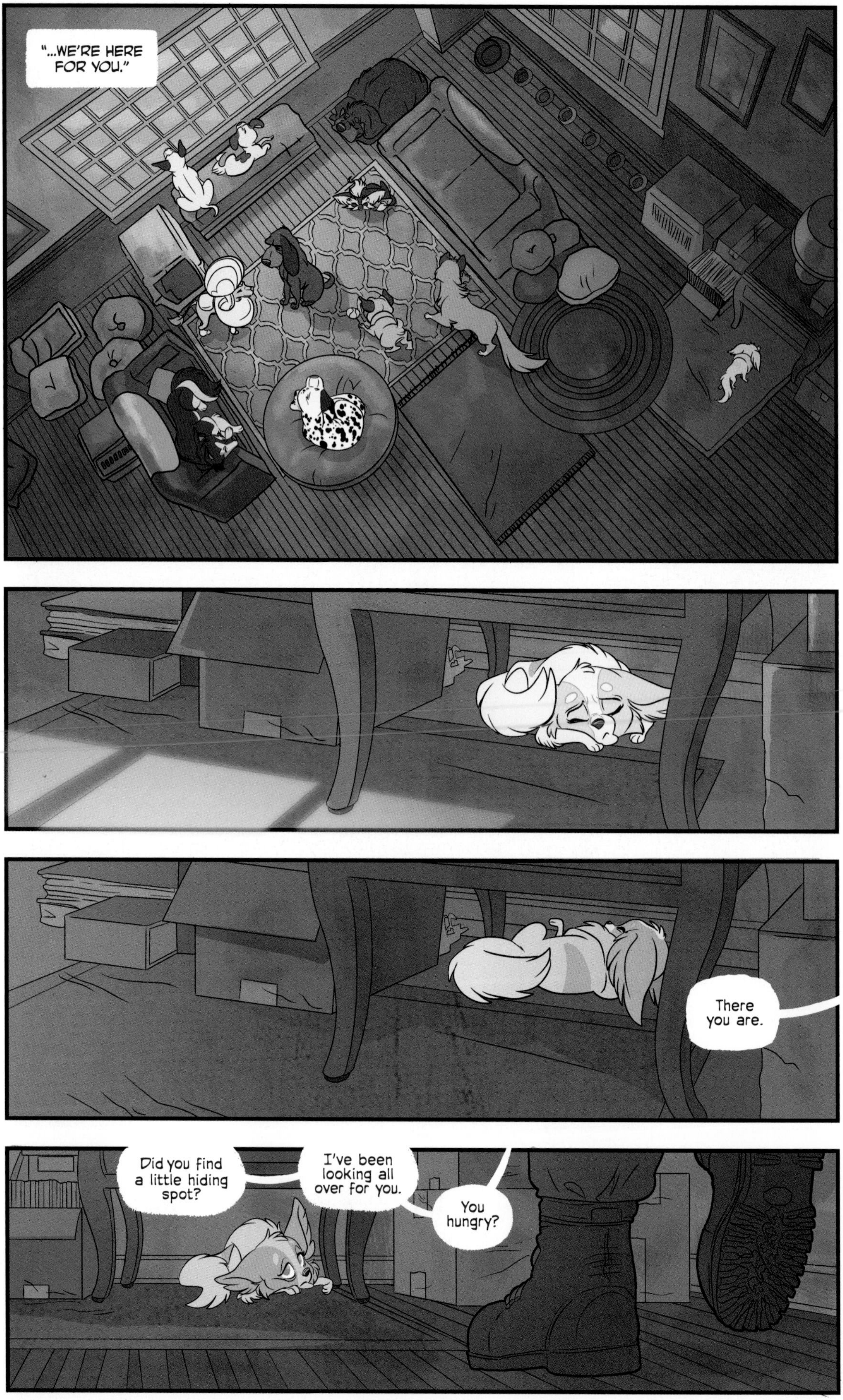
"...WE'RE HERE FOR YOU."
There you are.
Did you find a little hiding spot?
I've been looking all over for you.
You hungry?

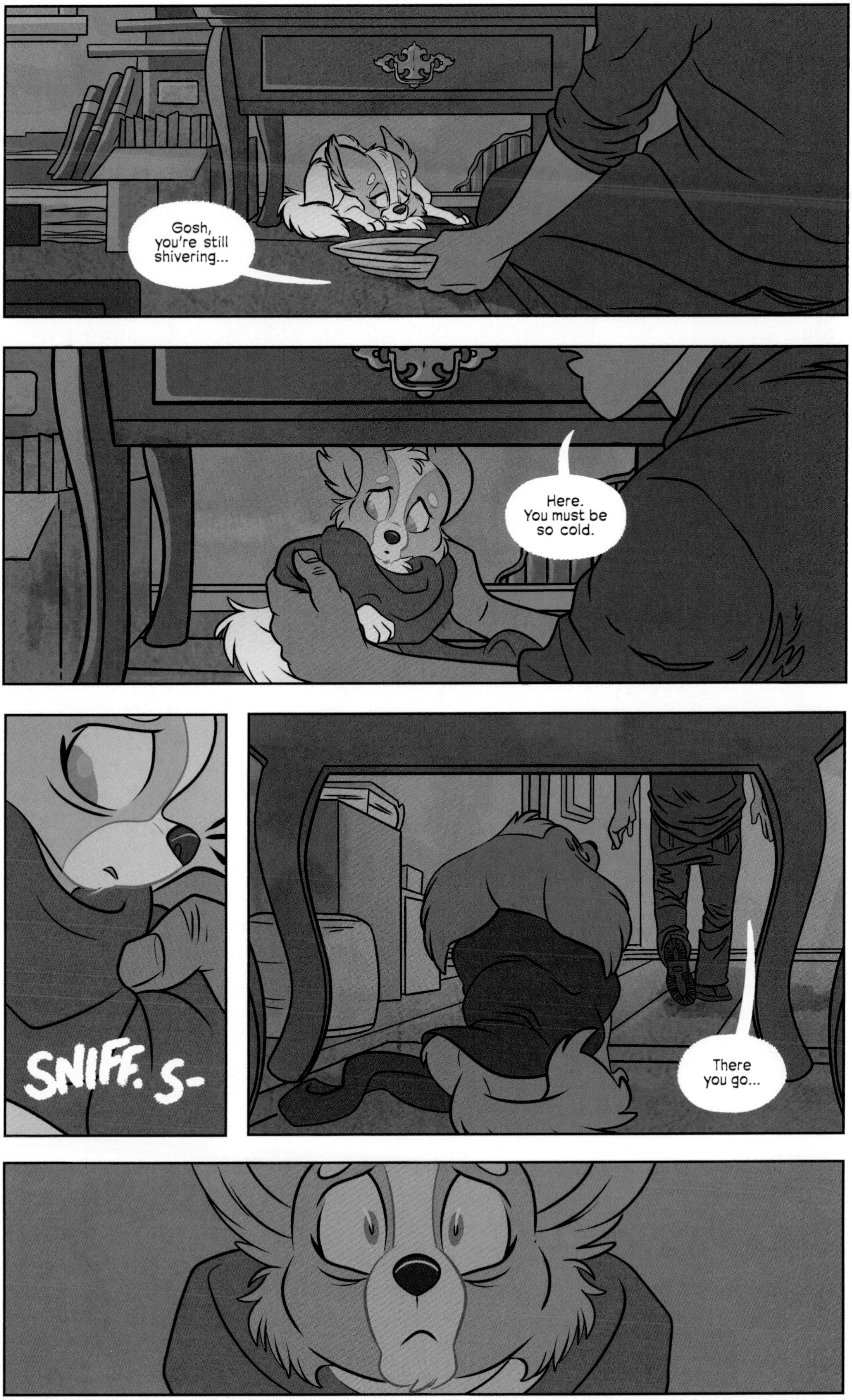
Gosh, you're still shivering...
Here. You must be so cold.
SNIFF. S-
There you go...

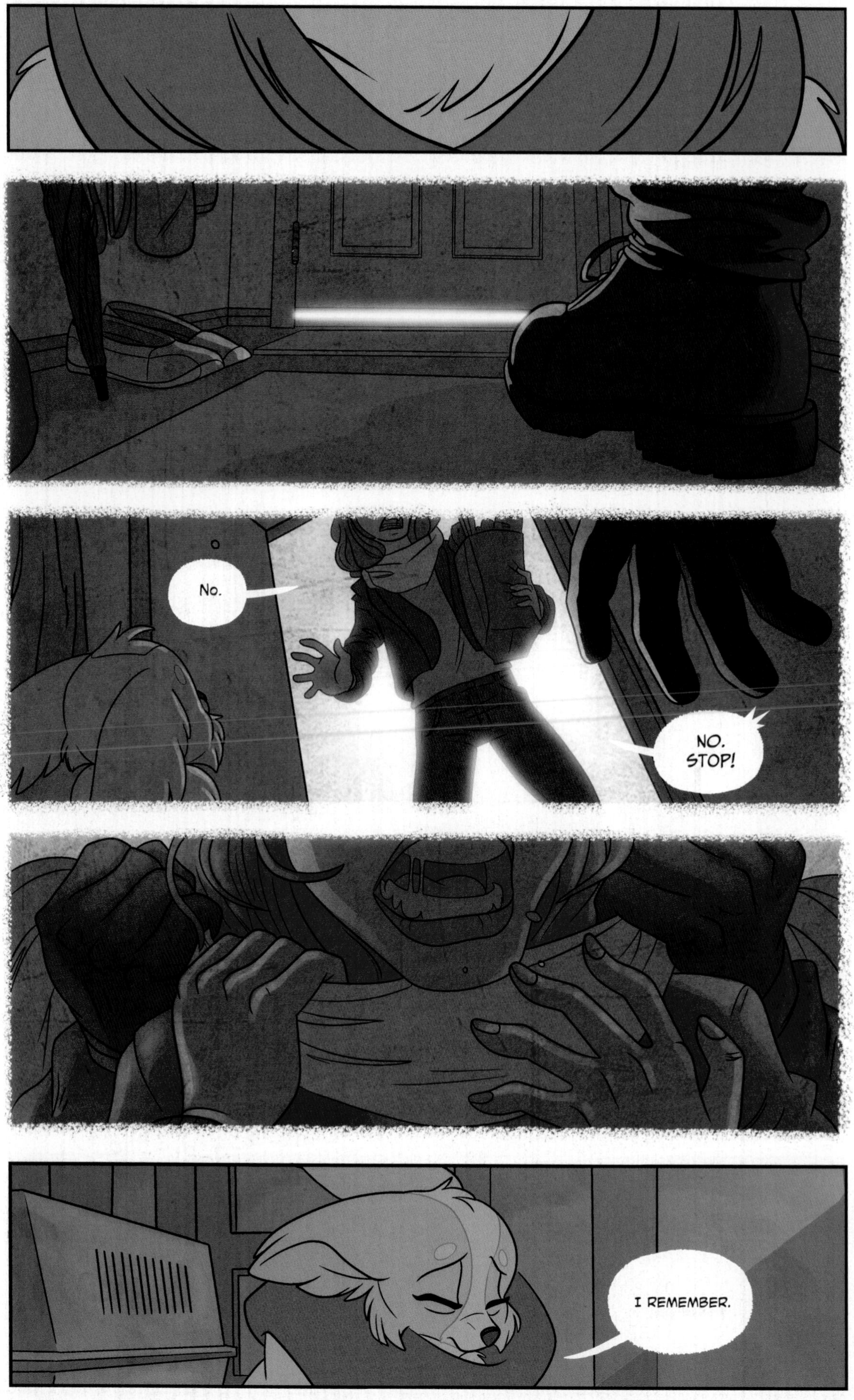
No.
NO. STOP!
I REMEMBER.

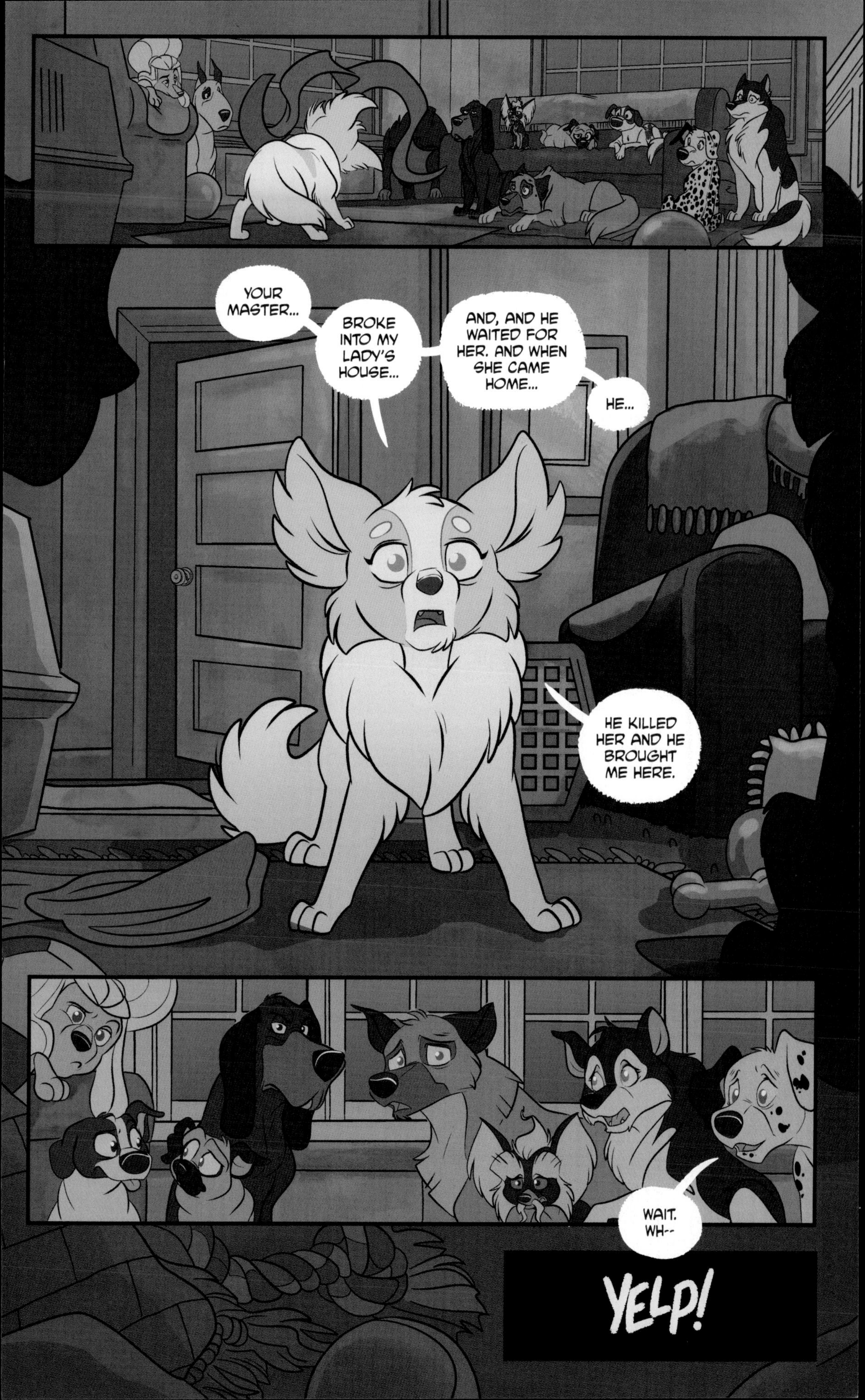
YOUR MASTER...
BROKE INTO MY LADY'S HOUSE...
AND, AND HE WAITED FOR HER. AND WHEN SHE CAME HOME...
HE...
HE KILLED HER AND HE BROUGHT ME HERE.
WAIT. WH--
YELP!

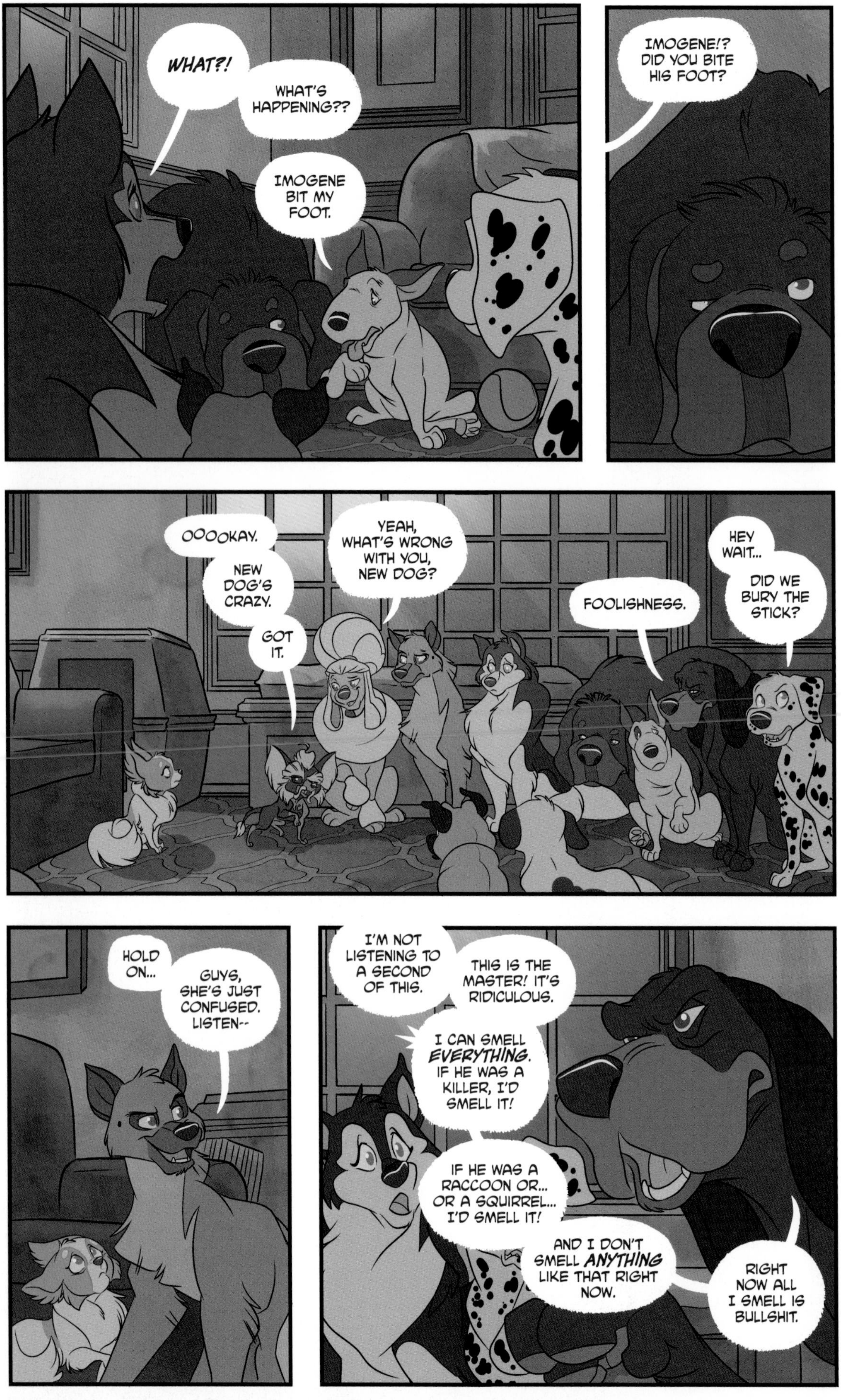
WHAT?!
WHAT'S HAPPENING??
IMOGENE BIT MY FOOT.
IMOGENE!? DID YOU BITE HIS FOOT?
OOOOKAY.
NEW DOG'S CRAZY.
GOT IT.
YEAH, WHAT'S WRONG WITH YOU, NEW DOG?
FOOLISHNESS.
HEY WAIT...
DID WE BURY THE STICK?
HOLD ON...
GUYS, SHE'S JUST CONFUSED. LISTEN--
I'M NOT LISTENING TO A SECOND OF THIS.
THIS IS THE MASTER! IT'S RIDICULOUS.
I CAN SMELL EVERYTHING. IF HE WAS A KILLER, I'D SMELL IT!
IF HE WAS A RACCOON OR... OR A SQUIRREL... I'D SMELL IT!
AND I DON'T SMELL ANYTHING LIKE THAT RIGHT NOW.
RIGHT NOW ALL I SMELL IS BULLSHIT.

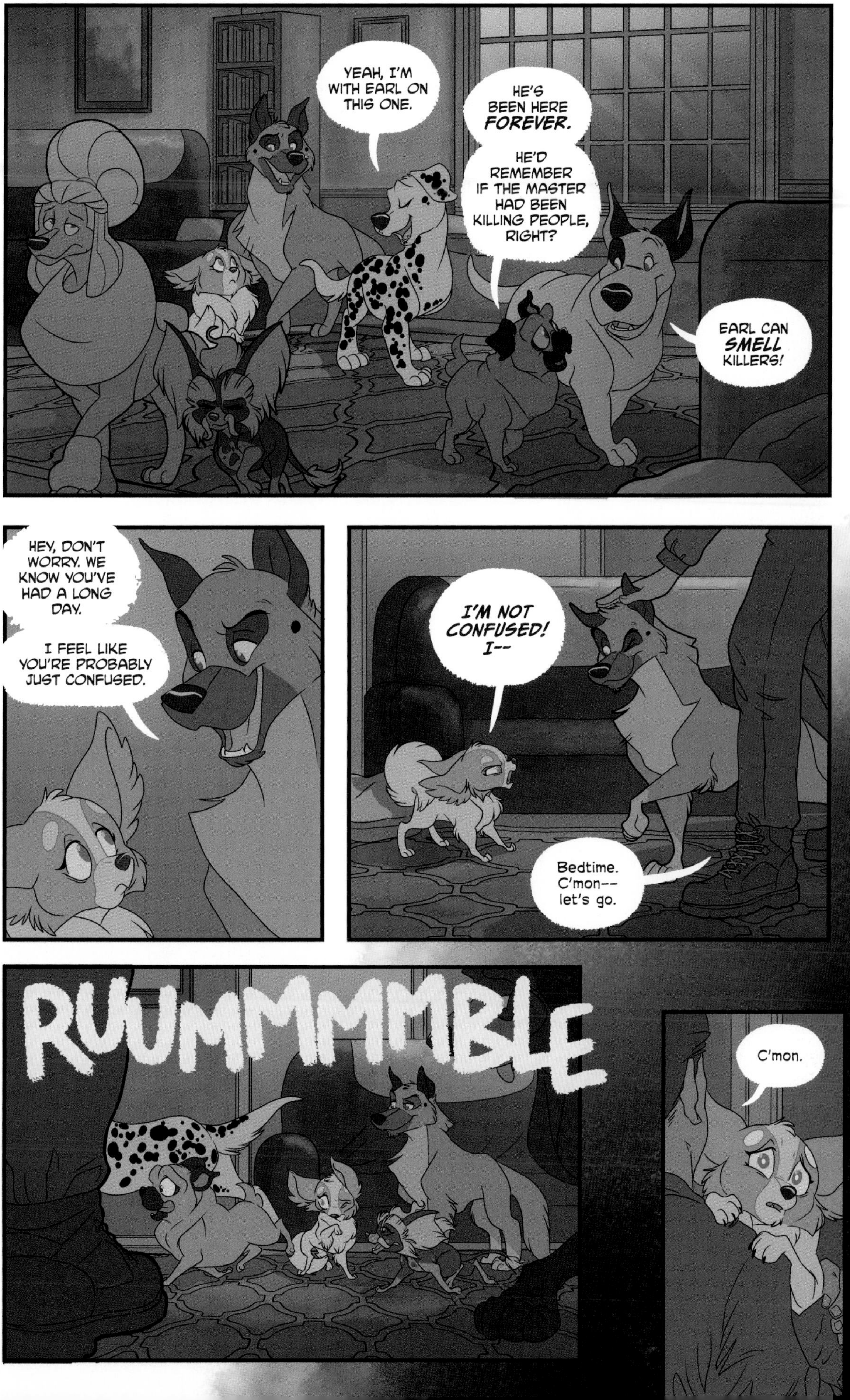
YEAH, I'M WITH EARL ON THIS ONE.
HE'S BEEN HERE FOREVER.
HE'D REMEMBER IF THE MASTER HAD BEEN KILLING PEOPLE, RIGHT?
EARL CAN SMELL KILLERS!
HEY, DON'T WORRY. WE KNOW YOU'VE HAD A LONG DAY.
I FEEL LIKE YOU'RE PROBABLY JUST CONFUSED.
I'M NOT CONFUSED! I--
Bedtime. C'mon-- let's go.
RUUMMMMBLE
C'mon.

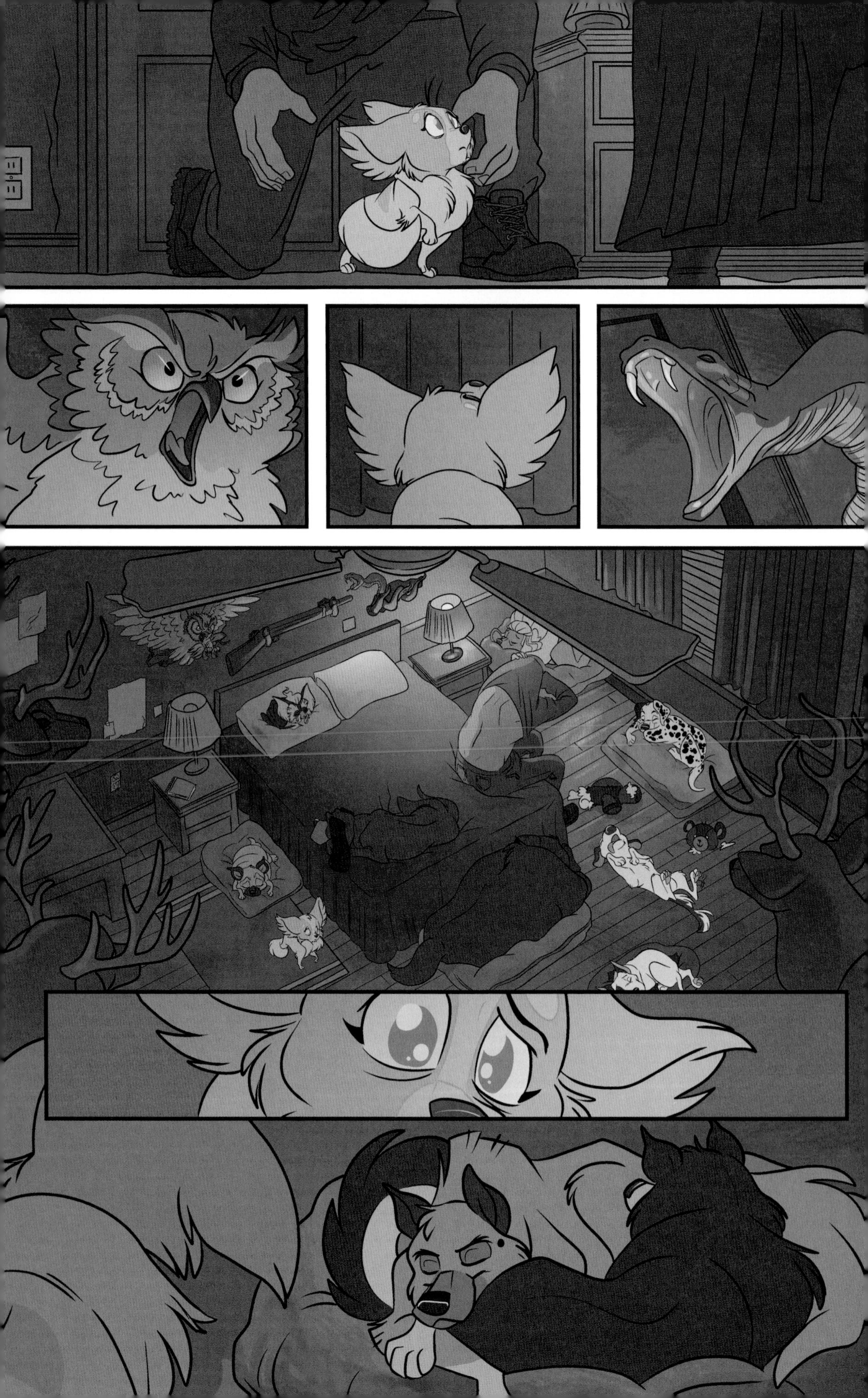

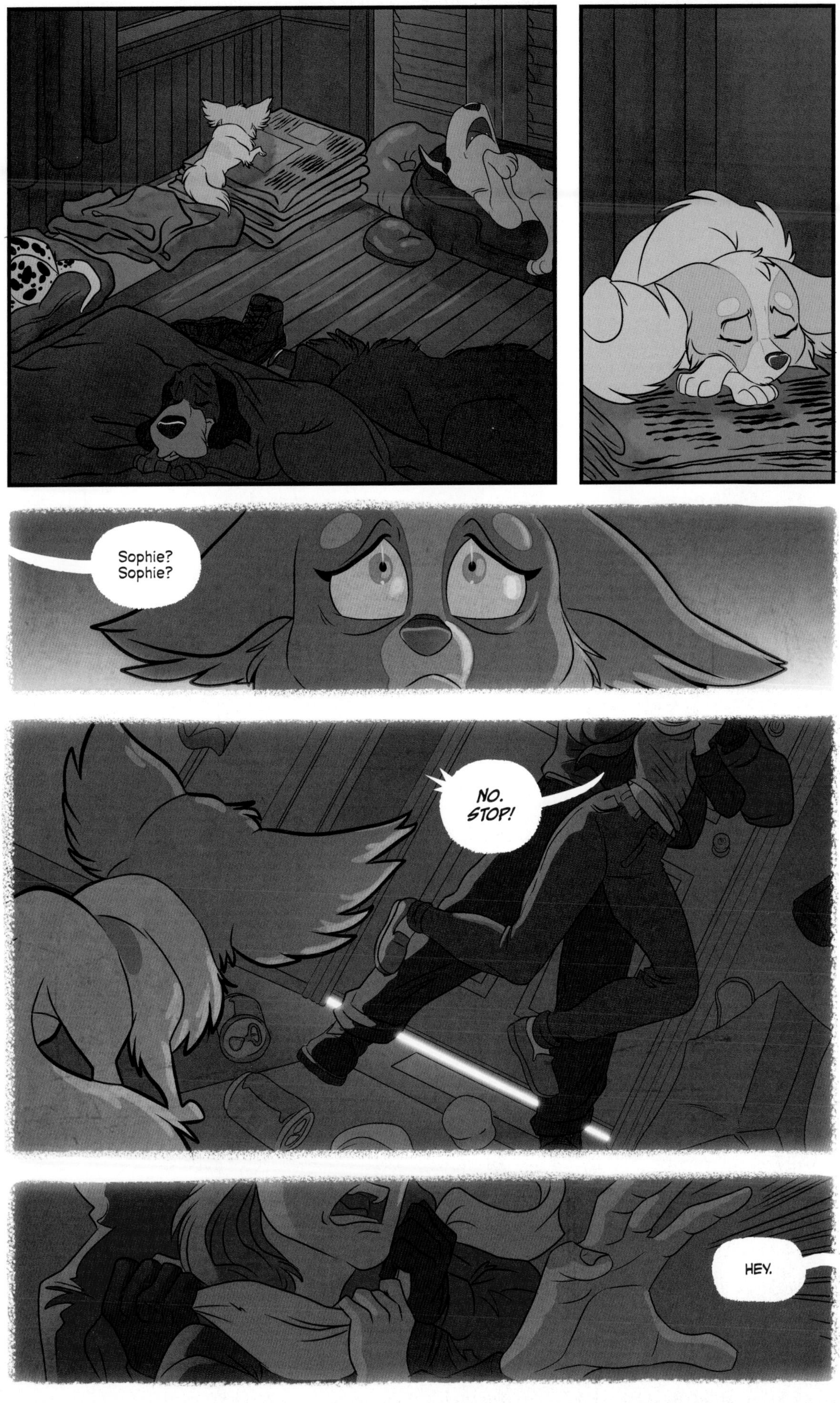
Sophie?
Sophie?
NO.
STOP!
HEY.

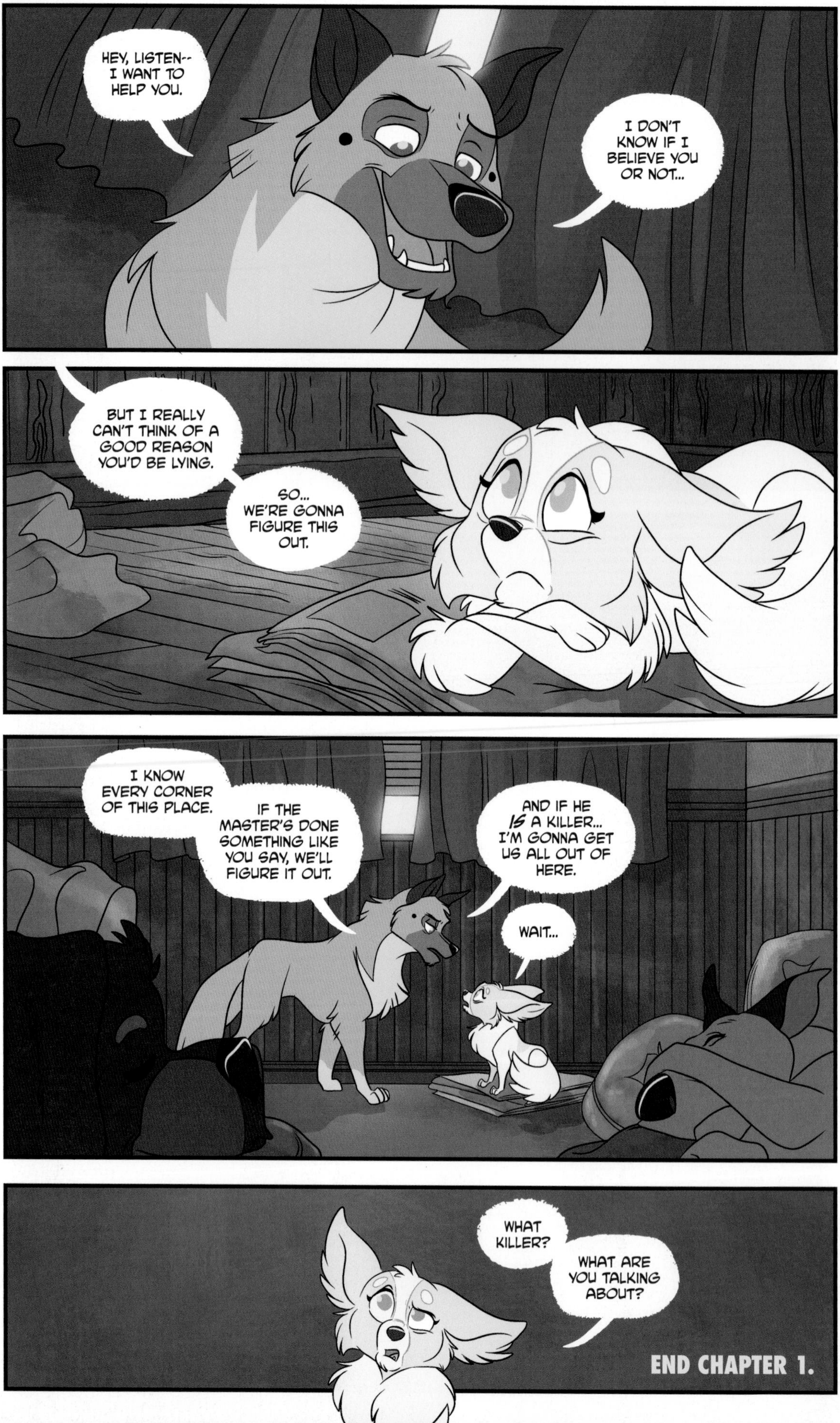
HEY, LISTEN-- I WANT TO HELP YOU.
I DON'T KNOW IF I BELIEVE YOU OR NOT...
BUT I REALLY CAN'T THINK OF A GOOD REASON YOU'D BE LYING.
SO... WE'RE GONNA FIGURE THIS OUT.
I KNOW EVERY CORNER OF THIS PLACE.
IF THE MASTER'S DONE SOMETHING LIKE YOU SAY, WE'LL FIGURE IT OUT.
AND IF HE *IS* A KILLER... I'M GONNA GET US ALL OUT OF HERE.
WAIT...
WHAT KILLER?
WHAT ARE YOU TALKING ABOUT?
END CHAPTER 1.

Chapter 2:
STAY

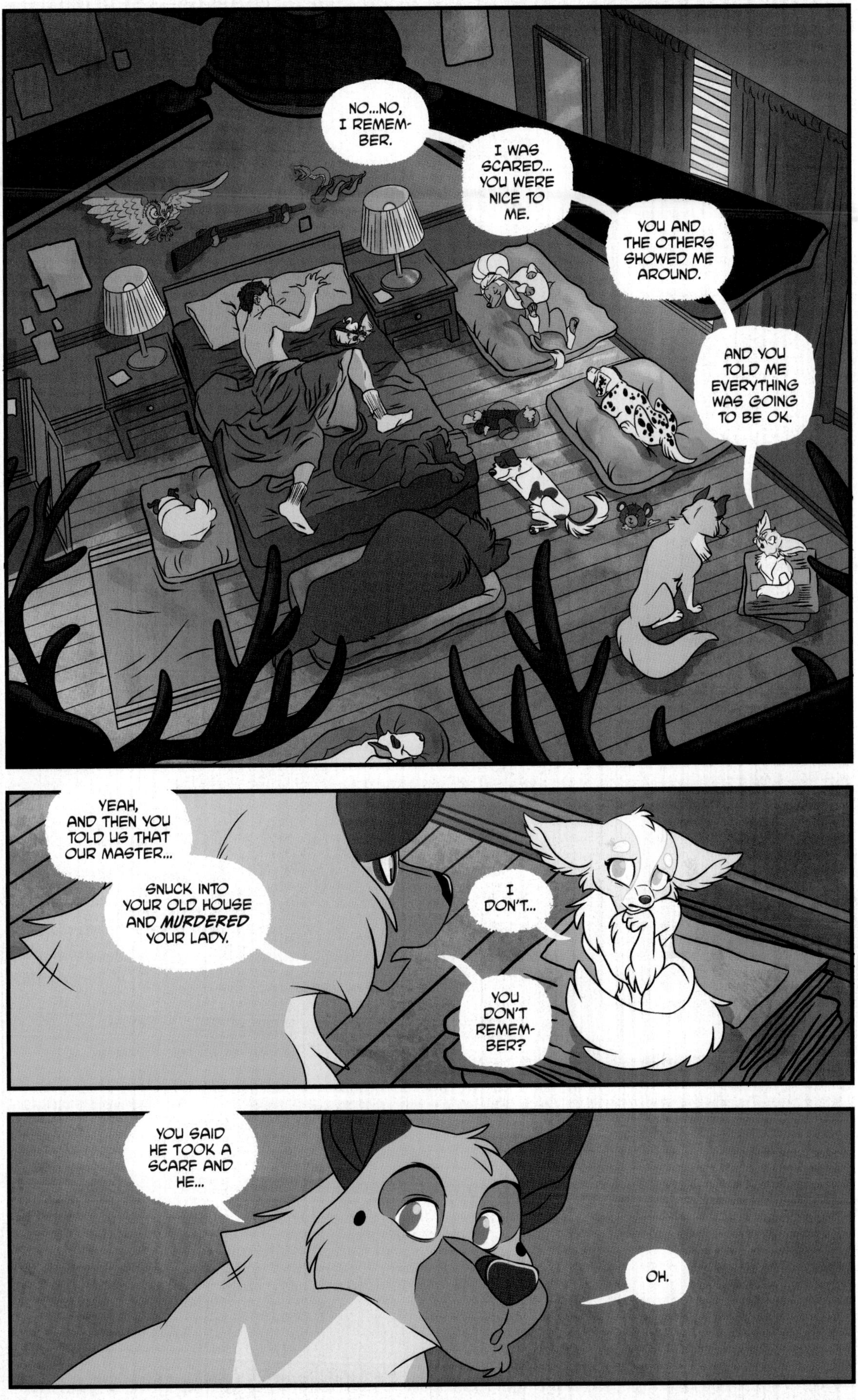
NO...NO, I REMEMBER.
I WAS SCARED... YOU WERE NICE TO ME.
YOU AND THE OTHERS SHOWED ME AROUND.
AND YOU TOLD ME EVERYTHING WAS GOING TO BE OK.
YEAH, AND THEN YOU TOLD US THAT OUR MASTER...
SNUCK INTO YOUR OLD HOUSE AND *MURDERED* YOUR LADY.
I DON'T...
YOU DON'T REMEMBER?
YOU SAID HE TOOK A SCARF AND HE...
OH.

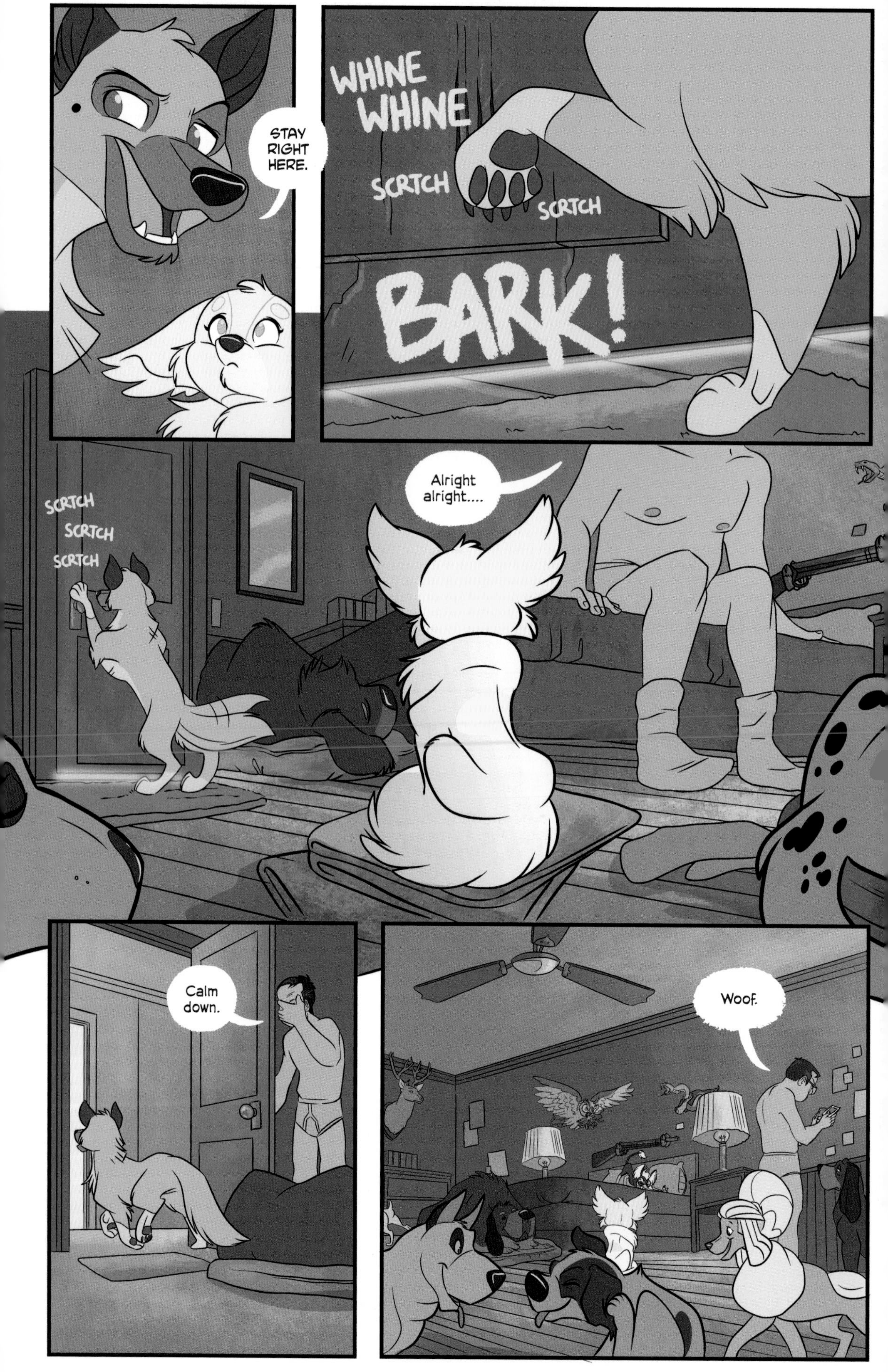
STAY RIGHT HERE.
WHINE WHINE
SCRTCH
SCRTCH
BARK!
SCRTCH
SCRTCH
SCRTCH
Alright alright....
Calm down.
Woof.

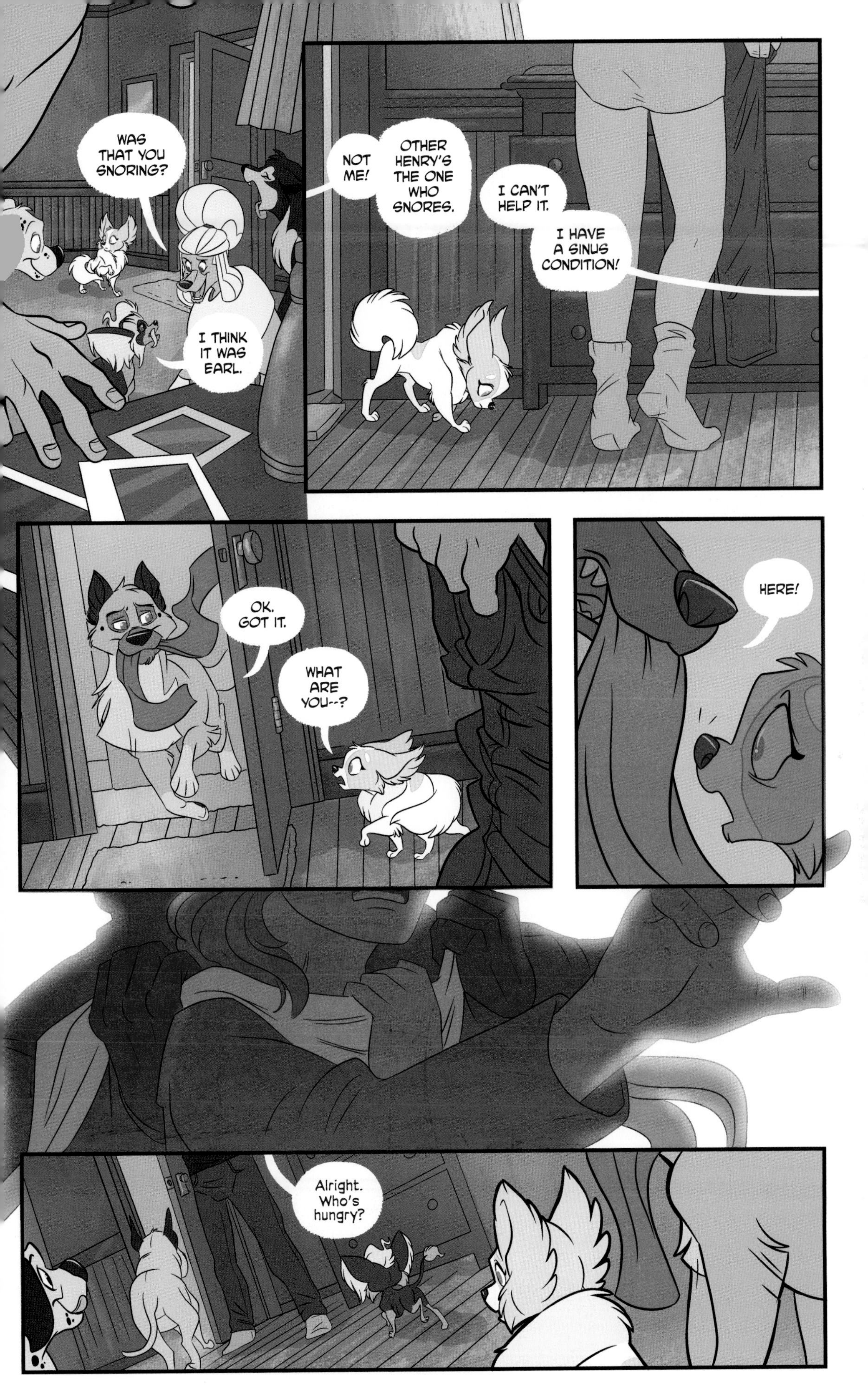
WAS THAT YOU SNORING?
I THINK IT WAS EARL.
NOT ME!
OTHER HENRY'S THE ONE WHO SNORES.
I CAN'T HELP IT.
I HAVE A SINUS CONDITION!
OK. GOT IT.
WHAT ARE YOU--?
HERE!
Alright. Who's hungry?

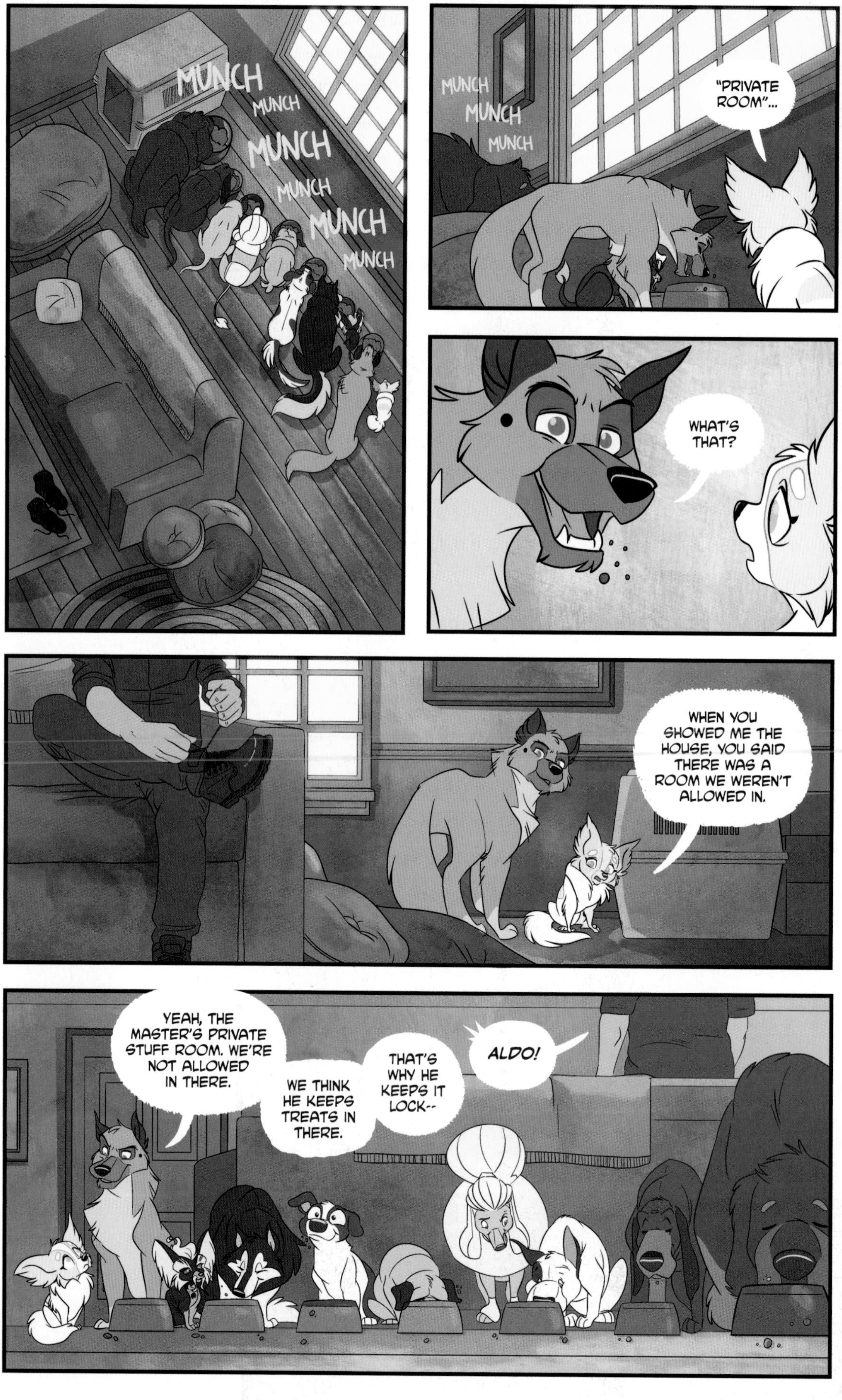
MUNCH
MUNCH
MUNCH
MUNCH
MUNCH
MUNCH
MUNCH
MUNCH
MUNCH
"PRIVATE ROOM"...
WHAT'S THAT?
WHEN YOU SHOWED ME THE HOUSE, YOU SAID THERE WAS A ROOM WE WEREN'T ALLOWED IN.
YEAH, THE MASTER'S PRIVATE STUFF ROOM. WE'RE NOT ALLOWED IN THERE.
WE THINK HE KEEPS TREATS IN THERE.
THAT'S WHY HE KEEPS IT LOCK--
ALDO!

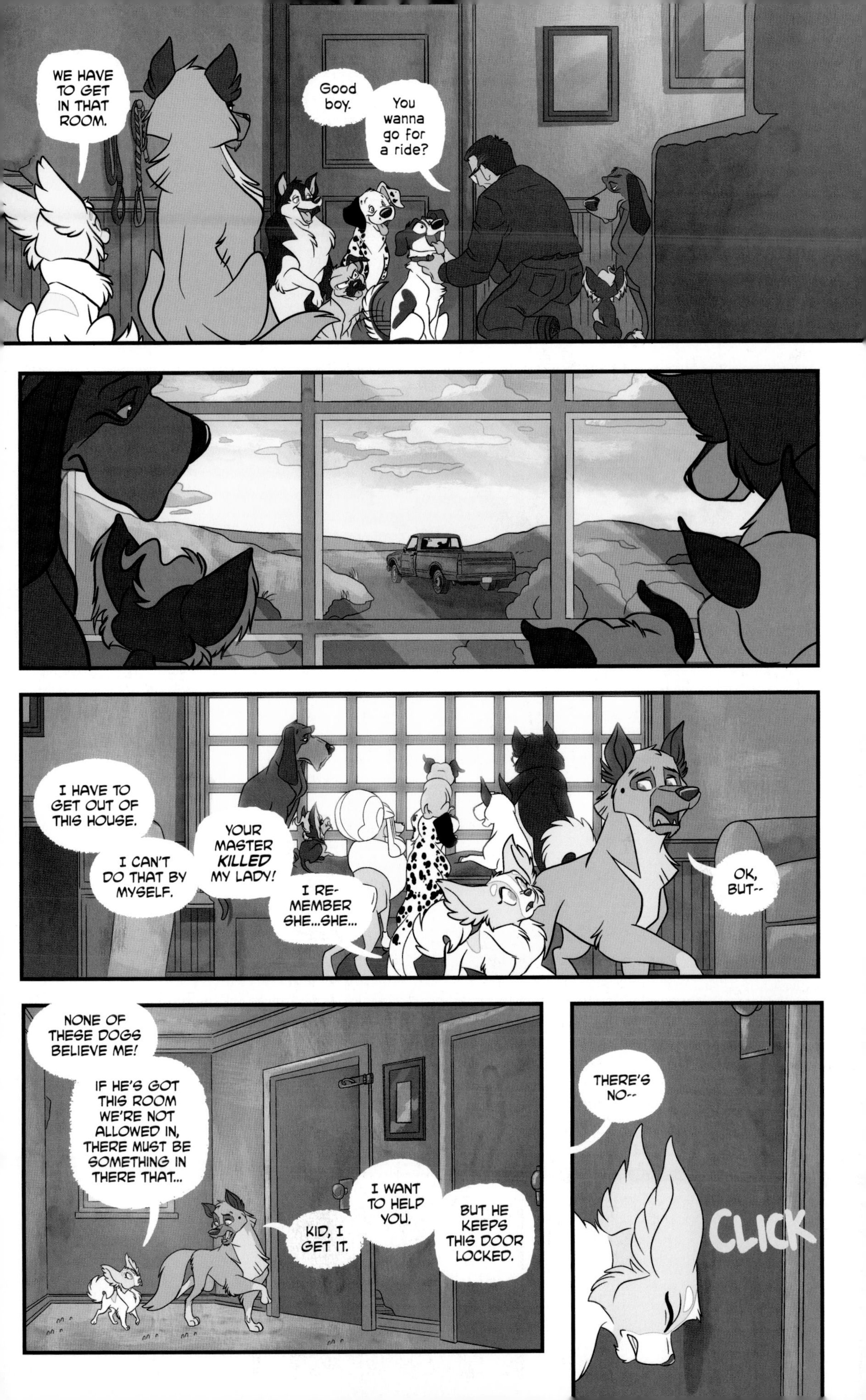
WE HAVE TO GET IN THAT ROOM.
Good boy.
You wanna go for a ride?
I HAVE TO GET OUT OF THIS HOUSE.
I CAN'T DO THAT BY MYSELF.
YOUR MASTER *KILLED* MY LADY!
I RE-MEMBER SHE...SHE...
OK, BUT--
NONE OF THESE DOGS BELIEVE ME!
IF HE'S GOT THIS ROOM WE'RE NOT ALLOWED IN, THERE MUST BE SOMETHING IN THERE THAT...
KID, I GET IT.
I WANT TO HELP YOU.
BUT HE KEEPS THIS DOOR LOCKED.
THERE'S NO--
CLICK

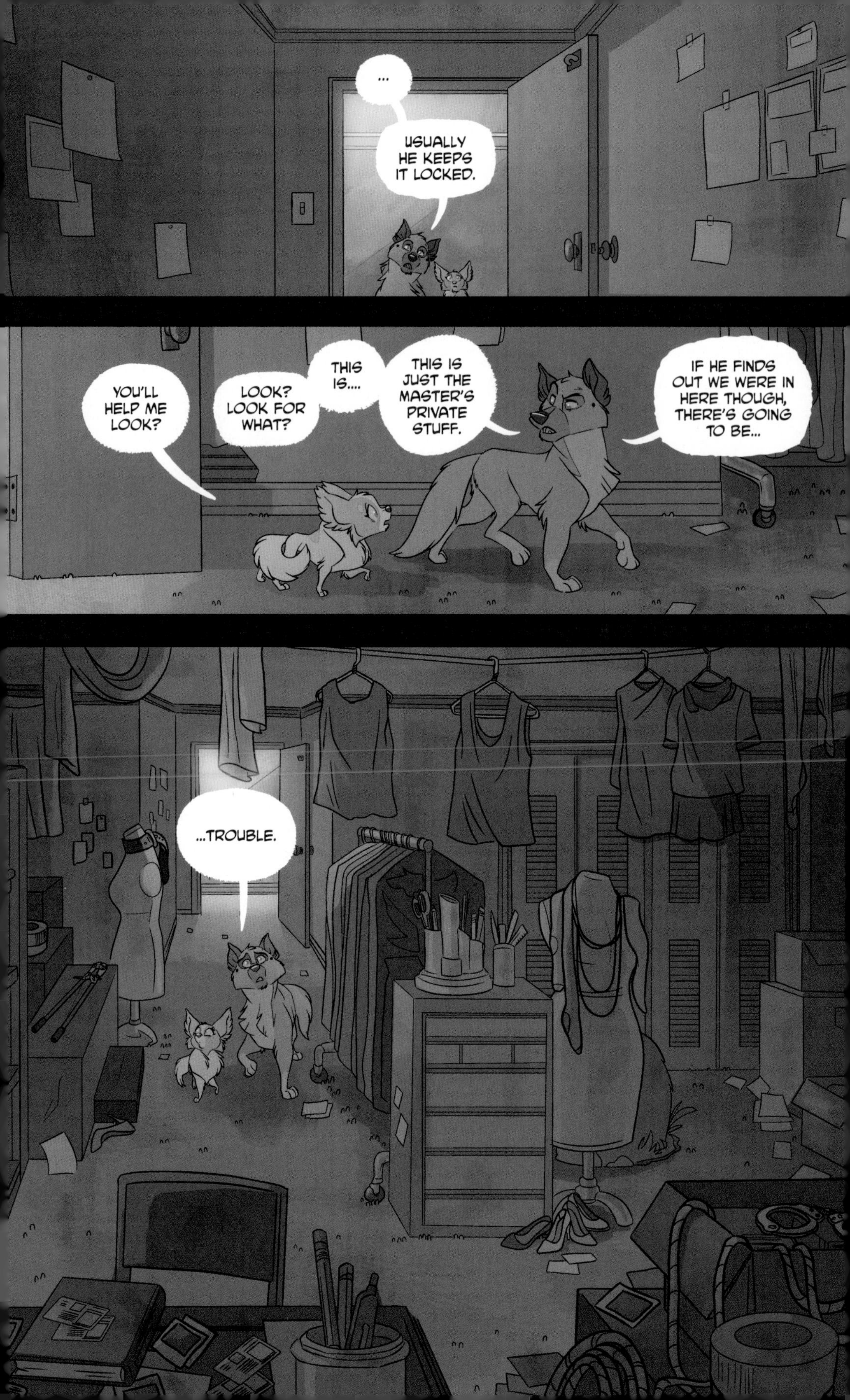
...
USUALLY HE KEEPS IT LOCKED.
YOU'LL HELP ME LOOK?
LOOK? LOOK FOR WHAT?
THIS IS....
THIS IS JUST THE MASTER'S PRIVATE STUFF.
IF HE FINDS OUT WE WERE IN HERE THOUGH, THERE'S GOING TO BE...
...TROUBLE.

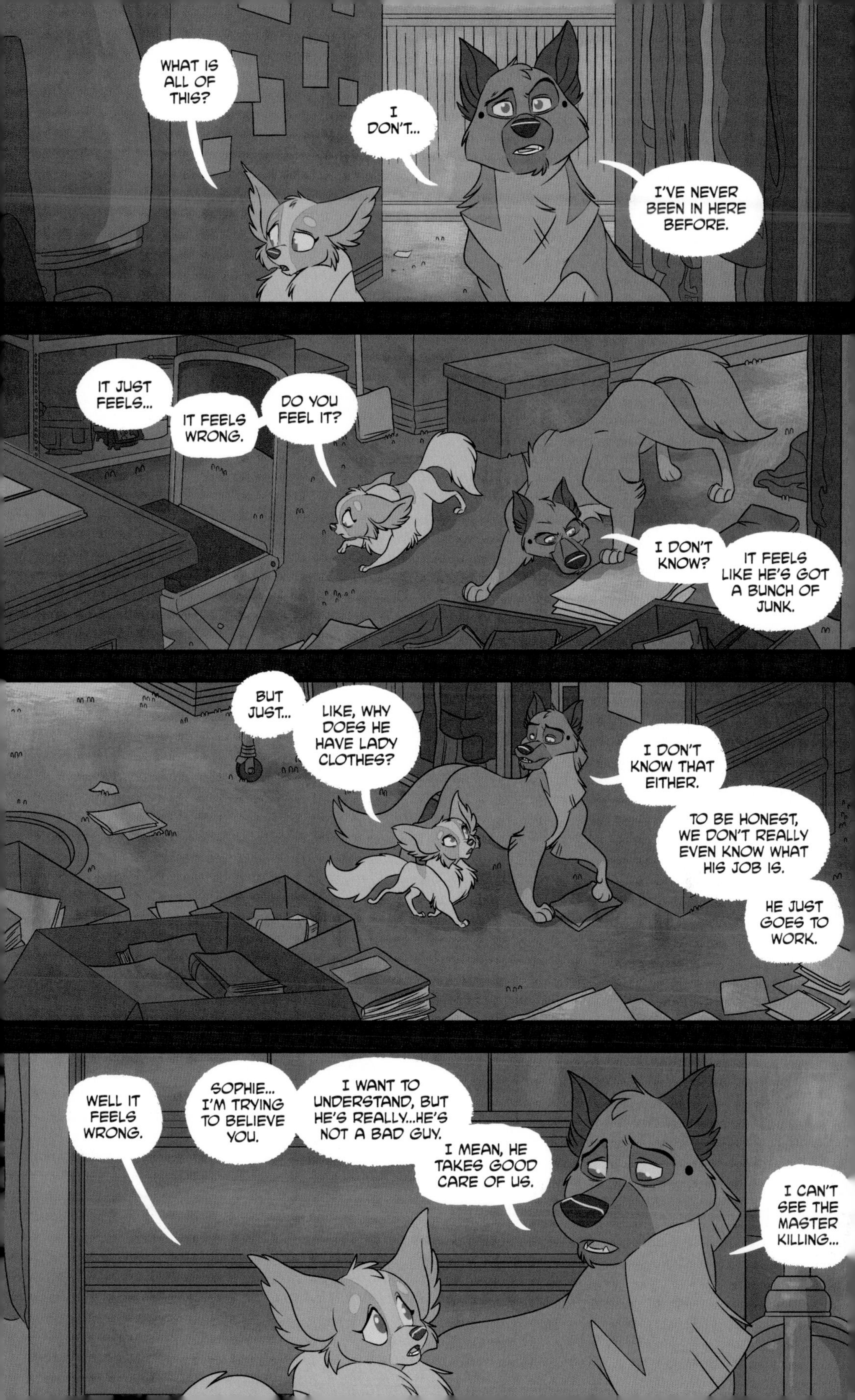
WHAT IS ALL OF THIS?
I DON'T...
I'VE NEVER BEEN IN HERE BEFORE.
IT JUST FEELS...
IT FEELS WRONG.
DO YOU FEEL IT?
I DON'T KNOW?
IT FEELS LIKE HE'S GOT A BUNCH OF JUNK.
BUT JUST...
LIKE, WHY DOES HE HAVE LADY CLOTHES?
I DON'T KNOW THAT EITHER.
TO BE HONEST, WE DON'T REALLY EVEN KNOW WHAT HIS JOB IS.
HE JUST GOES TO WORK.
WELL IT FEELS WRONG.
SOPHIE... I'M TRYING TO BELIEVE YOU.
I WANT TO UNDERSTAND, BUT HE'S REALLY...HE'S NOT A BAD GUY.
I MEAN, HE TAKES GOOD CARE OF US.
I CAN'T SEE THE MASTER KILLING...

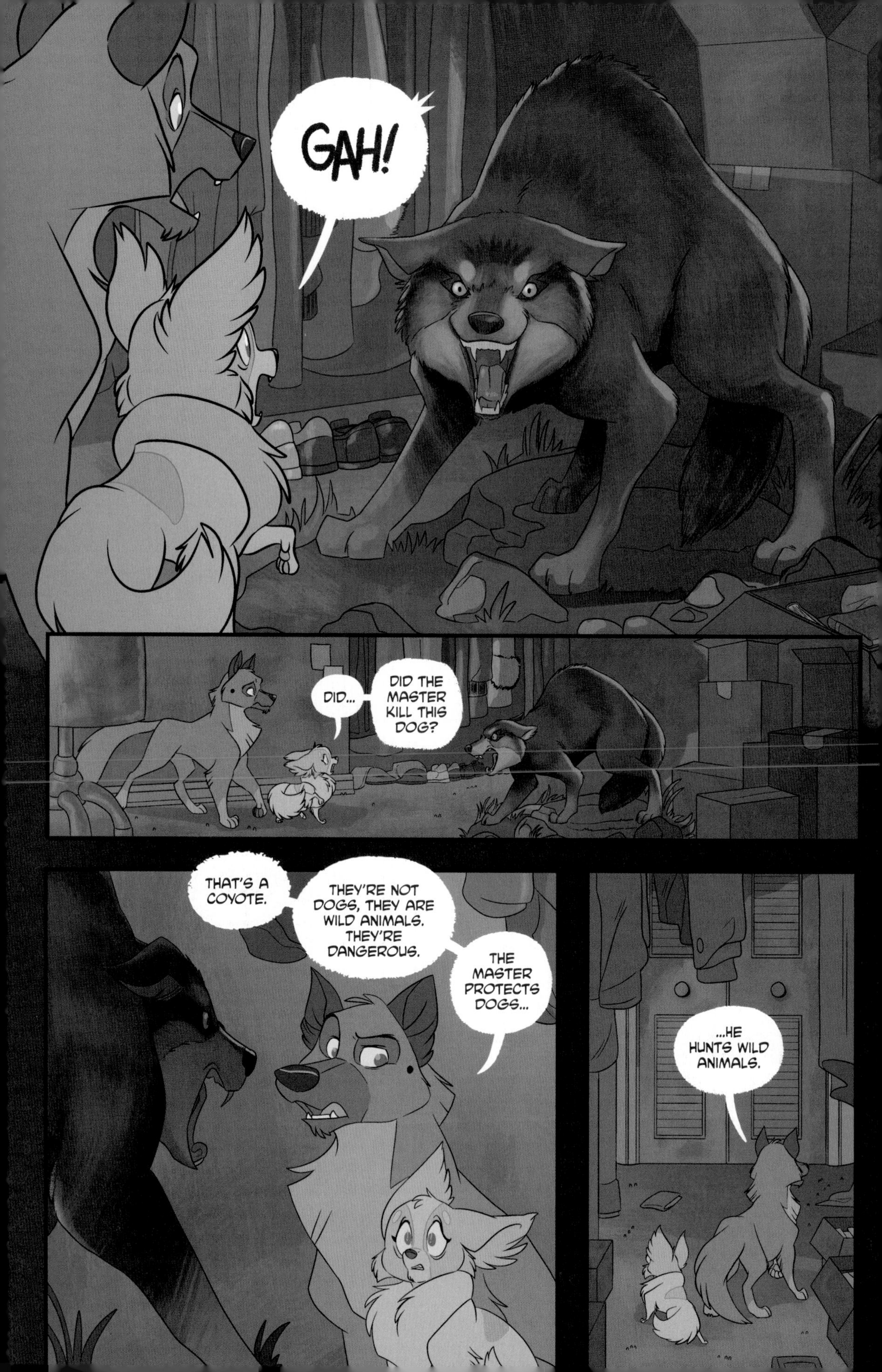
GAH!
DID...
DID THE MASTER KILL THIS DOG?
THAT'S A COYOTE.
THEY'RE NOT DOGS, THEY ARE WILD ANIMALS. THEY'RE DANGEROUS.
THE MASTER PROTECTS DOGS...
...HE HUNTS WILD ANIMALS.

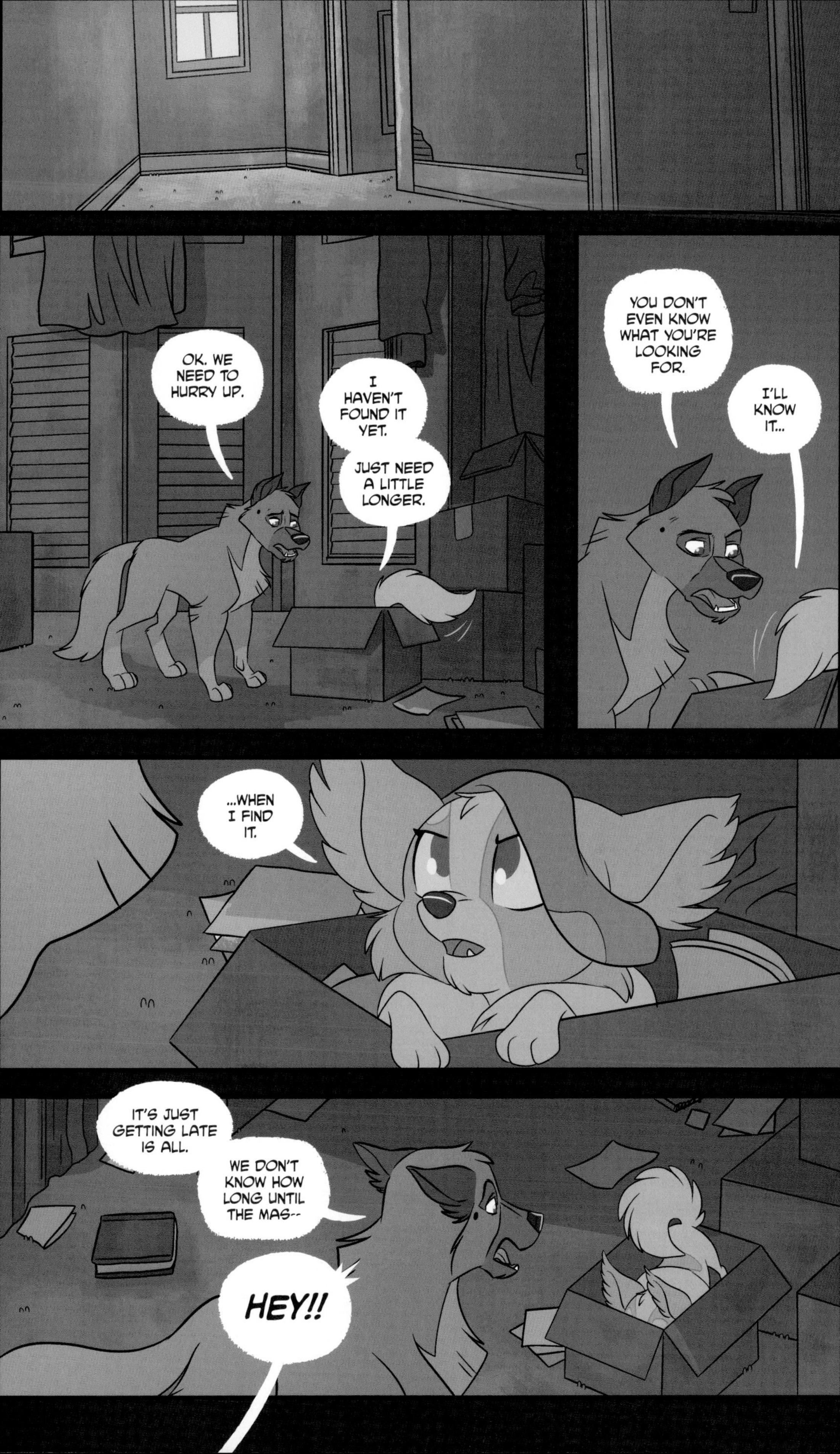
OK. WE NEED TO HURRY UP.
I HAVEN'T FOUND IT YET.
JUST NEED A LITTLE LONGER.
YOU DON'T EVEN KNOW WHAT YOU'RE LOOKING FOR.
I'LL KNOW IT...
...WHEN I FIND IT.
IT'S JUST GETTING LATE IS ALL.
WE DON'T KNOW HOW LONG UNTIL THE MAS--
HEY!!

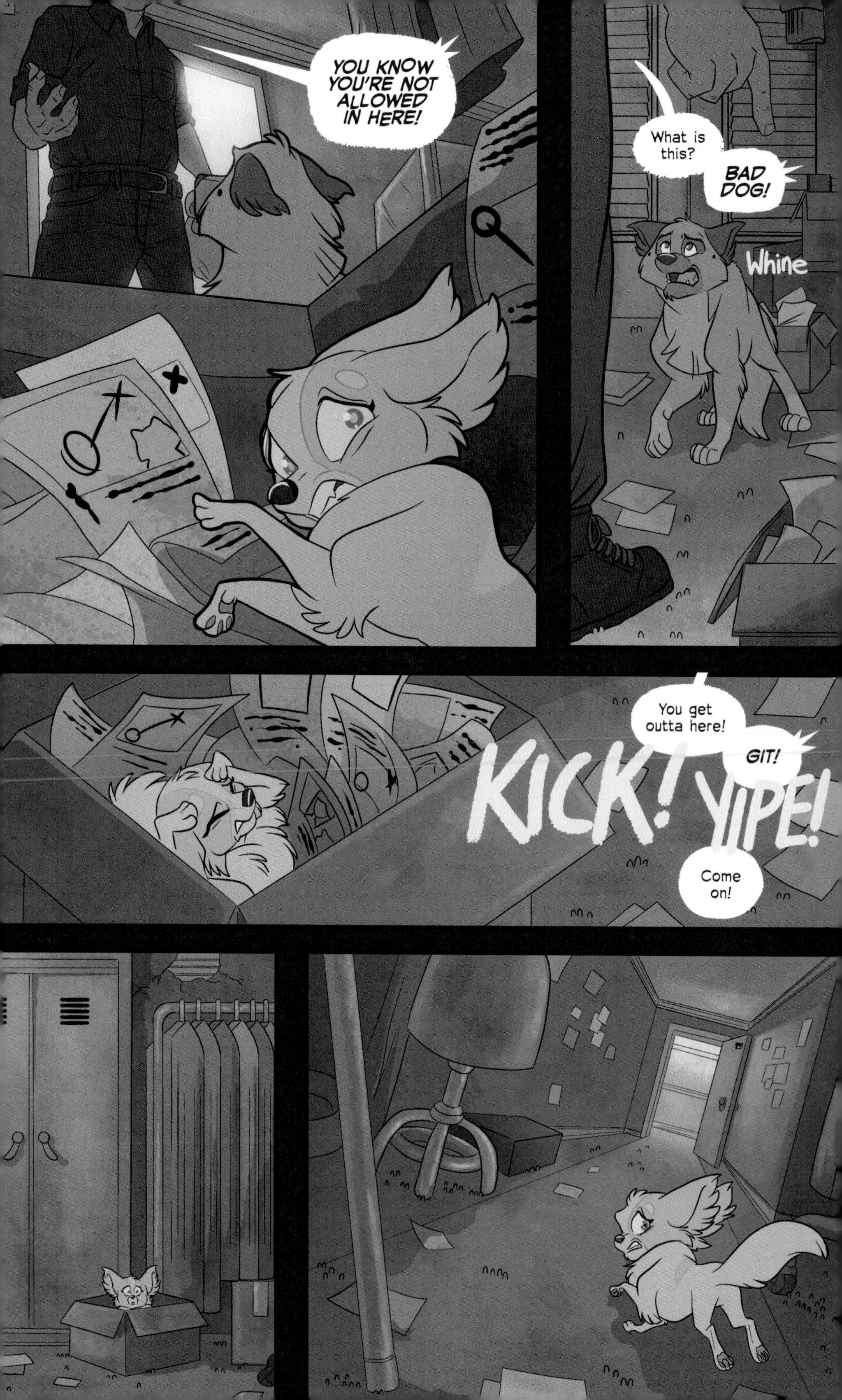

YOU KNOW YOU'RE NOT ALLOWED IN HERE!
What is this?
BAD DOG!
Whine
You get outta here!
GIT!
KICK!
YIPE!
Come on!

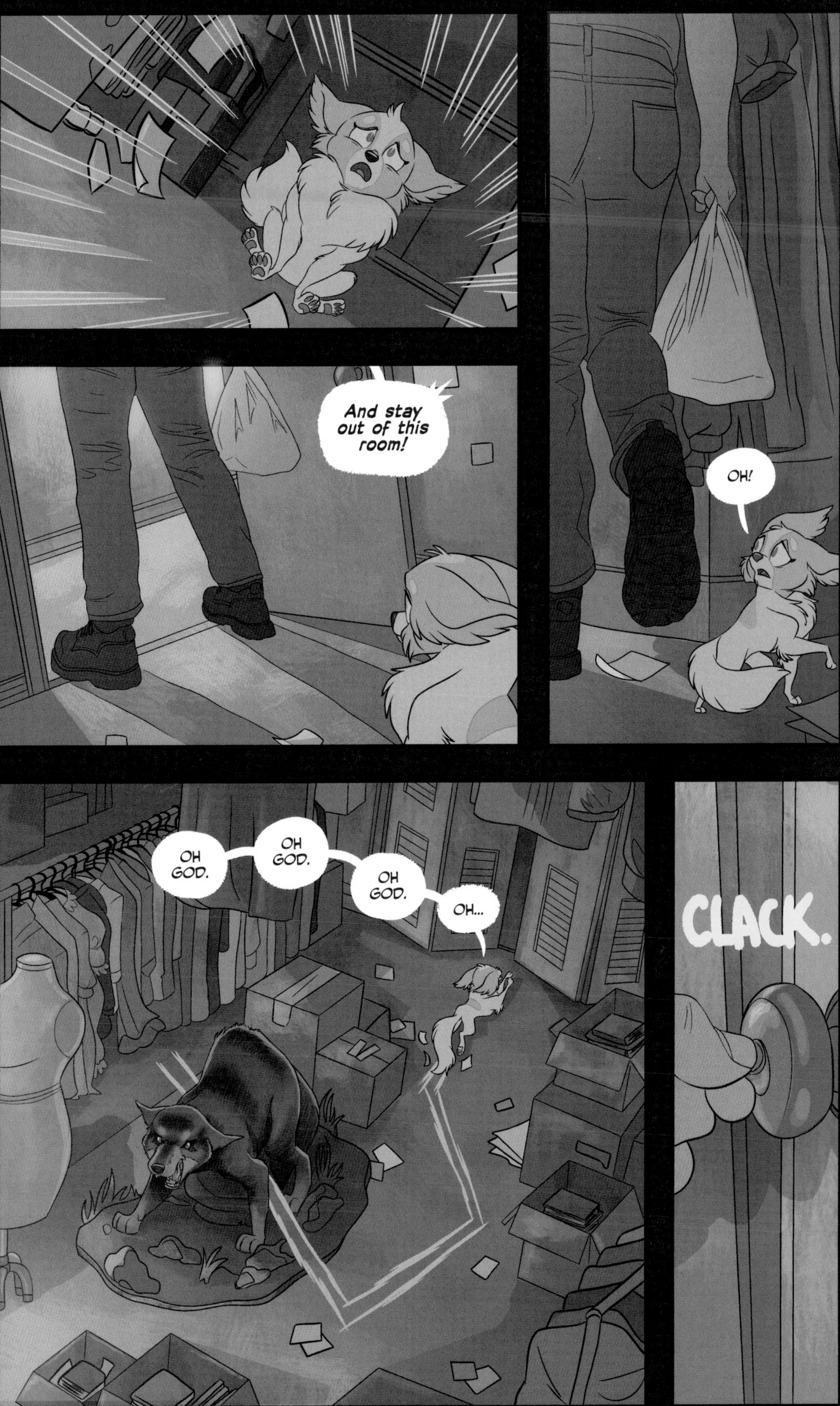
And stay out of this room!
OH!
OH GOD.
OH GOD.
OH GOD.
OH...
CLACK.

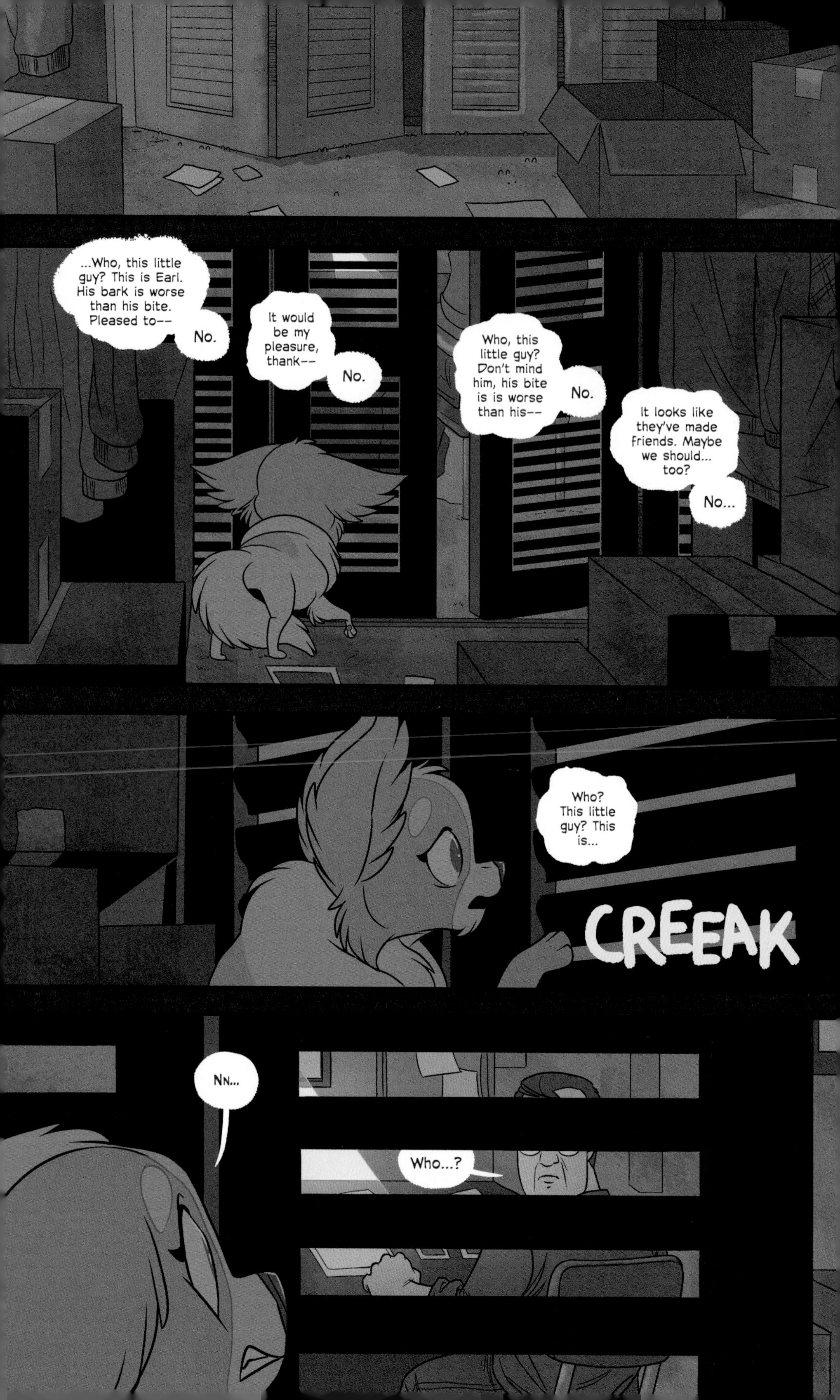

...Who, this little guy? This is Earl. His bark is worse than his bite. Pleased to--
No.
It would be my pleasure, thank--
No.
Who, this little guy? Don't mind him, his bite is is worse than his--
No.
It looks like they've made friends. Maybe we should... too?
No...
Who? This little guy? This is...
CREEAK
Nn...
Who...?

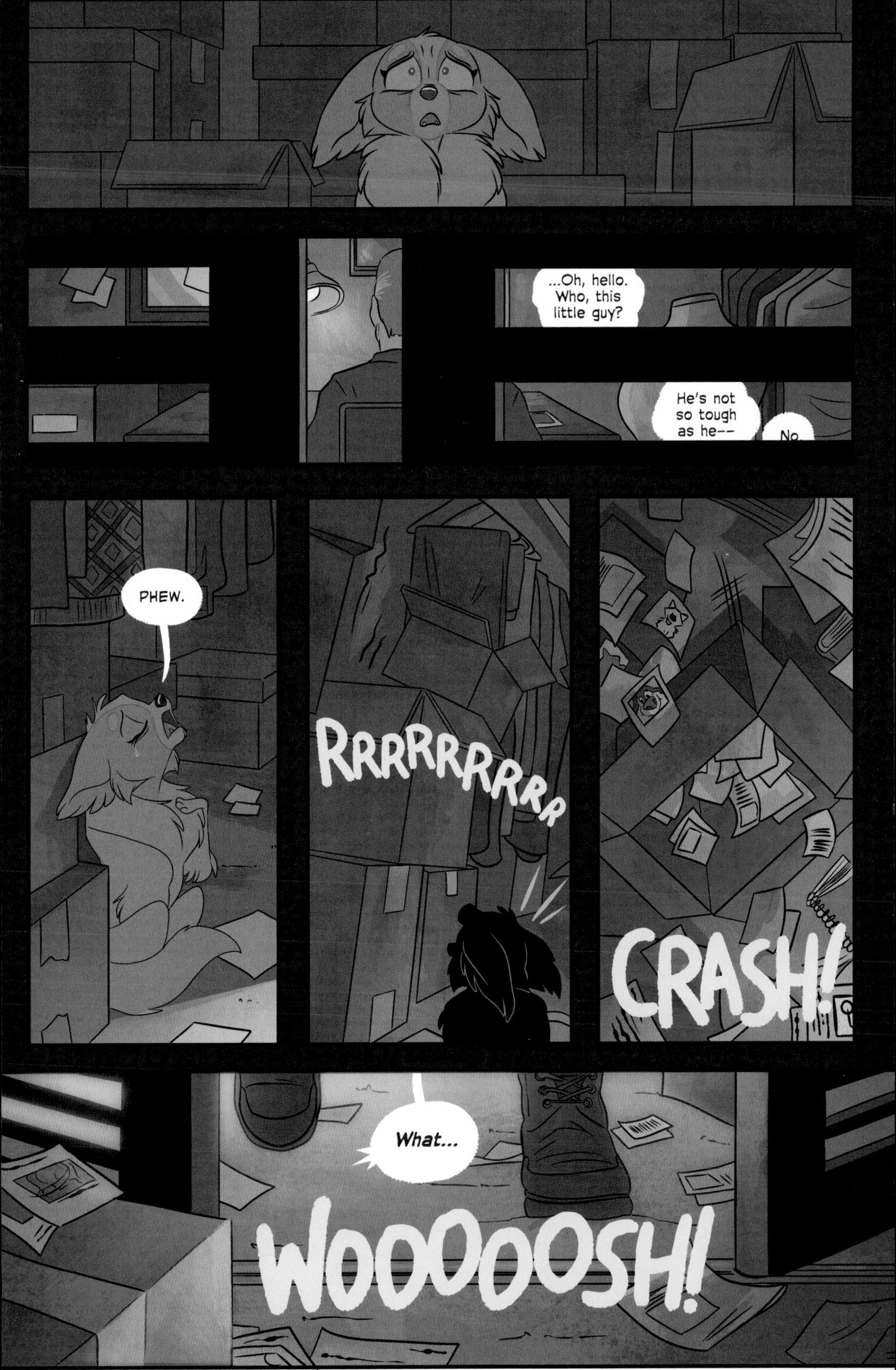
...Oh, hello. Who, this little guy?
He's not so tough as he--
No.
PHEW.
RRRRRRRRRR
CRASH!
What...
WOOOOOSH!

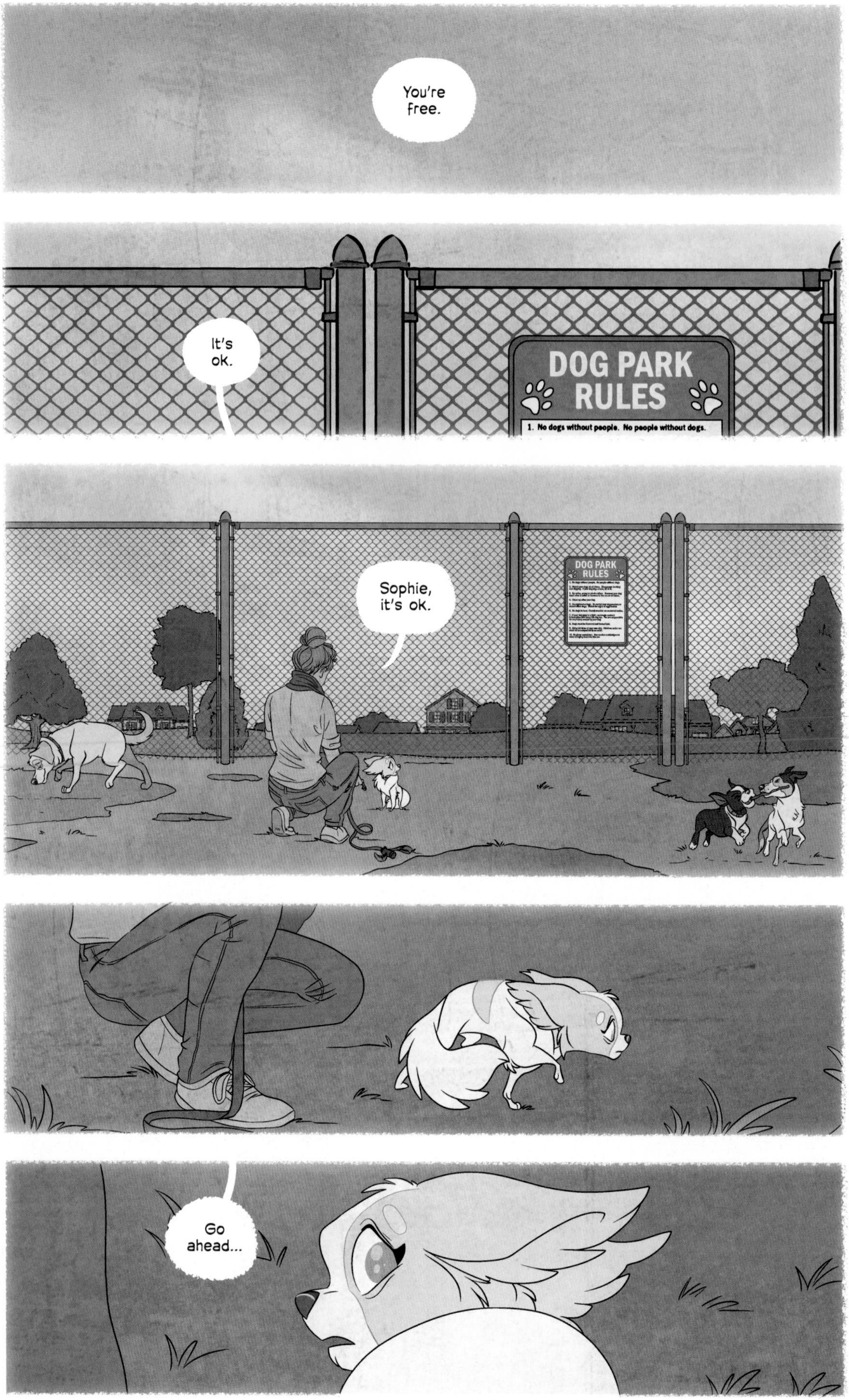
You're free.
It's ok.
DOG PARK RULES
1. No dogs without people. No people without dogs.
DOG PARK RULES
Sophie, it's ok.
Go ahead...

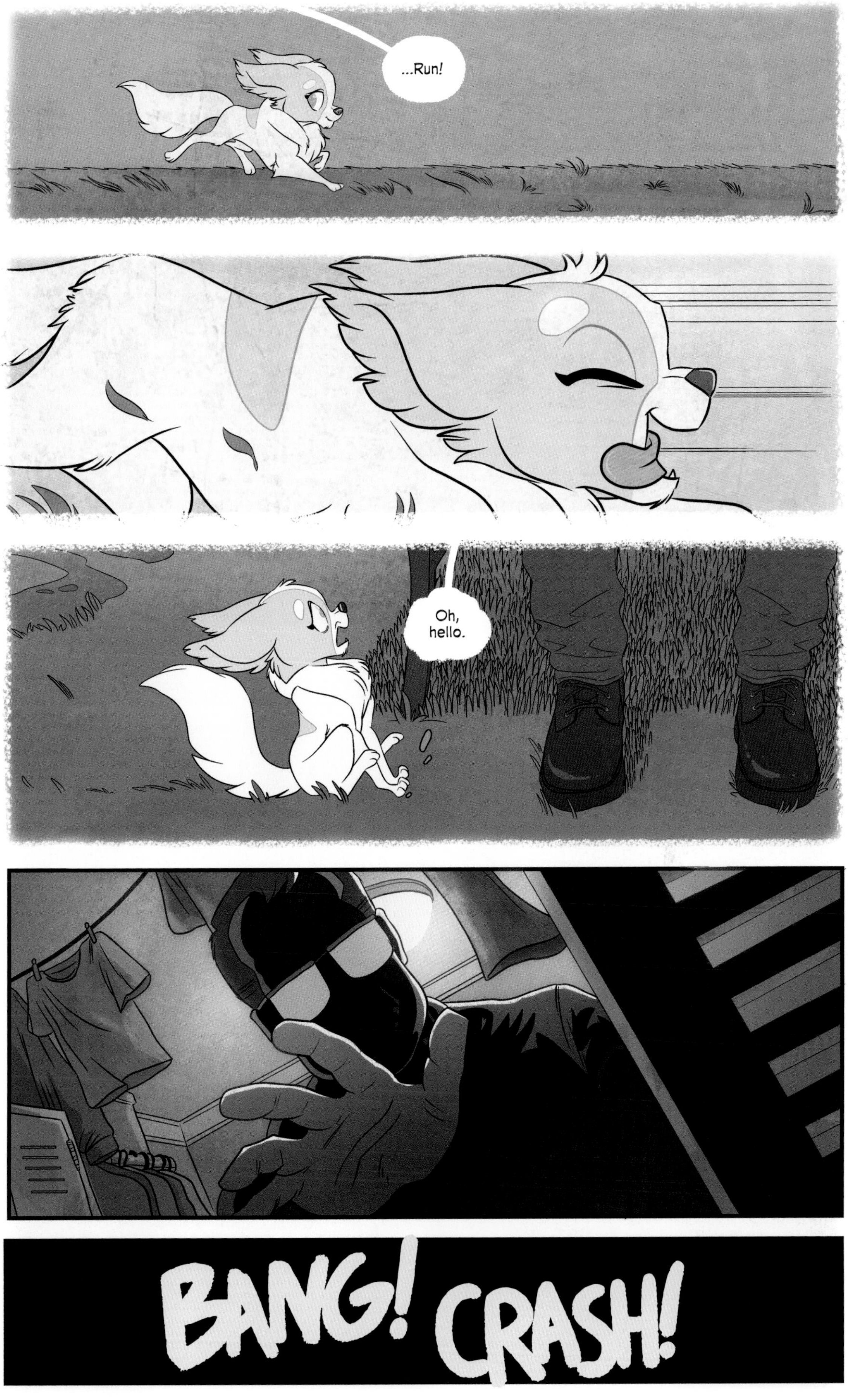
...Run!
Oh, hello.
BANG! CRASH!

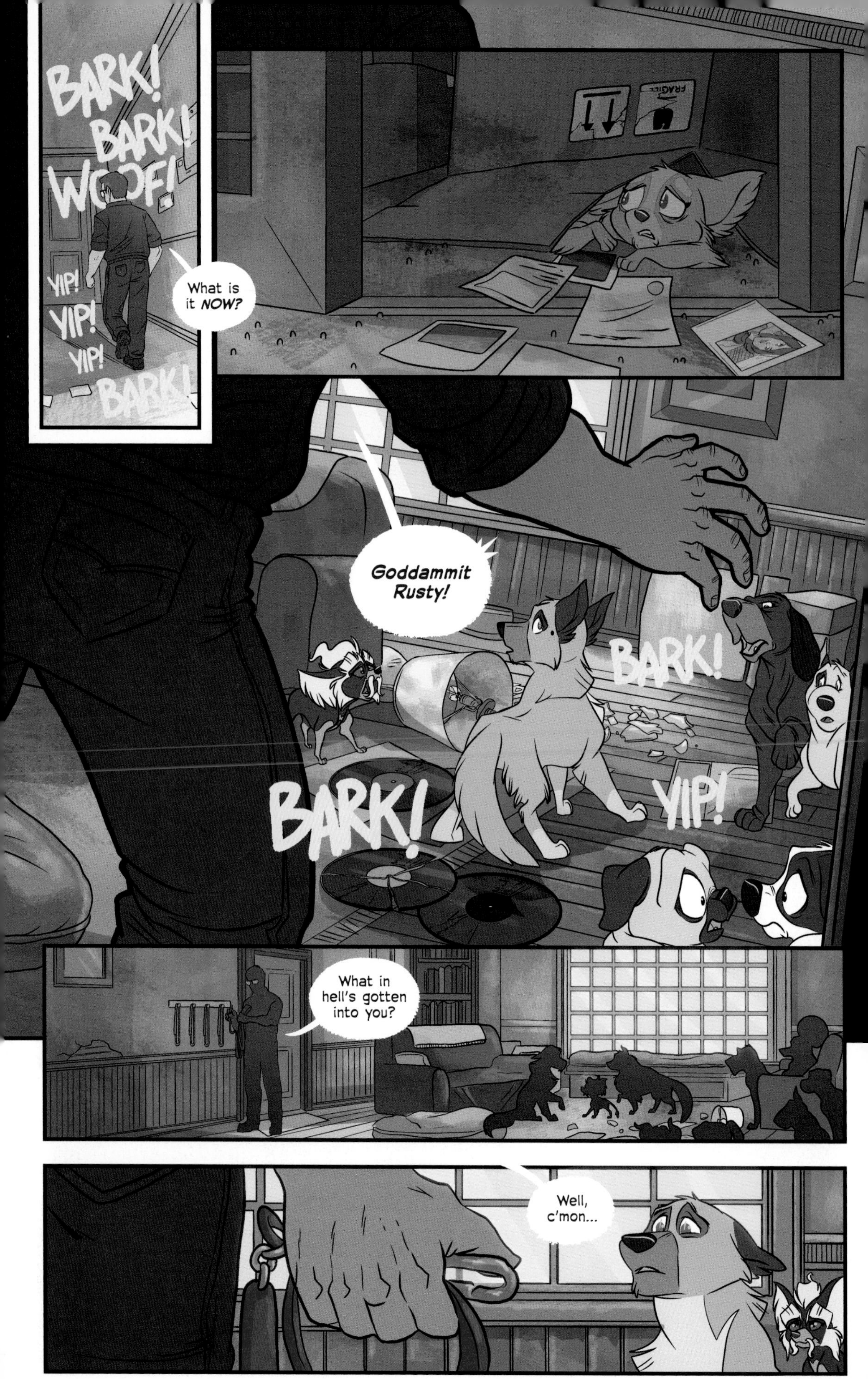
BARK!
BARK!
WOOF!
YIP!
YIP!
YIP!
BARK!
What is it NOW?
Goddammit Rusty!
BARK!
BARK!
YIP!
What in hell's gotten into you?
Well, c'mon...

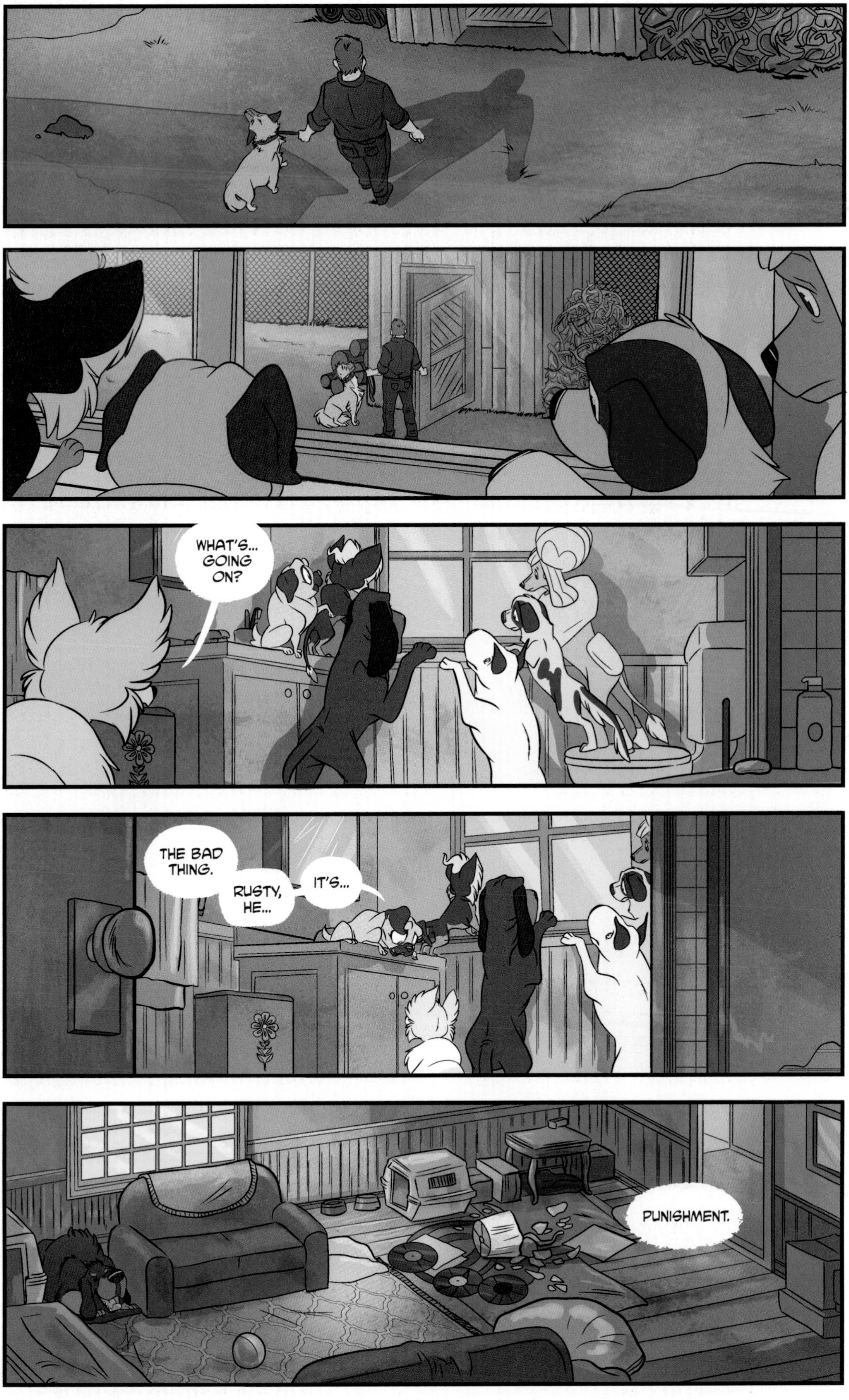
WHAT'S... GOING ON?
THE BAD THING.
RUSTY, HE...
IT'S...
PUNISHMENT.

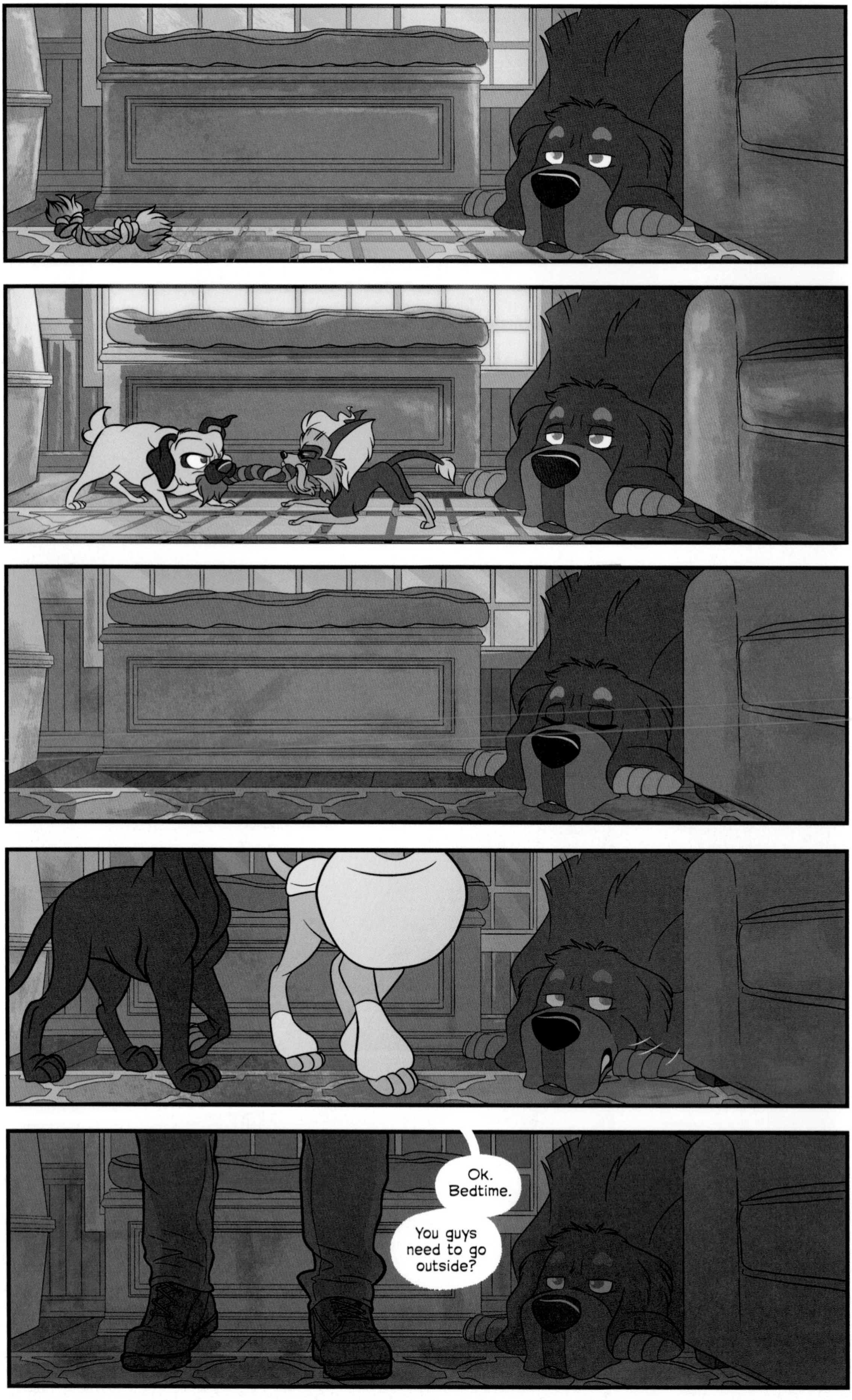
Ok. Bedtime.
You guys need to go outside?

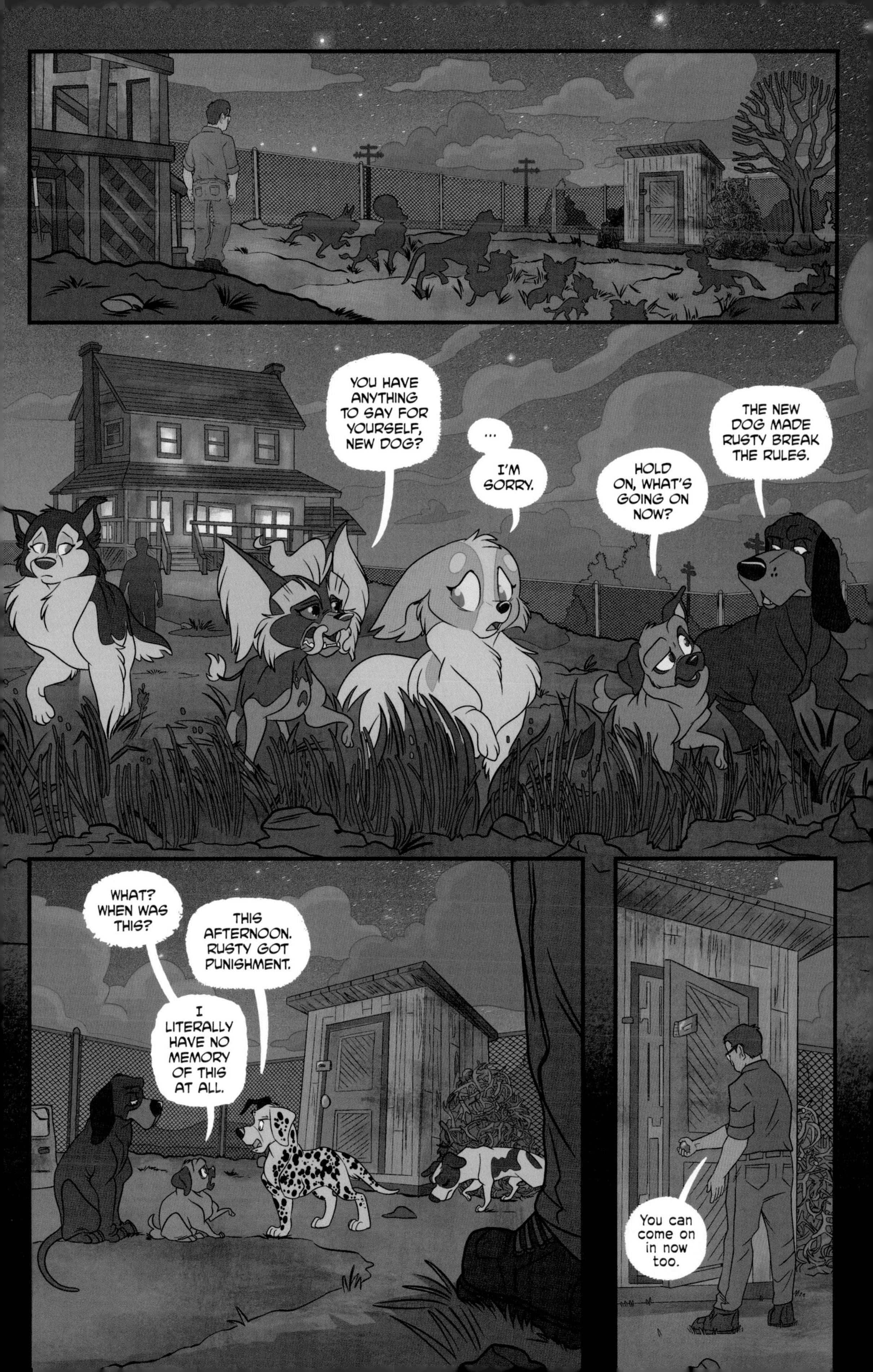
YOU HAVE ANYTHING TO SAY FOR YOURSELF, NEW DOG?
...
I'M SORRY.
HOLD ON, WHAT'S GOING ON NOW?
THE NEW DOG MADE RUSTY BREAK THE RULES.
WHAT? WHEN WAS THIS?
THIS AFTERNOON. RUSTY GOT PUNISHMENT.
I LITERALLY HAVE NO MEMORY OF THIS AT ALL.
You can come on in now too.

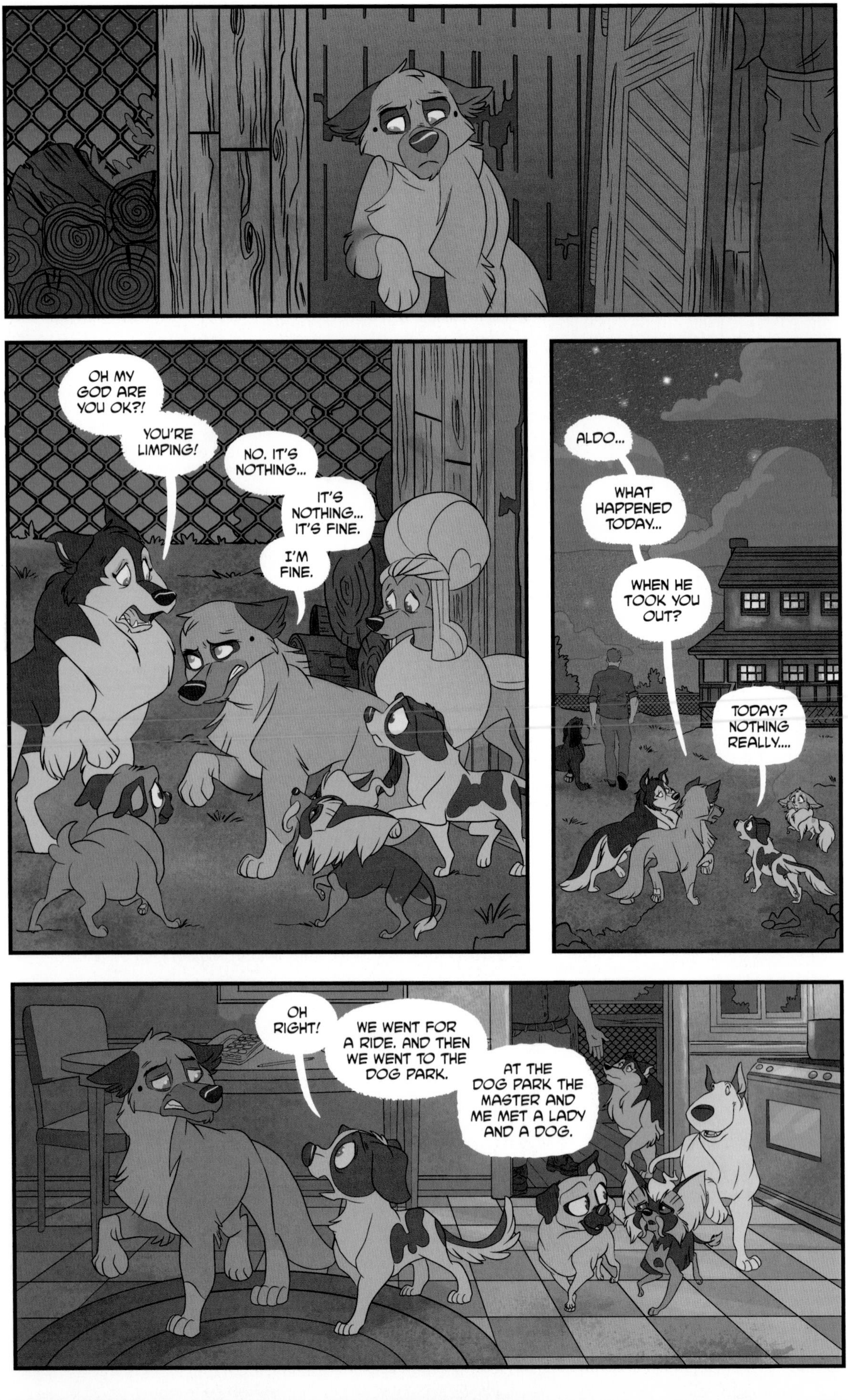
OH MY GOD ARE YOU OK?!
YOU'RE LIMPING!
NO. IT'S NOTHING...
IT'S NOTHING... IT'S FINE.
I'M FINE.
ALDO...
WHAT HAPPENED TODAY...
WHEN HE TOOK YOU OUT?
TODAY? NOTHING REALLY....
OH RIGHT!
WE WENT FOR A RIDE. AND THEN WE WENT TO THE DOG PARK.
AT THE DOG PARK THE MASTER AND ME MET A LADY AND A DOG.

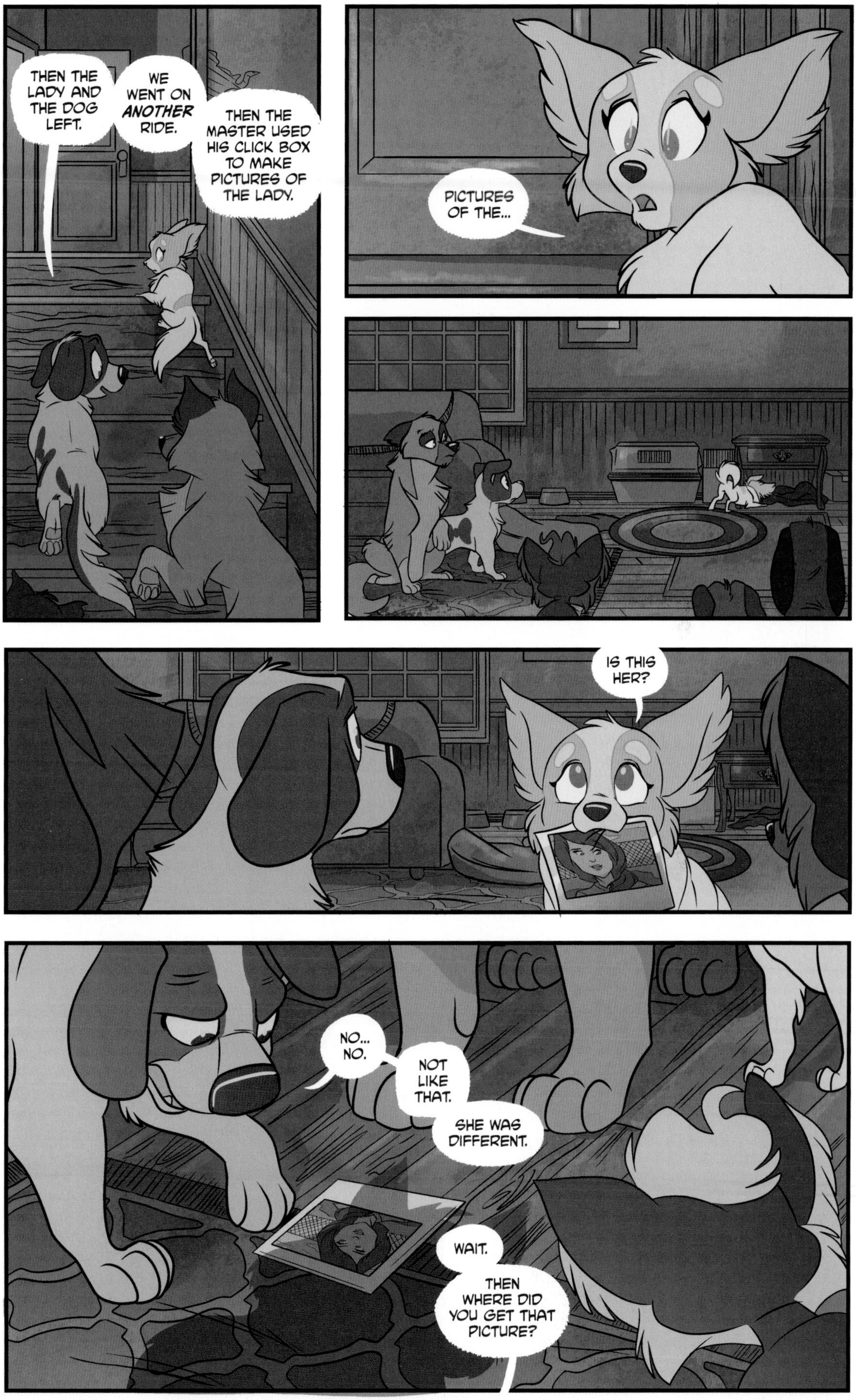
THEN THE LADY AND THE DOG LEFT.
WE WENT ON *ANOTHER* RIDE.
THEN THE MASTER USED HIS CLICK BOX TO MAKE PICTURES OF THE LADY.
PICTURES OF THE...
IS THIS HER?
NO... NO.
NOT LIKE THAT.
SHE WAS DIFFERENT.
WAIT.
THEN WHERE DID YOU GET THAT PICTURE?

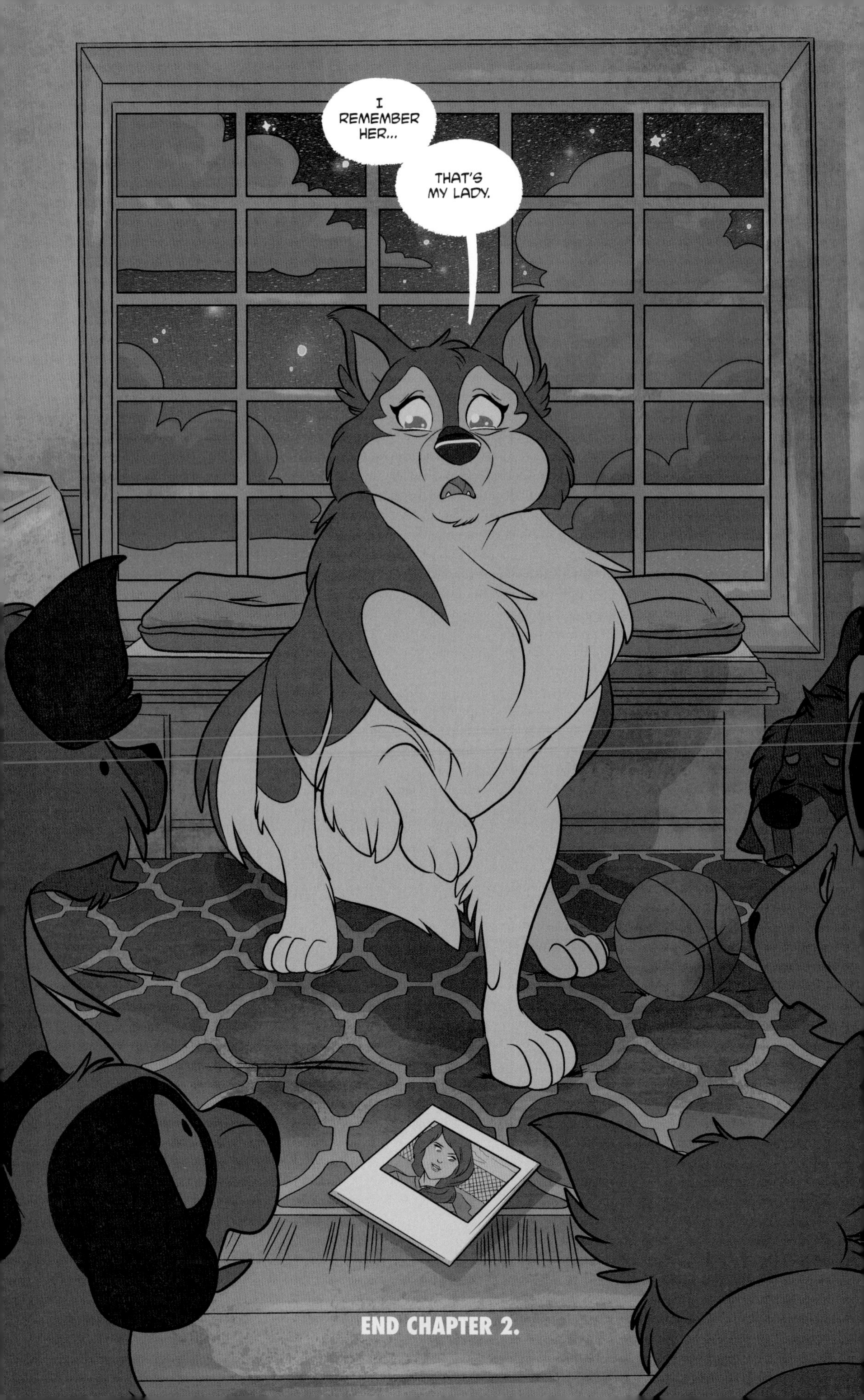
I REMEMBER HER...
THAT'S MY LADY.
END CHAPTER 2.

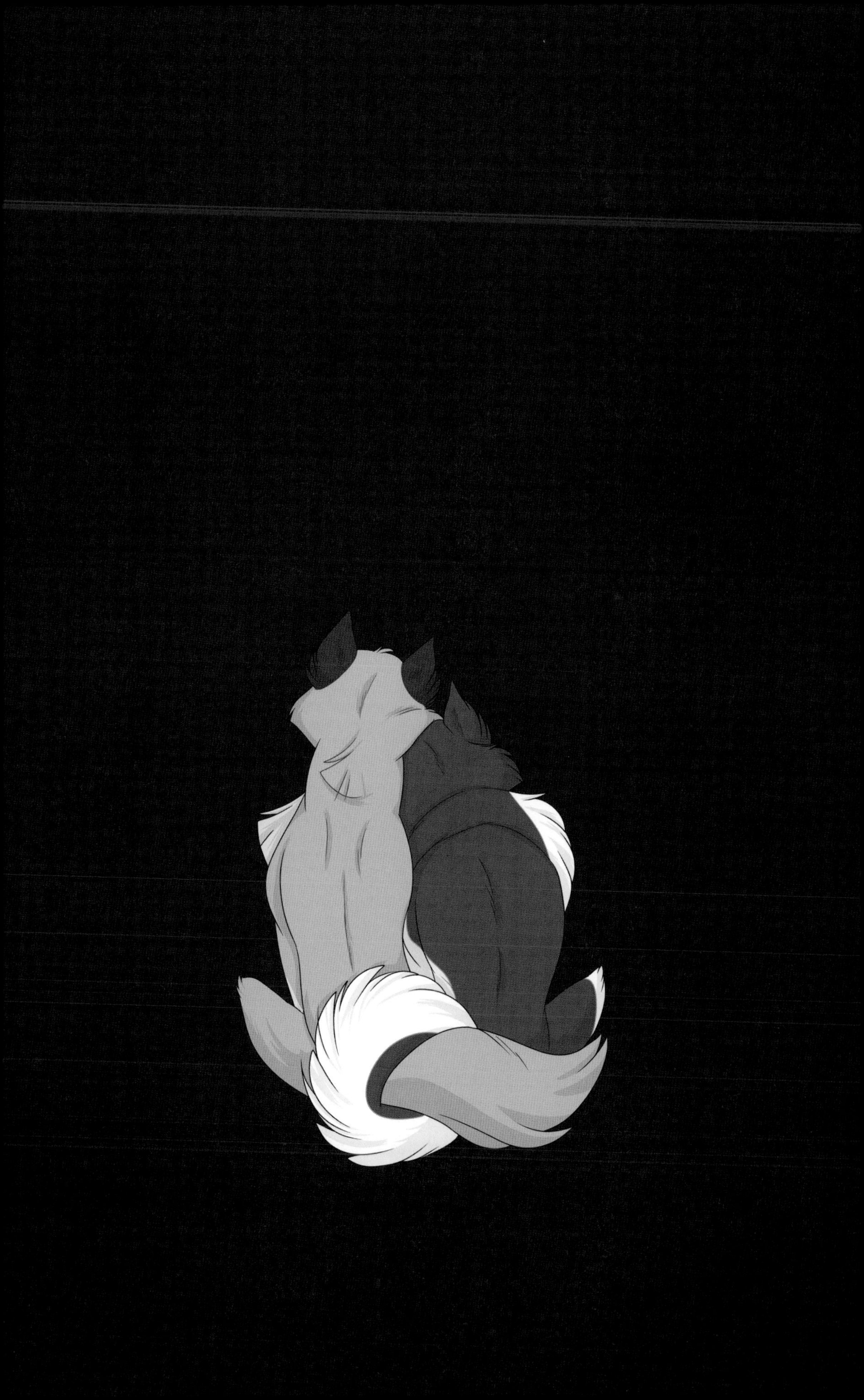

Chapter 3:
LIE DOWN

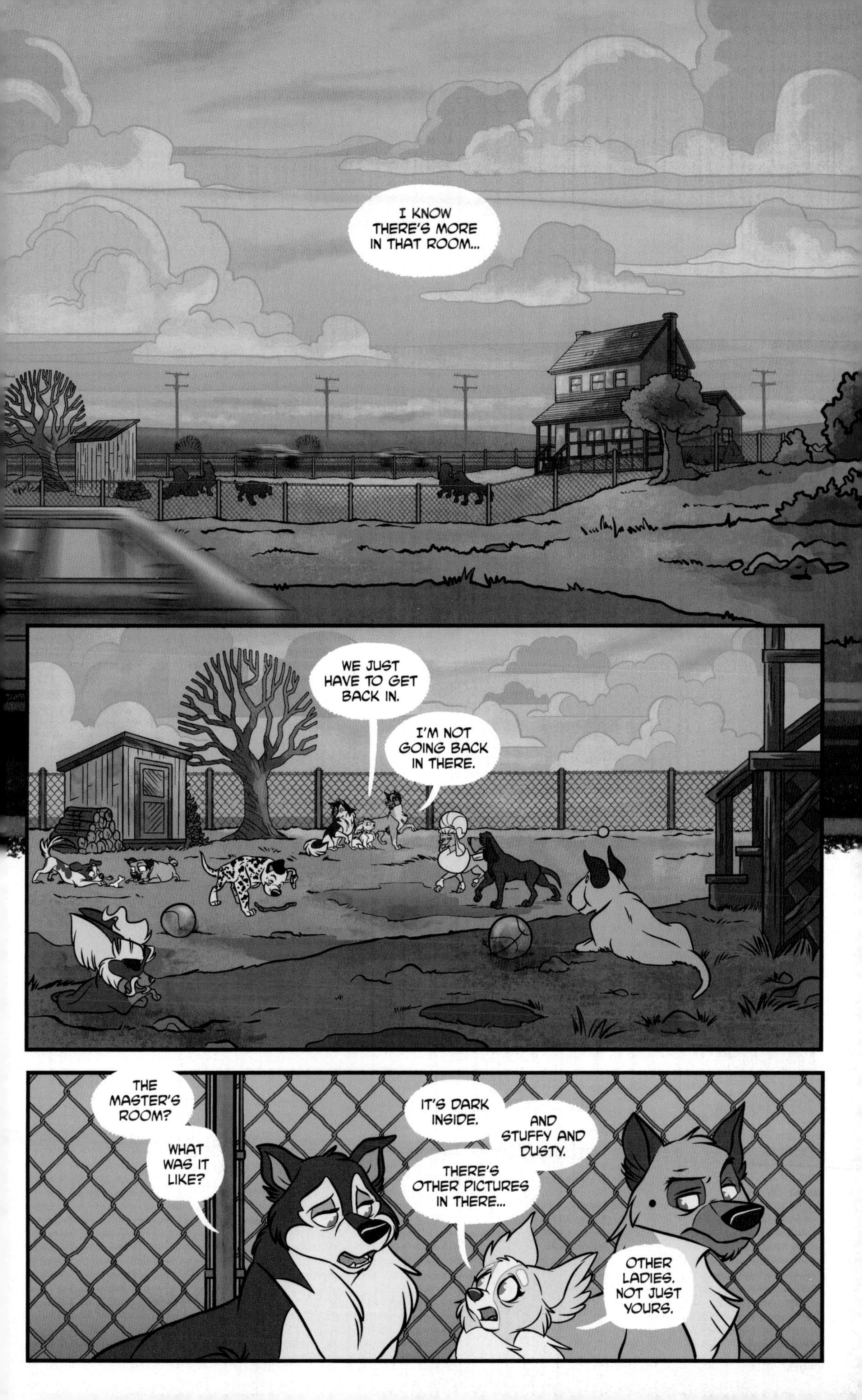
I KNOW THERE'S MORE IN THAT ROOM...
WE JUST HAVE TO GET BACK IN.
I'M NOT GOING BACK IN THERE.
THE MASTER'S ROOM?
WHAT WAS IT LIKE?
IT'S DARK INSIDE.
AND STUFFY AND DUSTY.
THERE'S OTHER PICTURES IN THERE...
OTHER LADIES. NOT JUST YOURS.

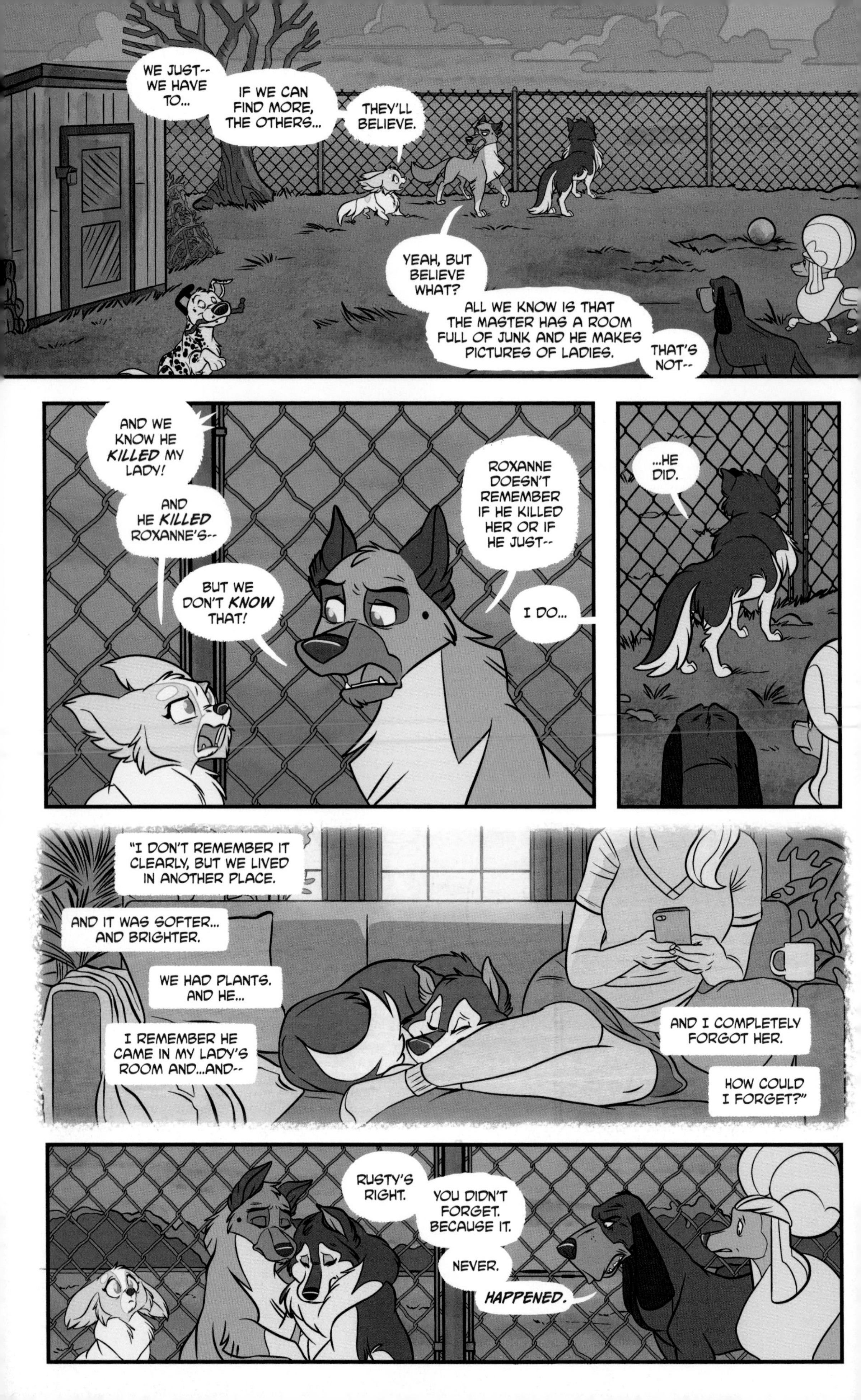
WE JUST-- WE HAVE TO...
IF WE CAN FIND MORE, THE OTHERS...
THEY'LL BELIEVE.
YEAH, BUT BELIEVE WHAT?
ALL WE KNOW IS THAT THE MASTER HAS A ROOM FULL OF JUNK AND HE MAKES PICTURES OF LADIES.
THAT'S NOT--
AND WE KNOW HE *KILLED* MY LADY!
AND HE *KILLED* ROXANNE'S--
BUT WE DON'T *KNOW* THAT!
ROXANNE DOESN'T REMEMBER IF HE KILLED HER OR IF HE JUST--
I DO...
...HE DID.
"I DON'T REMEMBER IT CLEARLY, BUT WE LIVED IN ANOTHER PLACE.
AND IT WAS SOFTER... AND BRIGHTER.
WE HAD PLANTS. AND HE...
I REMEMBER HE CAME IN MY LADY'S ROOM AND...AND--
AND I COMPLETELY FORGOT HER.
HOW COULD I FORGET?"
RUSTY'S RIGHT.
YOU DIDN'T FORGET. BECAUSE IT.
NEVER.
HAPPENED.

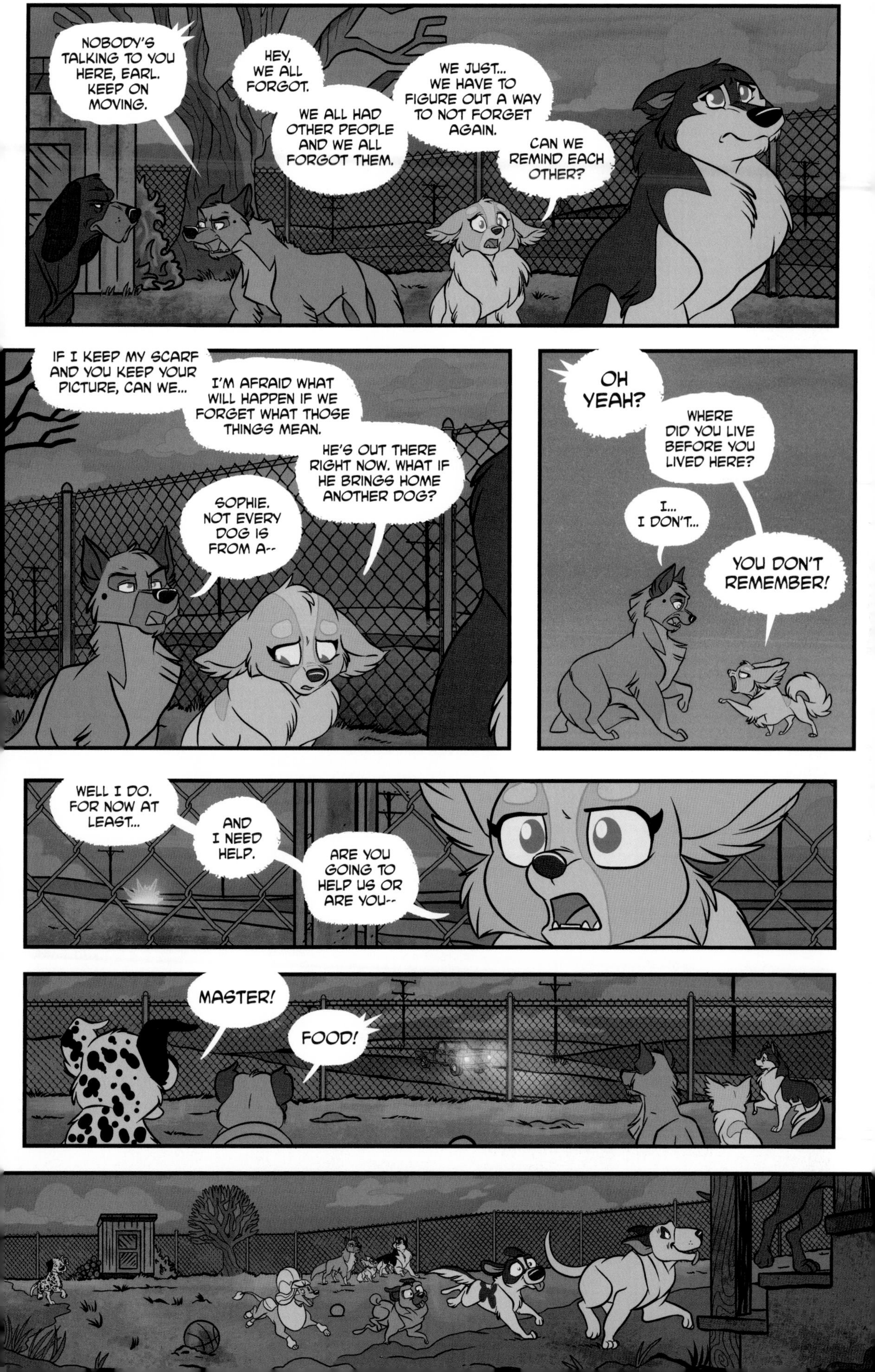
NOBODY'S TALKING TO YOU HERE, EARL. KEEP ON MOVING.
HEY, WE ALL FORGOT.
WE ALL HAD OTHER PEOPLE AND WE ALL FORGOT THEM.
WE JUST... WE HAVE TO FIGURE OUT A WAY TO NOT FORGET AGAIN.
CAN WE REMIND EACH OTHER?
IF I KEEP MY SCARF AND YOU KEEP YOUR PICTURE, CAN WE...
I'M AFRAID WHAT WILL HAPPEN IF WE FORGET WHAT THOSE THINGS MEAN.
HE'S OUT THERE RIGHT NOW. WHAT IF HE BRINGS HOME ANOTHER DOG?
SOPHIE. NOT EVERY DOG IS FROM A--
OH YEAH?
WHERE DID YOU LIVE BEFORE YOU LIVED HERE?
I... I DON'T...
YOU DON'T REMEMBER!
WELL I DO. FOR NOW AT LEAST...
AND I NEED HELP.
ARE YOU GOING TO HELP US OR ARE YOU--
MASTER!
FOOD!

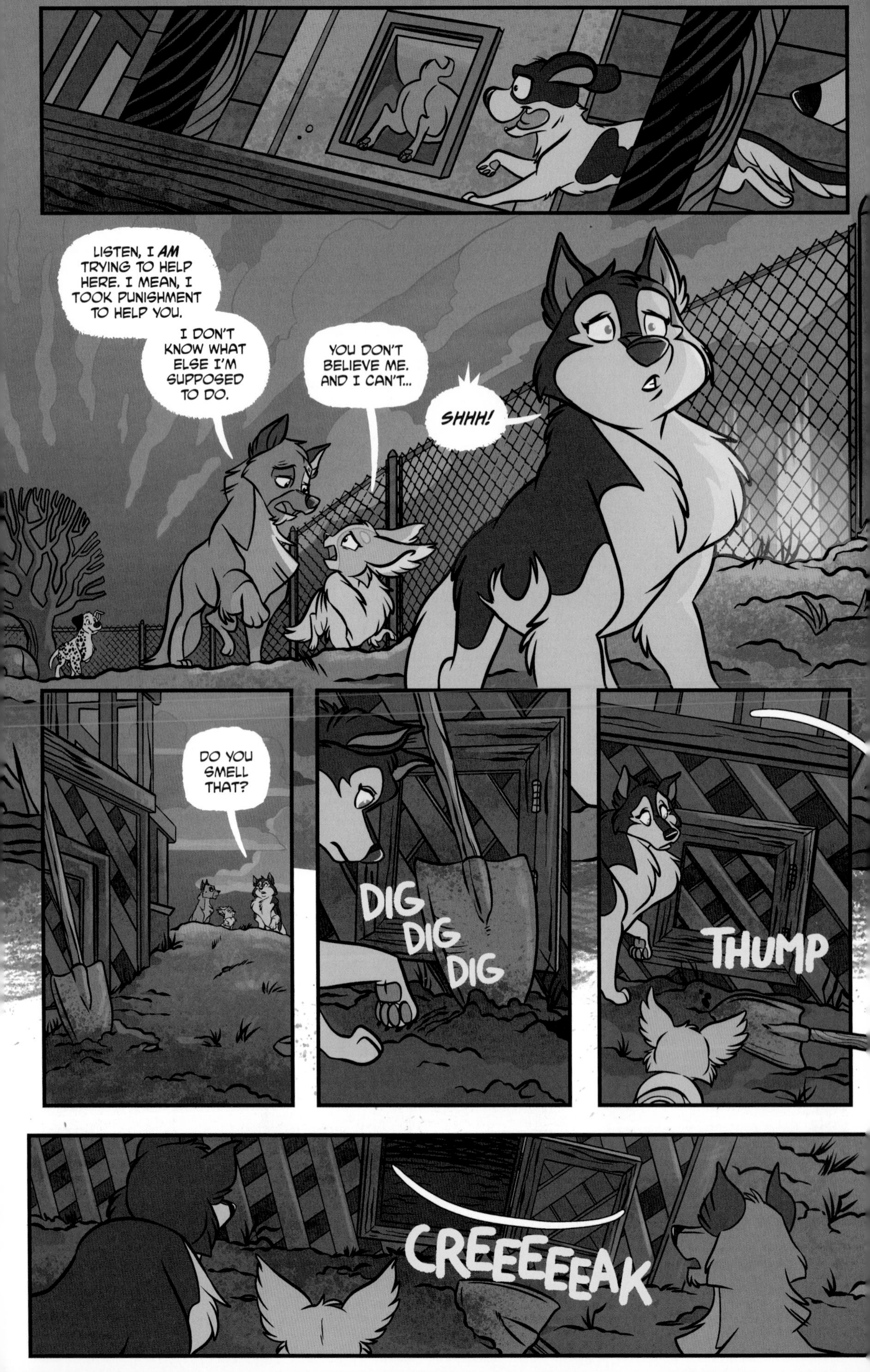
LISTEN, I AM TRYING TO HELP HERE. I MEAN, I TOOK PUNISHMENT TO HELP YOU.
I DON'T KNOW WHAT ELSE I'M SUPPOSED TO DO.
YOU DON'T BELIEVE ME. AND I CAN'T...
SHHH!
DO YOU SMELL THAT?
DIG DIG DIG
THUMP
CREEEEEEAK

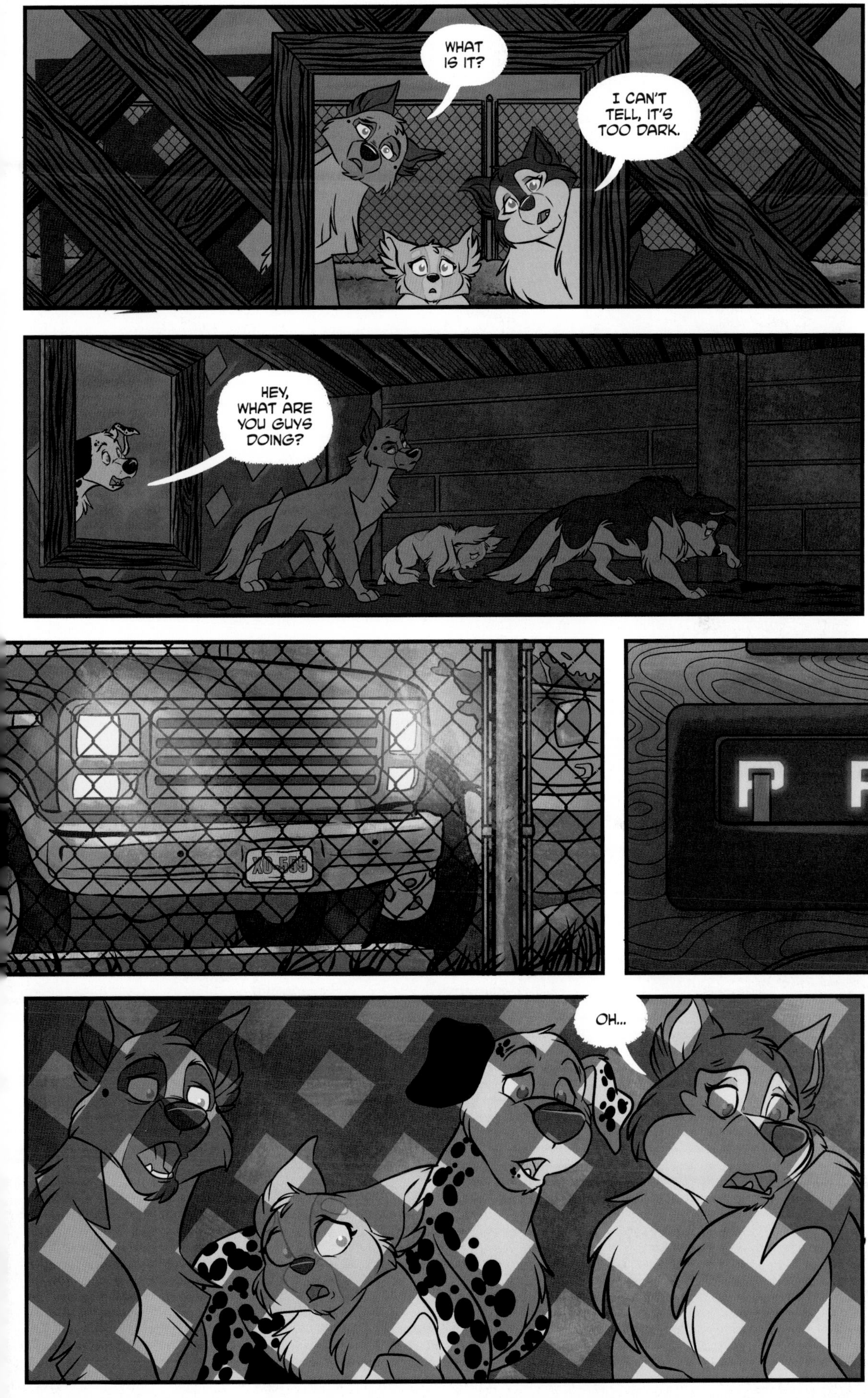
WHAT IS IT?
I CAN'T TELL, IT'S TOO DARK.
HEY, WHAT ARE YOU GUYS DOING?
XO-555
OH...

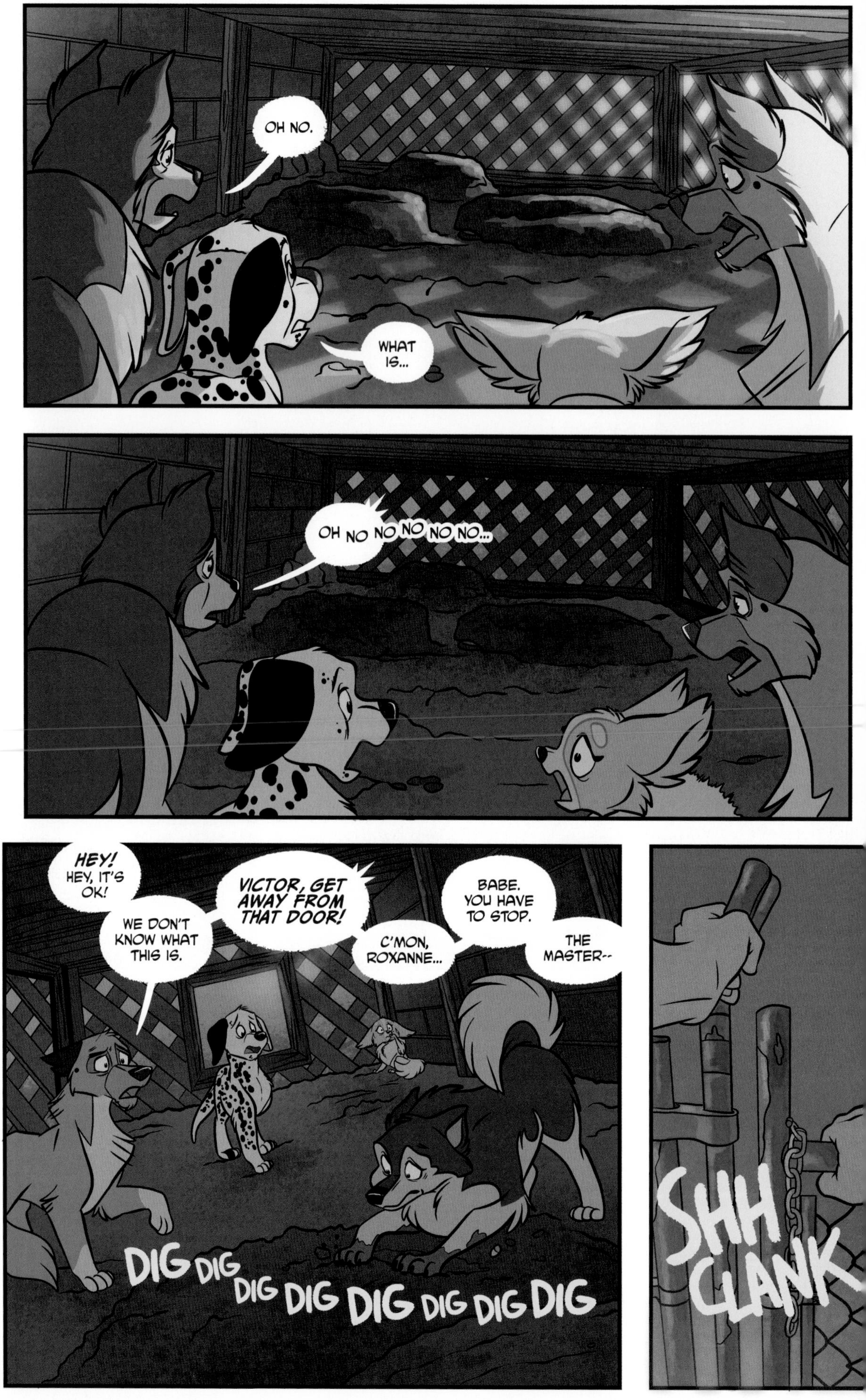
OH NO.
WHAT IS...
OH NO NO NO NO NO...
HEY! HEY, IT'S OK!
WE DON'T KNOW WHAT THIS IS.
VICTOR, GET AWAY FROM THAT DOOR!
C'MON, ROXANNE...
BABE. YOU HAVE TO STOP.
THE MASTER--
DIG DIG DIG DIG DIG DIG DIG DIG
SHH CLANK

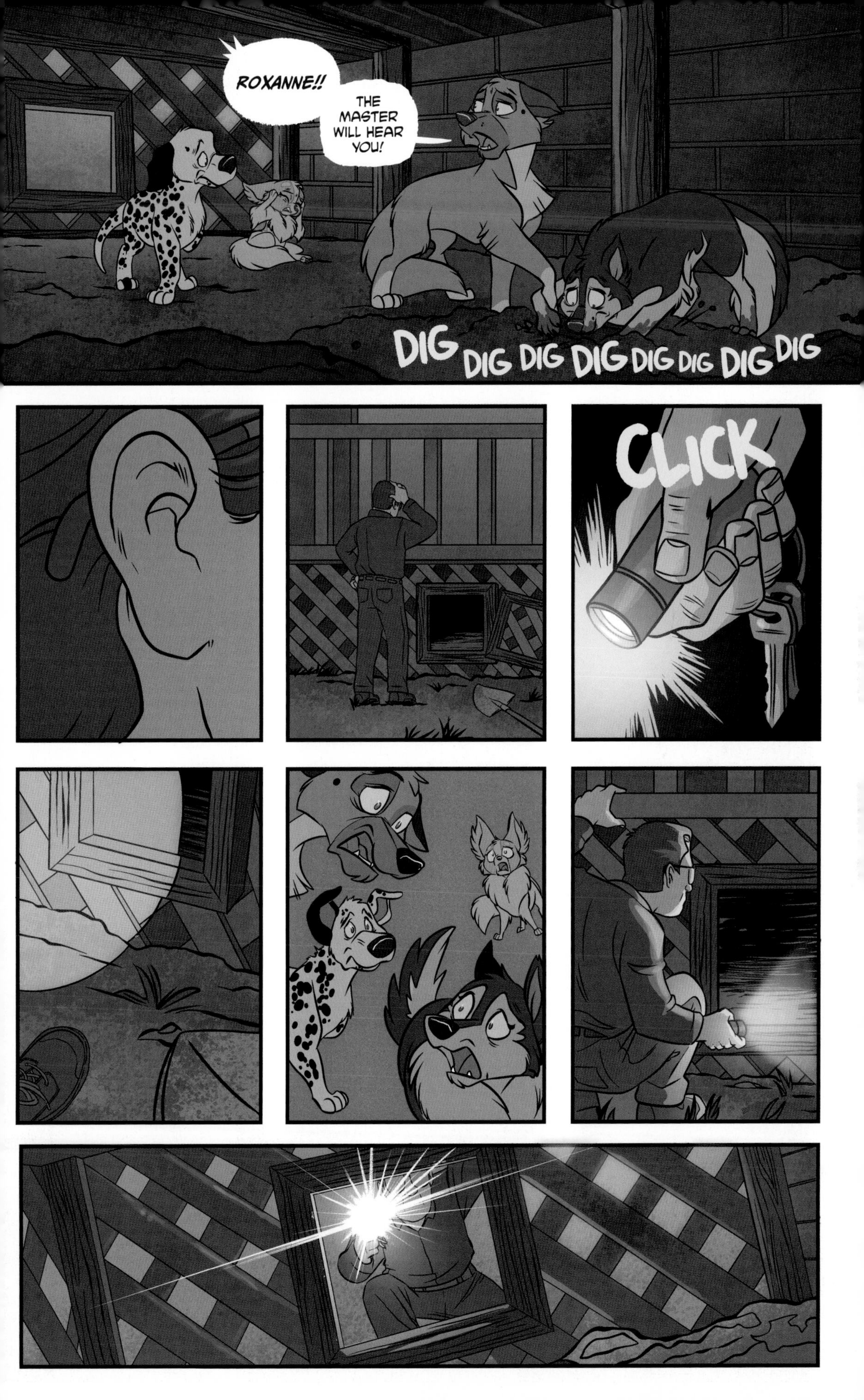
ROXANNE!!
THE MASTER WILL HEAR YOU!
DIG DIG DIG DIG DIG DIG DIG DIG
CLICK

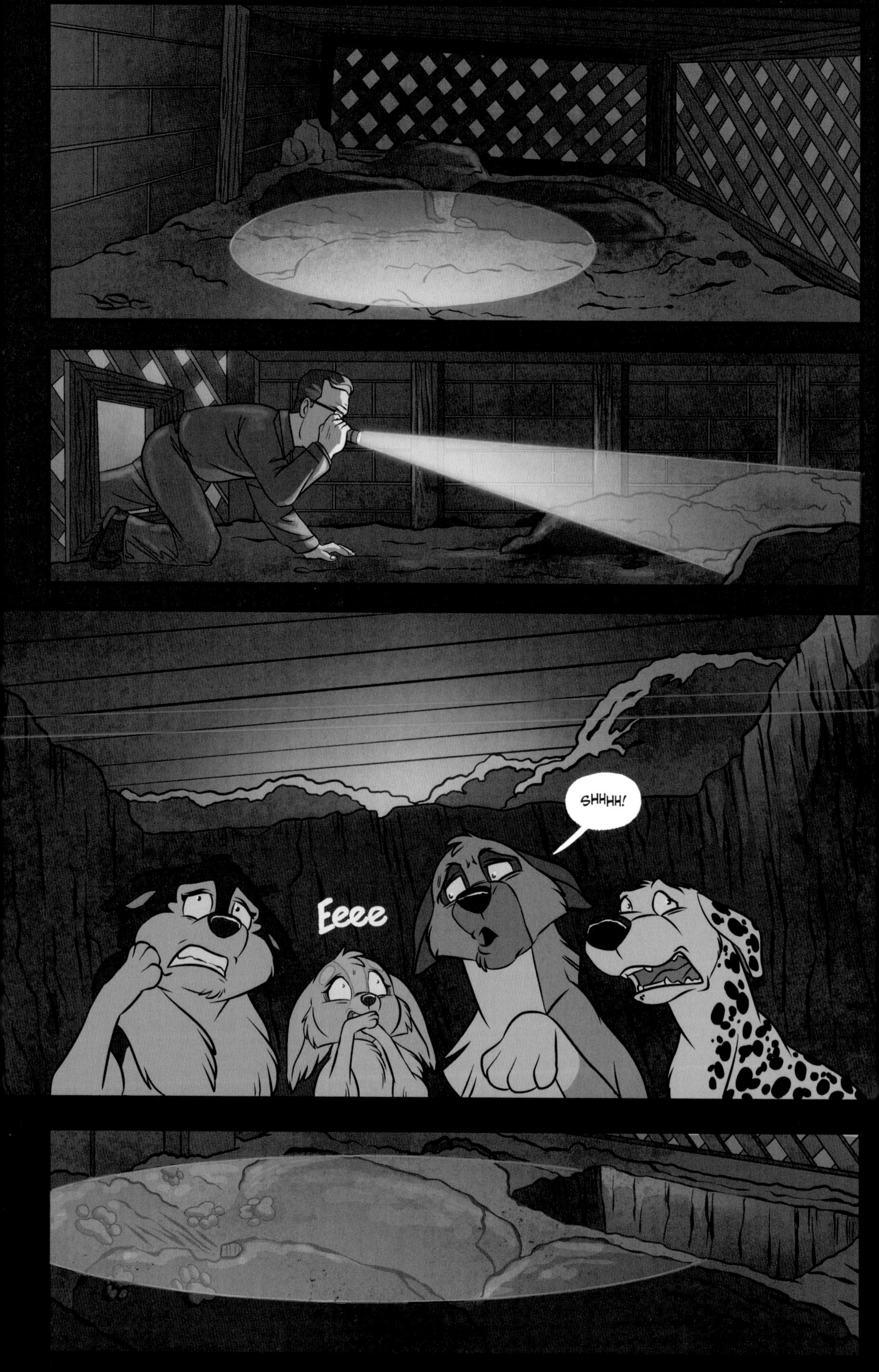
Eeee
SHHHH!

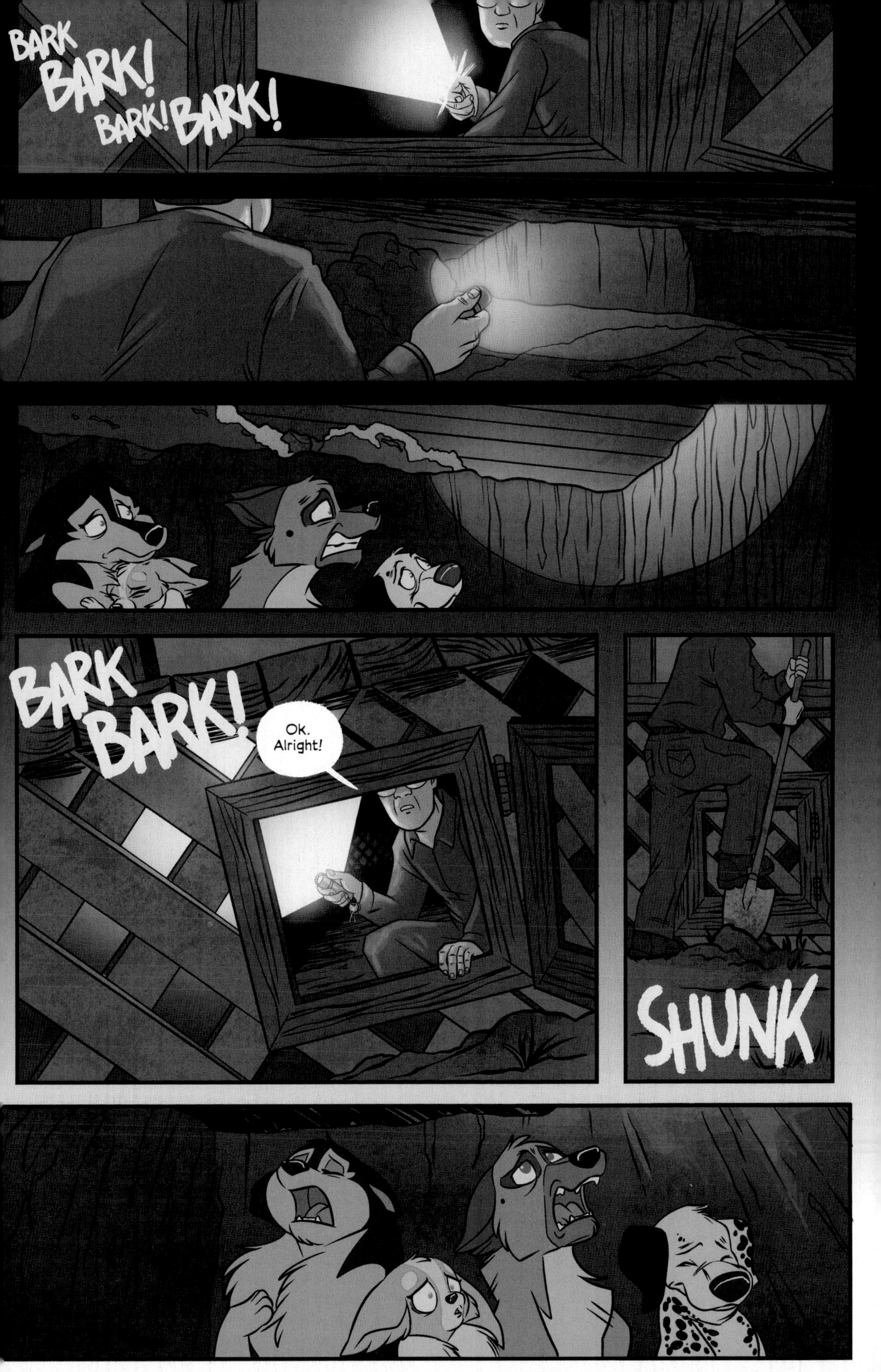
BARK
BARK!
BARK! BARK!
BARK
BARK!
Ok. Alright!
SHUNK

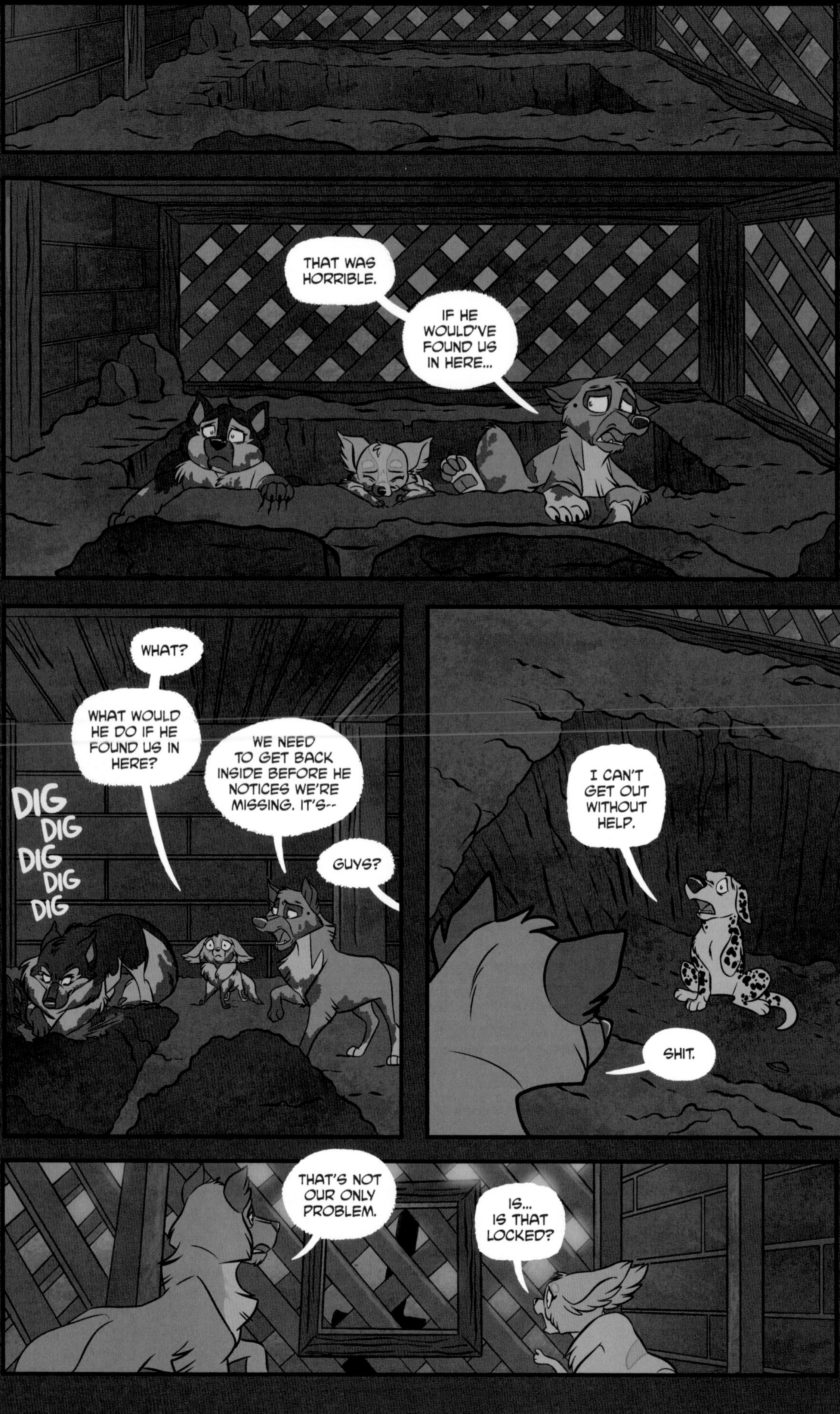
THAT WAS HORRIBLE.
IF HE WOULD'VE FOUND US IN HERE...
WHAT?
WHAT WOULD HE DO IF HE FOUND US IN HERE?
WE NEED TO GET BACK INSIDE BEFORE HE NOTICES WE'RE MISSING. IT'S--
DIG DIG DIG DIG DIG
GUYS?
I CAN'T GET OUT WITHOUT HELP.
SHIT.
THAT'S NOT OUR ONLY PROBLEM.
IS... IS THAT LOCKED?

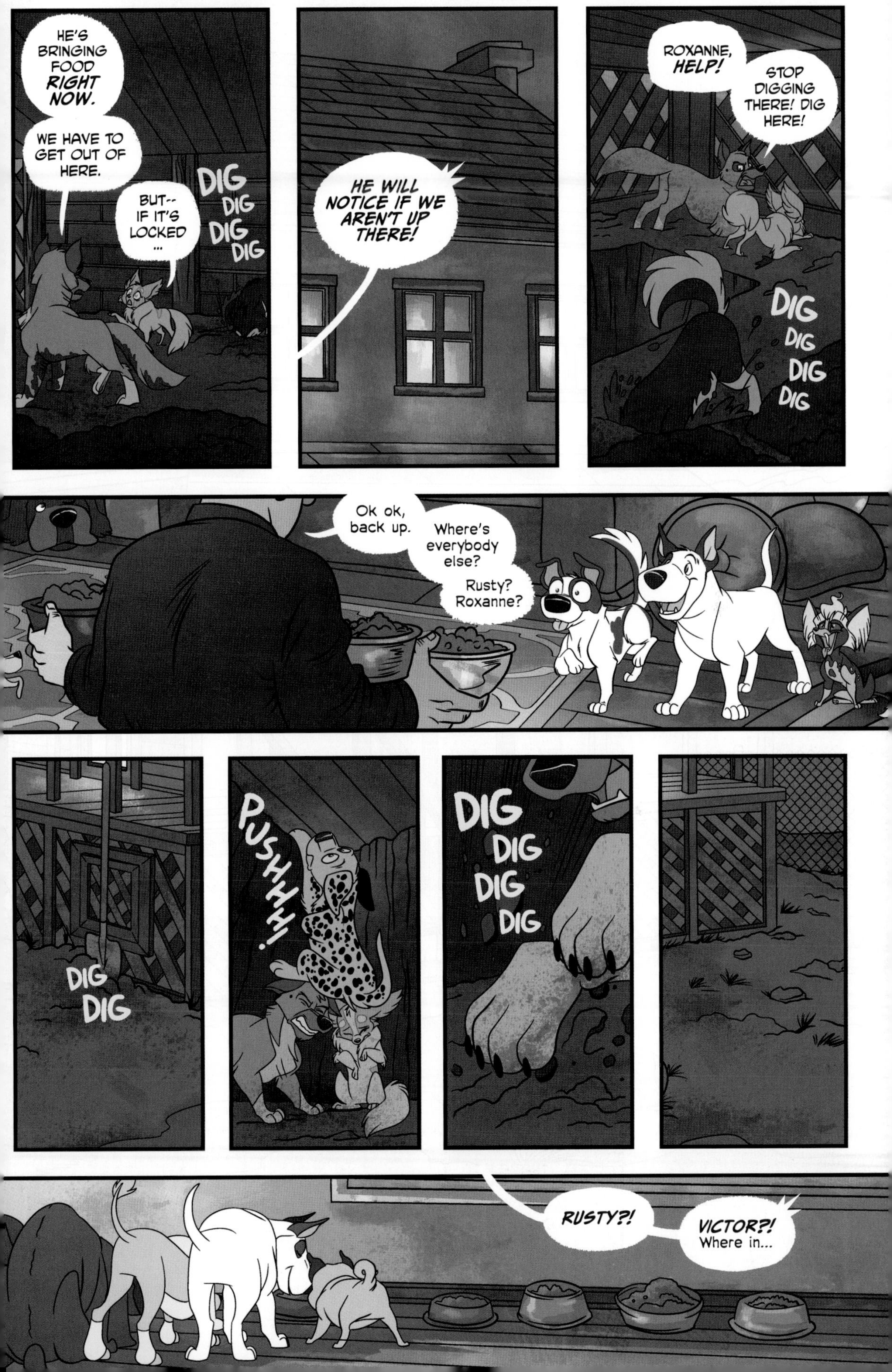
HE'S BRINGING FOOD RIGHT NOW.
WE HAVE TO GET OUT OF HERE.
BUT-- IF IT'S LOCKED ...
DIG DIG DIG DIG
HE WILL NOTICE IF WE AREN'T UP THERE!
ROXANNE, HELP!
STOP DIGGING THERE! DIG HERE!
DIG DIG DIG DIG
Ok ok, back up.
Where's everybody else?
Rusty? Roxanne?
DIG DIG
PUSHHH!
DIG DIG DIG DIG
RUSTY?!
VICTOR?! Where in...

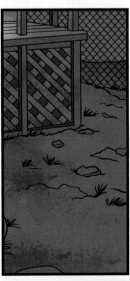

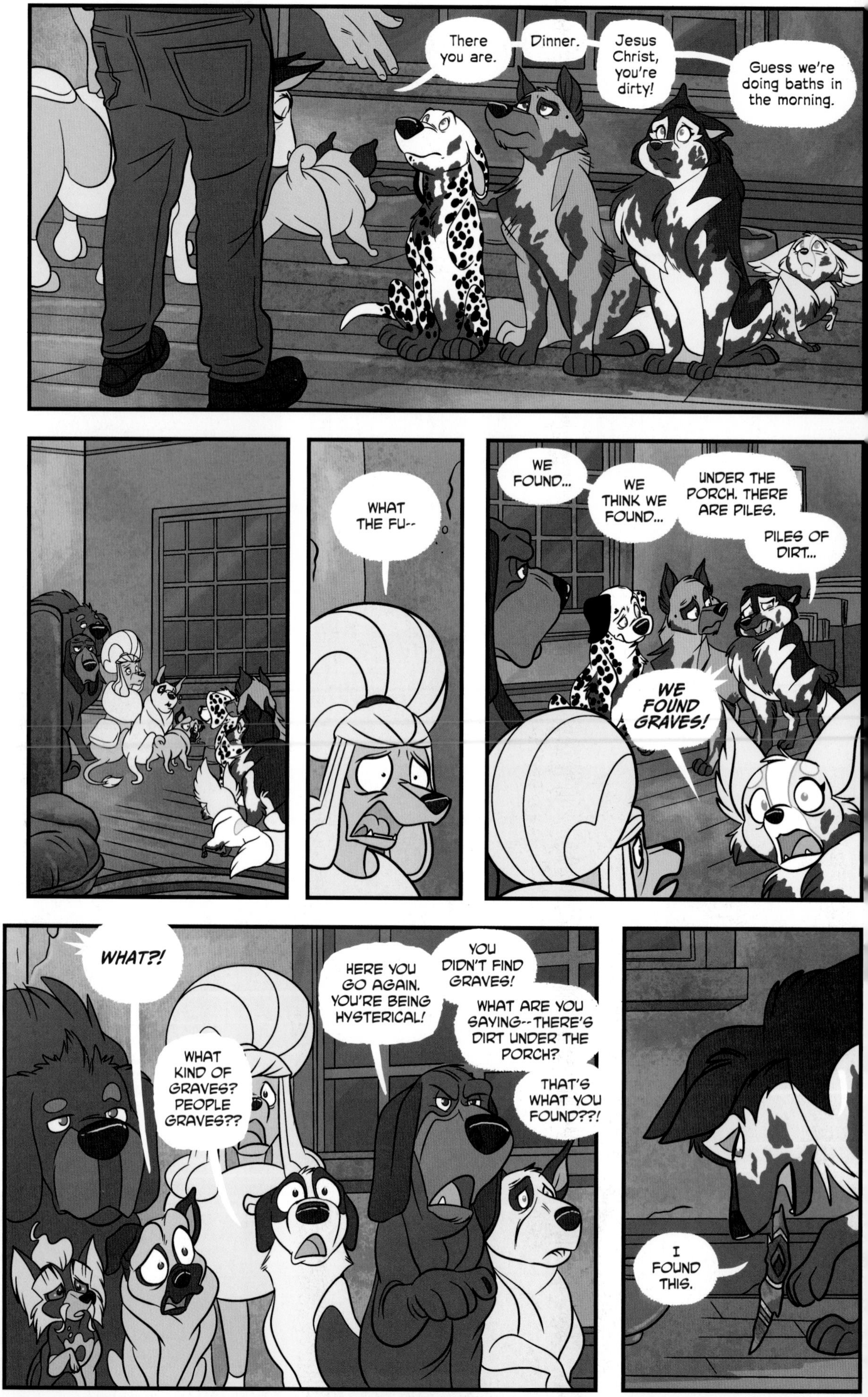
There you are.
Dinner.
Jesus Christ, you're dirty!
Guess we're doing baths in the morning.
WHAT THE FU--
WE FOUND...
WE THINK WE FOUND...
UNDER THE PORCH. THERE ARE PILES.
PILES OF DIRT...
WE FOUND GRAVES!
WHAT?!
WHAT KIND OF GRAVES? PEOPLE GRAVES??
HERE YOU GO AGAIN. YOU'RE BEING HYSTERICAL!
YOU DIDN'T FIND GRAVES!
WHAT ARE YOU SAYING--THERE'S DIRT UNDER THE PORCH?
THAT'S WHAT YOU FOUND??!
I FOUND THIS.

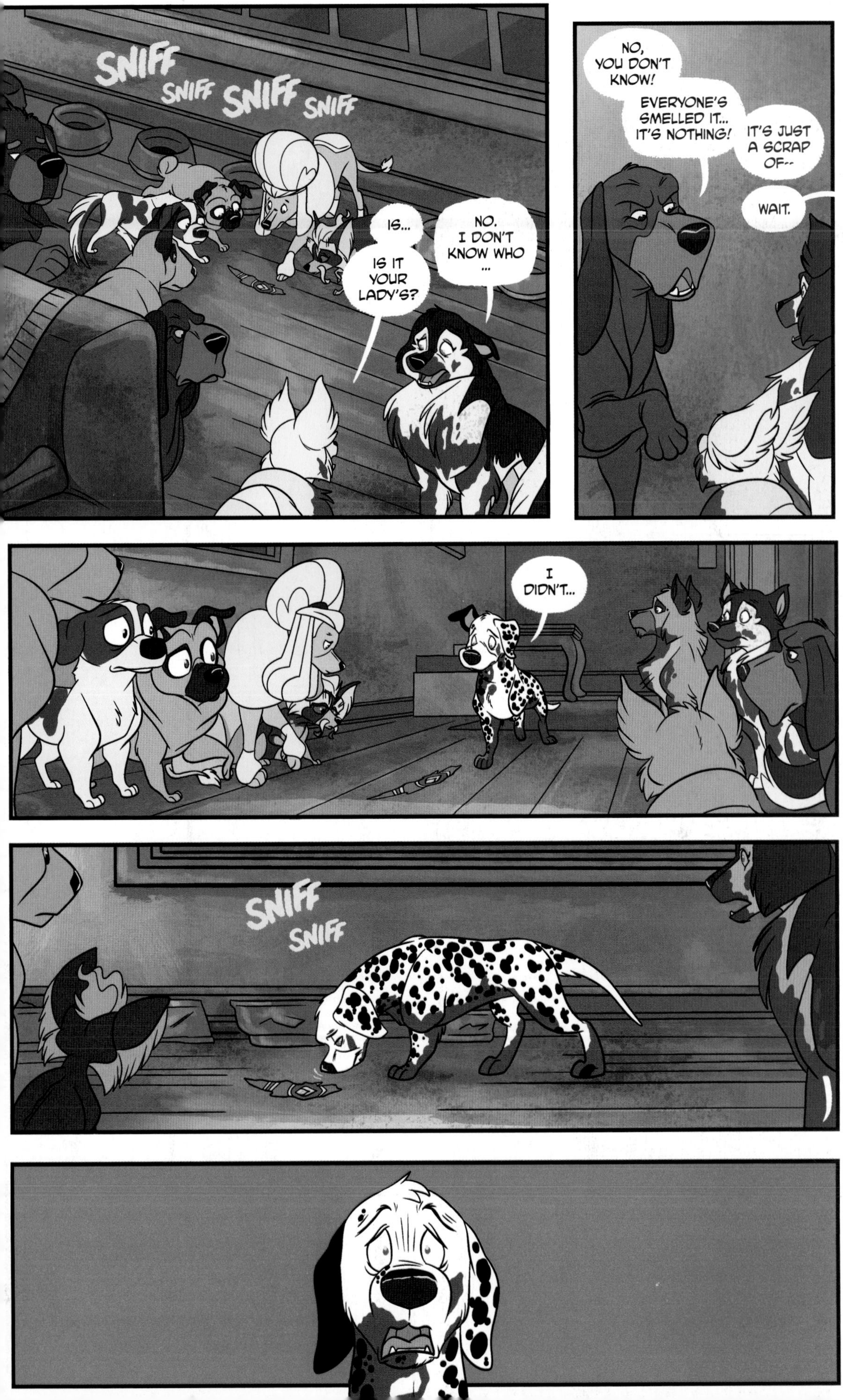
SNIFF
SNIFF
SNIFF
SNIFF
IS...
IS IT YOUR LADY'S?
NO. I DON'T KNOW WHO ...
NO, YOU DON'T KNOW!
EVERYONE'S SMELLED IT... IT'S NOTHING!
IT'S JUST A SCRAP OF--
WAIT.
I DIDN'T...
SNIFF
SNIFF

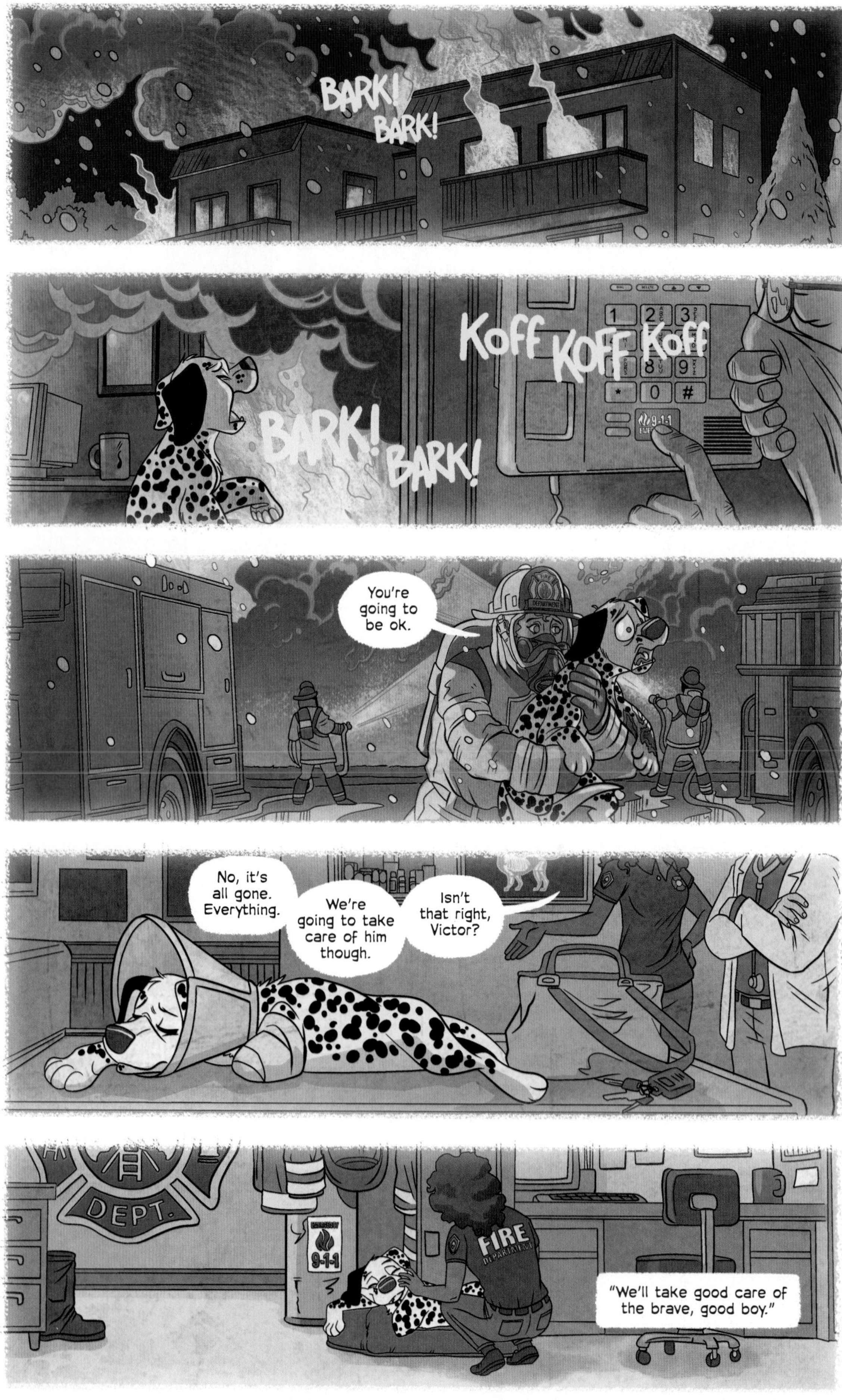
BARK!
BARK!
BARK!
BARK!
Koff KOFF Koff
You're going to be ok.
No, it's all gone. Everything.
We're going to take care of him though.
Isn't that right, Victor?
DEPT.
9-1-1
FIRE
"We'll take good care of the brave, good boy."

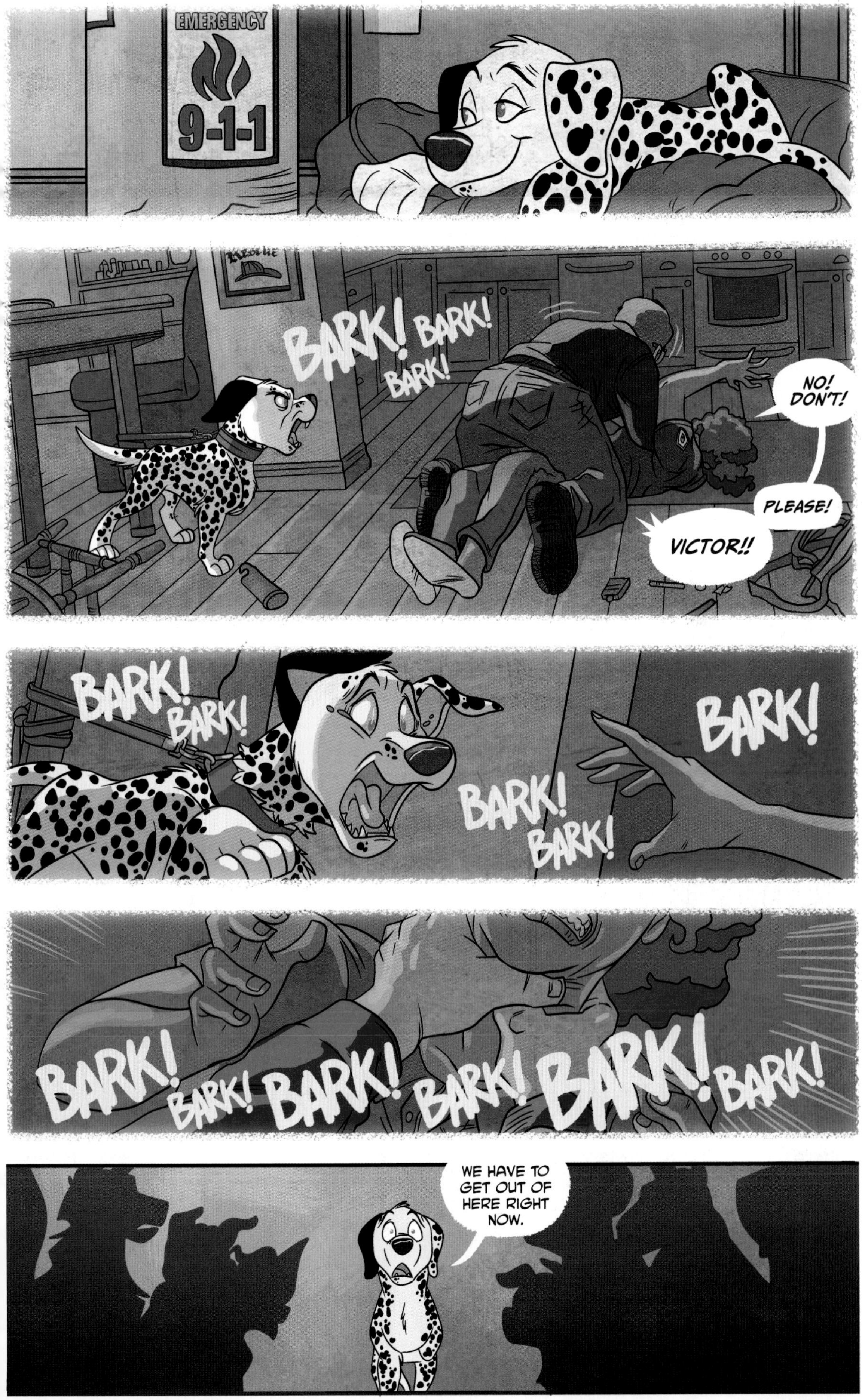
EMERGENCY
9-1-1
BARK! BARK!
BARK!
NO! DON'T!
PLEASE!
VICTOR!!
BARK!
BARK!
BARK!
BARK!
BARK!
BARK!
BARK!
BARK!
BARK!
BARK!
BARK!
WE HAVE TO GET OUT OF HERE RIGHT NOW.

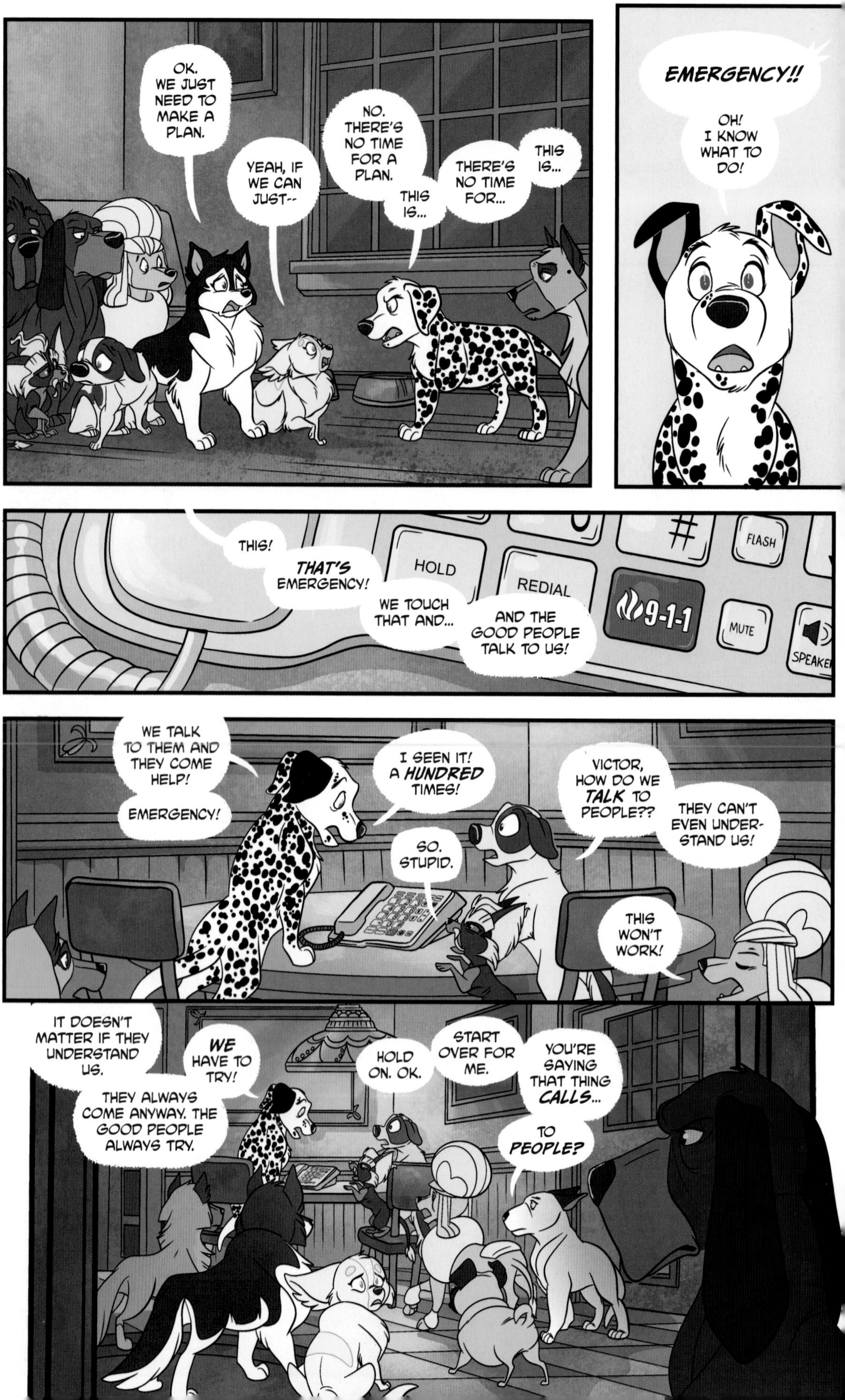
OK. WE JUST NEED TO MAKE A PLAN.
YEAH, IF WE CAN JUST--
NO. THERE'S NO TIME FOR A PLAN.
THIS IS...
THERE'S NO TIME FOR...
THIS IS...
EMERGENCY!!
OH! I KNOW WHAT TO DO!
THIS!
THAT'S EMERGENCY!
WE TOUCH THAT AND...
AND THE GOOD PEOPLE TALK TO US!
HOLD
REDIAL
FLASH
9-1-1
MUTE
SPEAKER
WE TALK TO THEM AND THEY COME HELP!
EMERGENCY!
I SEEN IT! A HUNDRED TIMES!
SO. STUPID.
VICTOR, HOW DO WE TALK TO PEOPLE??
THEY CAN'T EVEN UNDER-STAND US!
THIS WON'T WORK!
IT DOESN'T MATTER IF THEY UNDERSTAND US.
THEY ALWAYS COME ANYWAY. THE GOOD PEOPLE ALWAYS TRY.
WE HAVE TO TRY!
HOLD ON. OK.
START OVER FOR ME.
YOU'RE SAYING THAT THING CALLS...
TO PEOPLE?

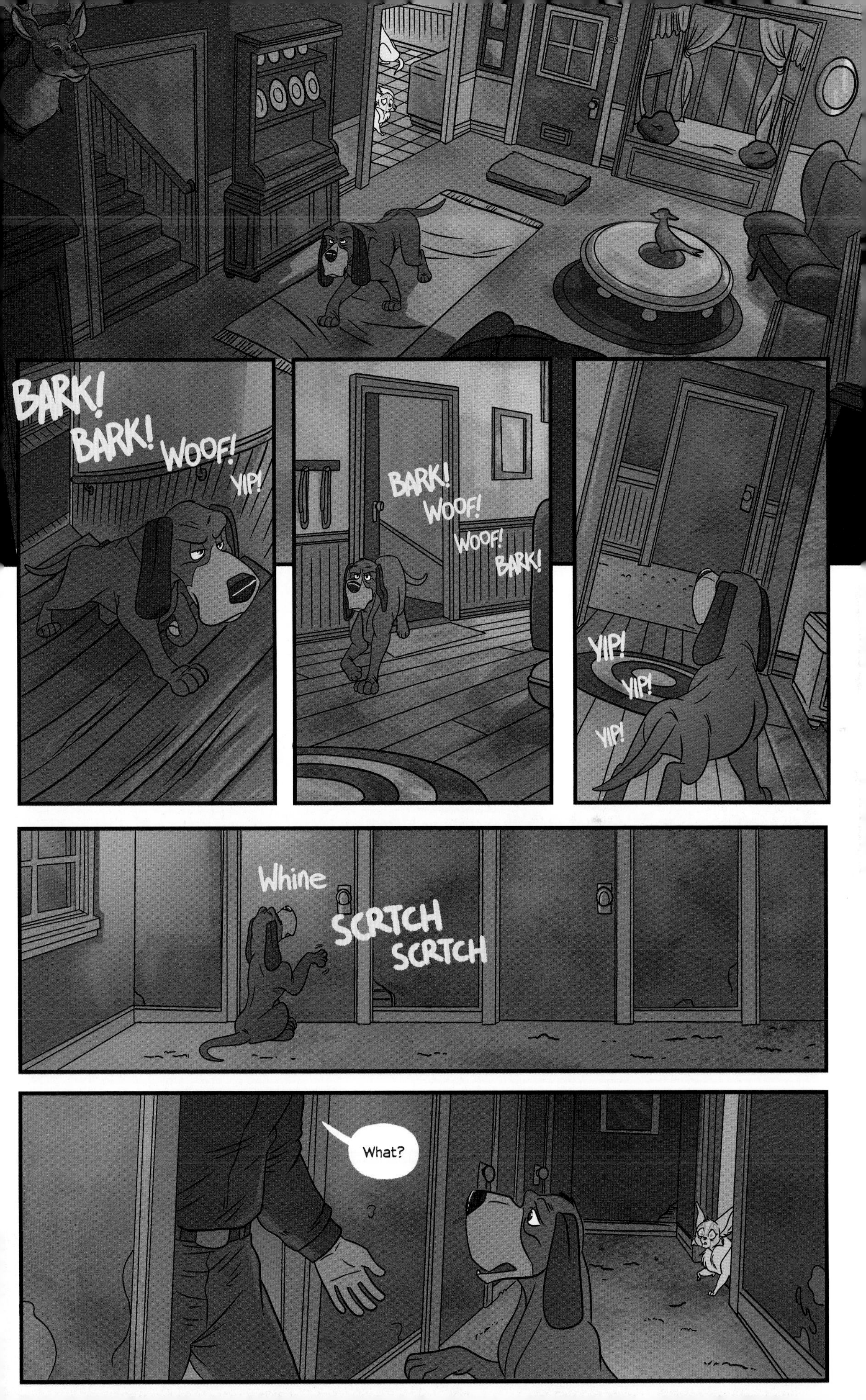
BARK!
BARK!
WOOF!
YIP!
BARK!
WOOF!
WOOF!
BARK!
YIP!
YIP!
YIP!
Whine
SCRTCH
SCRTCH
What?

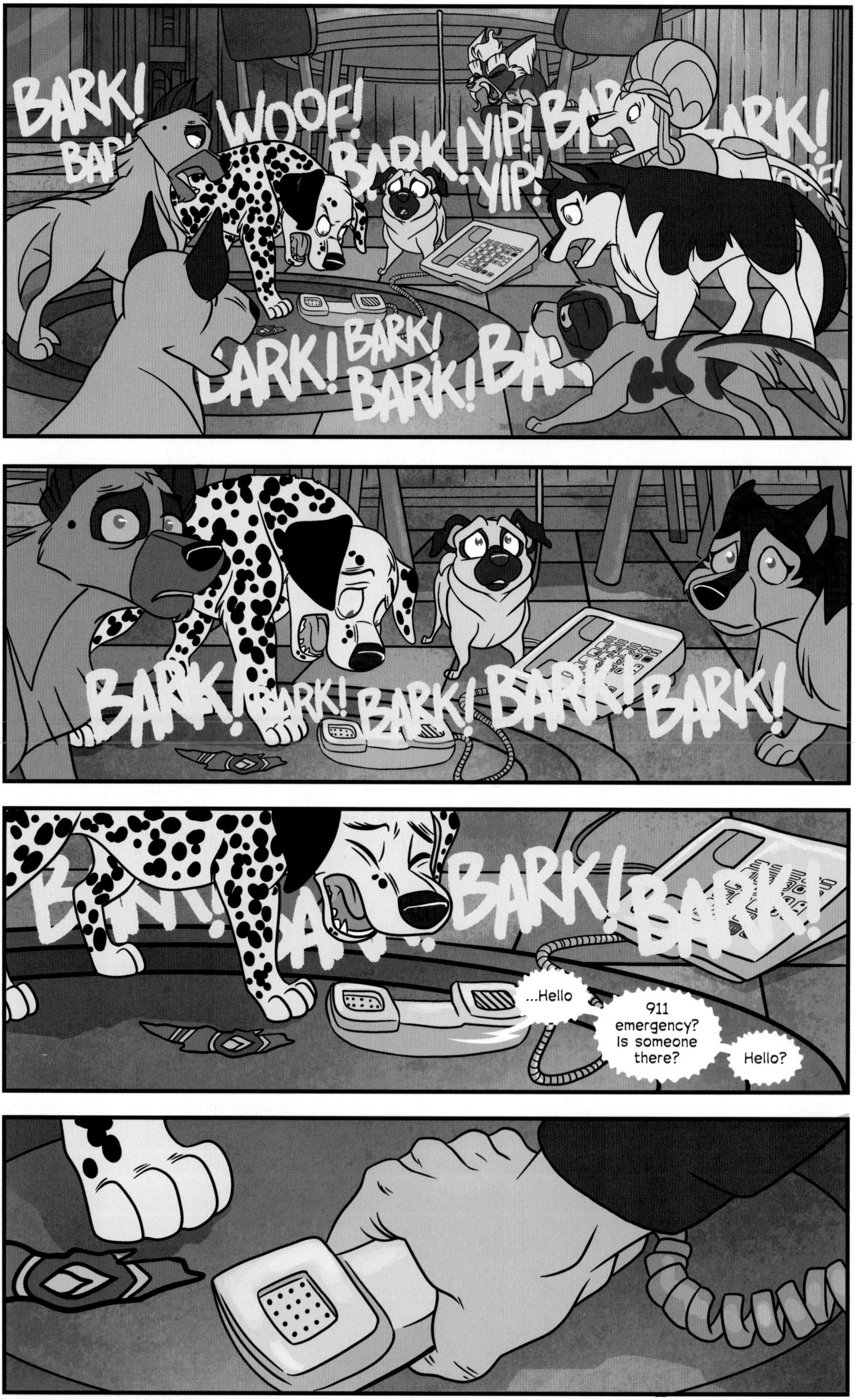
BARK!
WOOF!
BARK!
YIP!
YIP!
BARK!
BARK!
BARK!
BARK!
BARK!
BARK!
BARK!
BARK!
BARK!
BARK!
BARK!
...Hello
911 emergency? Is someone there?
Hello?

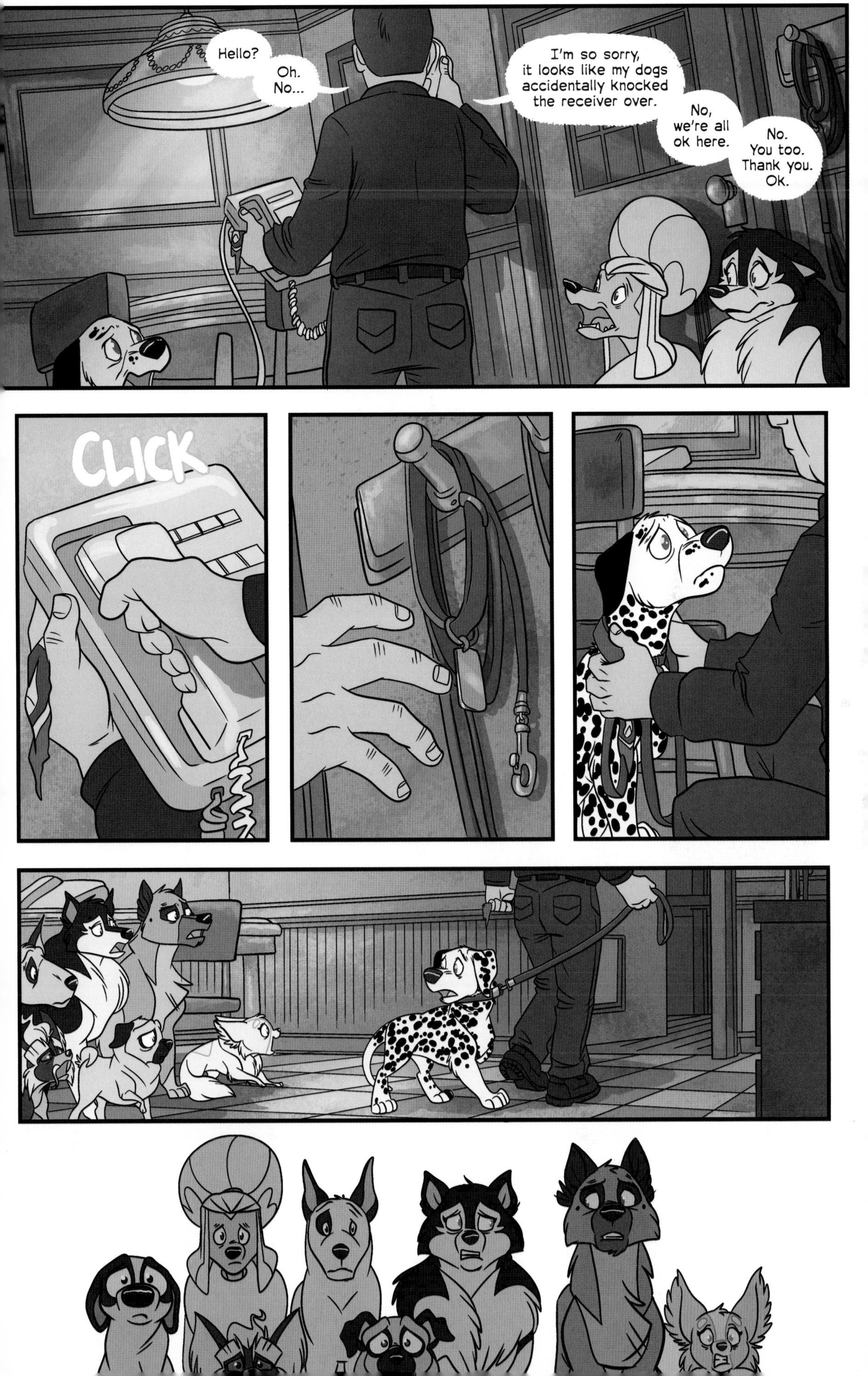
Hello?
Oh. No...
I'm so sorry, it looks like my dogs accidentally knocked the receiver over.
No, we're all ok here.
No. You too. Thank you. Ok.
CLICK

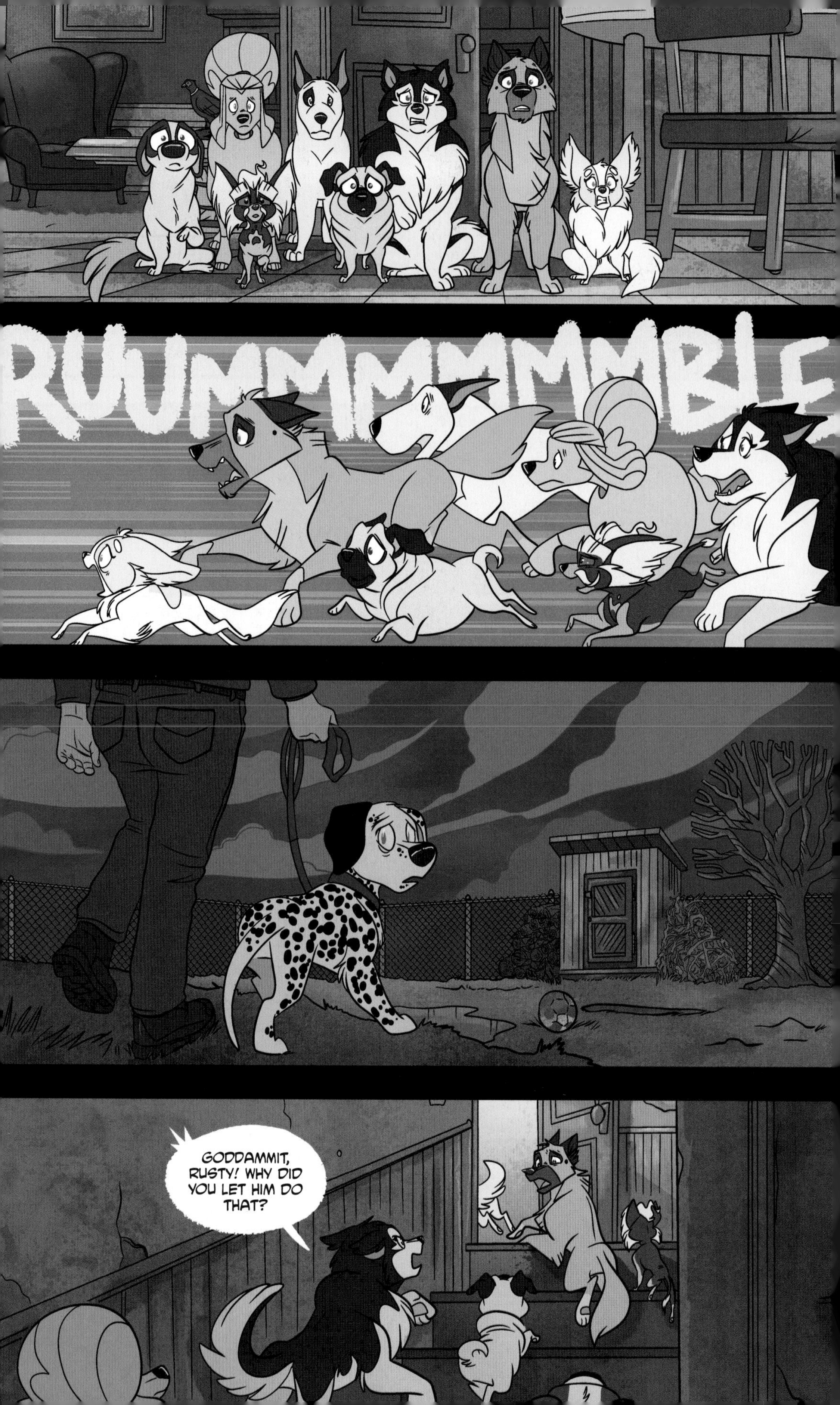
RUUMMMMMMMBLE
GODDAMMIT, RUSTY! WHY DID YOU LET HIM DO THAT?

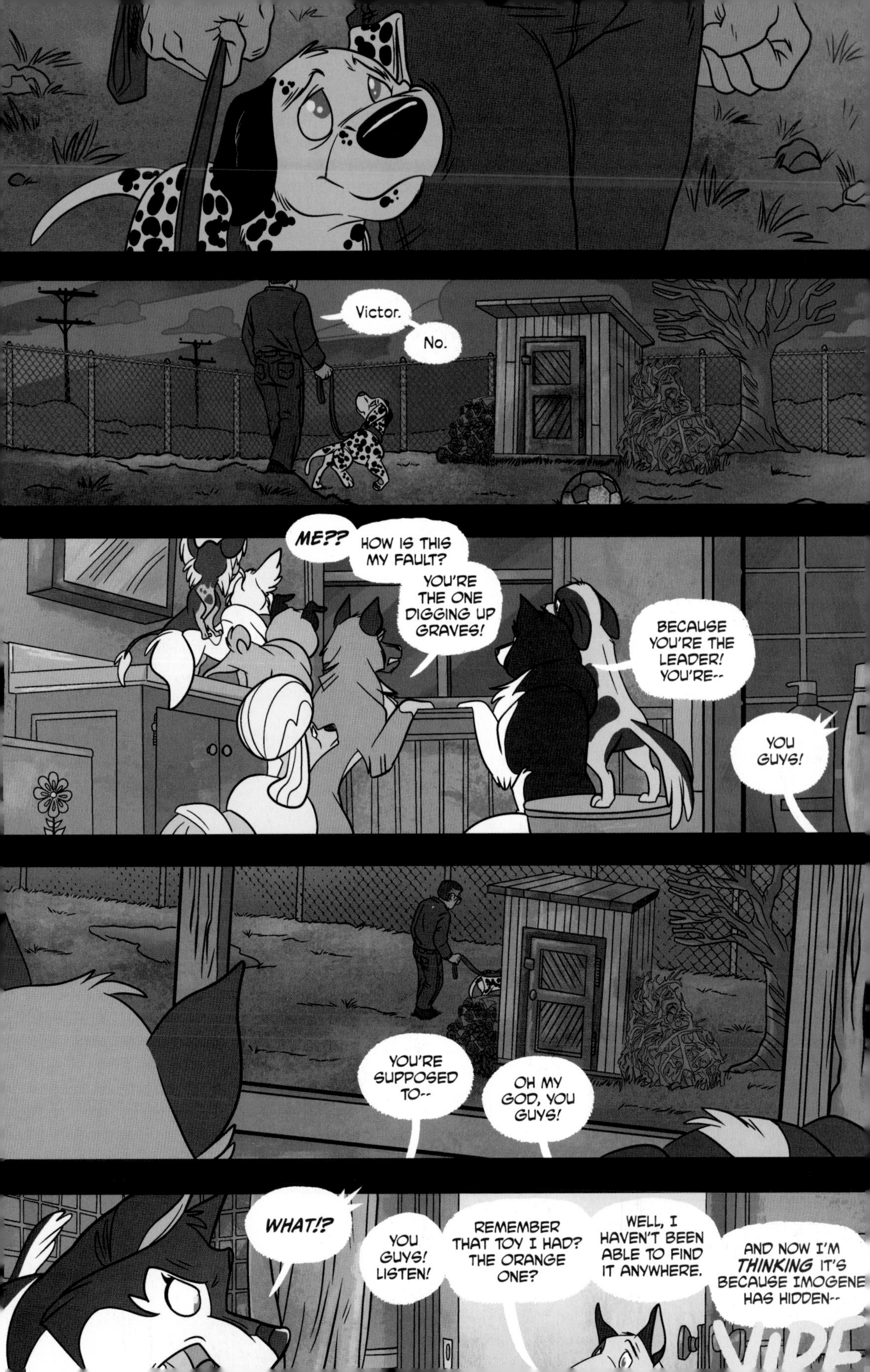
Victor.
No.
ME??
HOW IS THIS MY FAULT?
YOU'RE THE ONE DIGGING UP GRAVES!
BECAUSE YOU'RE THE LEADER! YOU'RE--
YOU GUYS!
YOU'RE SUPPOSED TO--
OH MY GOD, YOU GUYS!
WHAT!?
YOU GUYS! LISTEN!
REMEMBER THAT TOY I HAD? THE ORANGE ONE?
WELL, I HAVEN'T BEEN ABLE TO FIND IT ANYWHERE.
AND NOW I'M *THINKING* IT'S BECAUSE IMOGENE HAS HIDDEN--

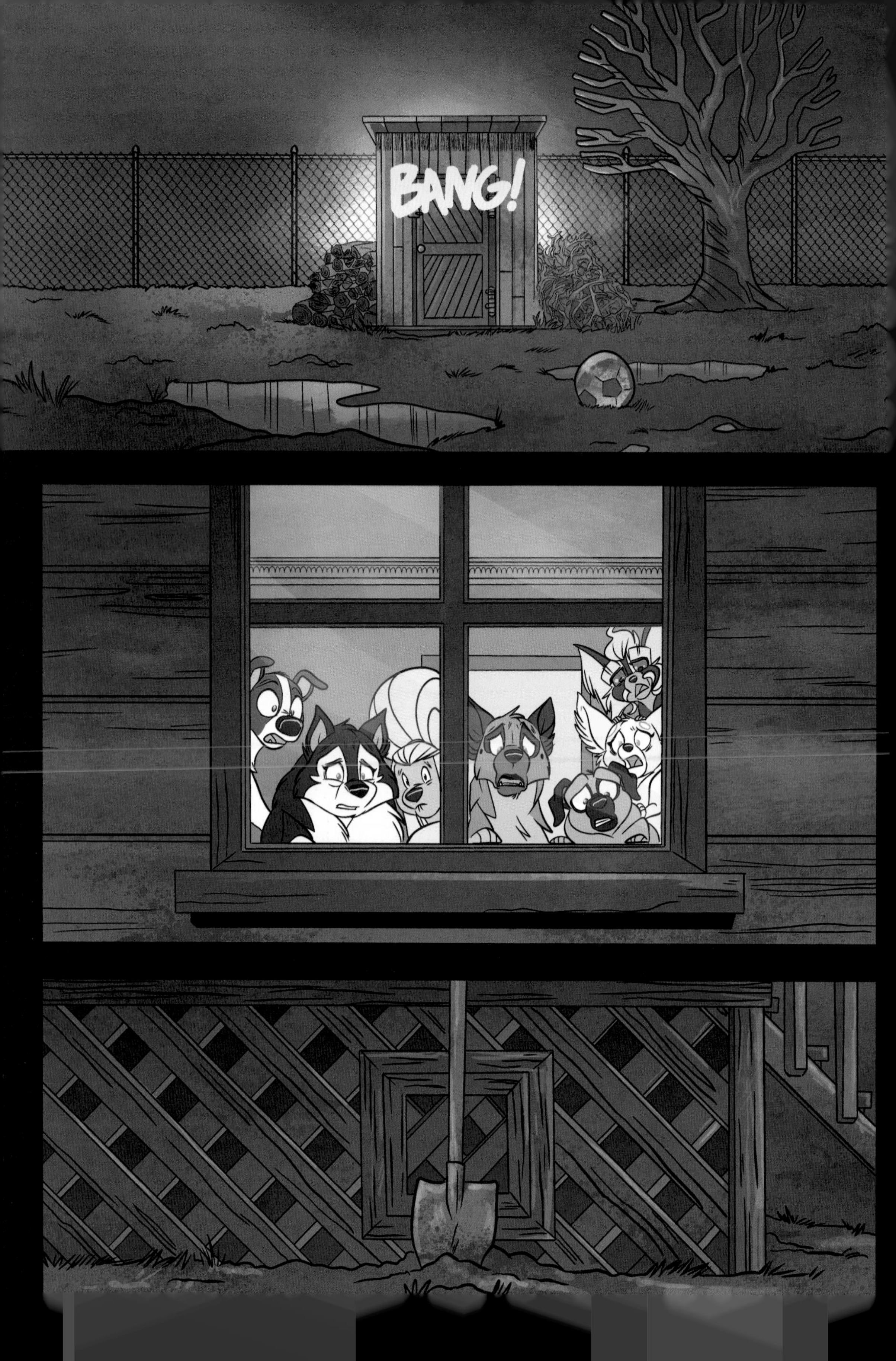
BANG!

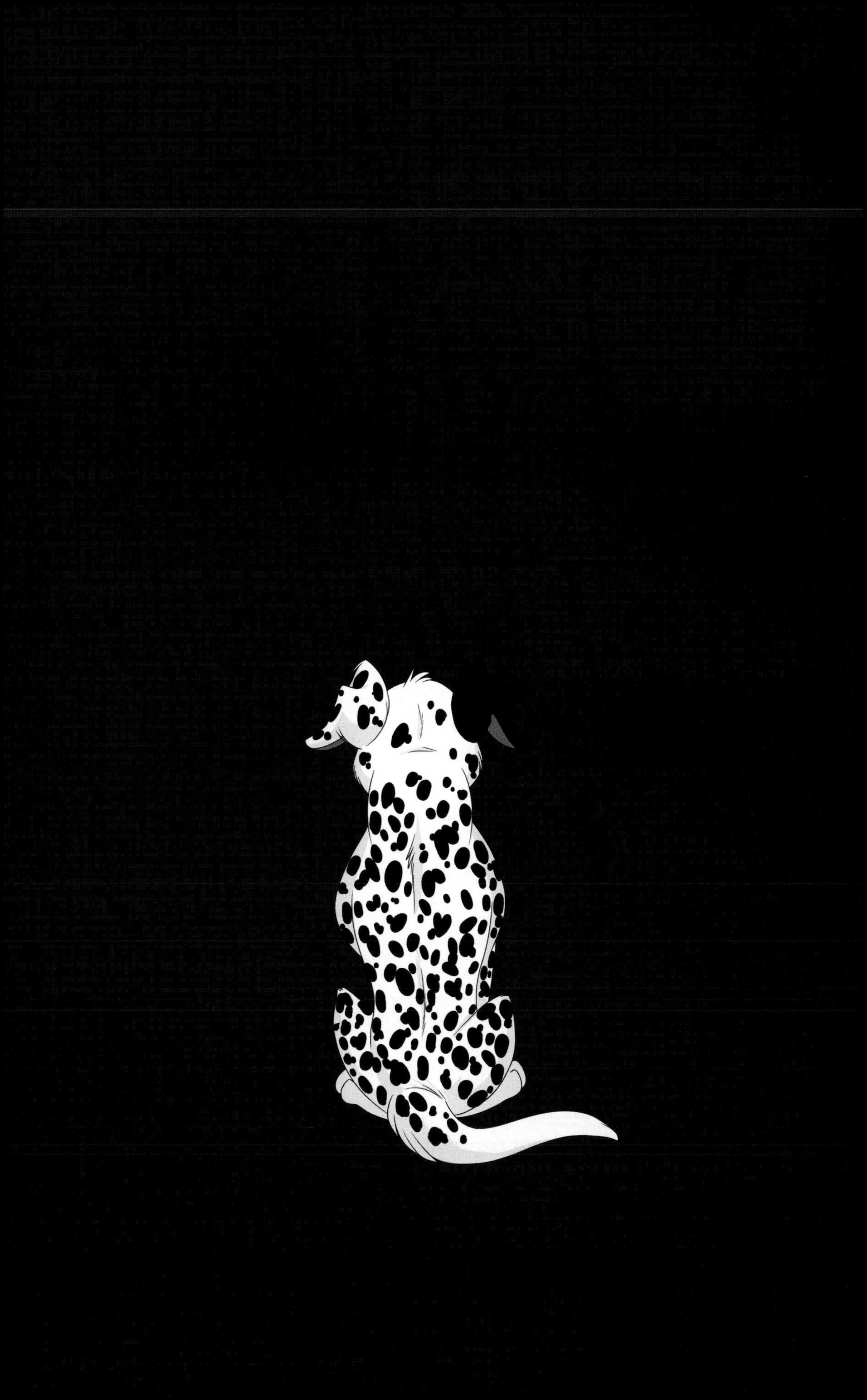

Chapter 4:
PLAY DEAD

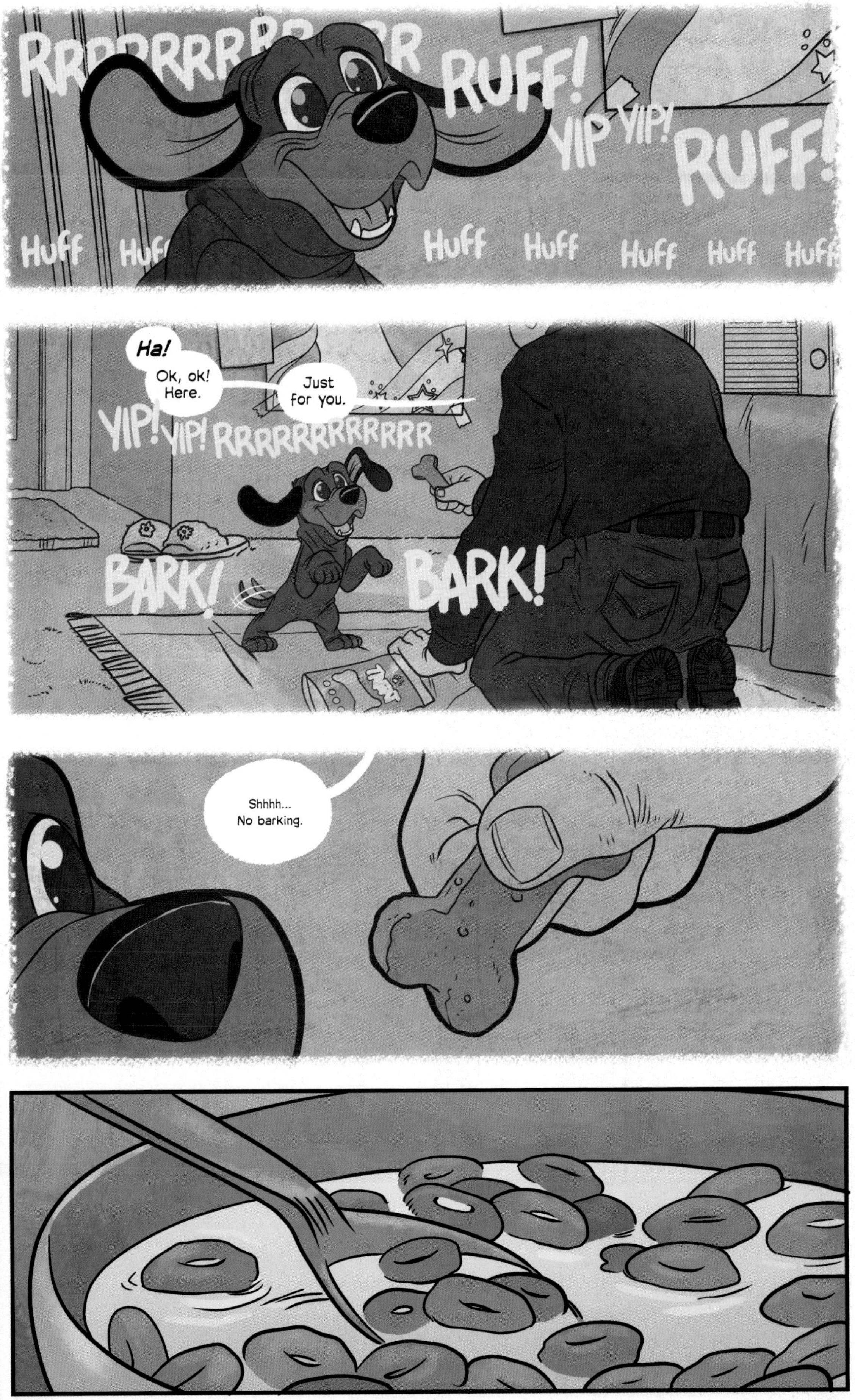
RRRRRRRRRRR
RUFF!
YIP YIP!
RUFF!
Huff Huff Huff Huff Huff Huff Huff
Ha!
Ok, ok! Here.
Just for you.
YIP! YIP! RRRRRRRRRRR
BARK!
BARK!
TREAT
Shhhh... No barking.

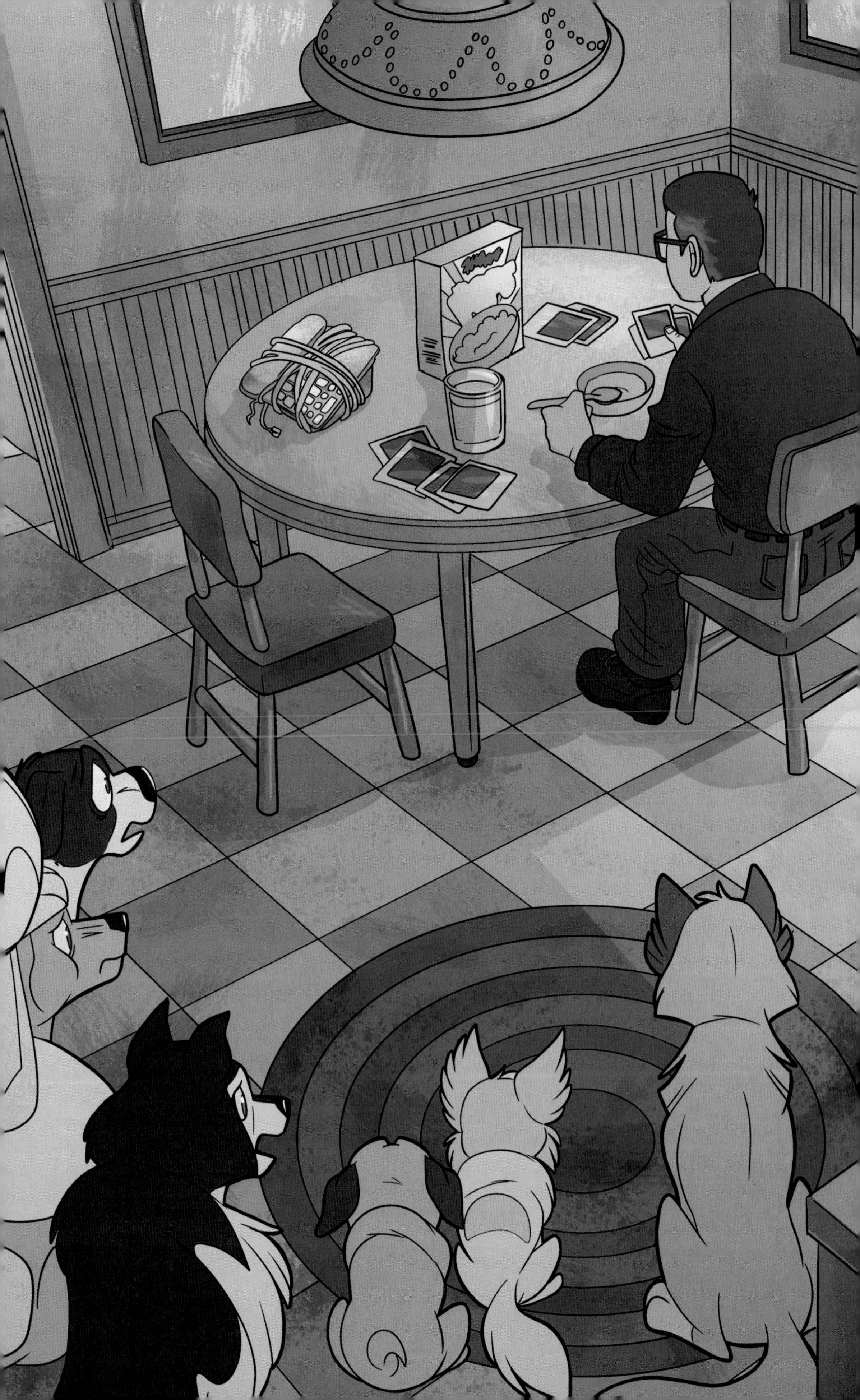

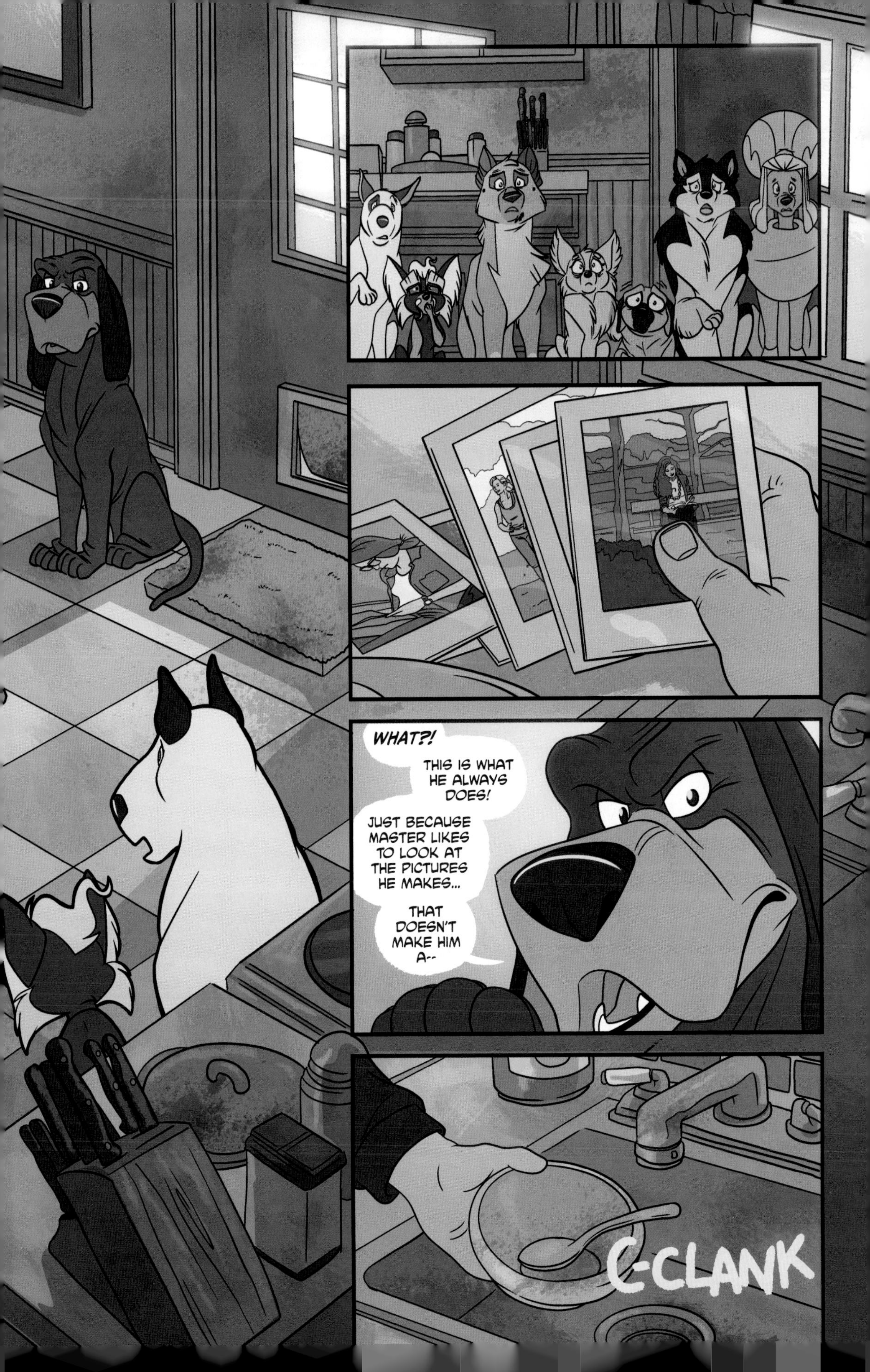
WHAT?!
THIS IS WHAT HE ALWAYS DOES!
JUST BECAUSE MASTER LIKES TO LOOK AT THE PICTURES HE MAKES...
THAT DOESN'T MAKE HIM A--
C-CLANK

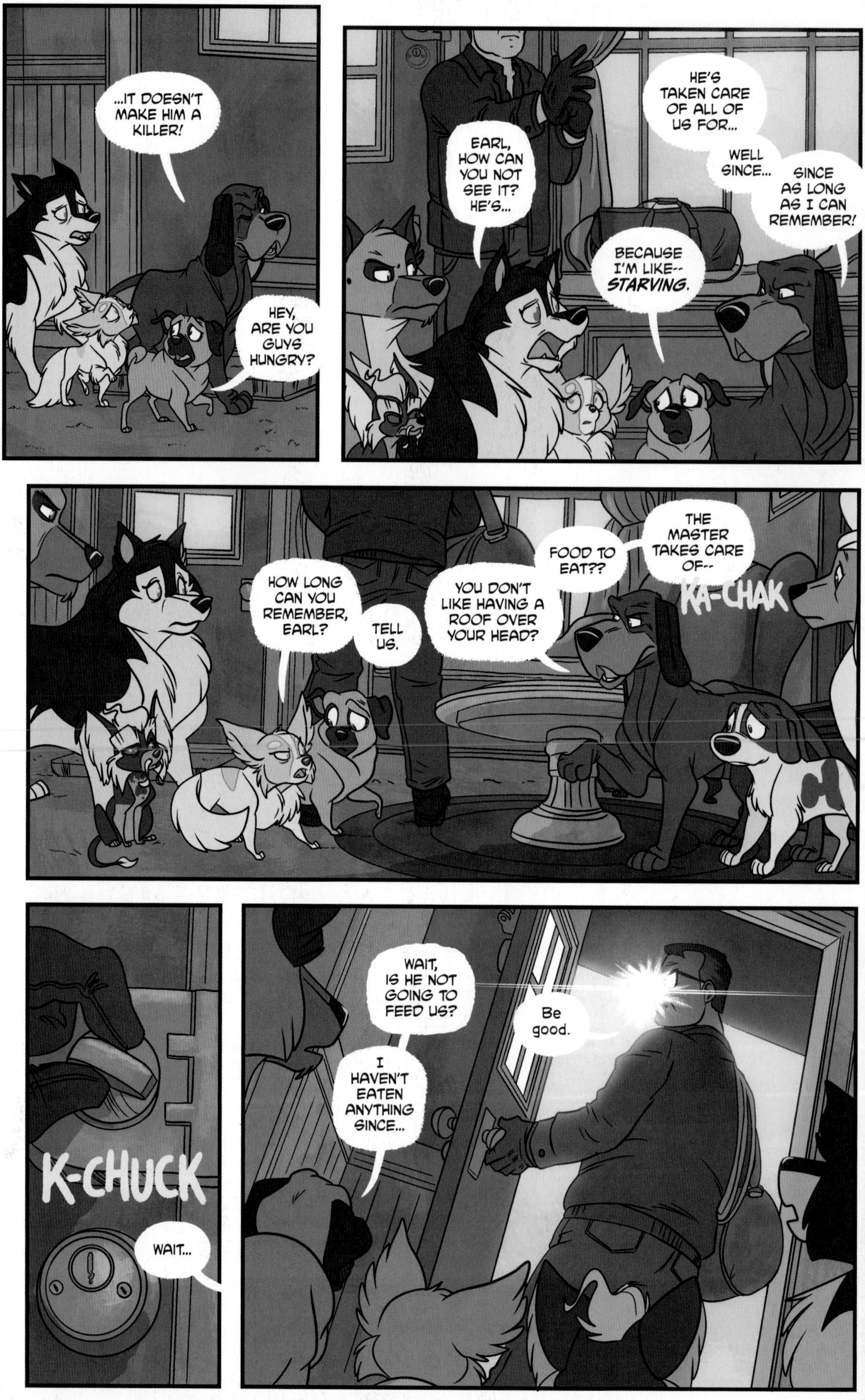
...IT DOESN'T MAKE HIM A KILLER!
HEY, ARE YOU GUYS HUNGRY?
EARL, HOW CAN YOU NOT SEE IT? HE'S...
HE'S TAKEN CARE OF ALL OF US FOR...
WELL SINCE...
SINCE AS LONG AS I CAN REMEMBER!
BECAUSE I'M LIKE-- STARVING.
HOW LONG CAN YOU REMEMBER, EARL?
TELL US.
YOU DON'T LIKE HAVING A ROOF OVER YOUR HEAD?
FOOD TO EAT??
THE MASTER TAKES CARE OF--
KA-CHAK
K-CHUCK
WAIT...
WAIT, IS HE NOT GOING TO FEED US?
I HAVEN'T EATEN ANYTHING SINCE...
Be good.

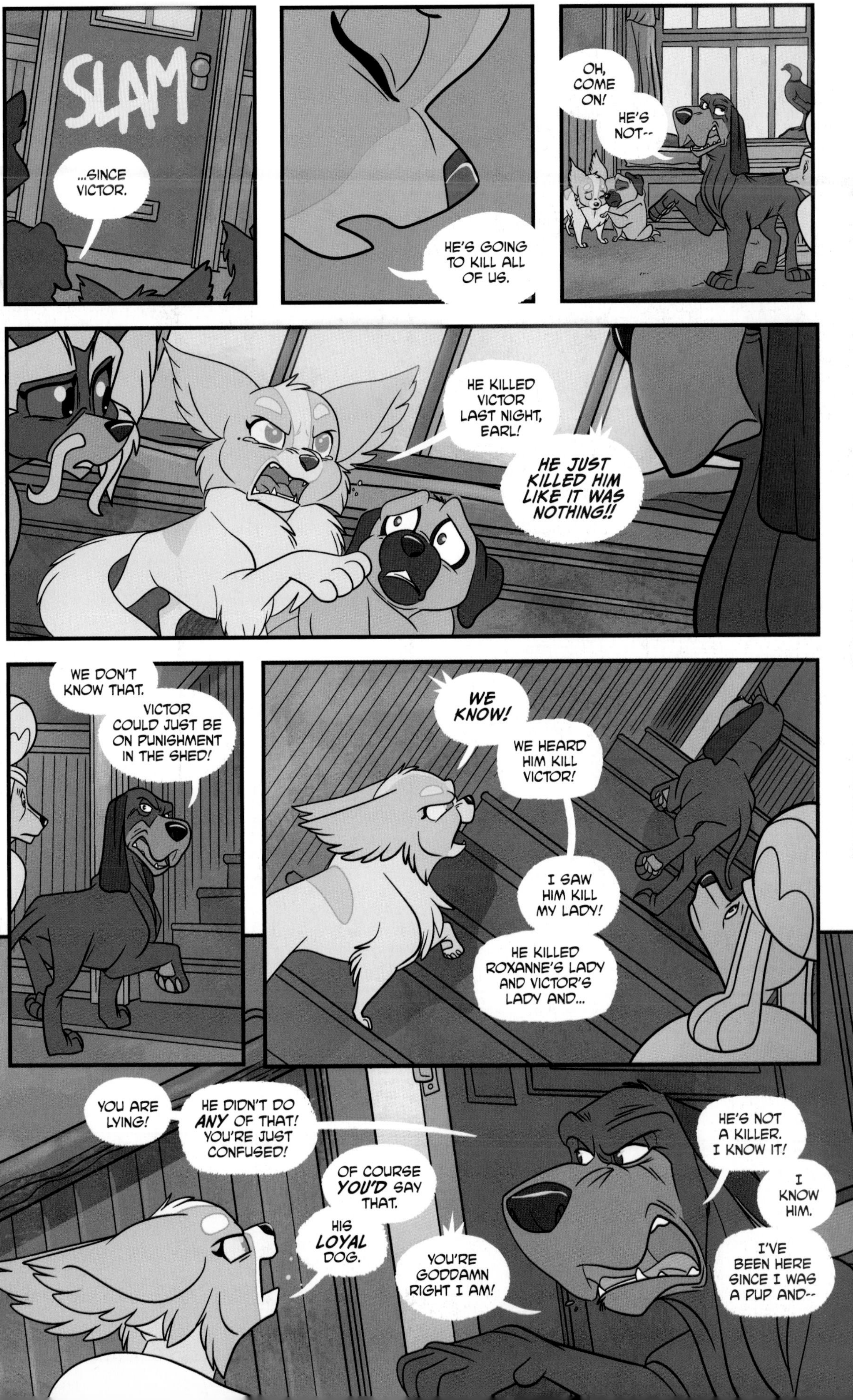
SLAM
...SINCE VICTOR.
HE'S GOING TO KILL ALL OF US.
OH, COME ON!
HE'S NOT--
HE KILLED VICTOR LAST NIGHT, EARL!
HE JUST KILLED HIM LIKE IT WAS NOTHING!!
WE DON'T KNOW THAT.
VICTOR COULD JUST BE ON PUNISHMENT IN THE SHED!
WE KNOW!
WE HEARD HIM KILL VICTOR!
I SAW HIM KILL MY LADY!
HE KILLED ROXANNE'S LADY AND VICTOR'S LADY AND...
YOU ARE LYING!
HE DIDN'T DO ANY OF THAT! YOU'RE JUST CONFUSED!
OF COURSE YOU'D SAY THAT.
HIS LOYAL DOG.
YOU'RE GODDAMN RIGHT I AM!
HE'S NOT A KILLER. I KNOW IT!
I KNOW HIM.
I'VE BEEN HERE SINCE I WAS A PUP AND--

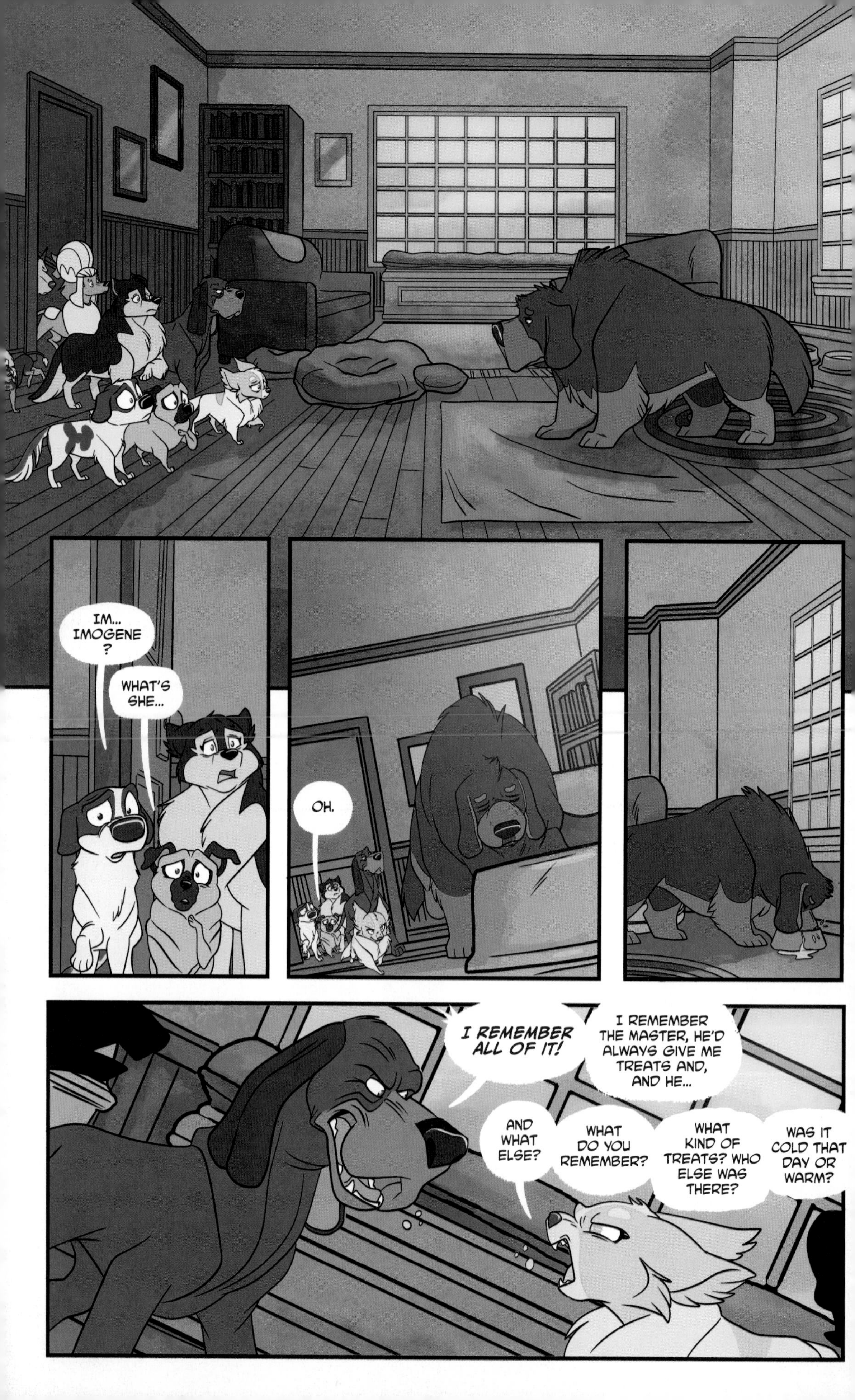
IM... IMOGENE ?
WHAT'S SHE...
OH.
I REMEMBER ALL OF IT!
I REMEMBER THE MASTER, HE'D ALWAYS GIVE ME TREATS AND, AND HE...
AND WHAT ELSE?
WHAT DO YOU REMEMBER?
WHAT KIND OF TREATS? WHO ELSE WAS THERE?
WAS IT COLD THAT DAY OR WARM?

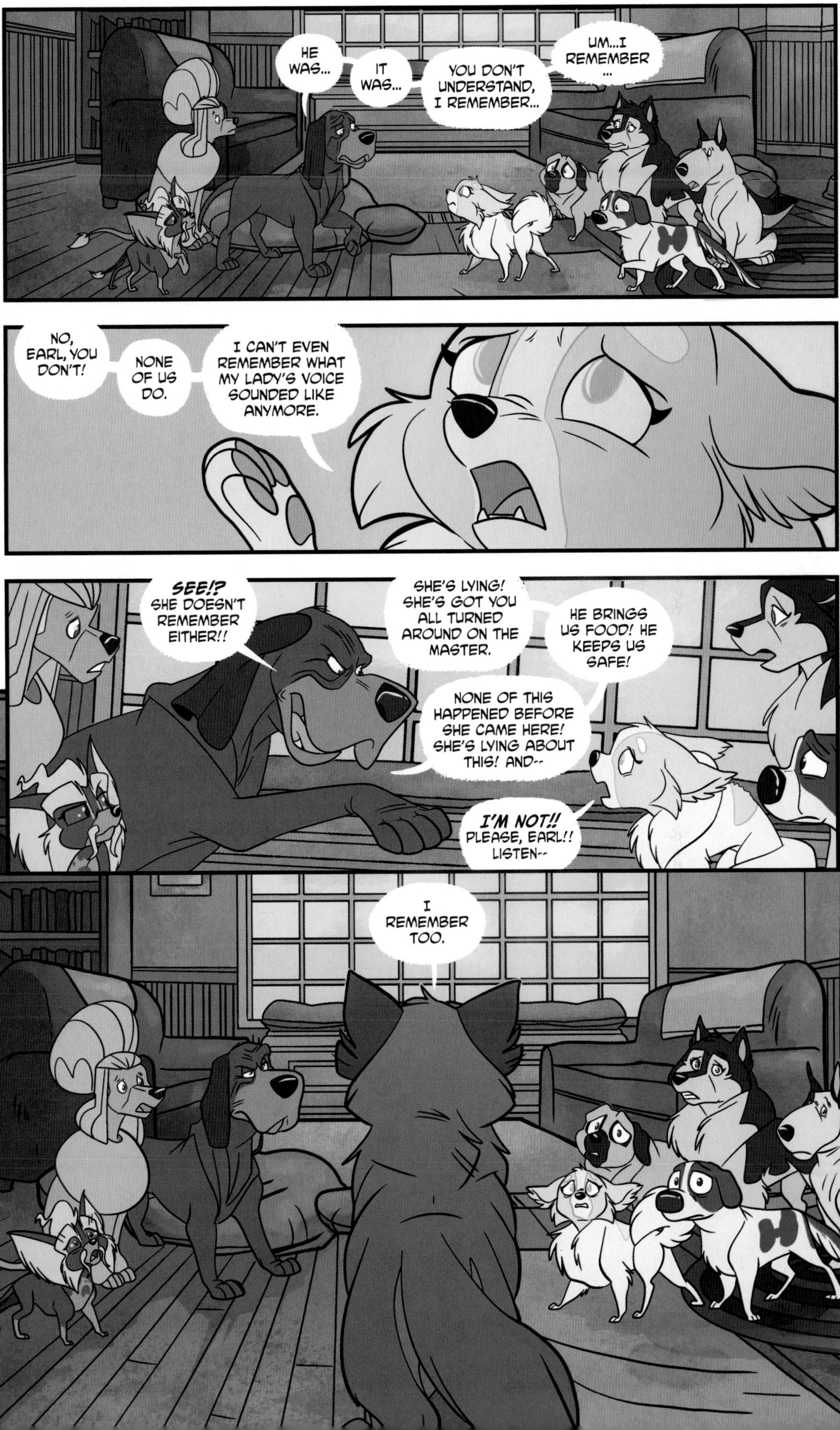
HE WAS...
IT WAS...
YOU DON'T UNDERSTAND, I REMEMBER...
UM...I REMEMBER ...
NO, EARL, YOU DON'T!
NONE OF US DO.
I CAN'T EVEN REMEMBER WHAT MY LADY'S VOICE SOUNDED LIKE ANYMORE.
SEE!? SHE DOESN'T REMEMBER EITHER!!
SHE'S LYING! SHE'S GOT YOU ALL TURNED AROUND ON THE MASTER.
HE BRINGS US FOOD! HE KEEPS US SAFE!
NONE OF THIS HAPPENED BEFORE SHE CAME HERE! SHE'S LYING ABOUT THIS! AND--
I'M NOT!! PLEASE, EARL!! LISTEN--
I REMEMBER TOO.

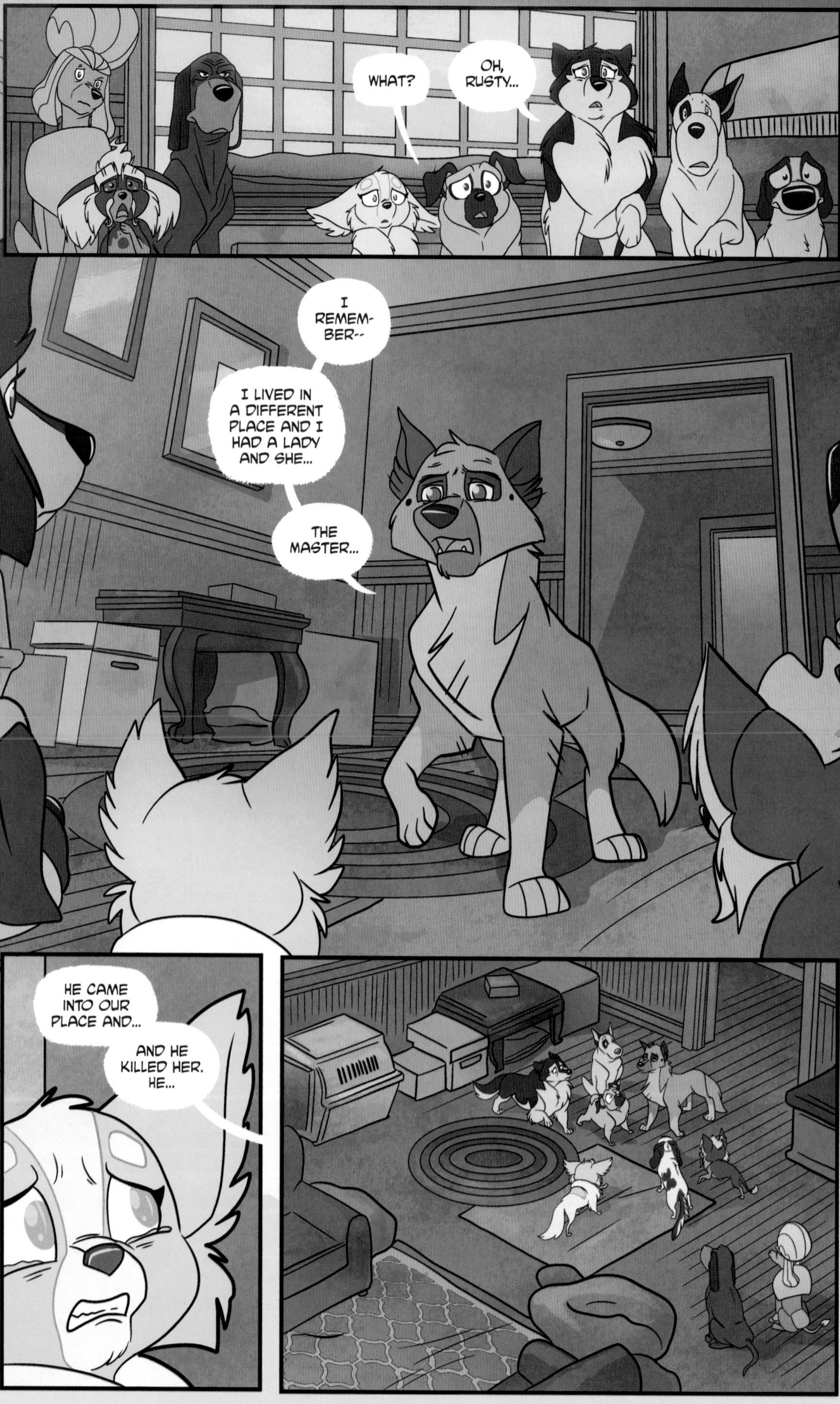
WHAT?
OH, RUSTY...
I REMEMBER--
I LIVED IN A DIFFERENT PLACE AND I HAD A LADY AND SHE...
THE MASTER...
HE CAME INTO OUR PLACE AND...
AND HE KILLED HER. HE...

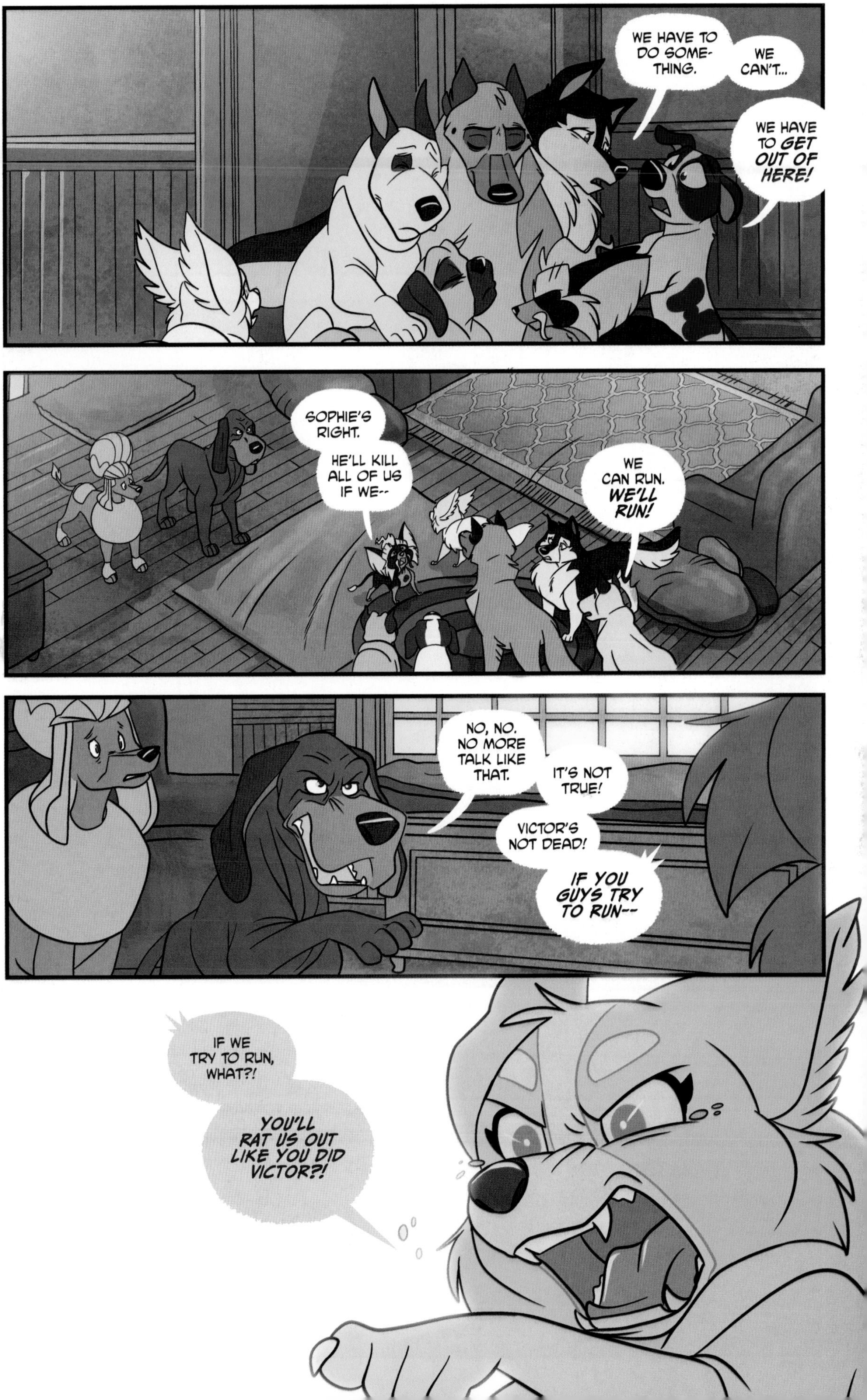
WE HAVE TO DO SOME-THING.
WE CAN'T...
WE HAVE TO GET OUT OF HERE!
SOPHIE'S RIGHT.
HE'LL KILL ALL OF US IF WE--
WE CAN RUN. WE'LL RUN!
NO, NO. NO MORE TALK LIKE THAT.
IT'S NOT TRUE!
VICTOR'S NOT DEAD!
IF YOU GUYS TRY TO RUN--
IF WE TRY TO RUN, WHAT?!
YOU'LL RAT US OUT LIKE YOU DID VICTOR?!

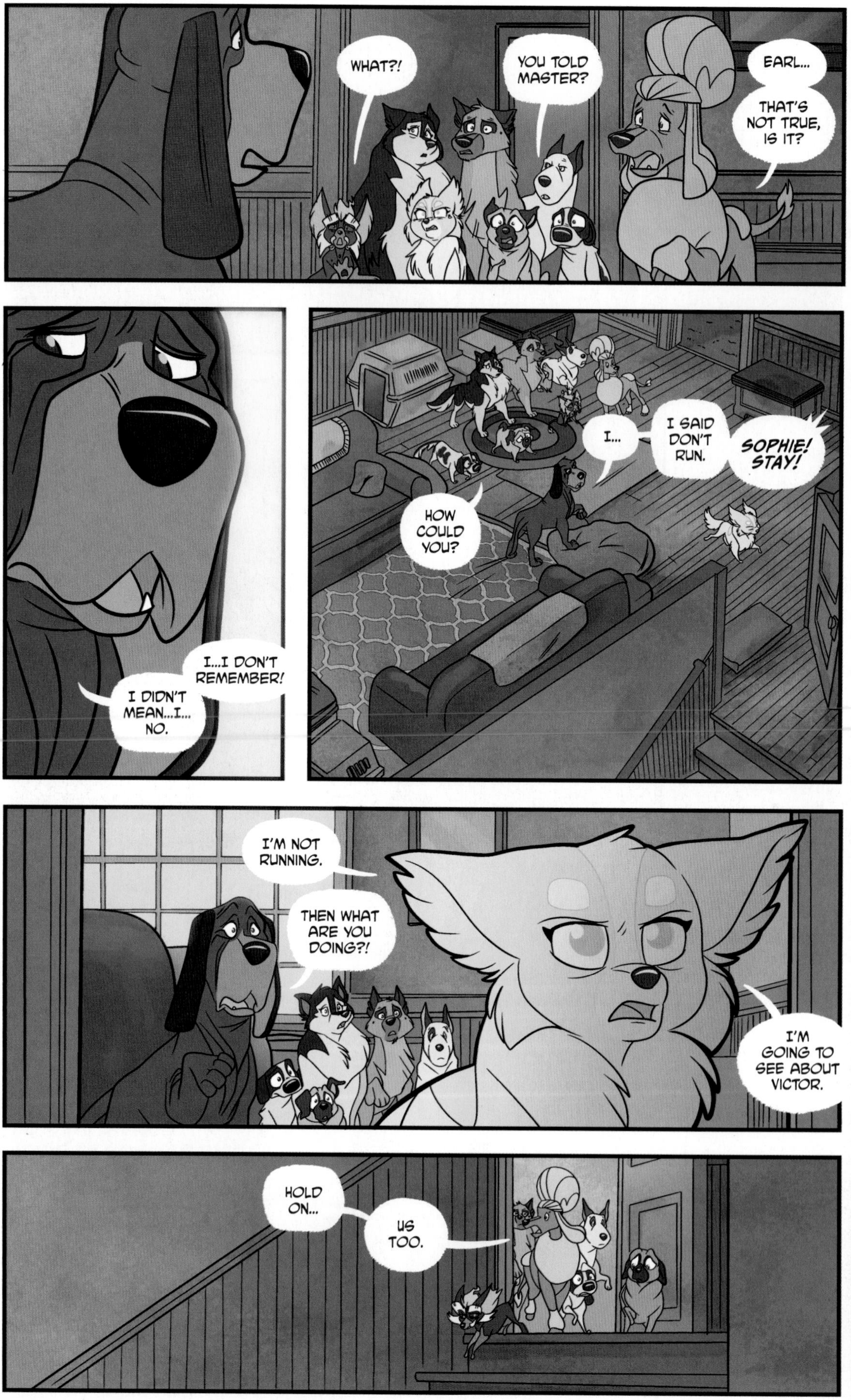
WHAT?!
YOU TOLD MASTER?
EARL...
THAT'S NOT TRUE, IS IT?
I...I DON'T REMEMBER!
I DIDN'T MEAN...I... NO.
HOW COULD YOU?
I...
I SAID DON'T RUN.
SOPHIE! STAY!
I'M NOT RUNNING.
THEN WHAT ARE YOU DOING?!
I'M GOING TO SEE ABOUT VICTOR.
HOLD ON...
US TOO.

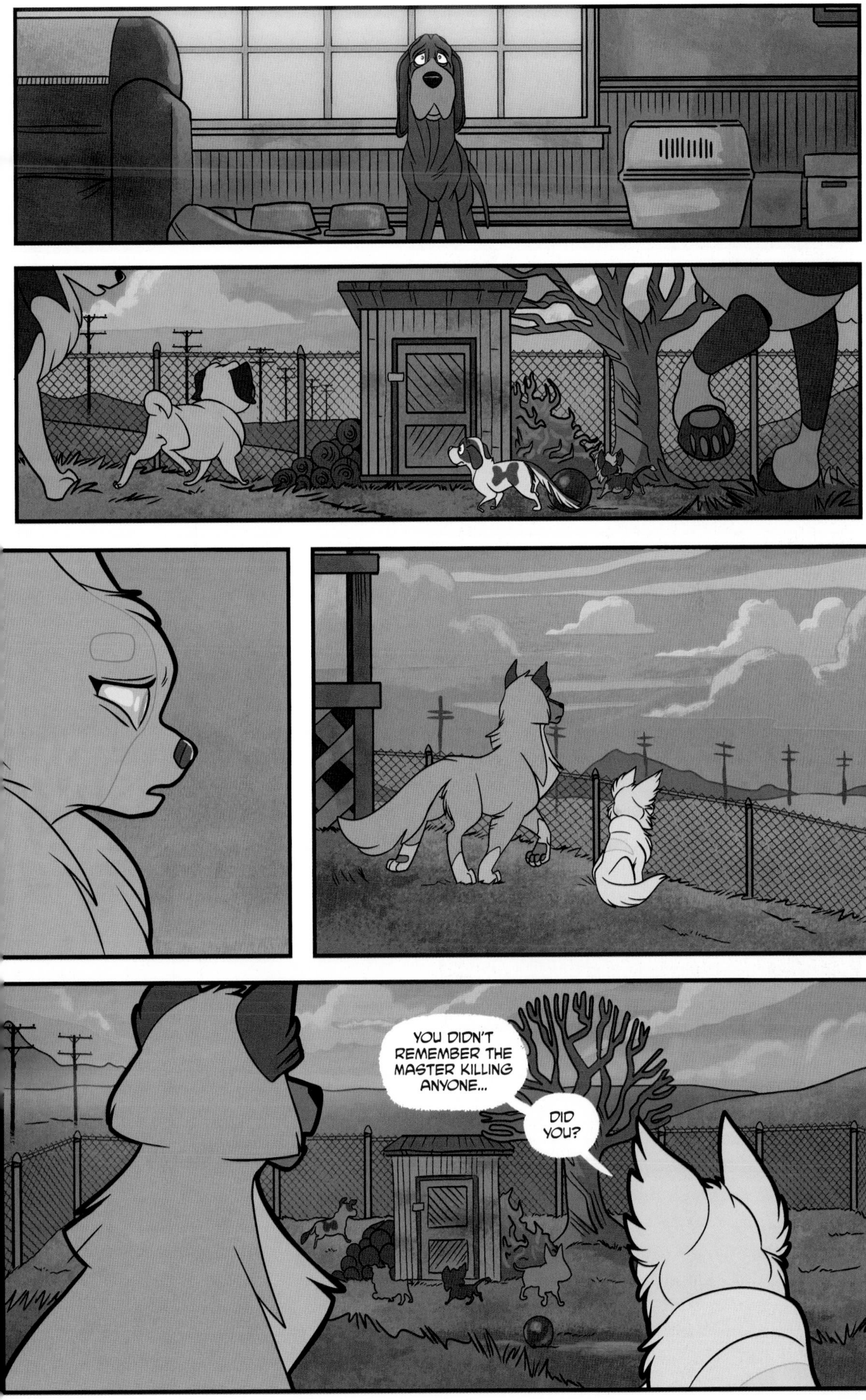
YOU DIDN'T REMEMBER THE MASTER KILLING ANYONE...
DID YOU?

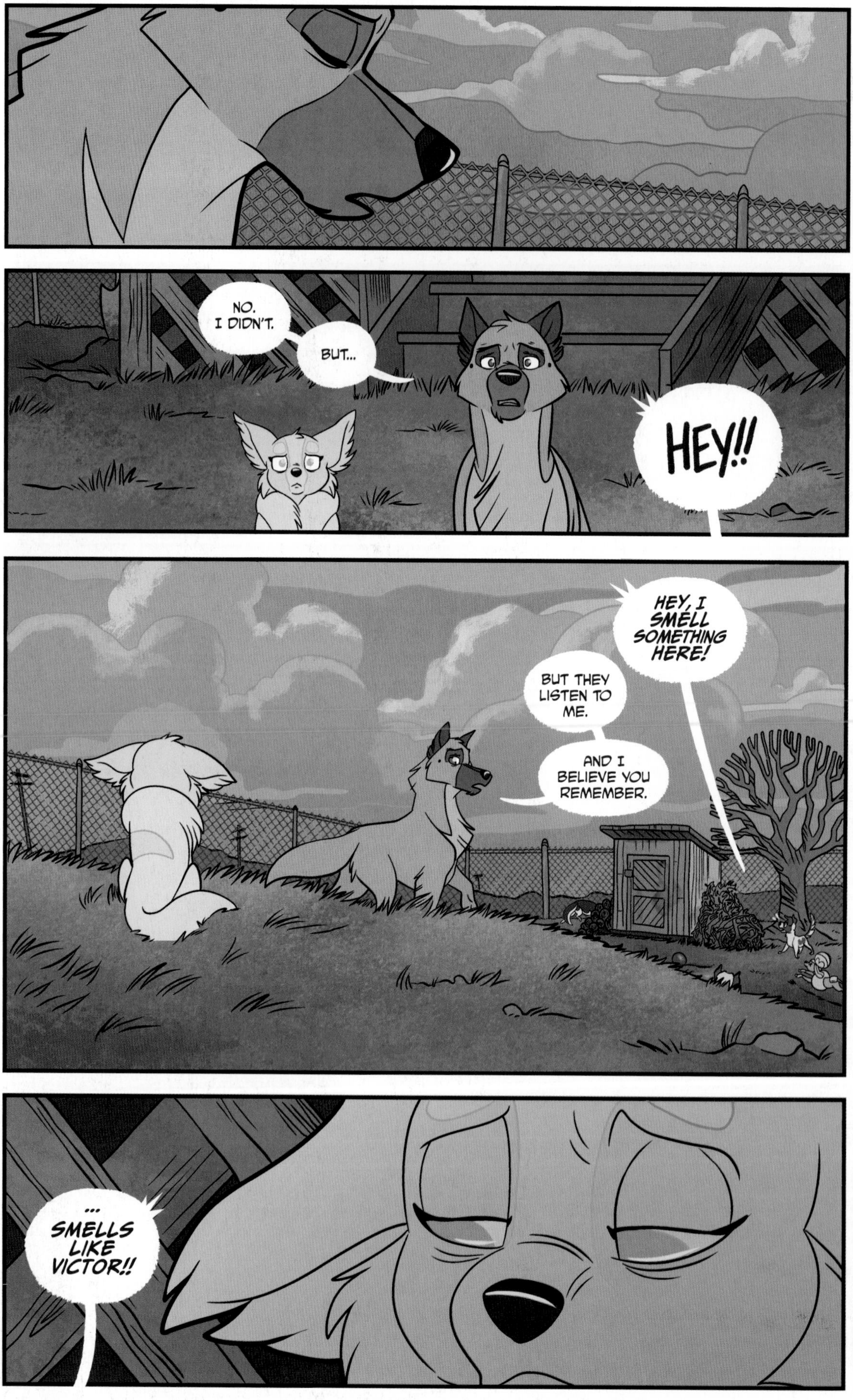
NO. I DIDN'T.
BUT...
HEY!!
HEY, I SMELL SOMETHING HERE!
BUT THEY LISTEN TO ME.
AND I BELIEVE YOU REMEMBER.
... SMELLS LIKE VICTOR!!

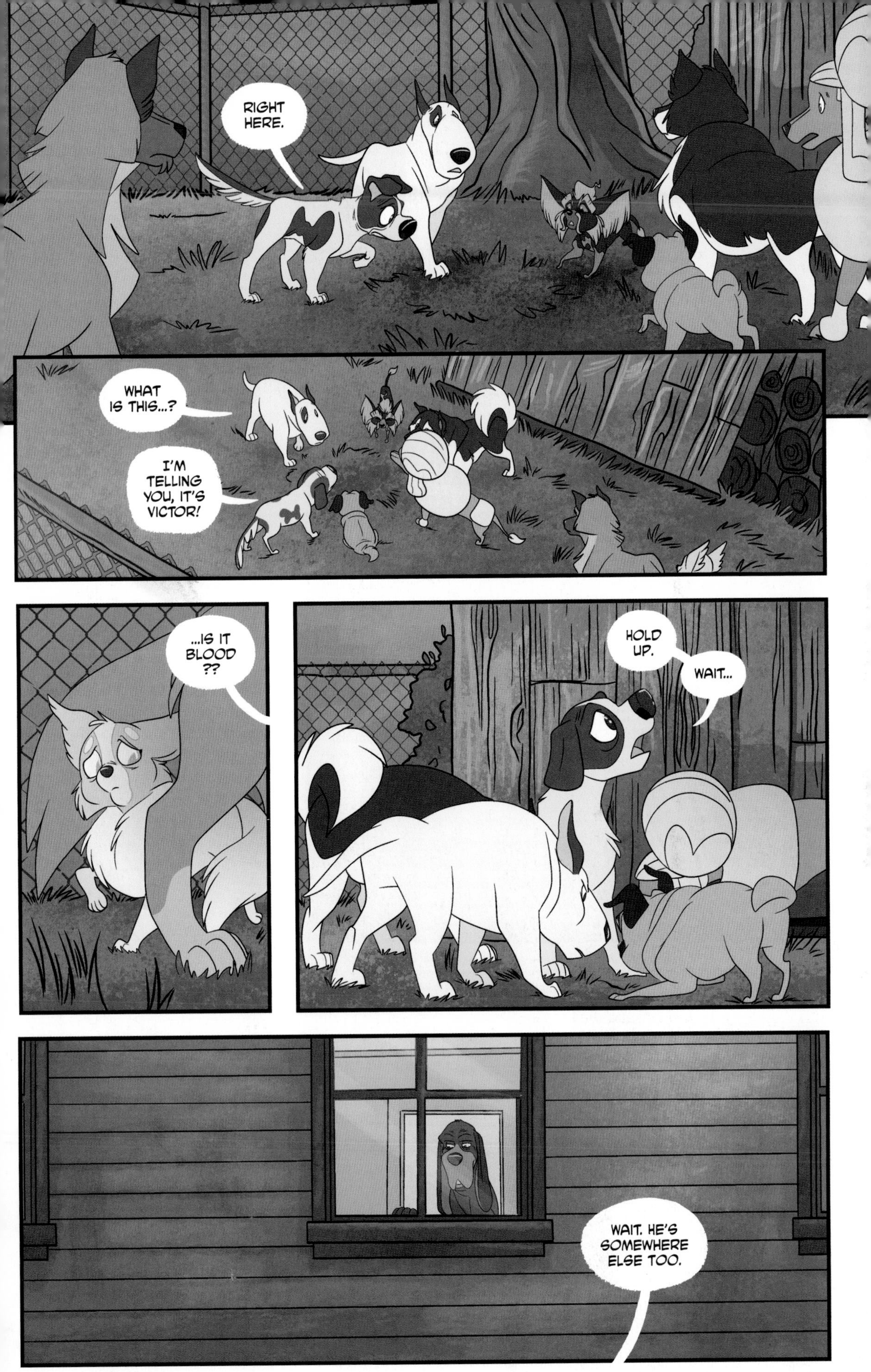
RIGHT HERE.
WHAT IS THIS...?
I'M TELLING YOU, IT'S VICTOR!
...IS IT BLOOD ??
HOLD UP.
WAIT...
WAIT. HE'S SOMEWHERE ELSE TOO.

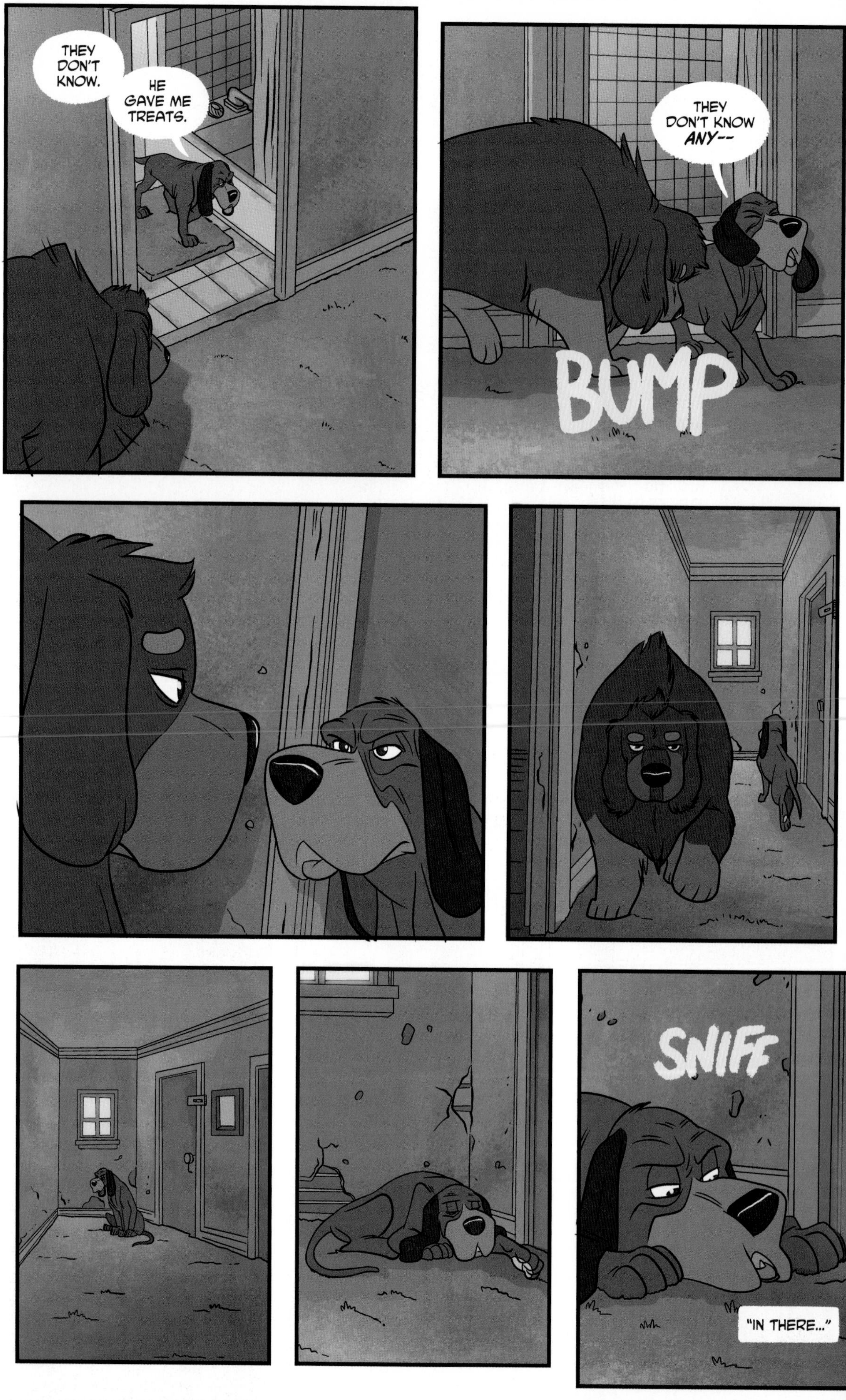
THEY DON'T KNOW.
HE GAVE ME TREATS.
THEY DON'T KNOW ANY--
BUMP
SNIFF
"IN THERE..."

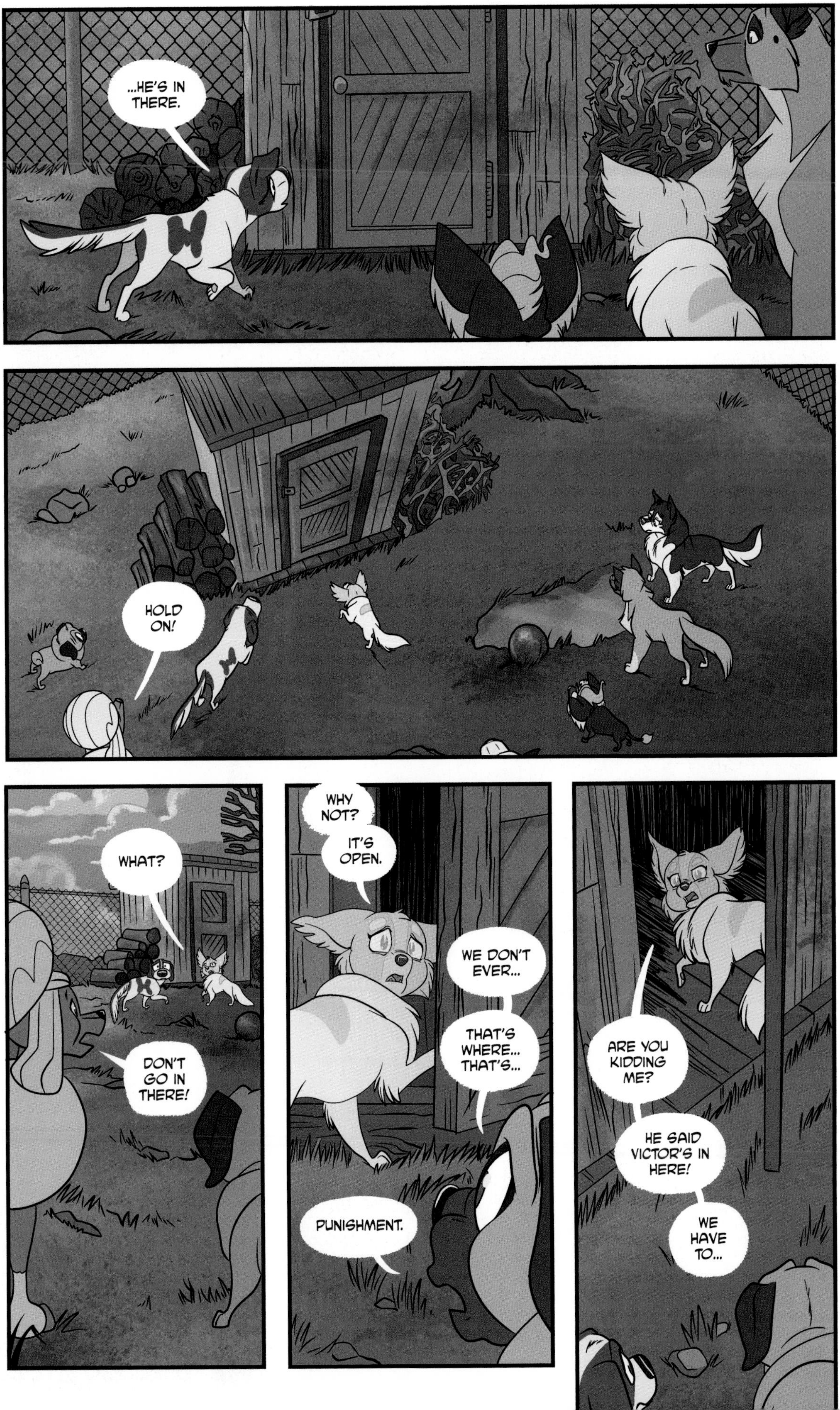
...HE'S IN THERE.
HOLD ON!
WHAT?
DON'T GO IN THERE!
WHY NOT?
IT'S OPEN.
WE DON'T EVER...
THAT'S WHERE... THAT'S...
PUNISHMENT.
ARE YOU KIDDING ME?
HE SAID VICTOR'S IN HERE!
WE HAVE TO...

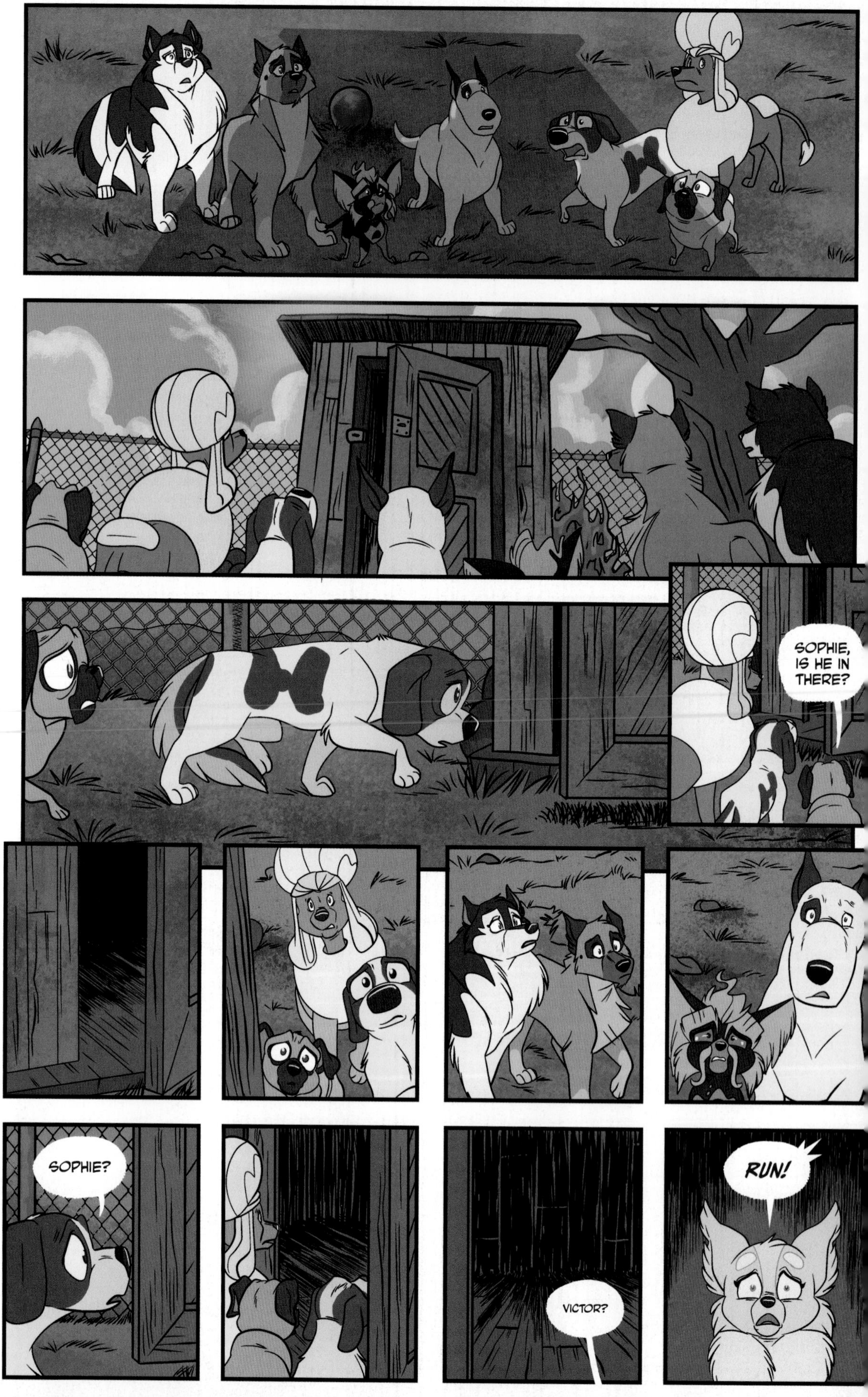
SOPHIE, IS HE IN THERE?
SOPHIE?
VICTOR?
RUN!

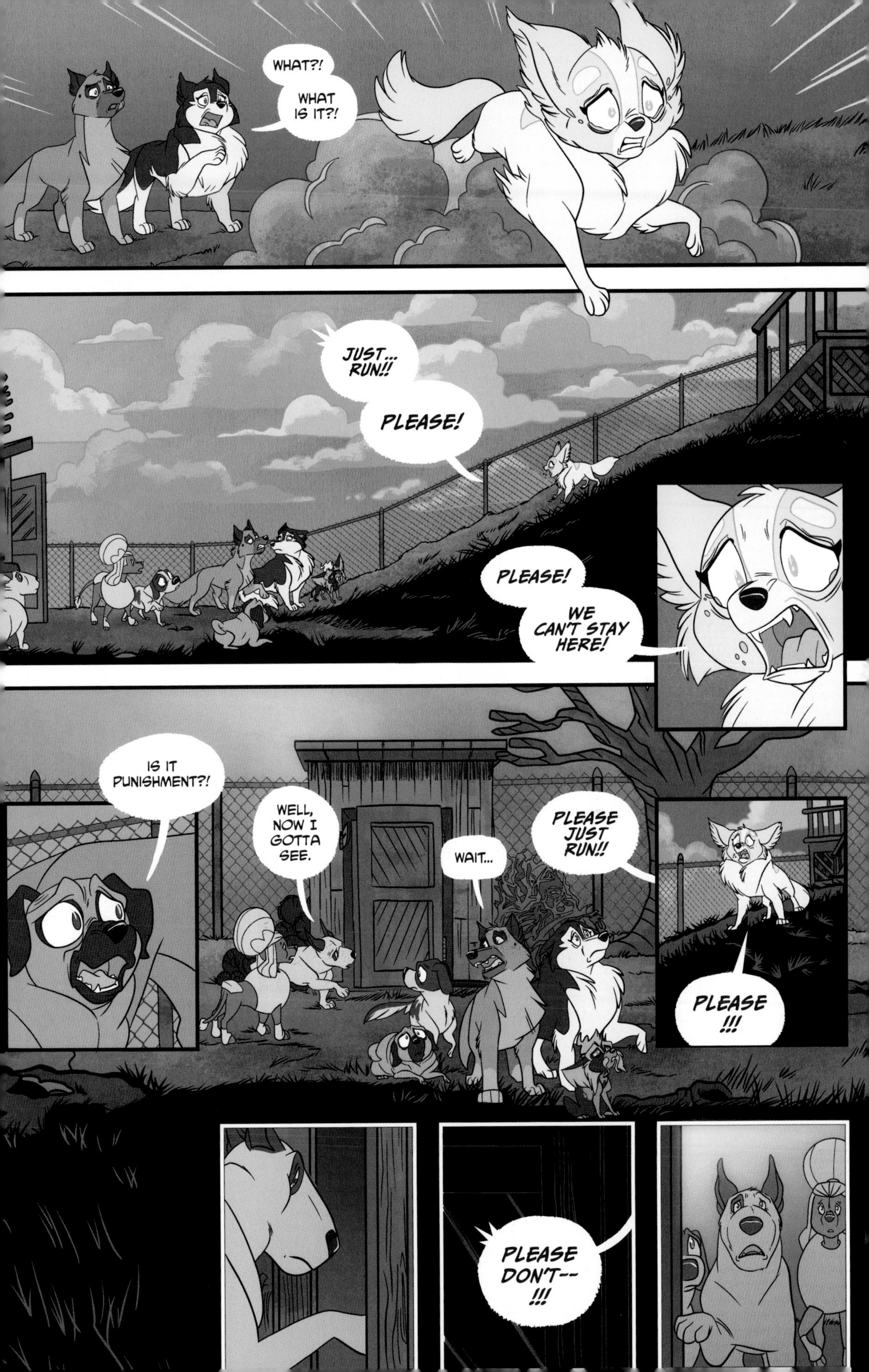
WHAT?!
WHAT IS IT?!
JUST... RUN!!
PLEASE!
PLEASE!
WE CAN'T STAY HERE!
IS IT PUNISHMENT?!
WELL, NOW I GOTTA SEE.
WAIT...
PLEASE JUST RUN!!
PLEASE !!!
PLEASE DON'T-- !!!

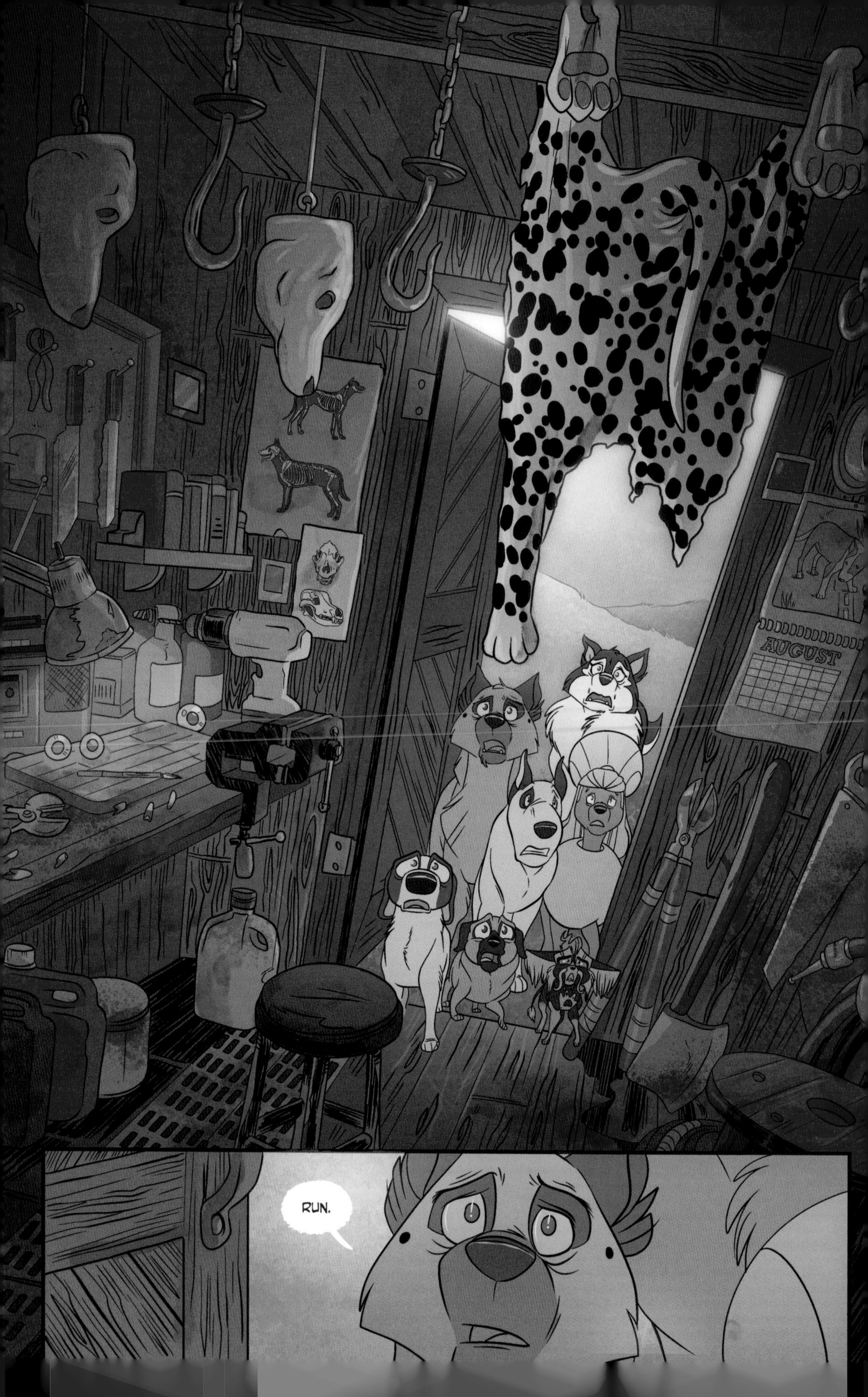
AUGUST
RUN.

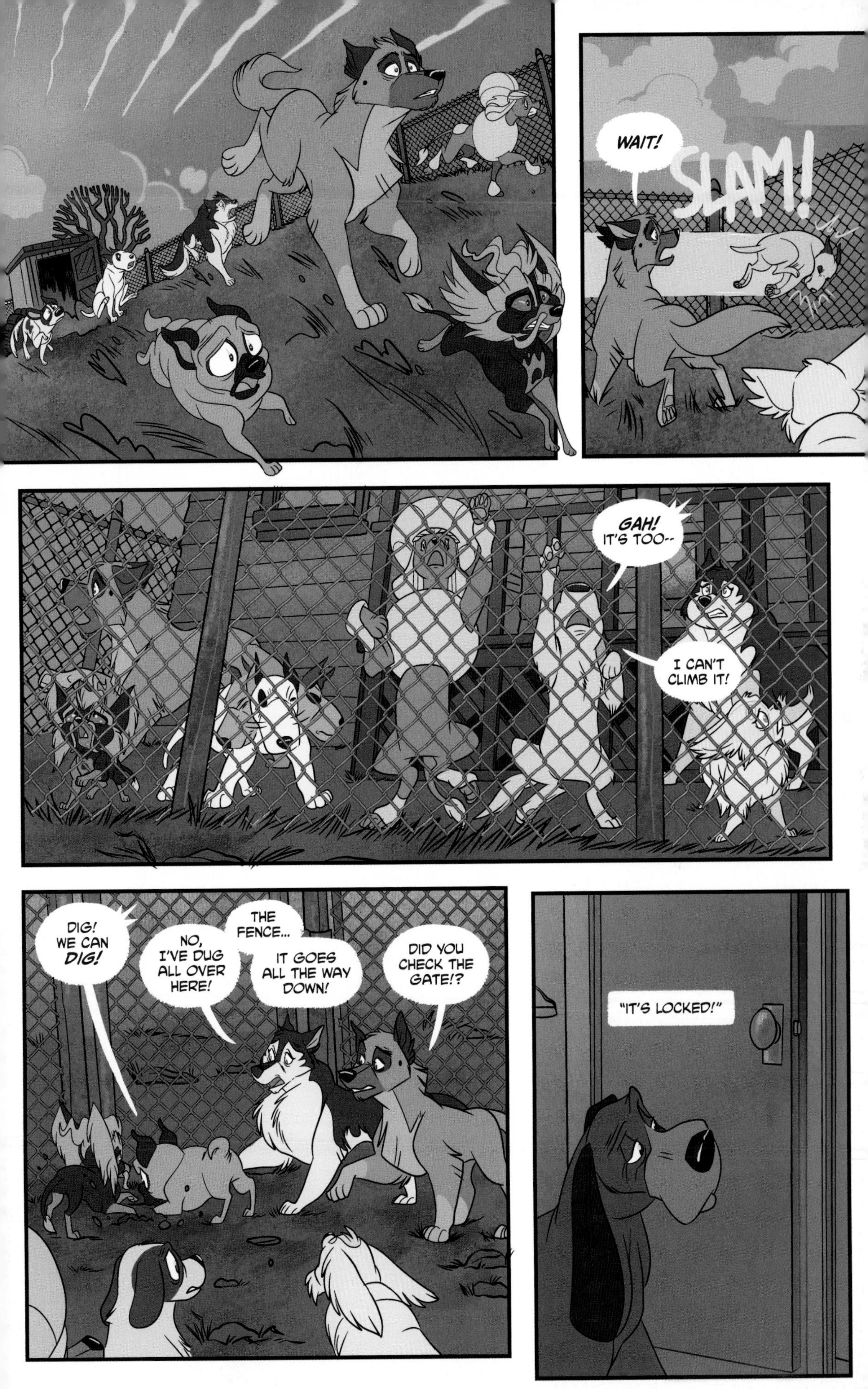
WAIT!
SLAM!
GAH! IT'S TOO--
I CAN'T CLIMB IT!
DIG! WE CAN DIG!
NO, I'VE DUG ALL OVER HERE!
THE FENCE...
IT GOES ALL THE WAY DOWN!
DID YOU CHECK THE GATE!?
"IT'S LOCKED!"

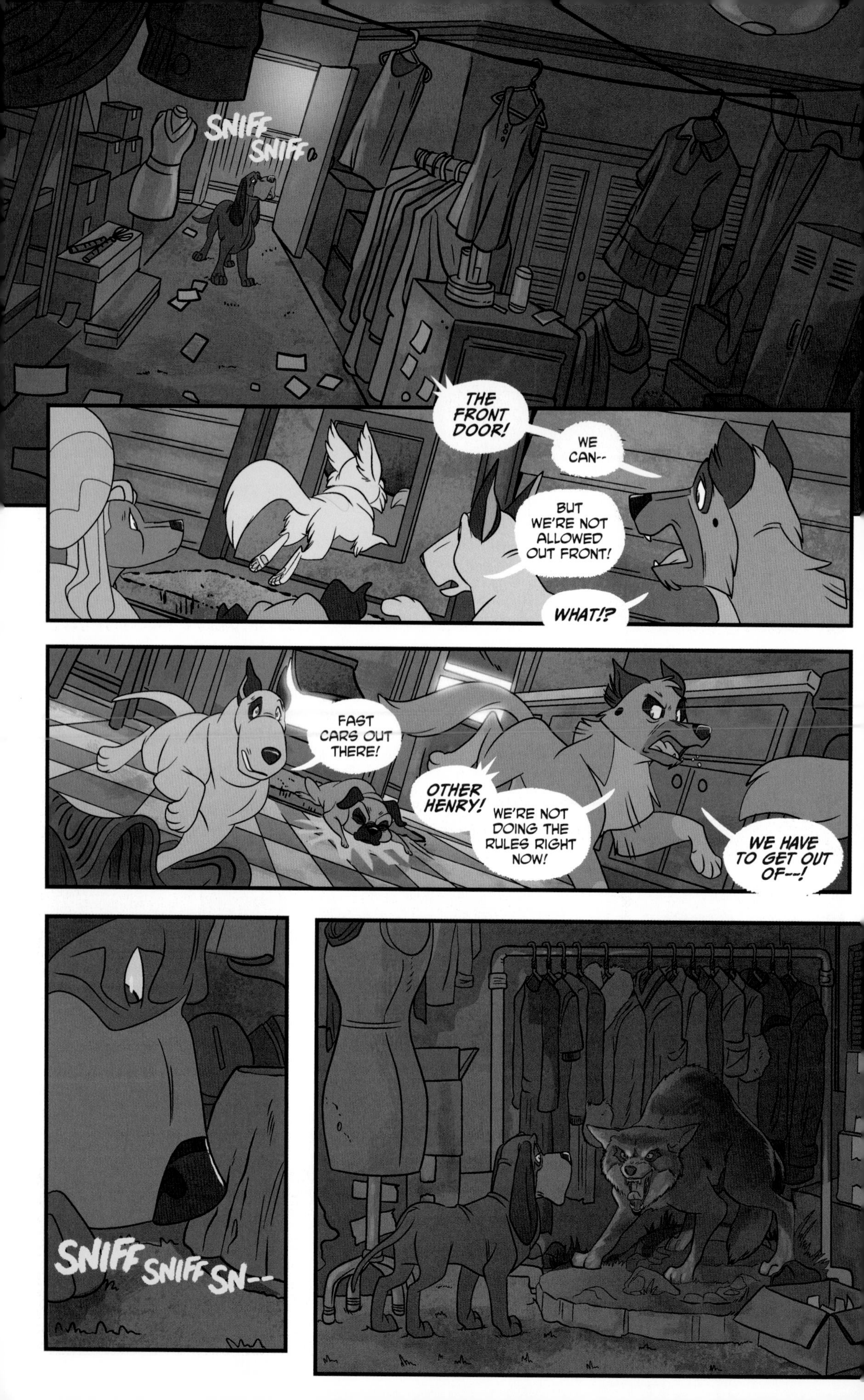
SNIFF
SNIFF
THE FRONT DOOR!
WE CAN--
BUT WE'RE NOT ALLOWED OUT FRONT!
WHAT!?
FAST CARS OUT THERE!
OTHER HENRY!
WE'RE NOT DOING THE RULES RIGHT NOW!
WE HAVE TO GET OUT OF--!
SNIFF SNIFF SN--

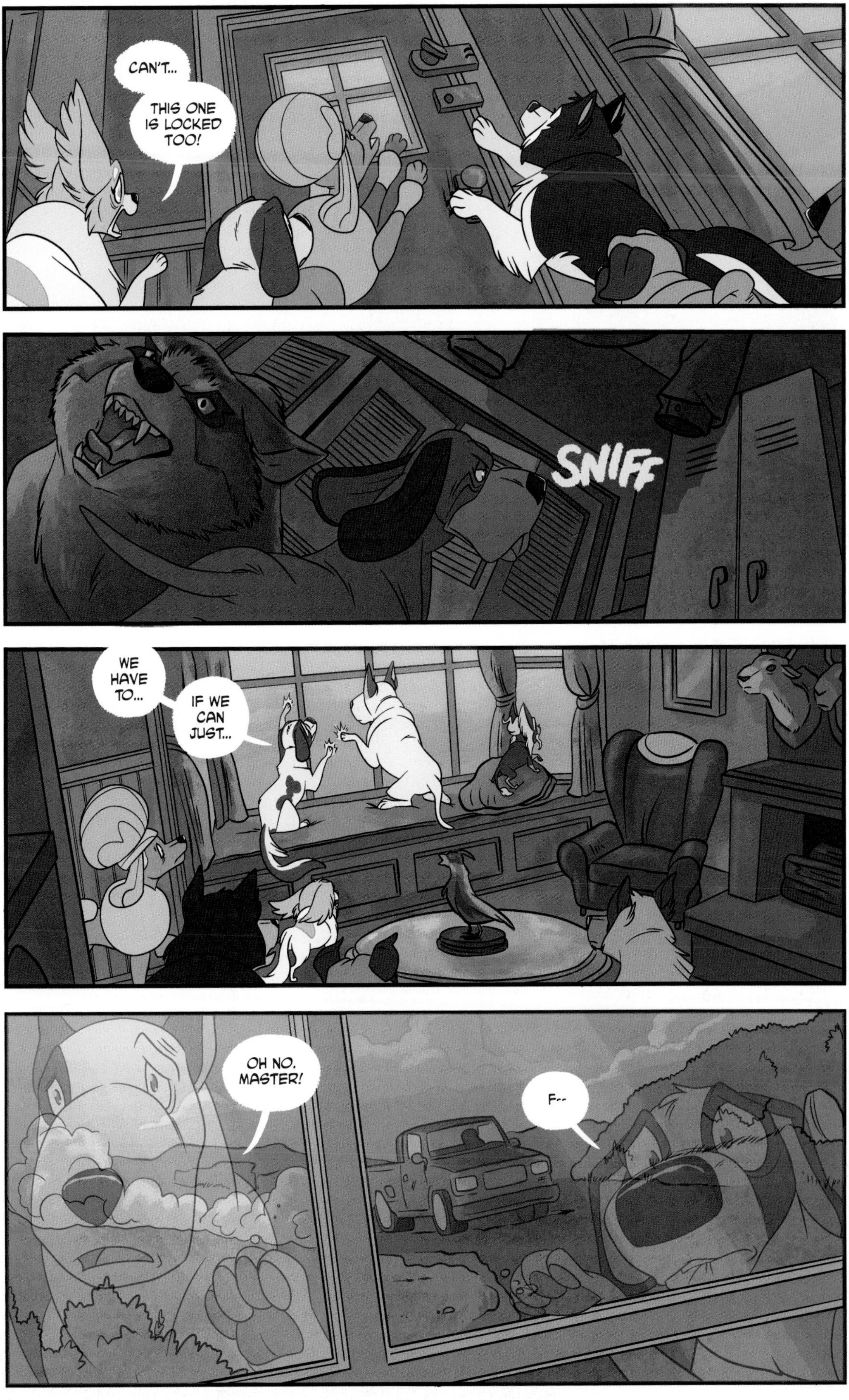
CAN'T...
THIS ONE IS LOCKED TOO!
SNIFF
WE HAVE TO...
IF WE CAN JUST...
OH NO. MASTER!
F--

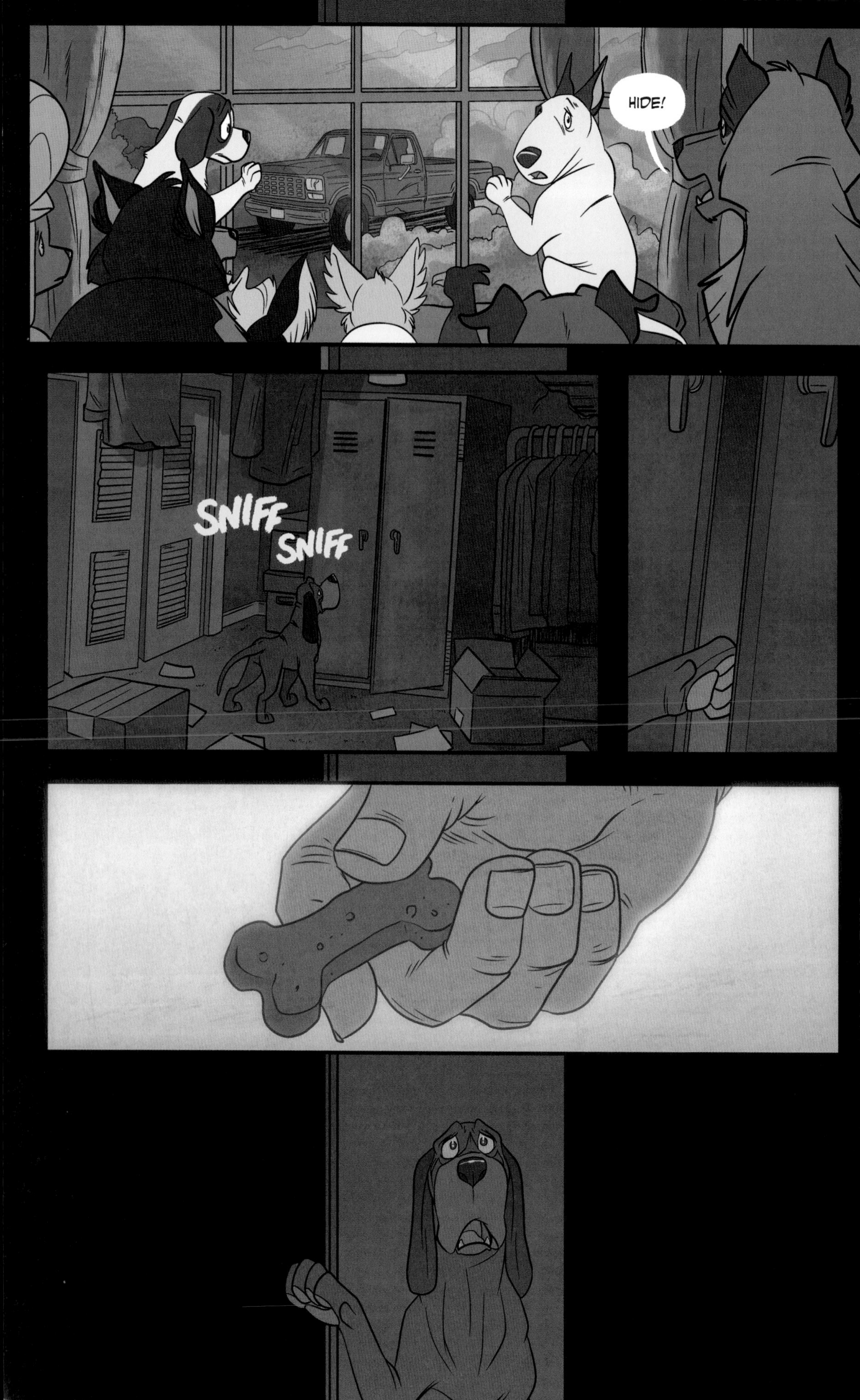
HIDE!
SNIFF
SNIFF

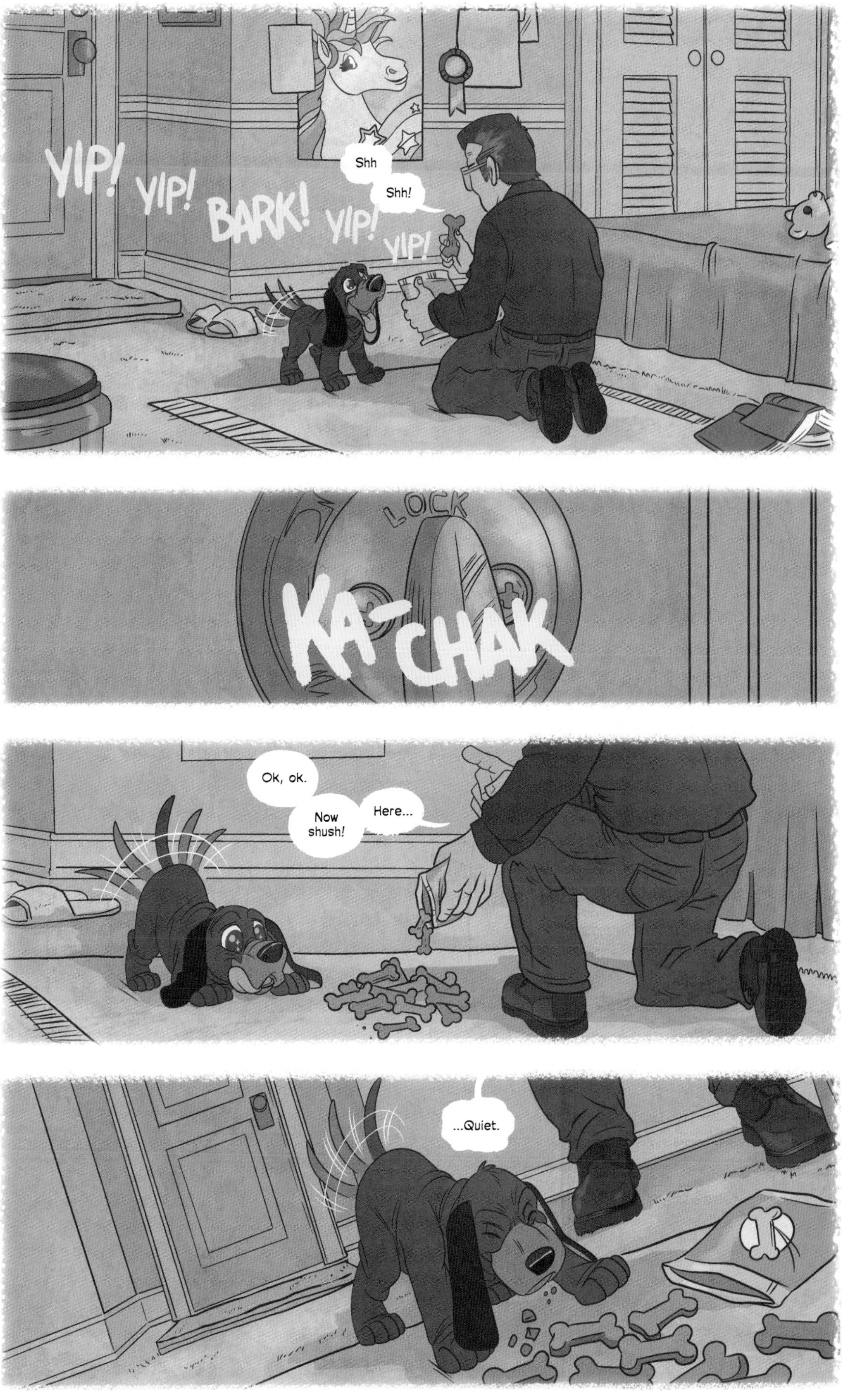
YIP! YIP! BARK! YIP! YIP!
Shh
Shh!
LOCK
KA-CHAK
Ok, ok.
Now shush!
Here...
...Quiet.

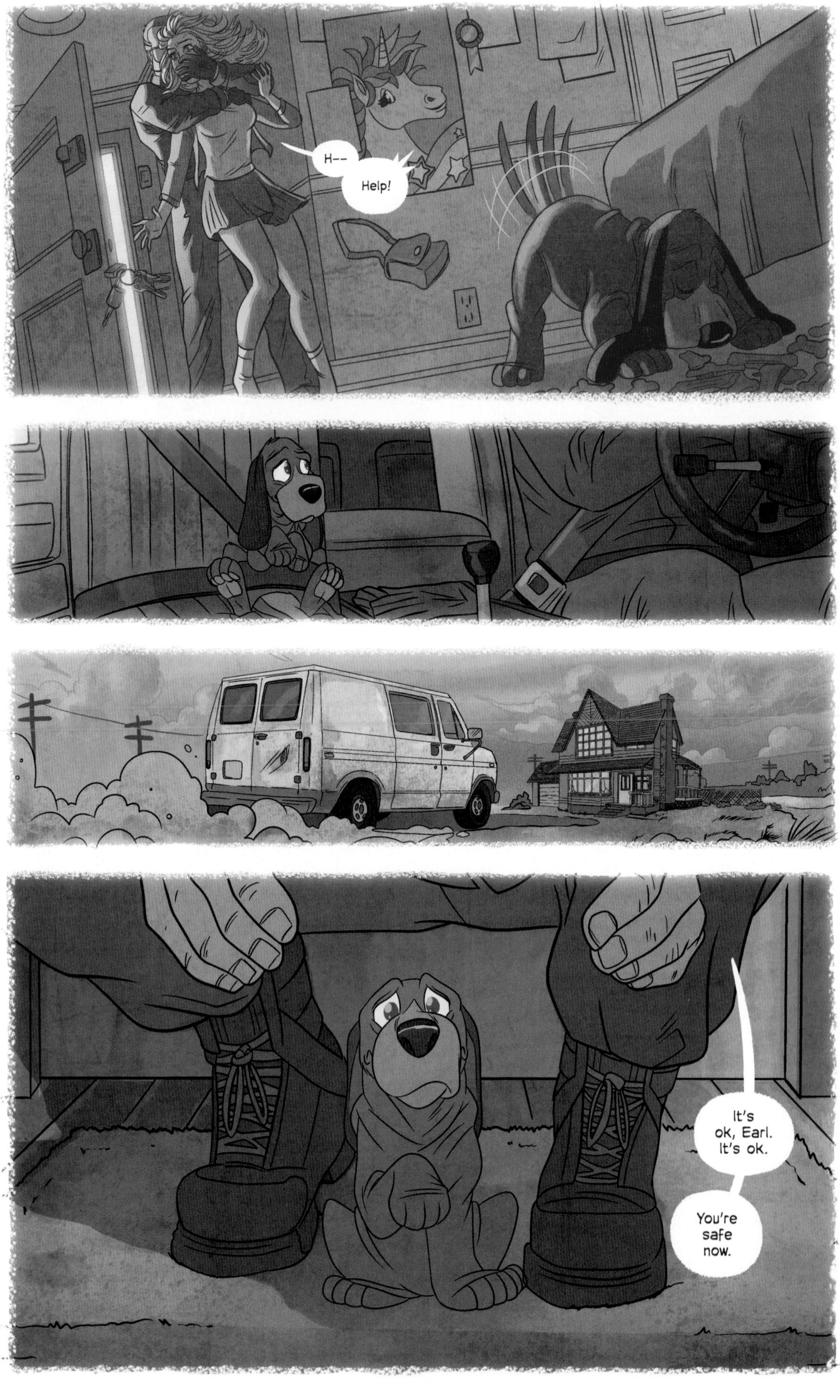
H--
Help!
It's ok, Earl. It's ok.
You're safe now.

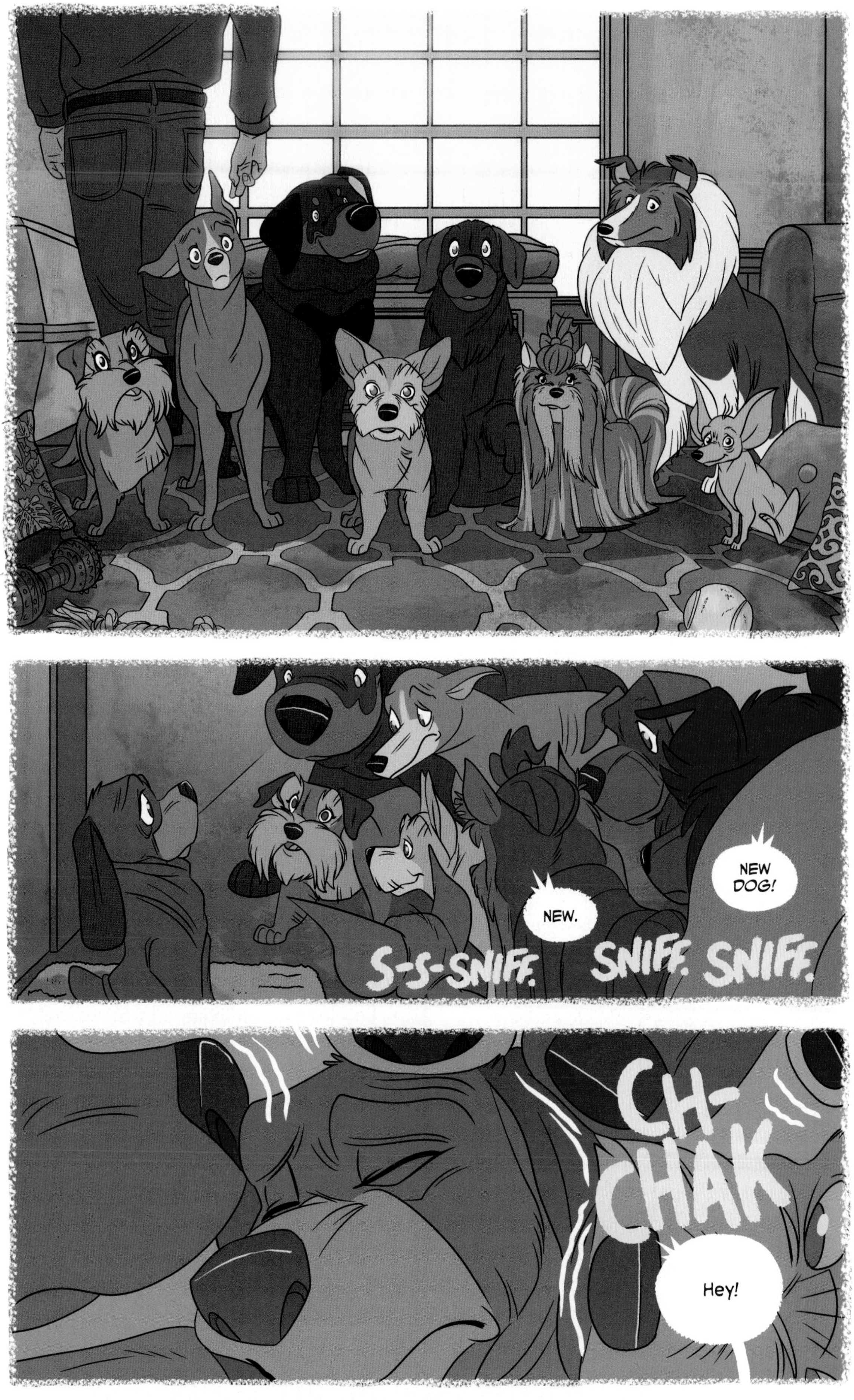
NEW.
NEW DOG!
S-S-SNIFF.
SNIFF. SNIFF.
CH-CHAK
Hey!

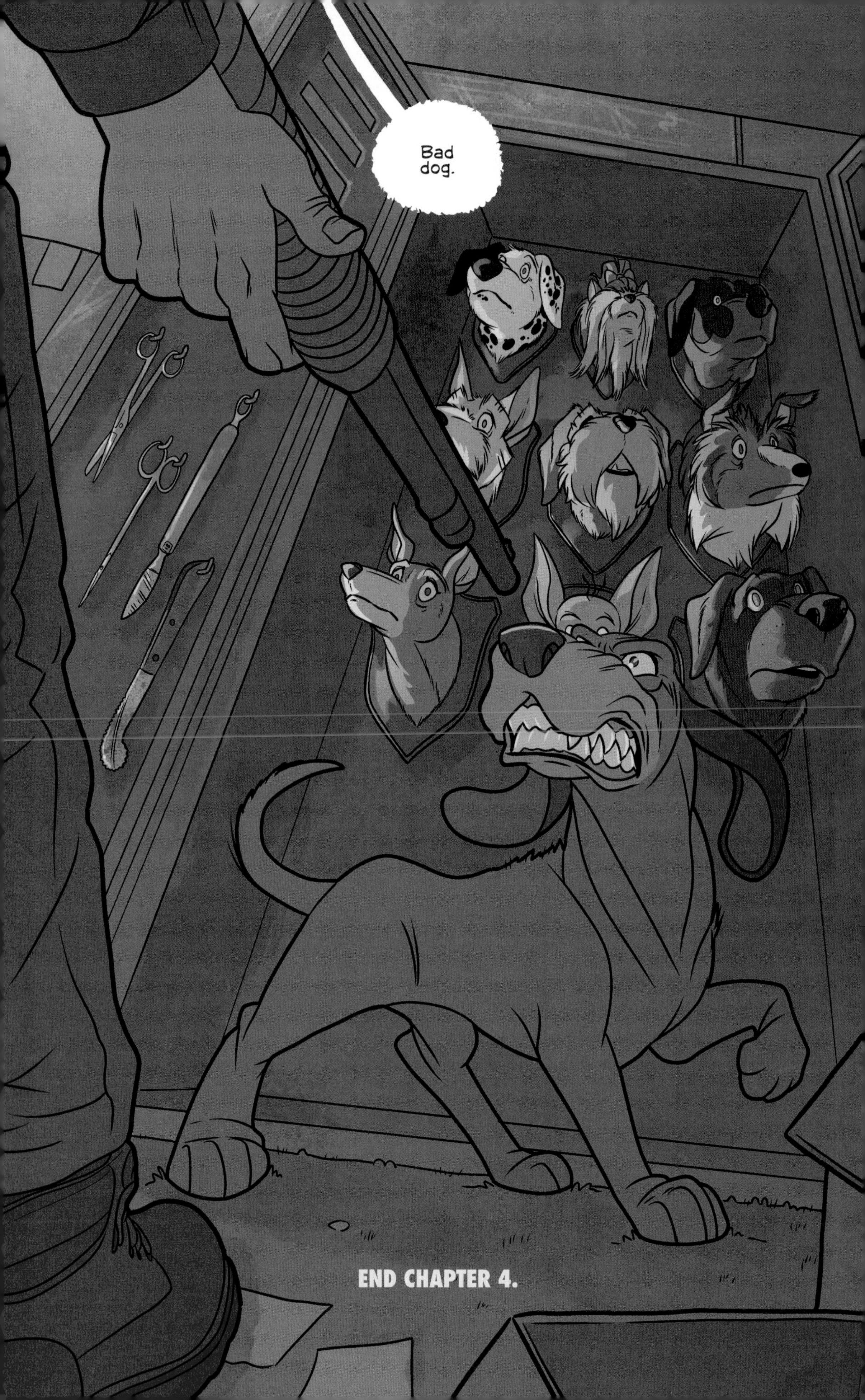
Bad dog.
END CHAPTER 4.

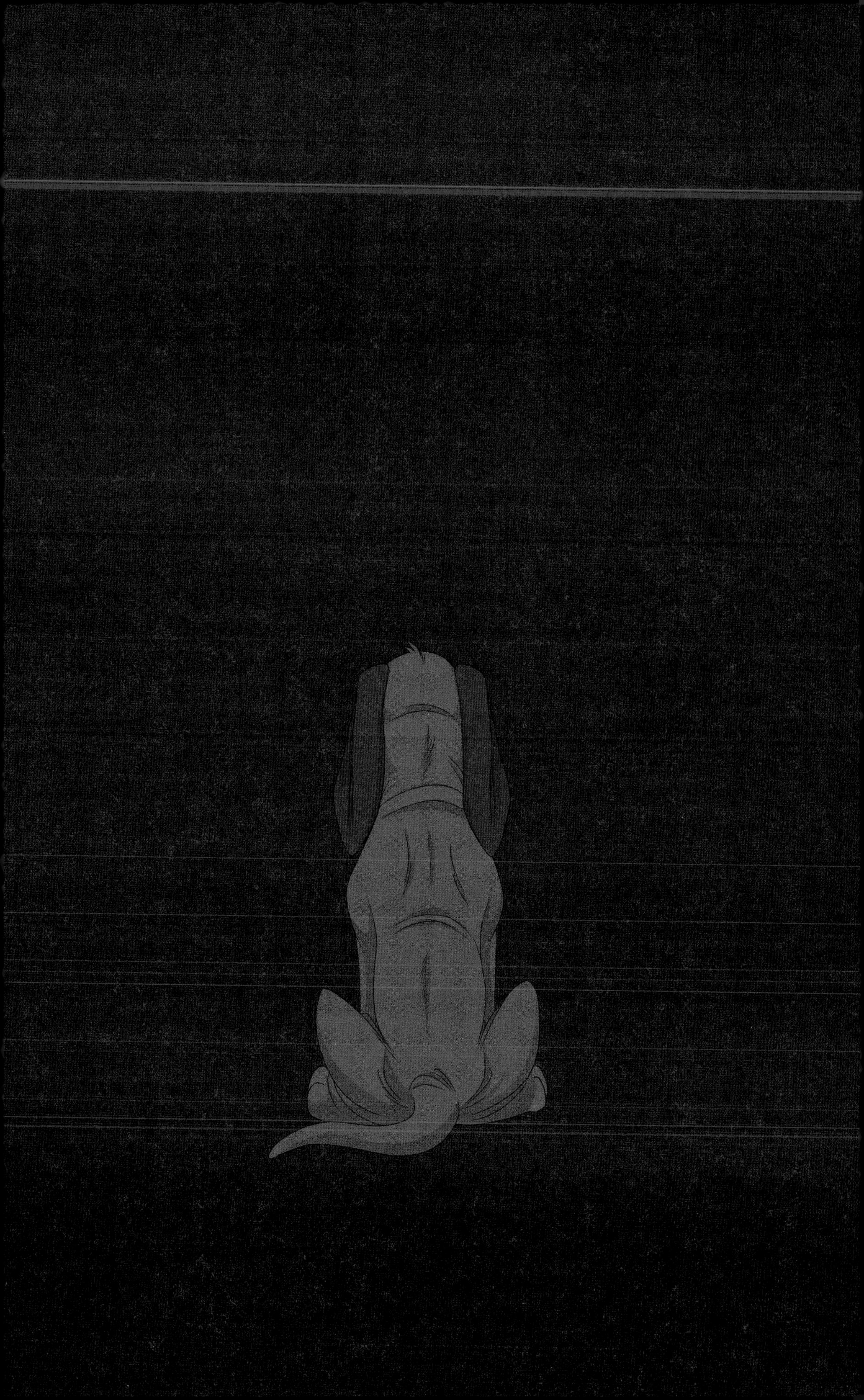

Chapter 5:
BAD DOG

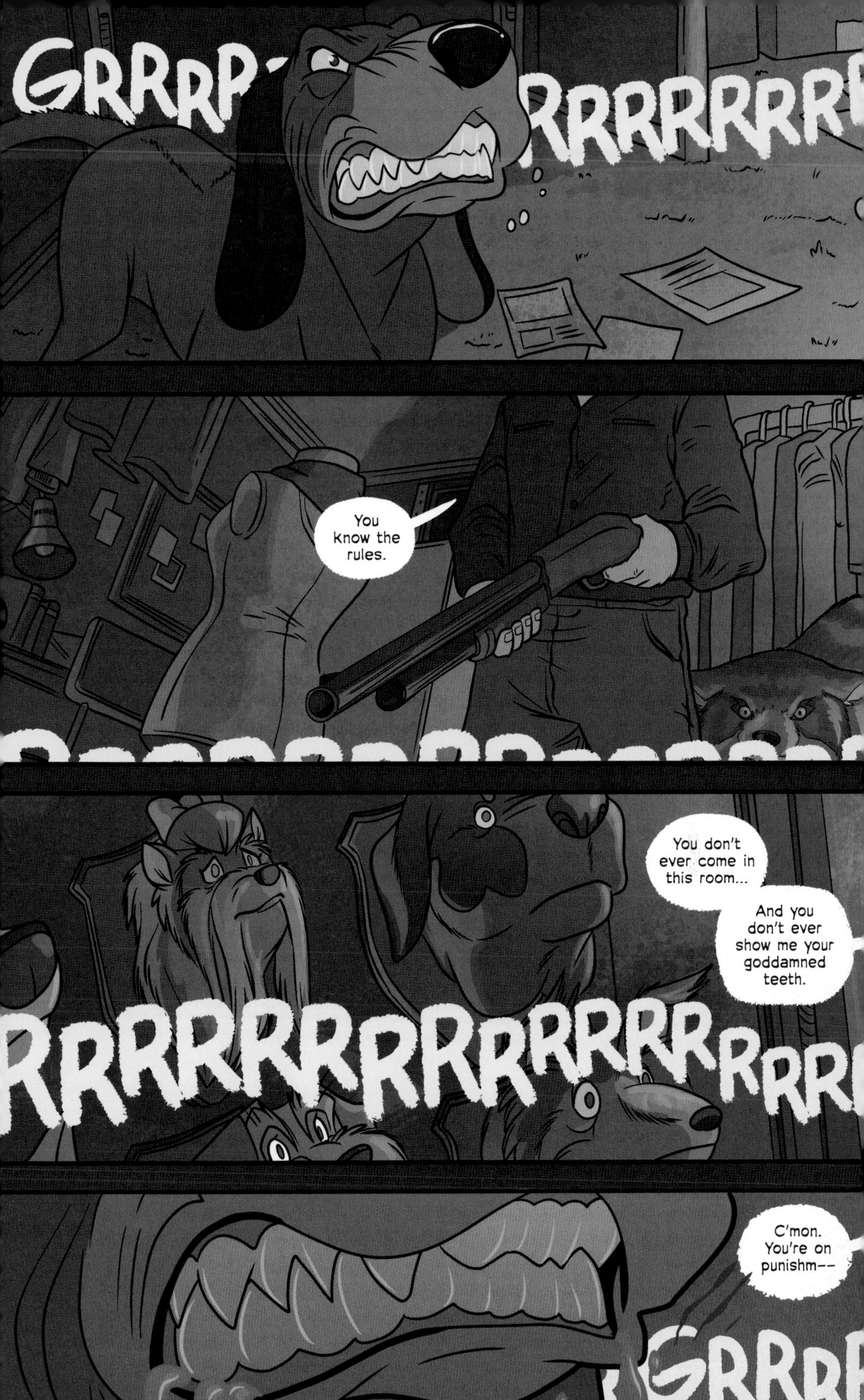

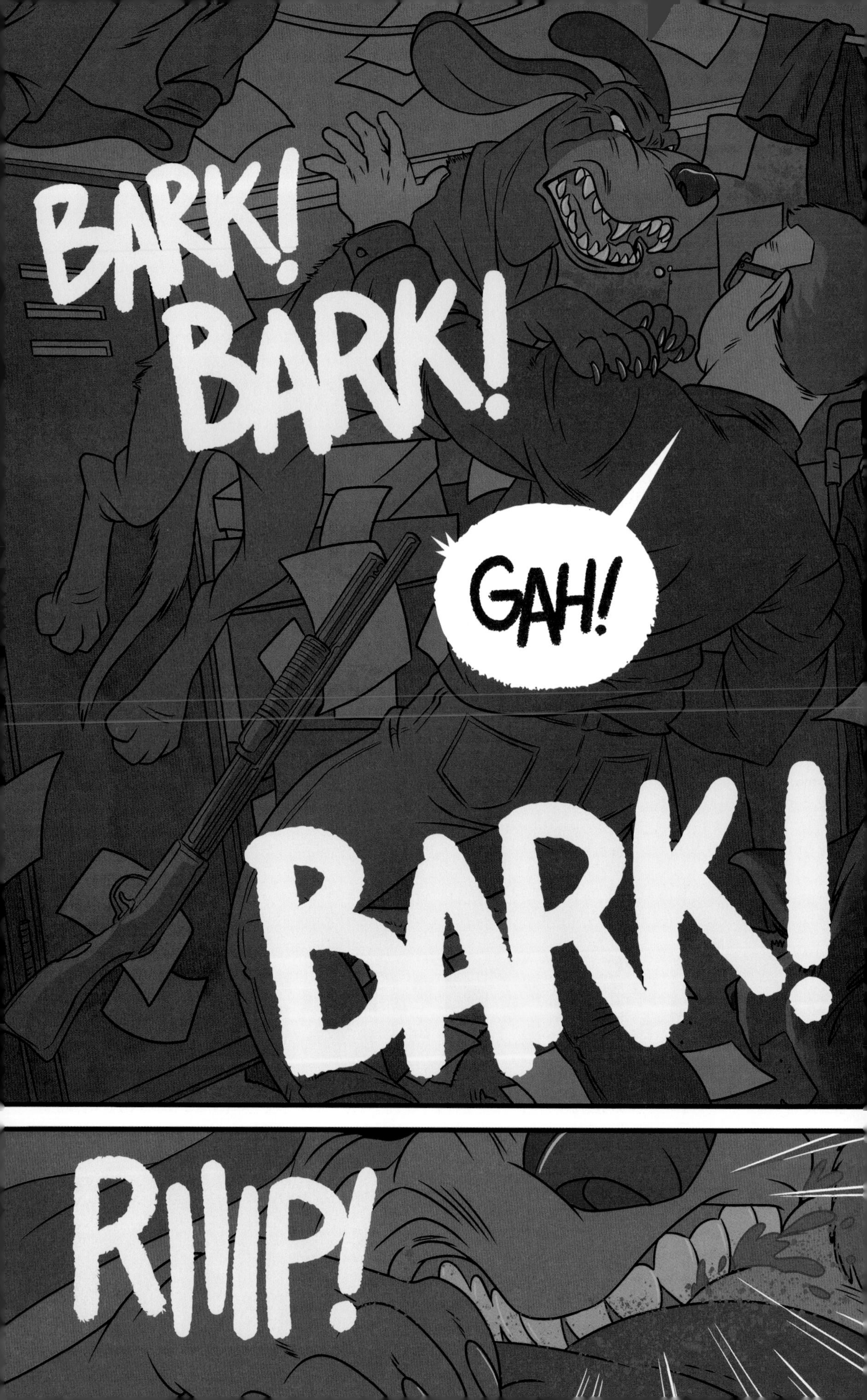
BARK!
BARK!
GAH!
BARK!
RIIIP!

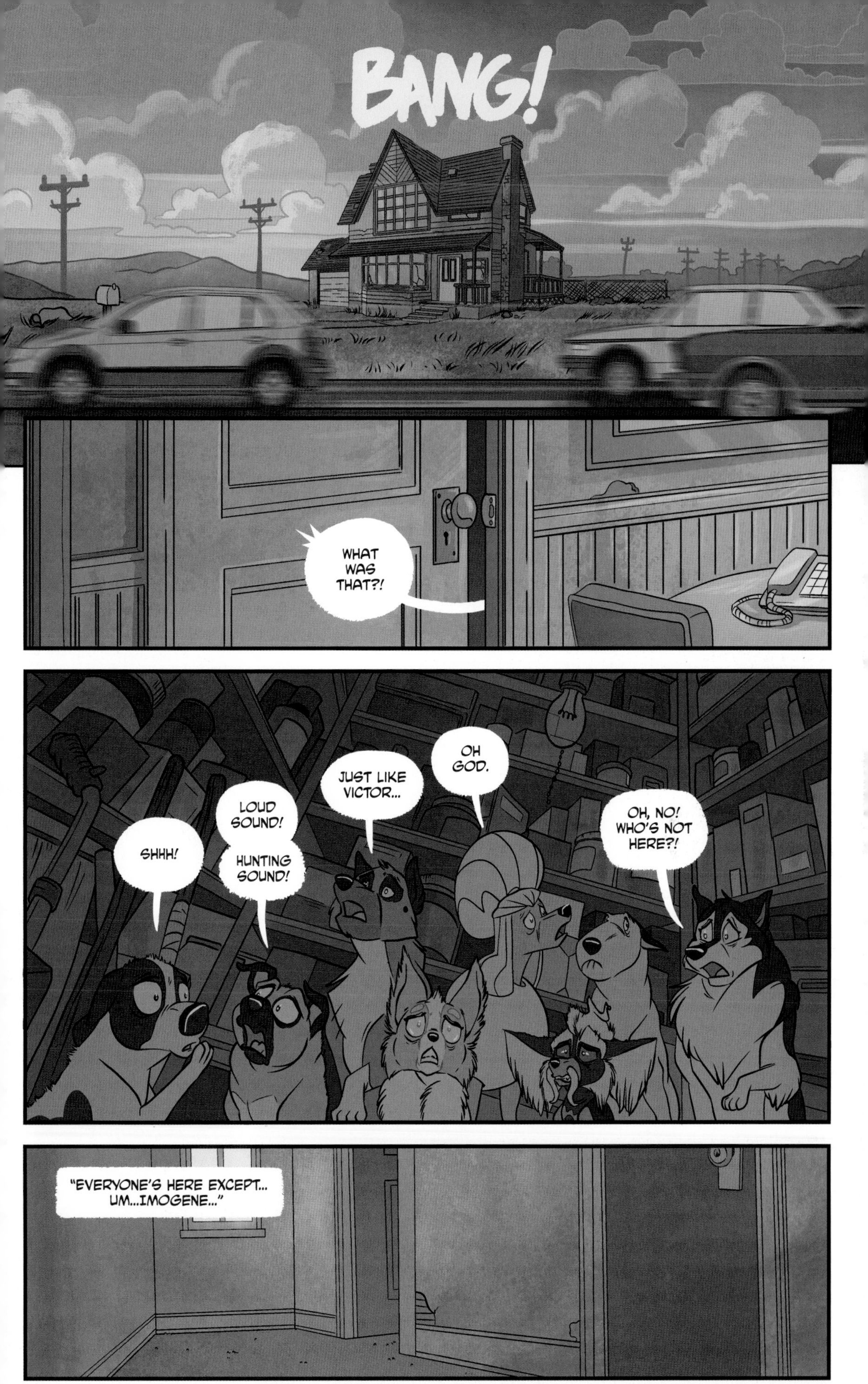
BANG!
WHAT WAS THAT?!
SHHH!
LOUD SOUND!
HUNTING SOUND!
JUST LIKE VICTOR...
OH GOD.
OH, NO! WHO'S NOT HERE?!
"EVERYONE'S HERE EXCEPT... UM...IMOGENE..."

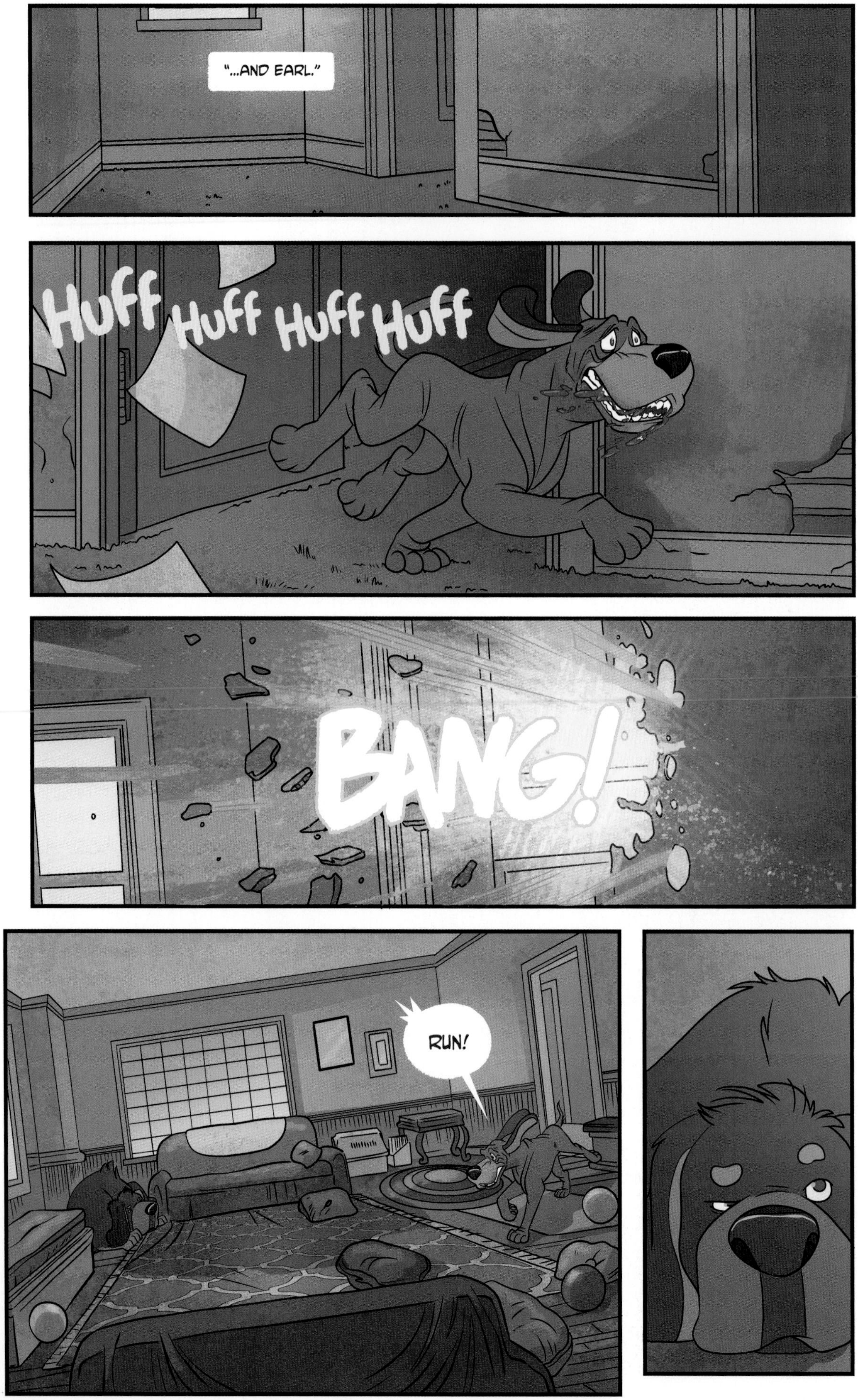
"...AND EARL."
HUFF HUFF HUFF HUFF
BANG!
RUN!

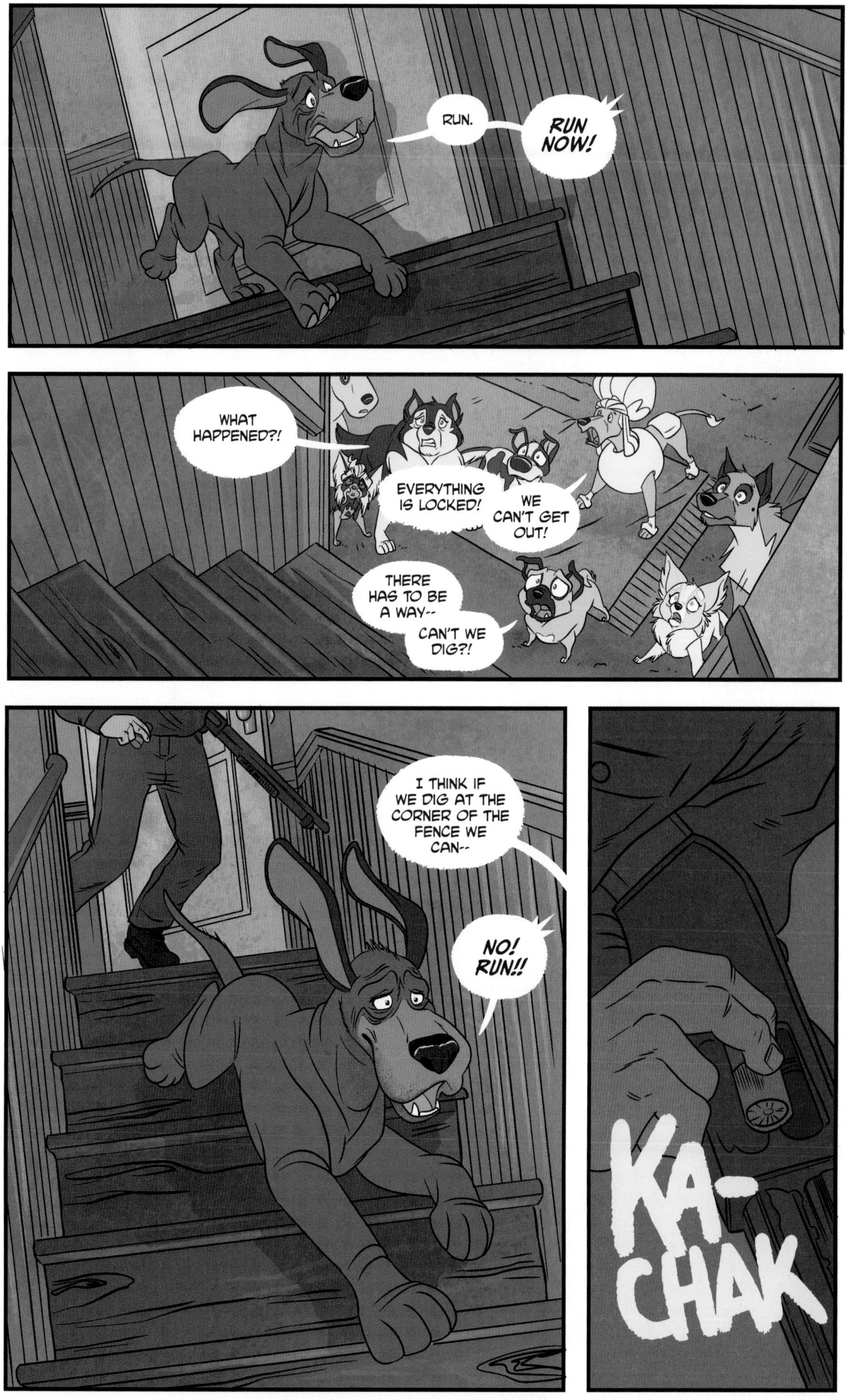
RUN.
RUN NOW!
WHAT HAPPENED?!
EVERYTHING IS LOCKED!
WE CAN'T GET OUT!
THERE HAS TO BE A WAY--
CAN'T WE DIG?!
I THINK IF WE DIG AT THE CORNER OF THE FENCE WE CAN--
NO! RUN!!
KA-CHAK

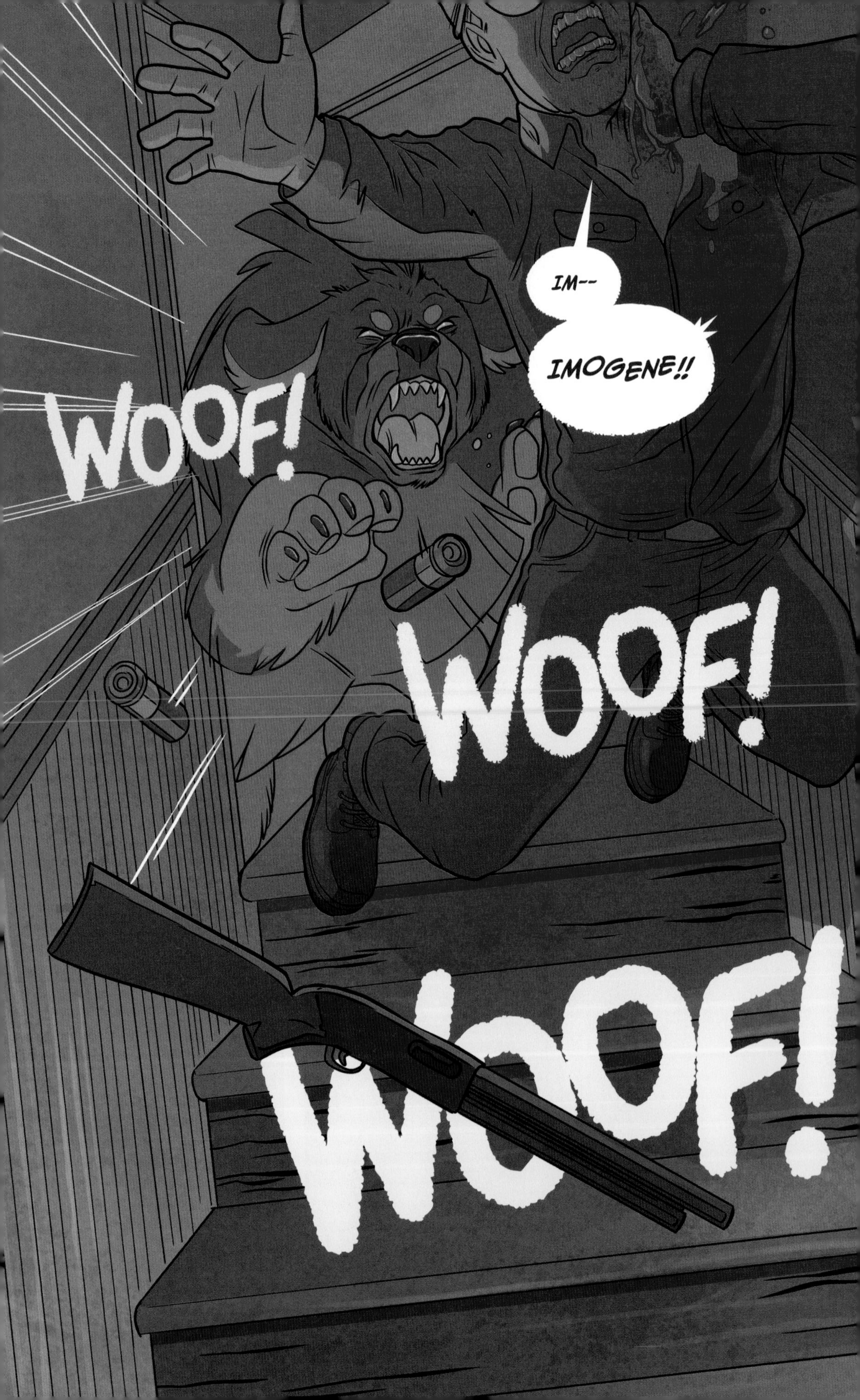
IM--
IMOGENE!!
WOOF!
WOOF!
WOOF!

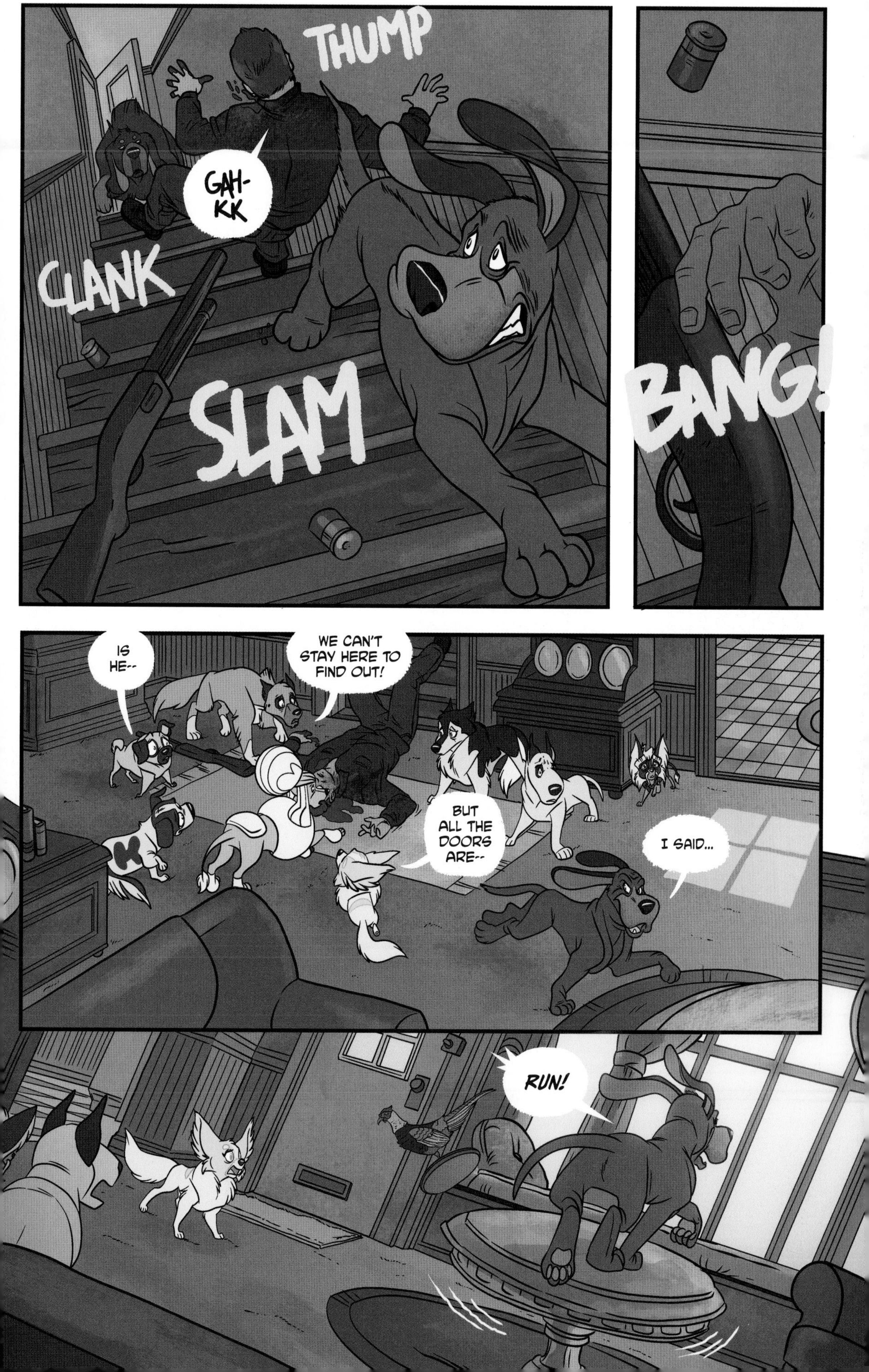
THUMP
GAH-KK
CLANK
SLAM
BANG!
IS HE--
WE CAN'T STAY HERE TO FIND OUT!
BUT ALL THE DOORS ARE--
I SAID...
RUN!

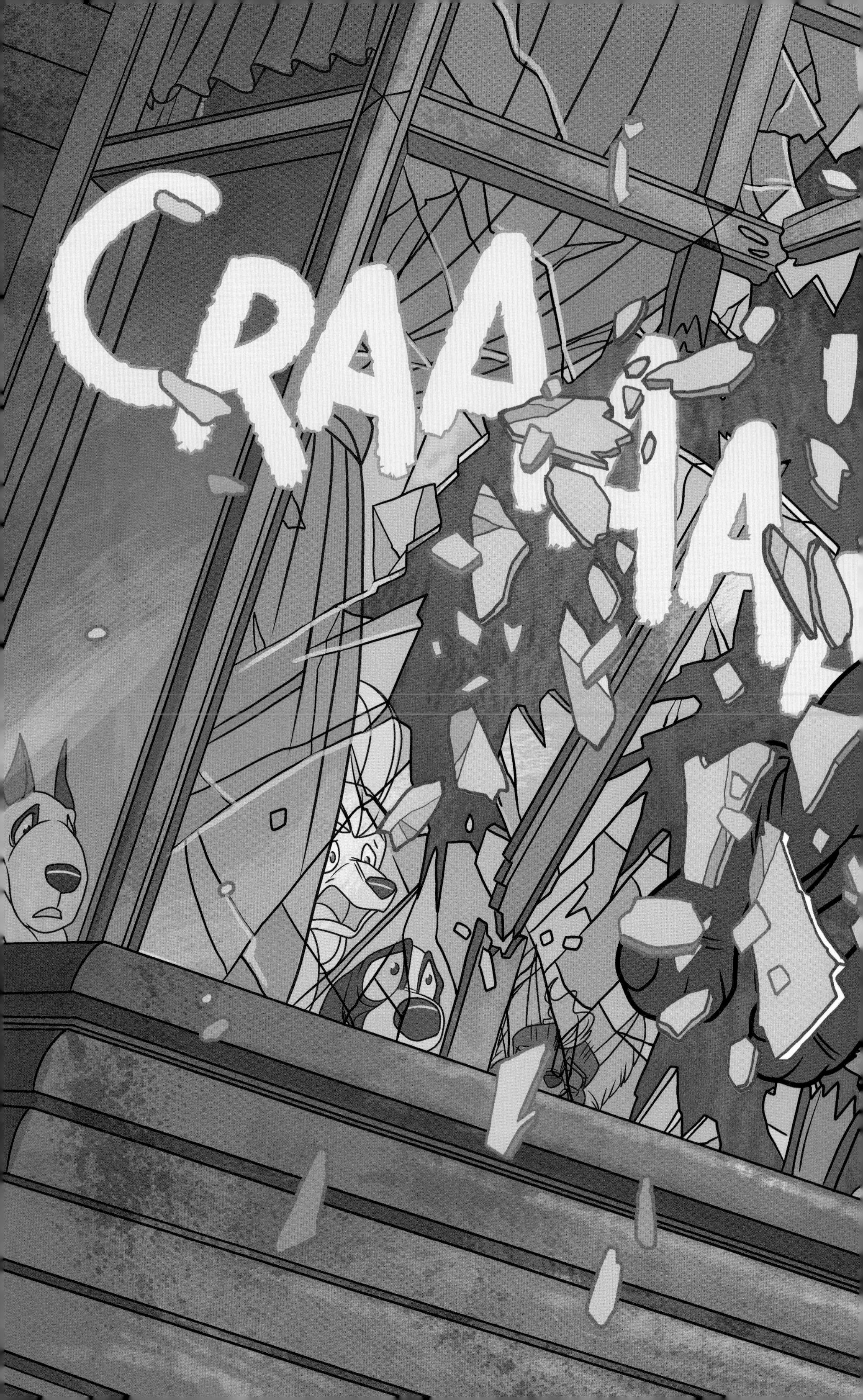
CRAAHA

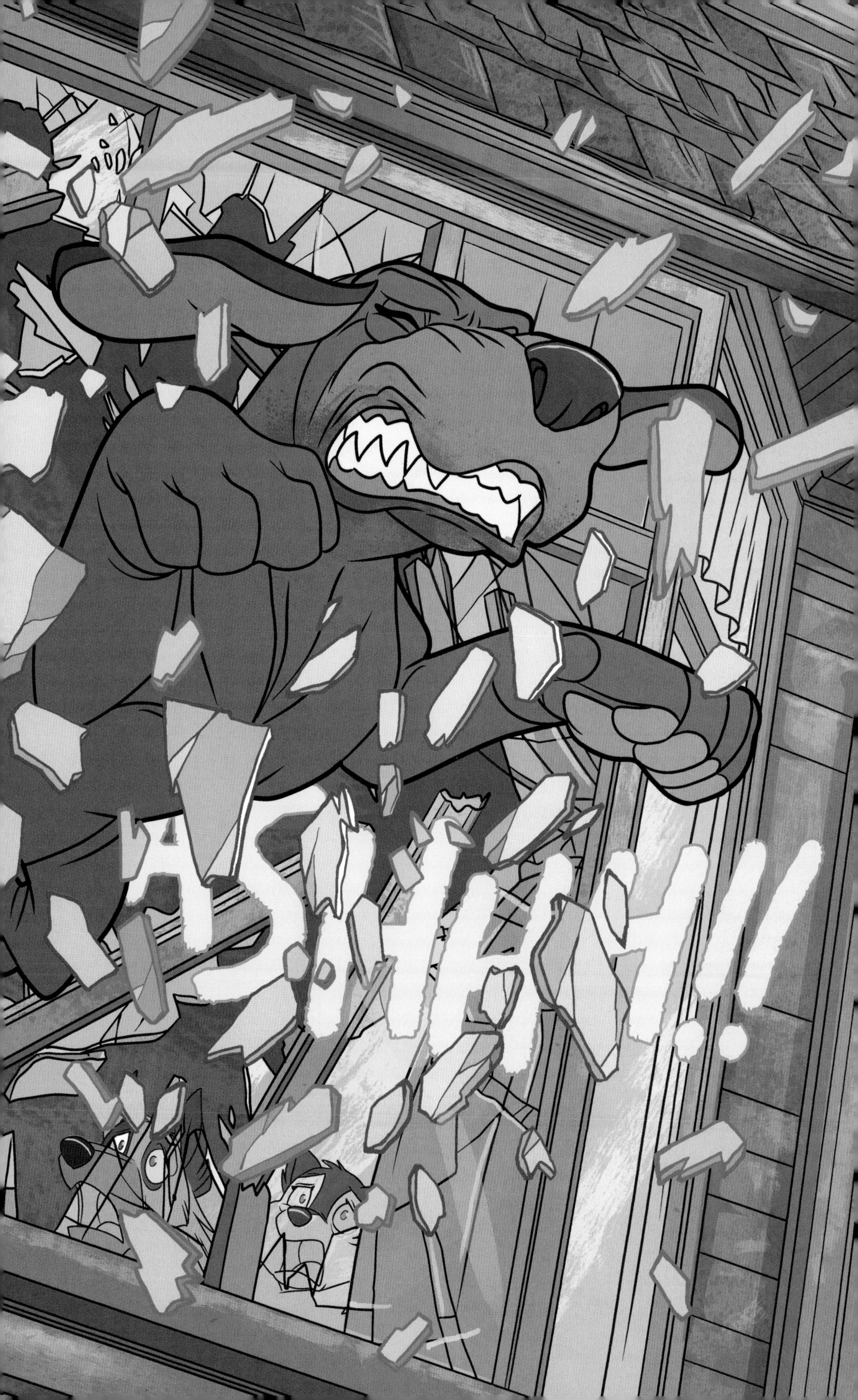

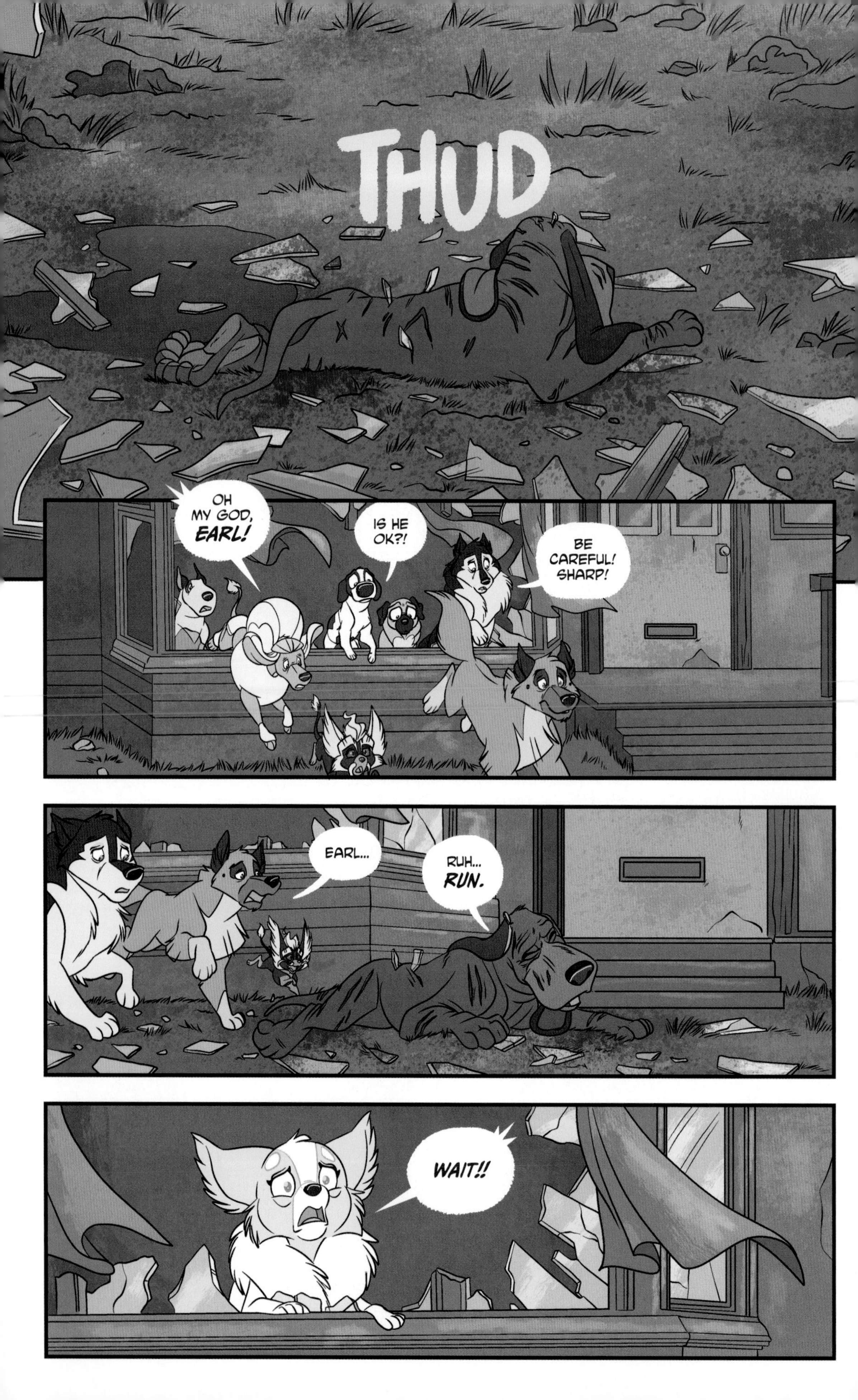
THUD
OH MY GOD, EARL!
IS HE OK?!
BE CAREFUL! SHARP!
EARL...
RUH... RUN.
WAIT!!

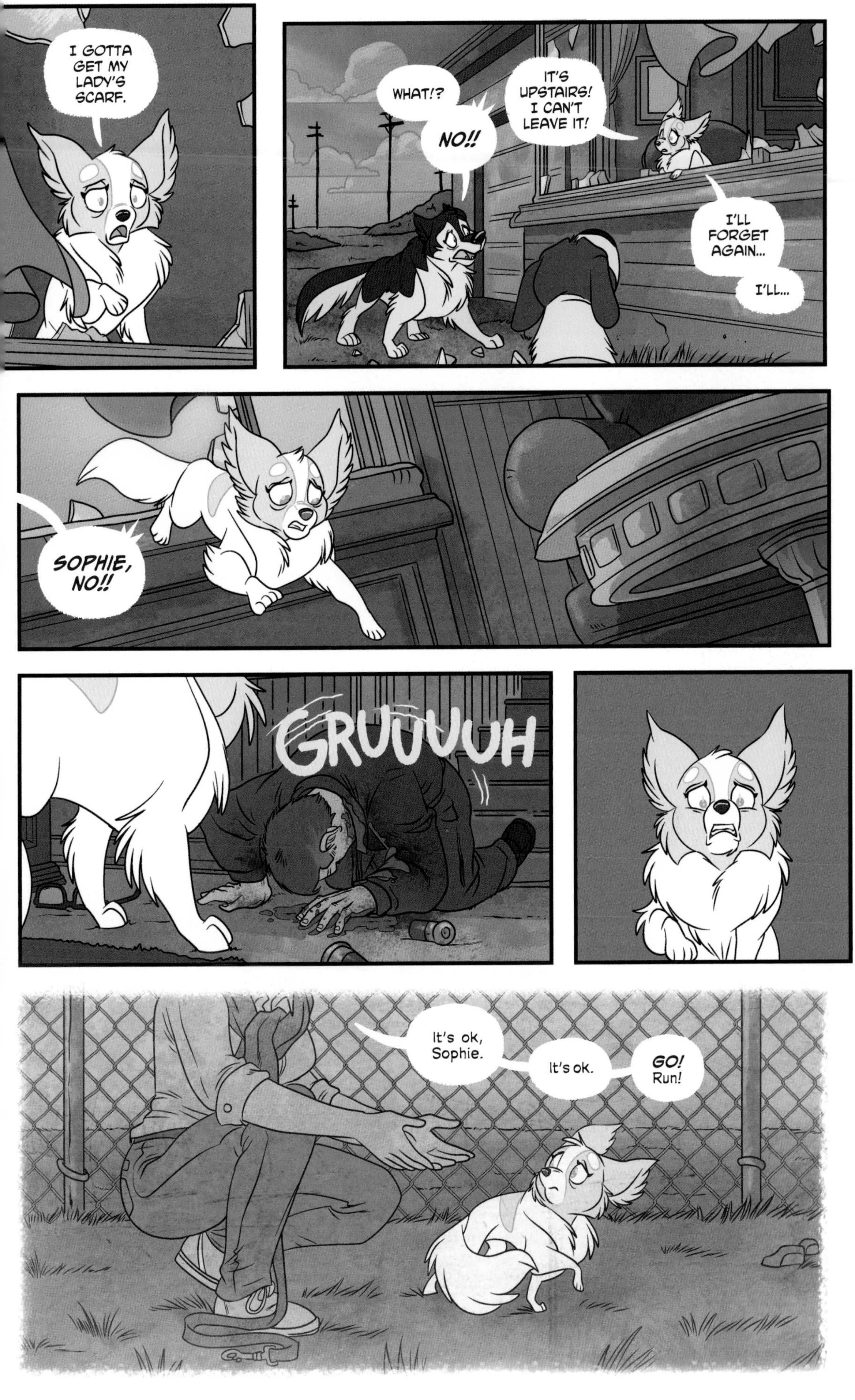
I GOTTA GET MY LADY'S SCARF.
WHAT!?
NO!!
IT'S UPSTAIRS! I CAN'T LEAVE IT!
I'LL FORGET AGAIN...
I'LL...
SOPHIE, NO!!
GRUUUUH
It's ok, Sophie.
It's ok.
GO! Run!

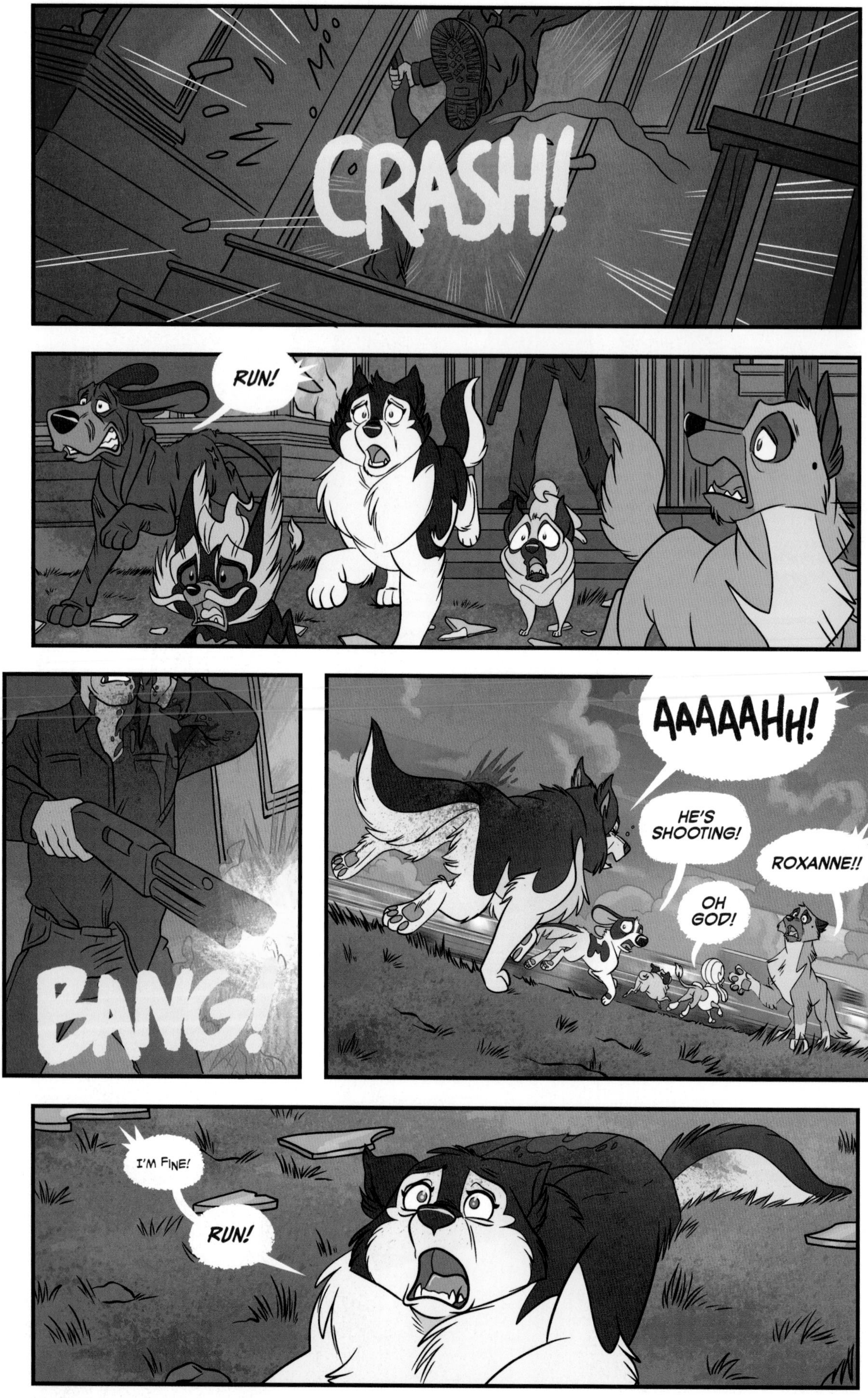
CRASH!
RUN!
BANG!
AAAAAHH!
HE'S SHOOTING!
ROXANNE!!
OH GOD!
I'M FINE!
RUN!

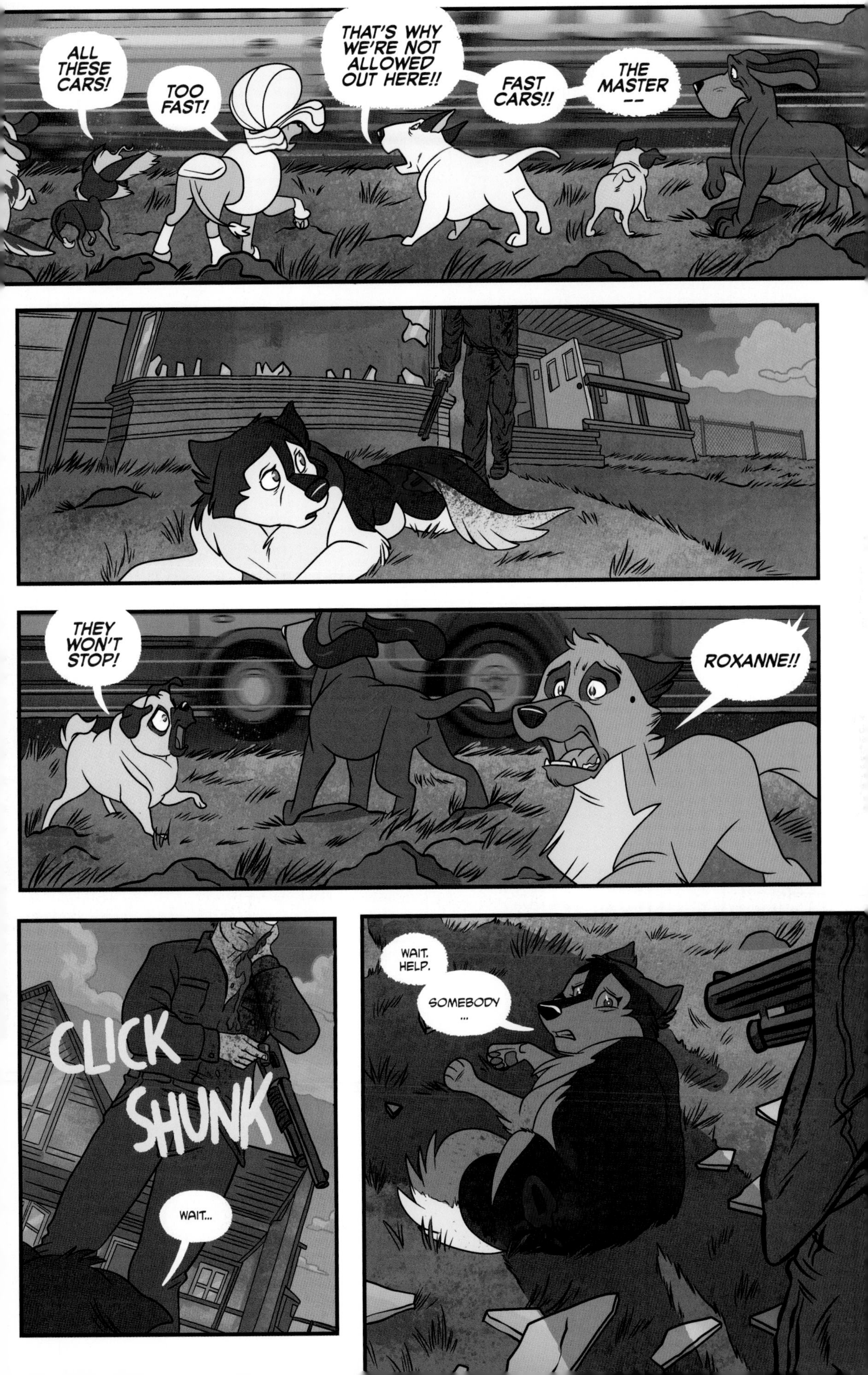
ALL THESE CARS!
TOO FAST!
THAT'S WHY WE'RE NOT ALLOWED OUT HERE!!
FAST CARS!!
THE MASTER --
THEY WON'T STOP!
ROXANNE!!
CLICK
SHUNK
WAIT...
WAIT. HELP.
SOMEBODY ...

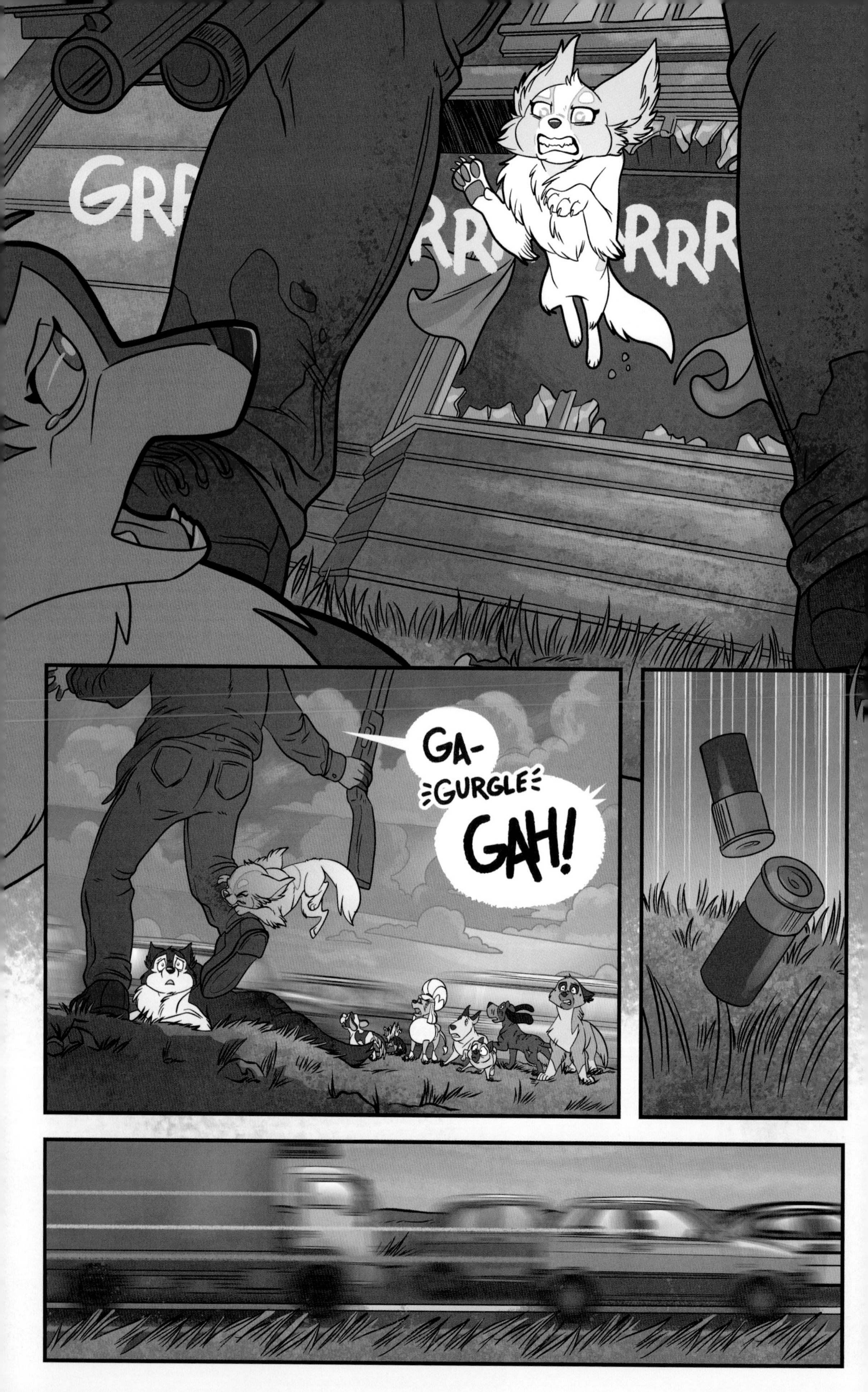
GRR
RR
RRR
GA-
GURGLE
GAH!

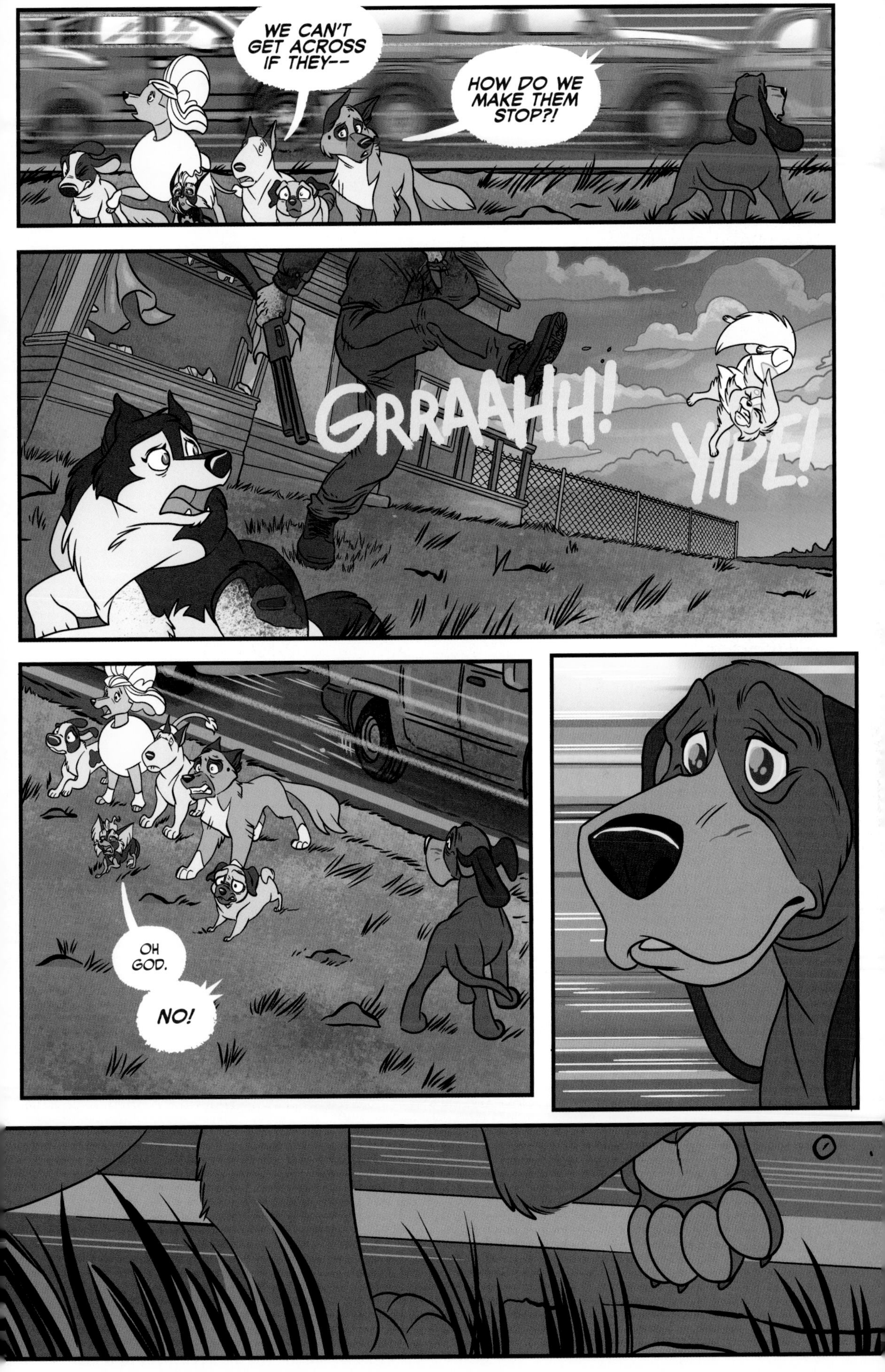
WE CAN'T GET ACROSS IF THEY--
HOW DO WE MAKE THEM STOP?!
GRRAAHH!
YIPE!
OH GOD.
NO!

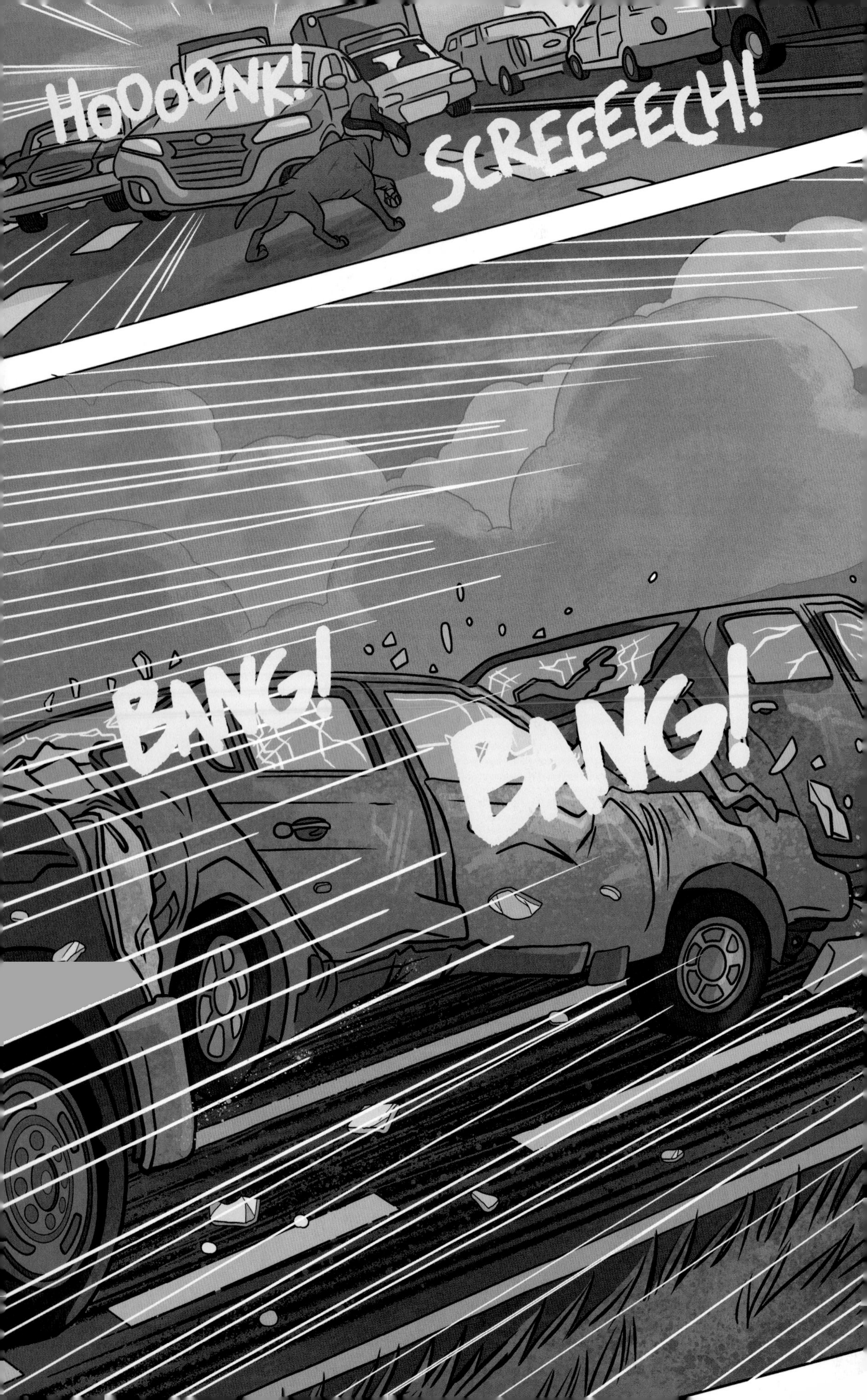
HOOOONK!
SCREEEECH!
BANG!
BANG!

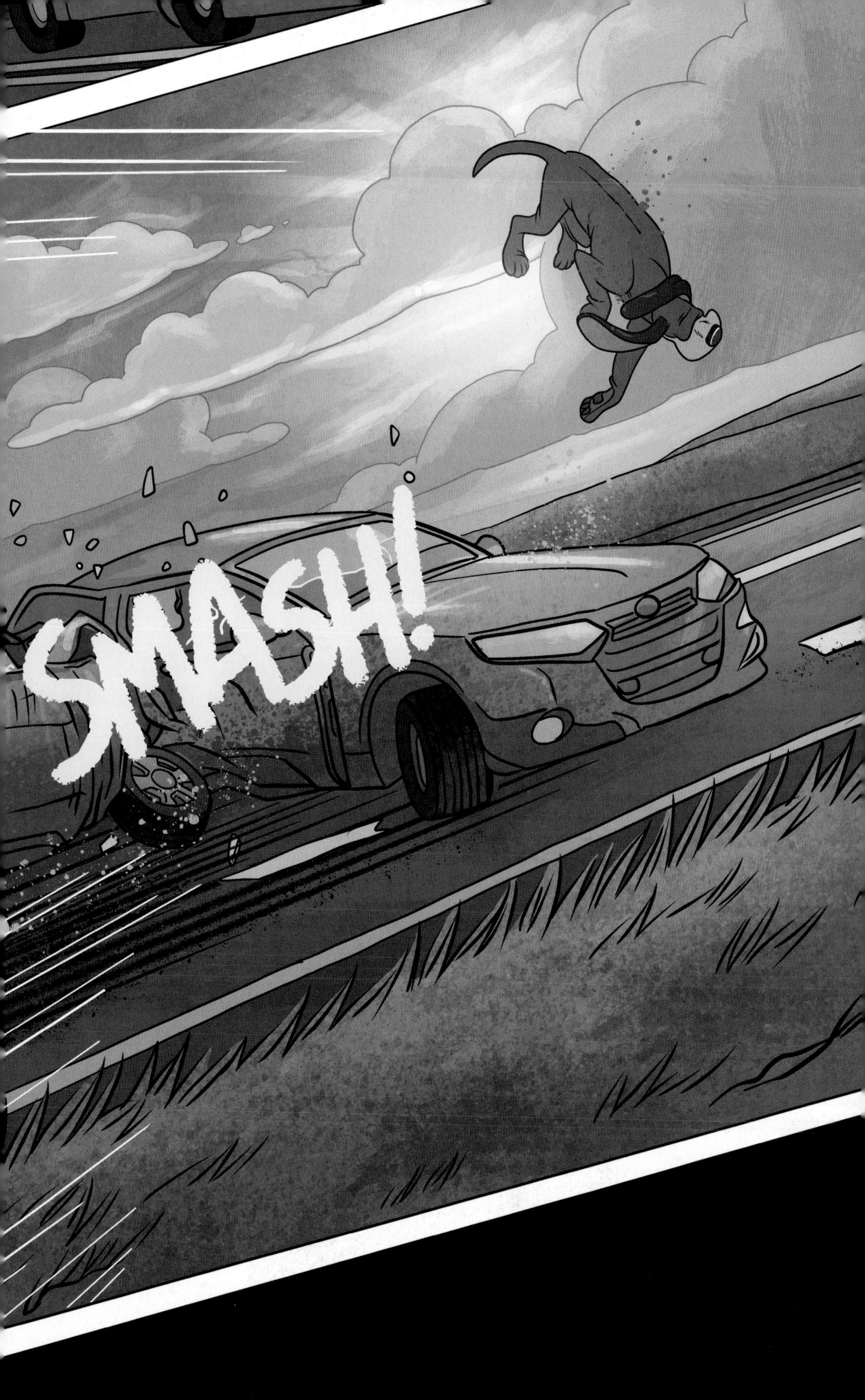
SMASH!

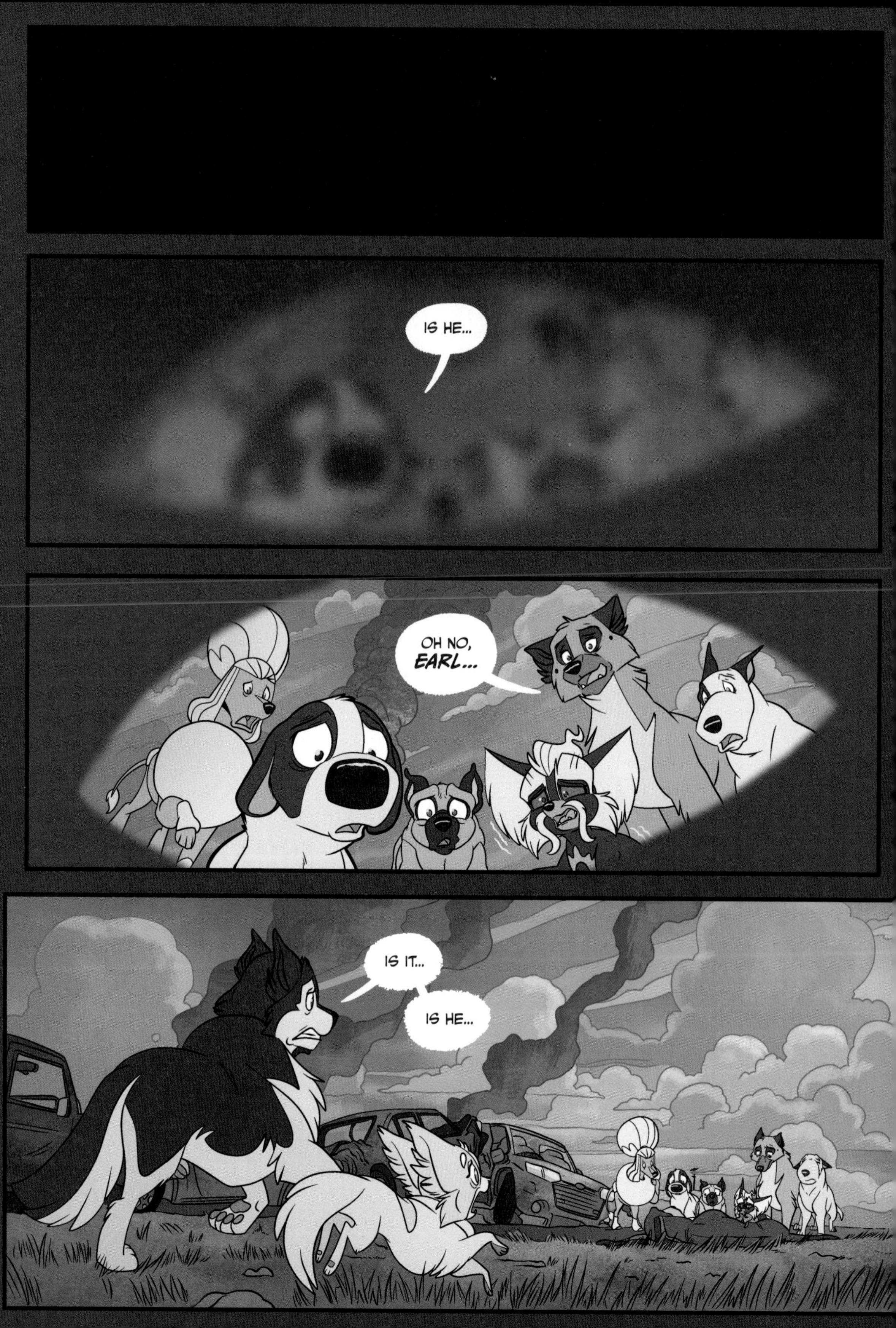
IS HE...
OH NO, EARL...
IS IT...
IS HE...

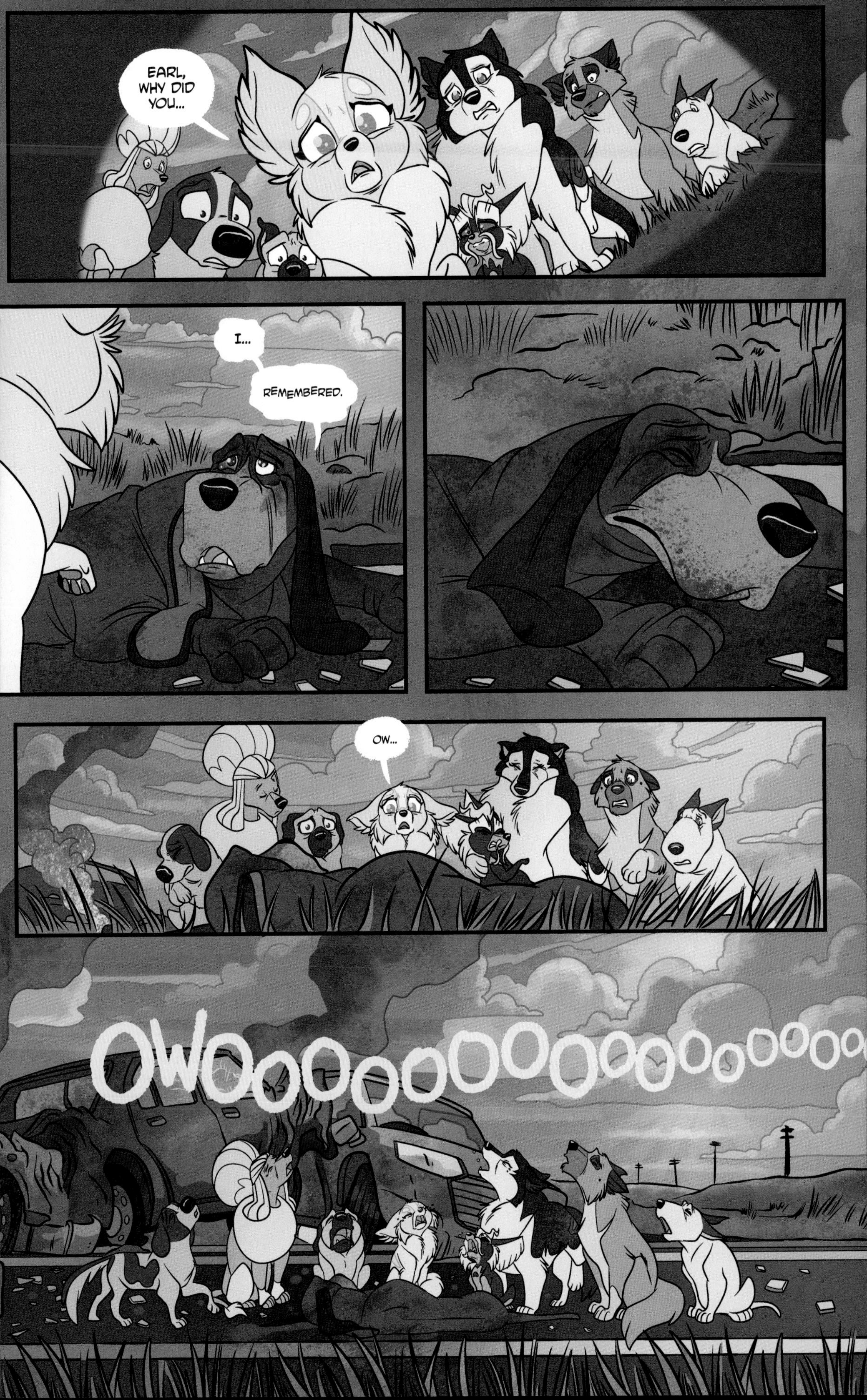
EARL, WHY DID YOU...
I...
REMEMBERED.
OW...
OWOOOOOOOOOOOOOOOOO

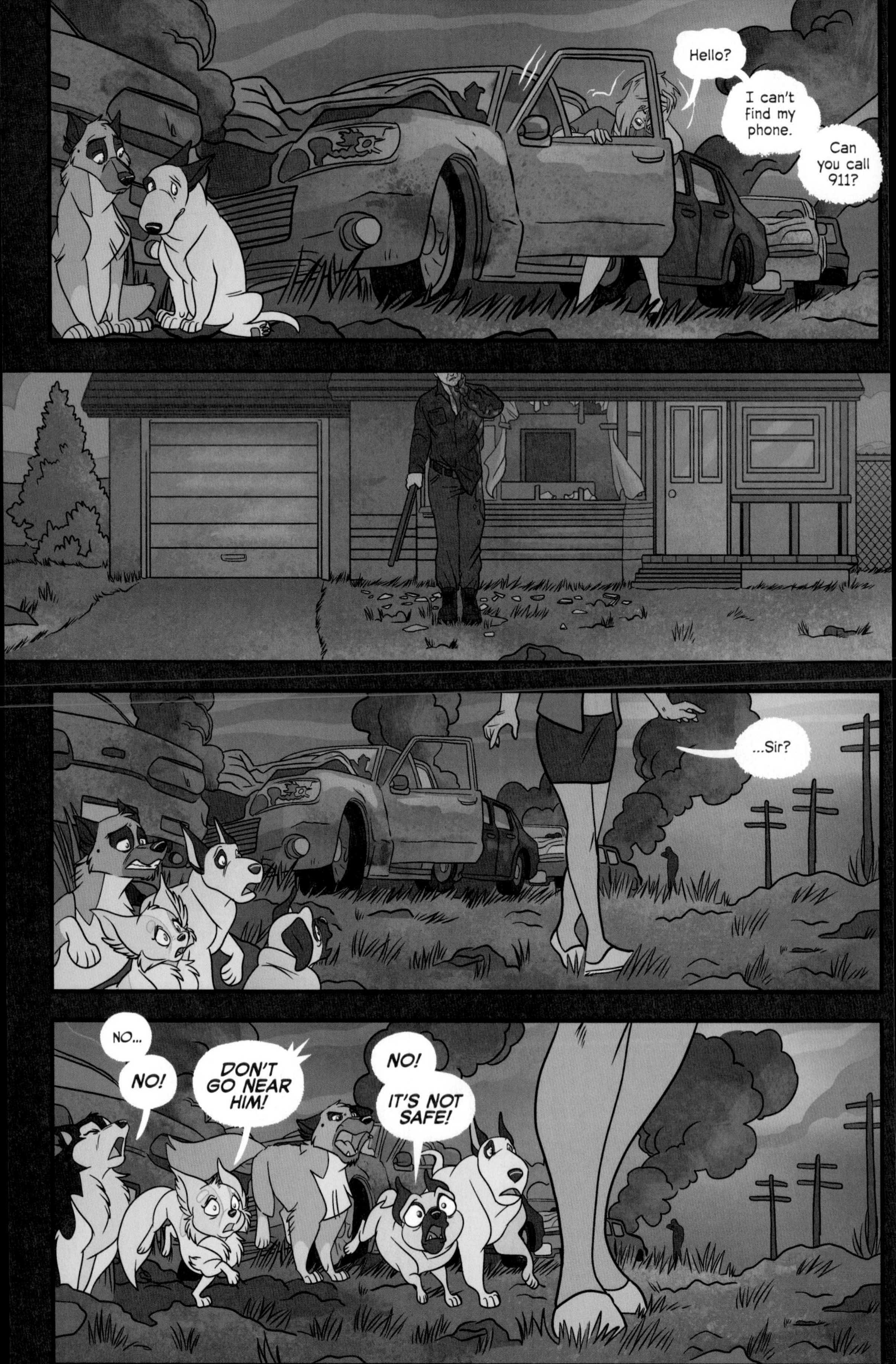
Hello?
I can't find my phone.
Can you call 911?
...Sir?
NO...
NO!
DON'T GO NEAR HIM!
NO!
IT'S NOT SAFE!

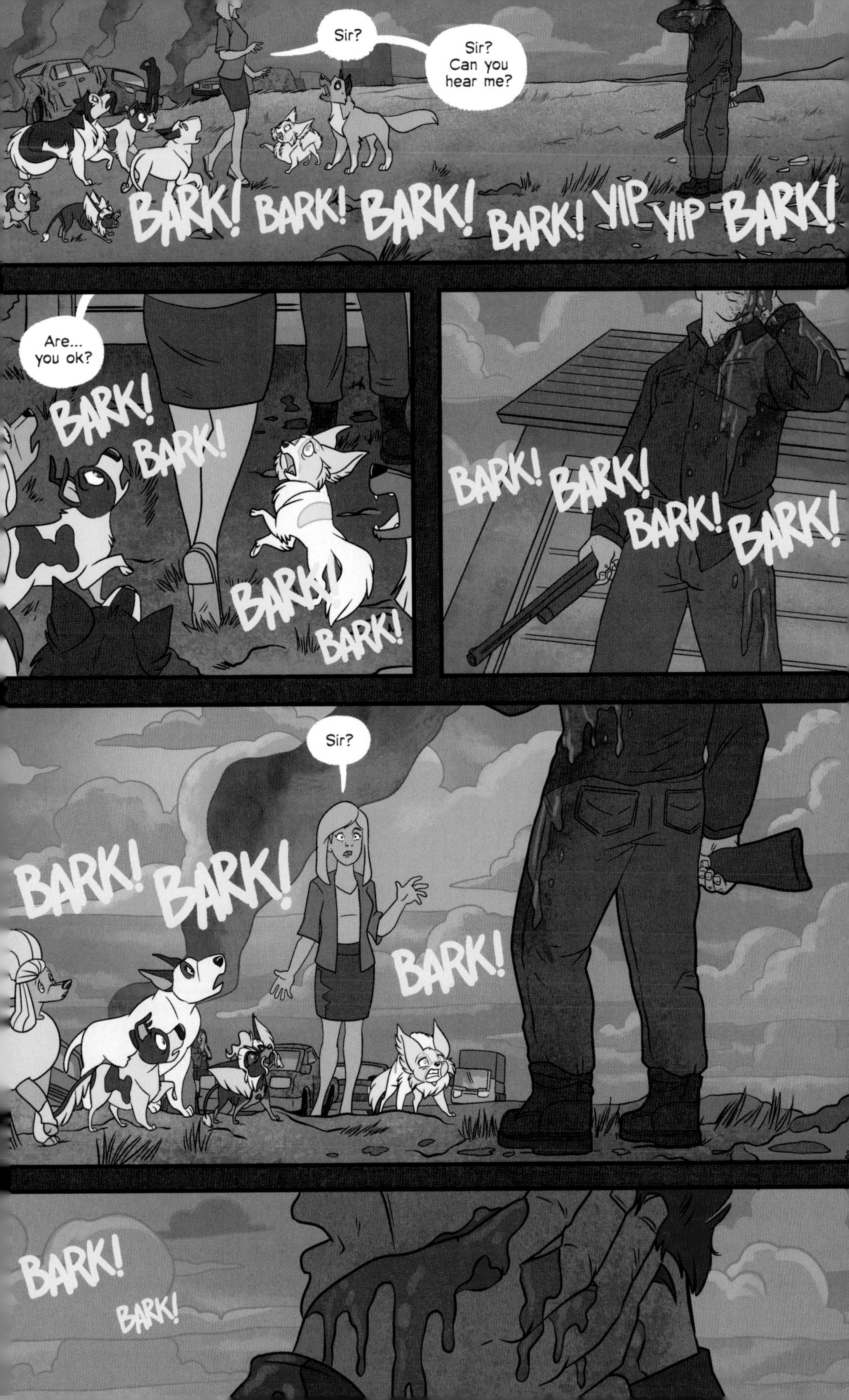
Sir?
Sir? Can you hear me?
BARK! BARK! BARK! BARK! YIP YIP BARK!
Are... you ok?
BARK! BARK!
BARK! BARK!
BARK! BARK! BARK! BARK!
Sir?
BARK! BARK!
BARK!
BARK!
BARK!

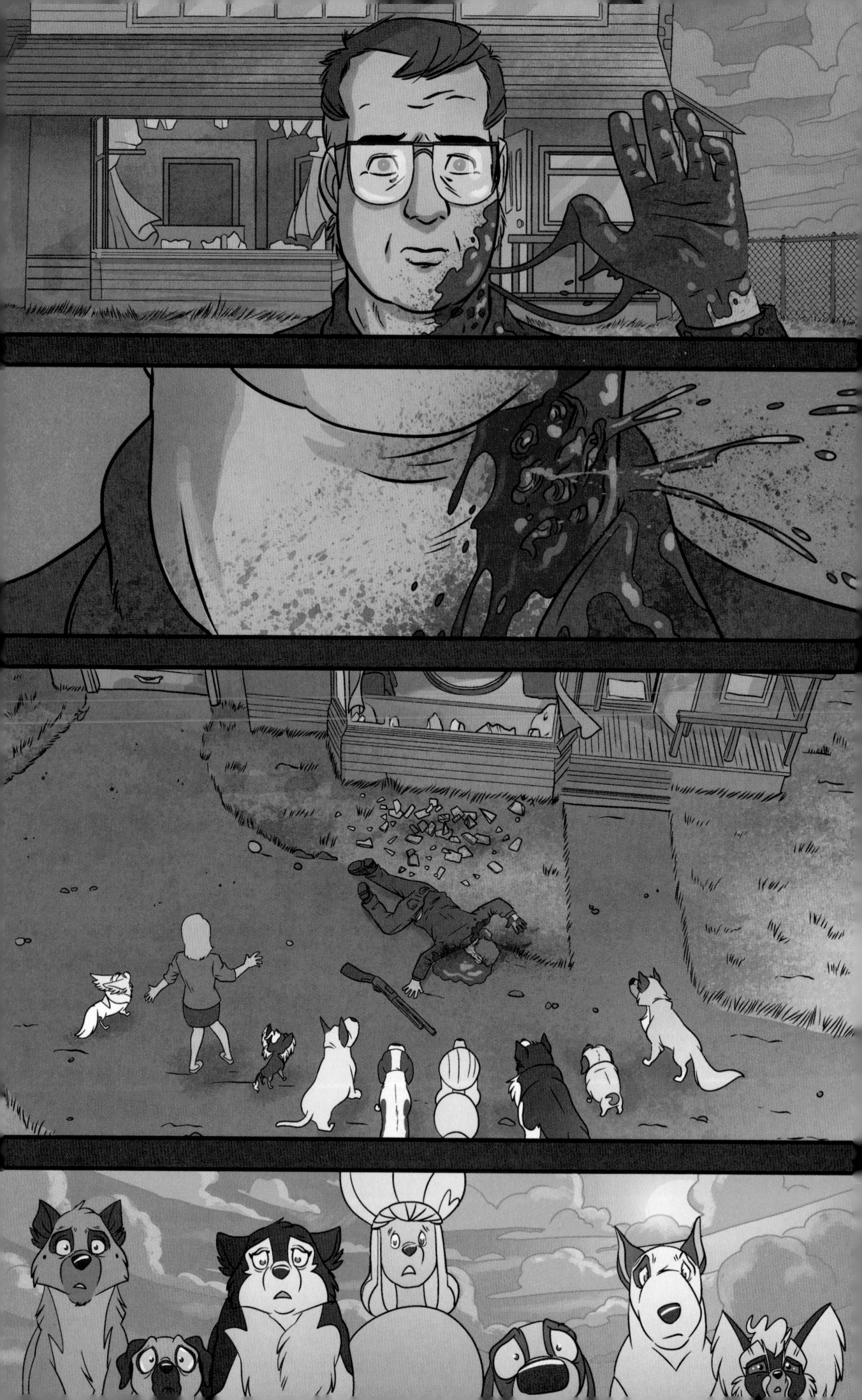

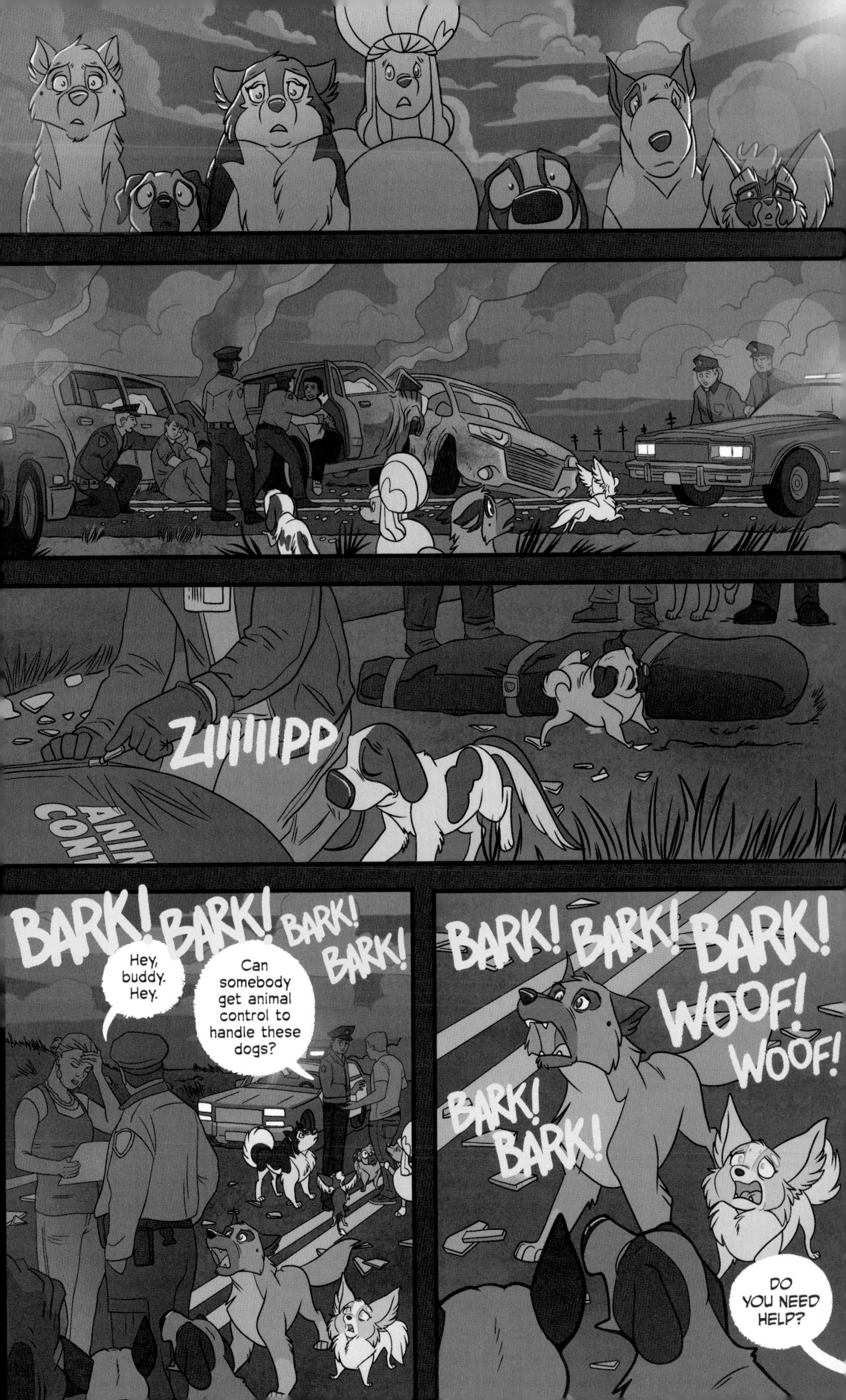
ZIIIIIPP
ANIM
CONT
BARK! BARK! BARK! BARK!
Hey, buddy. Hey.
Can somebody get animal control to handle these dogs?
BARK! BARK! BARK!
WOOF! WOOF!
BARK! BARK!
DO YOU NEED HELP?

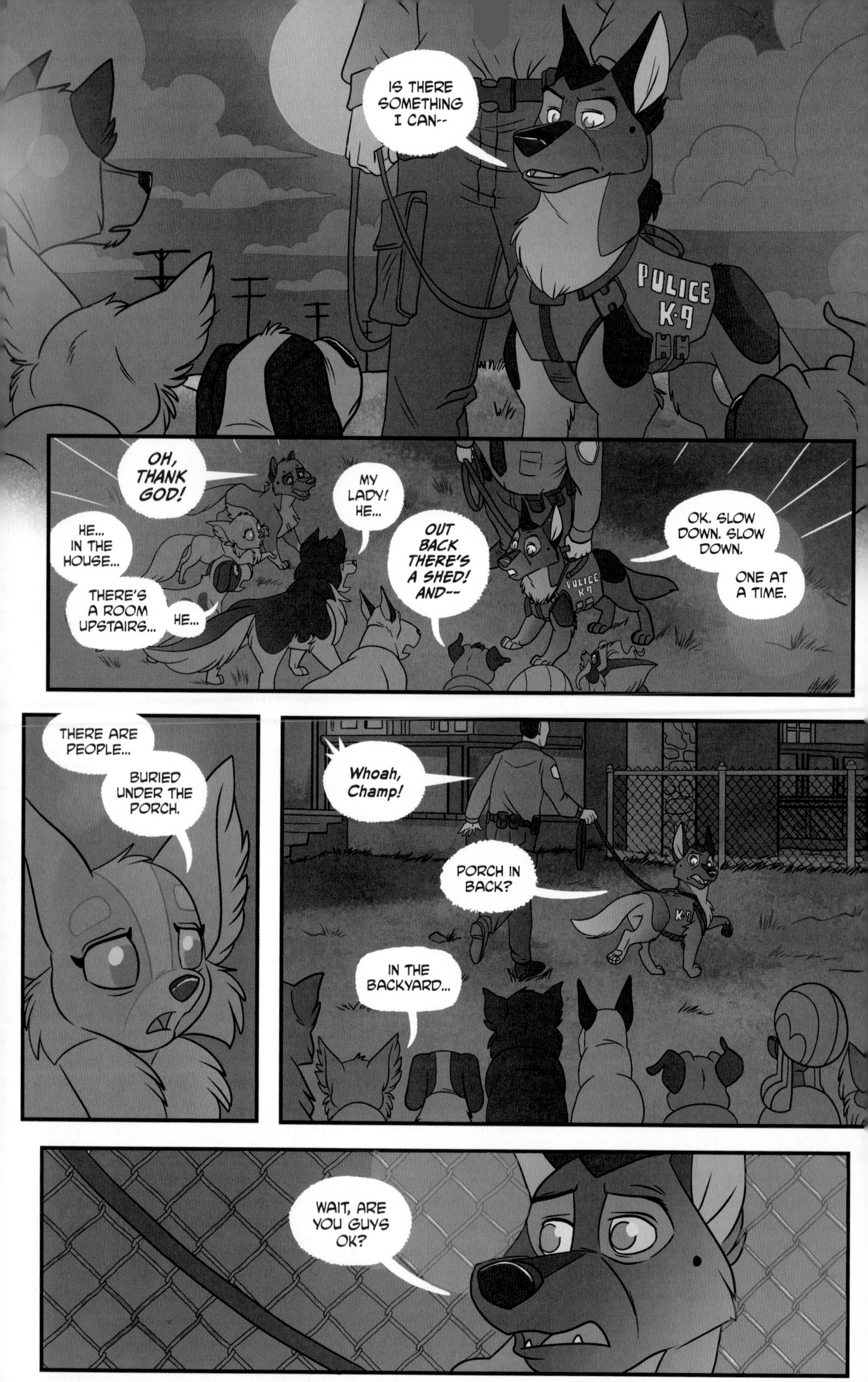
IS THERE SOMETHING I CAN--
OH, THANK GOD!
HE... IN THE HOUSE...
THERE'S A ROOM UPSTAIRS...
HE...
MY LADY! HE...
OUT BACK THERE'S A SHED! AND--
OK. SLOW DOWN. SLOW DOWN.
ONE AT A TIME.
THERE ARE PEOPLE...
BURIED UNDER THE PORCH.
Whoah, Champ!
PORCH IN BACK?
IN THE BACKYARD...
WAIT, ARE YOU GUYS OK?

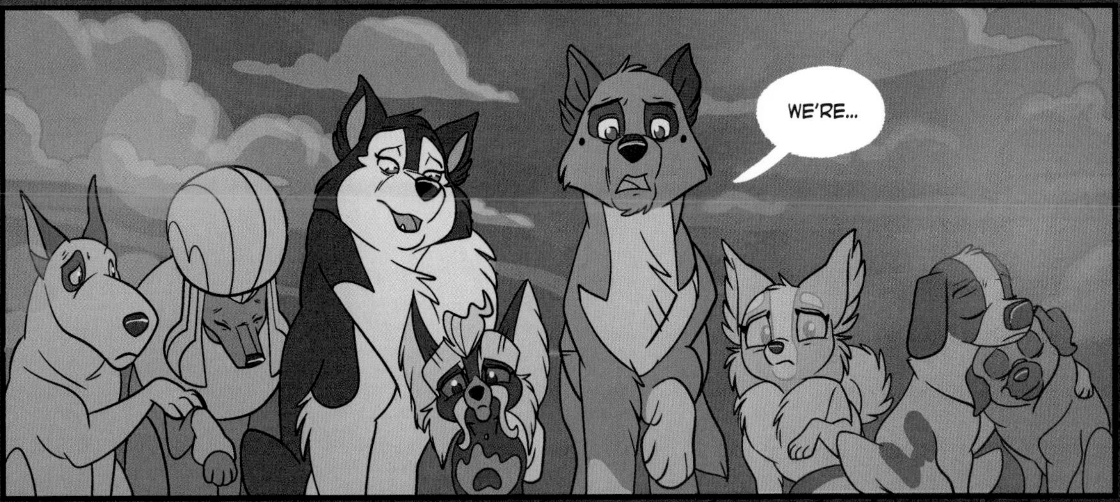
WE'RE...

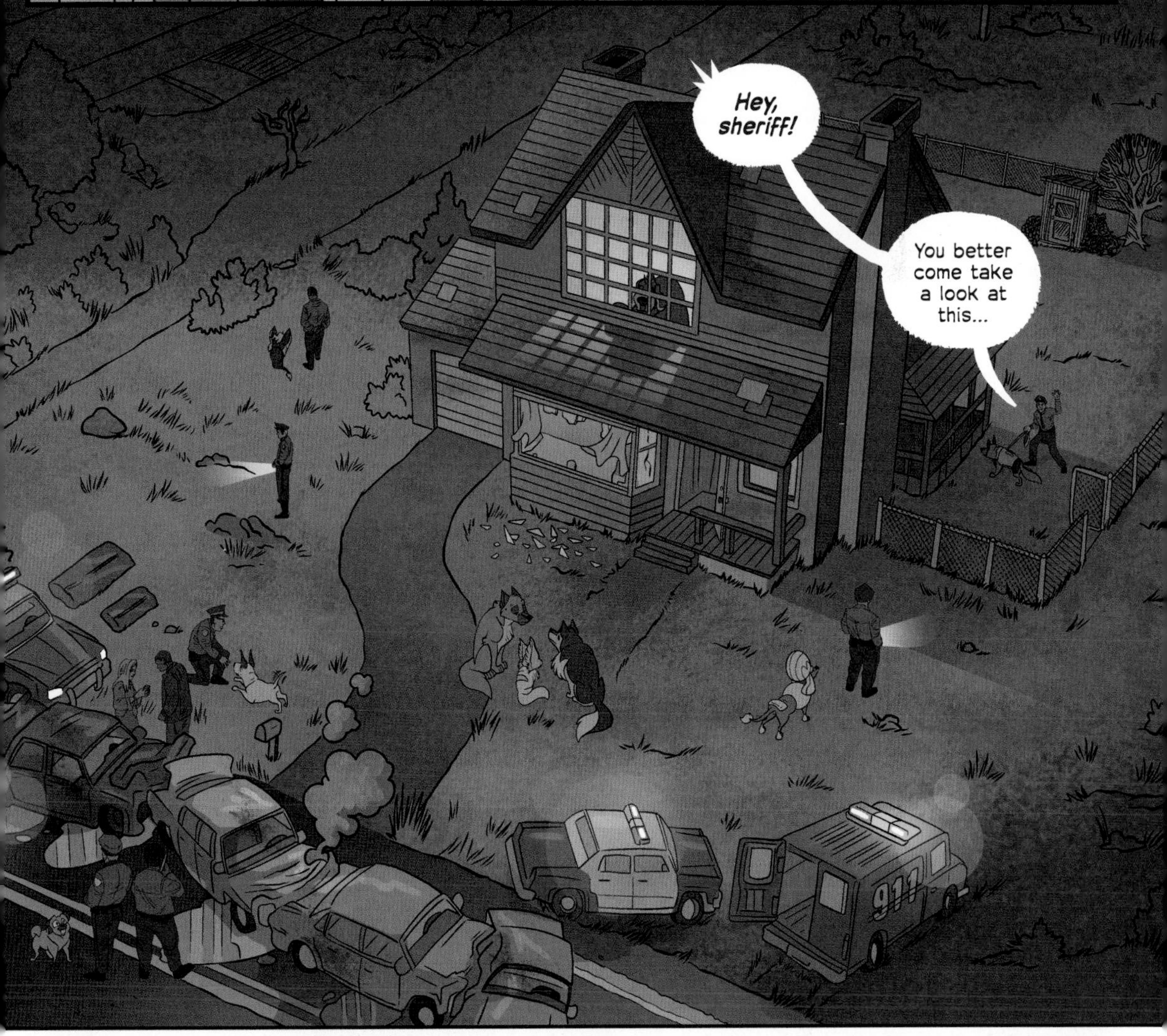
Hey, sheriff!
You better come take a look at this...

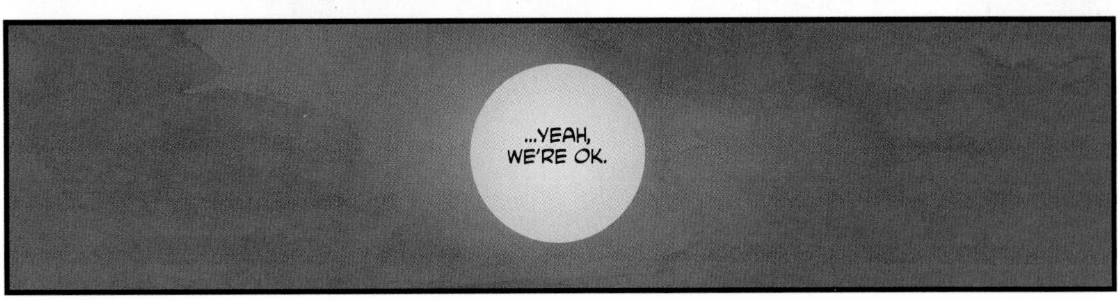
...YEAH, WE'RE OK.

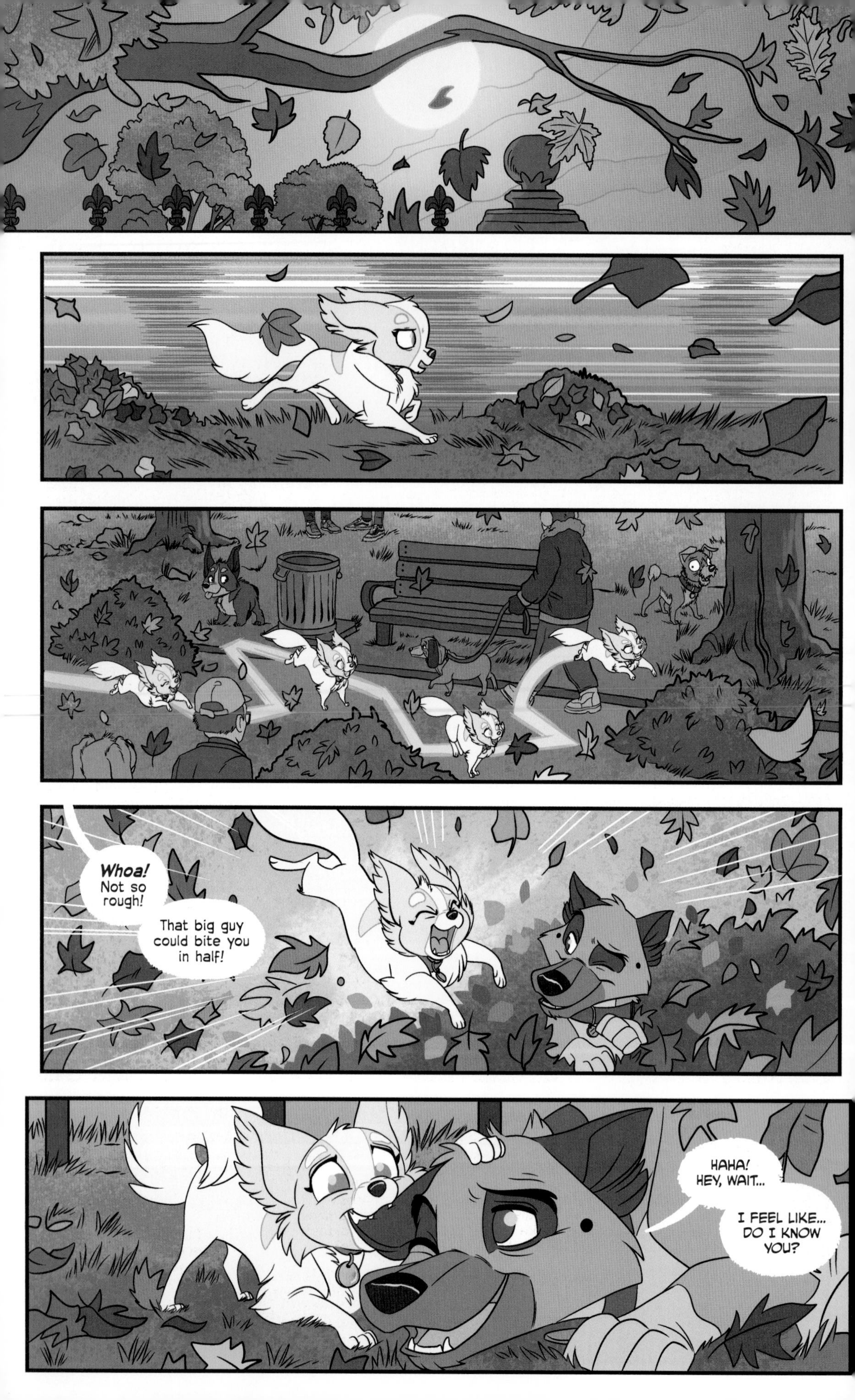
Whoa! Not so rough!
That big guy could bite you in half!
HAHA! HEY, WAIT...
I FEEL LIKE... DO I KNOW YOU?

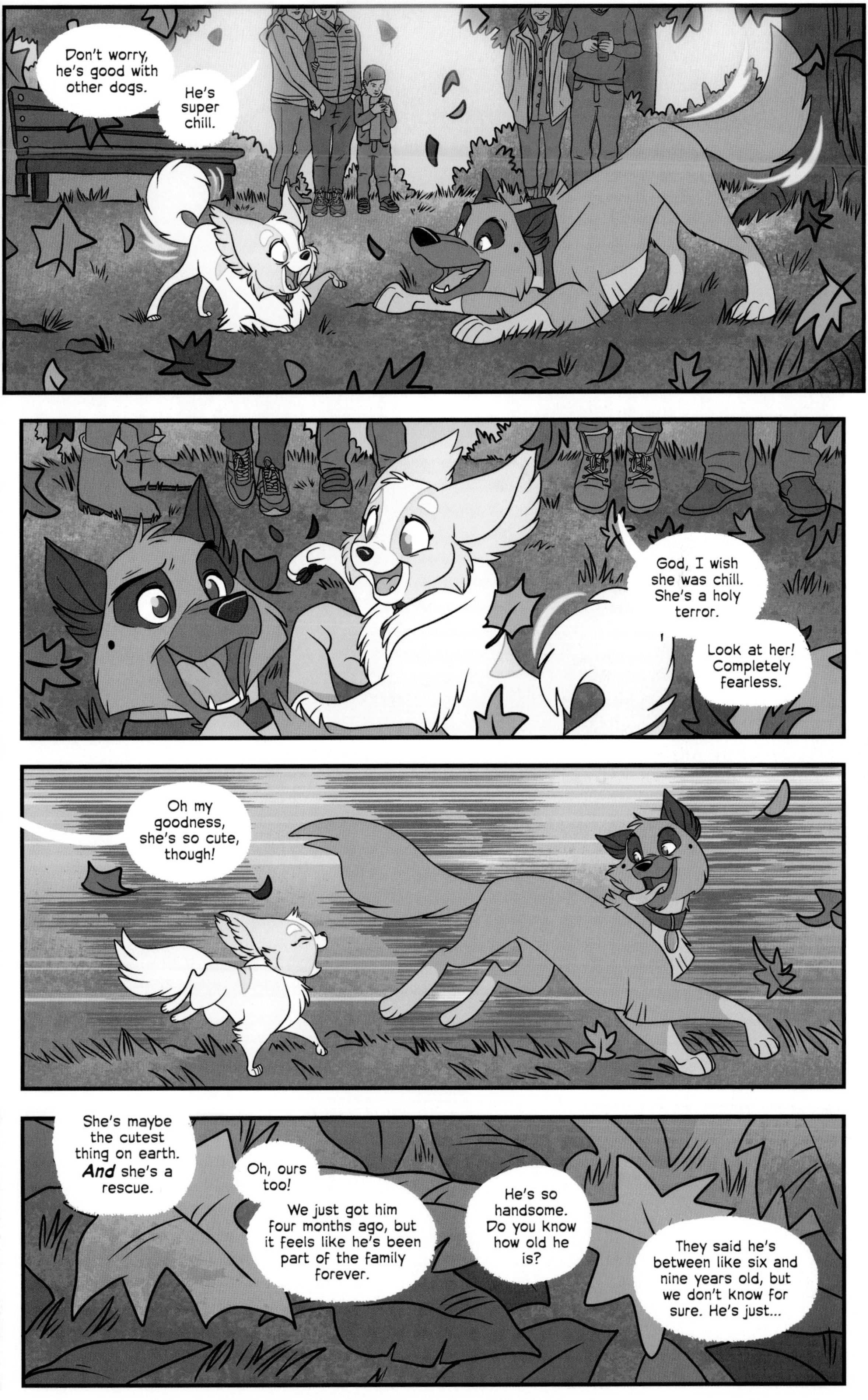

Don't worry, he's good with other dogs.
He's super chill.
God, I wish she was chill. She's a holy terror.
Look at her! Completely fearless.
Oh my goodness, she's so cute, though!
She's maybe the cutest thing on earth. ***And*** she's a rescue.
Oh, ours too!
We just got him four months ago, but it feels like he's been part of the family forever.
He's so handsome. Do you know how old he is?
They said he's between like six and nine years old, but we don't know for sure. He's just...

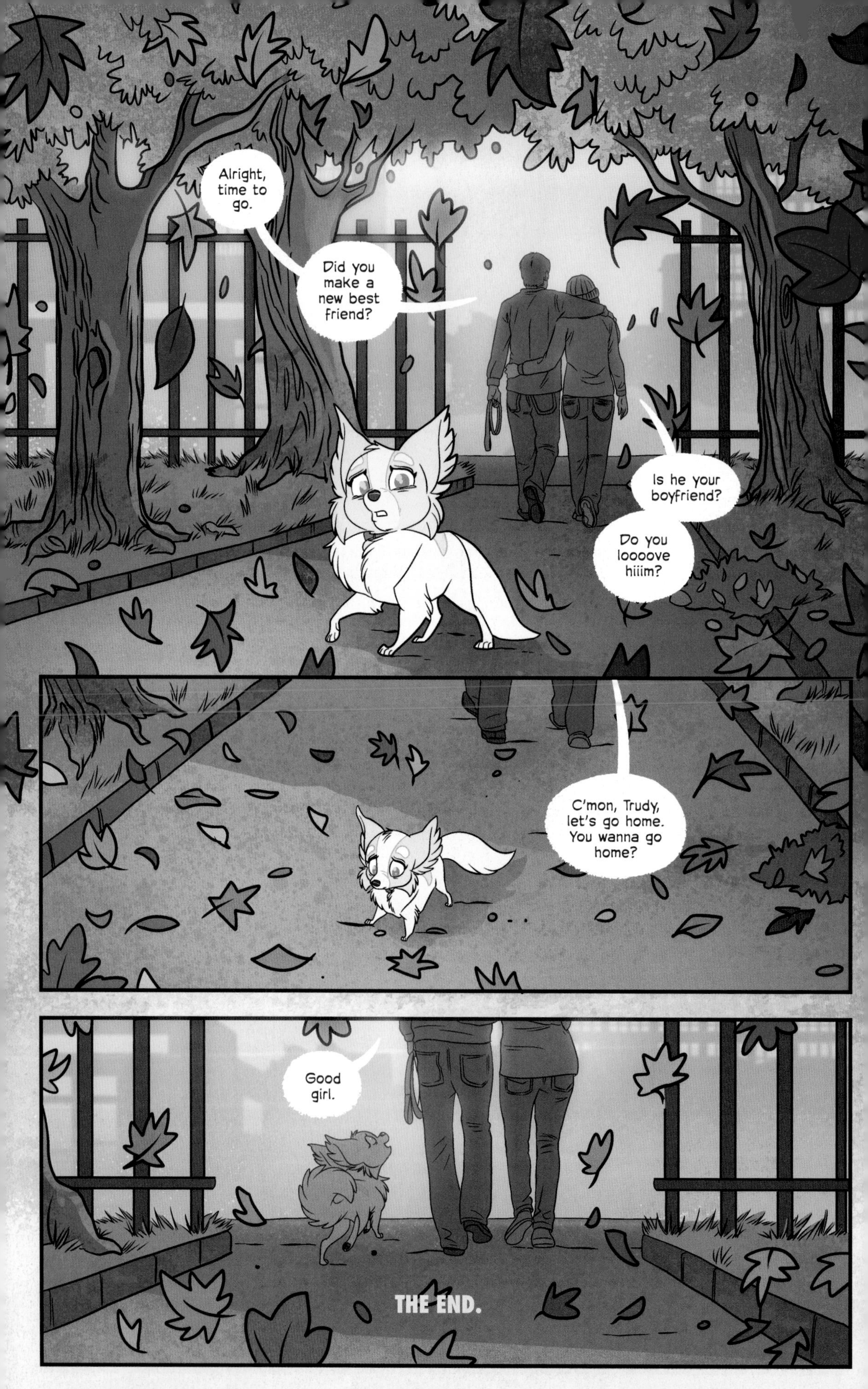
Alright, time to go.
Did you make a new best friend?
Is he your boyfriend?
Do you loooove hiiim?
C'mon, Trudy, let's go home. You wanna go home?
...
Good girl.
THE END.

STRAY DOGS

STRAY DOGS

COVER GALLERY

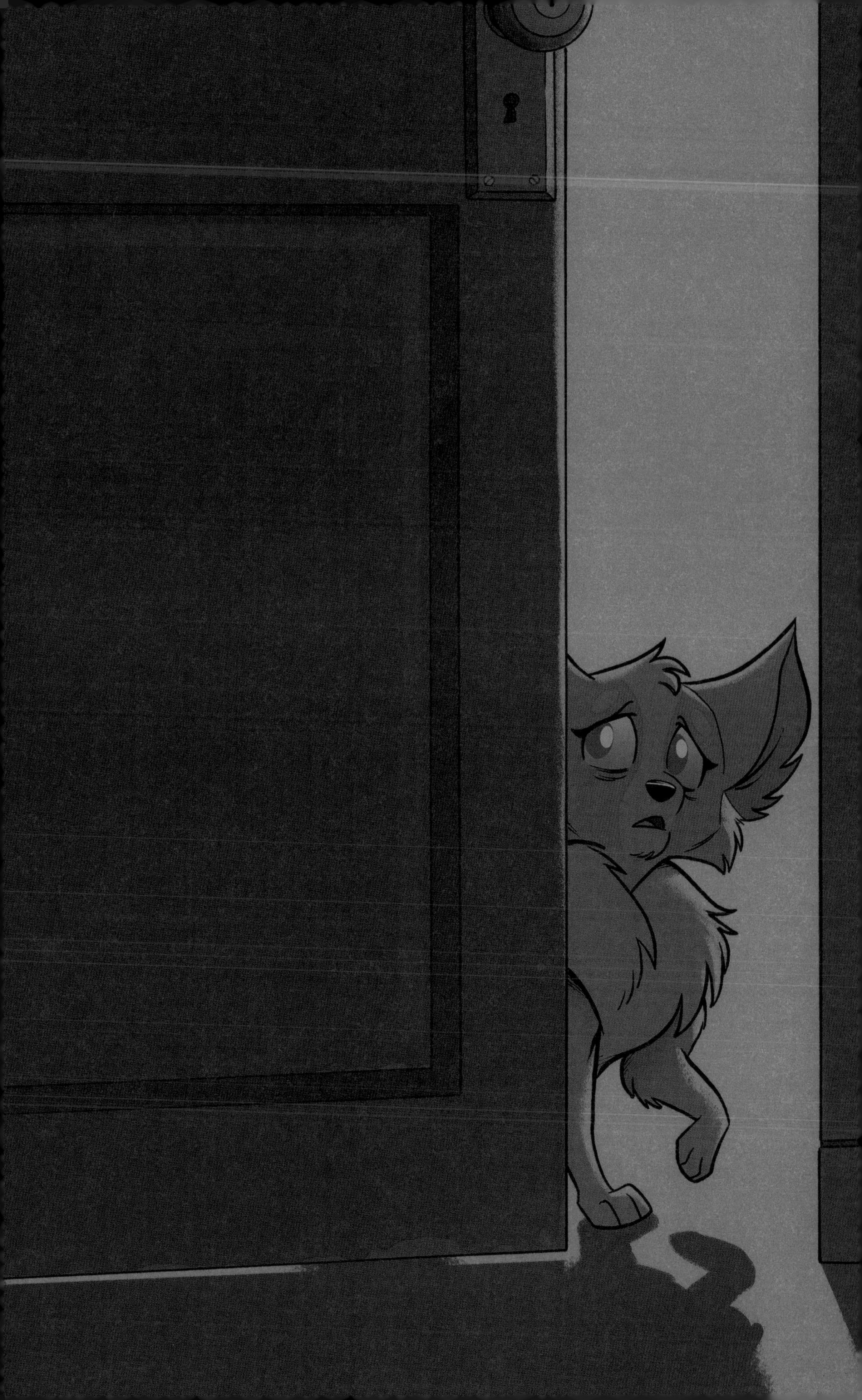

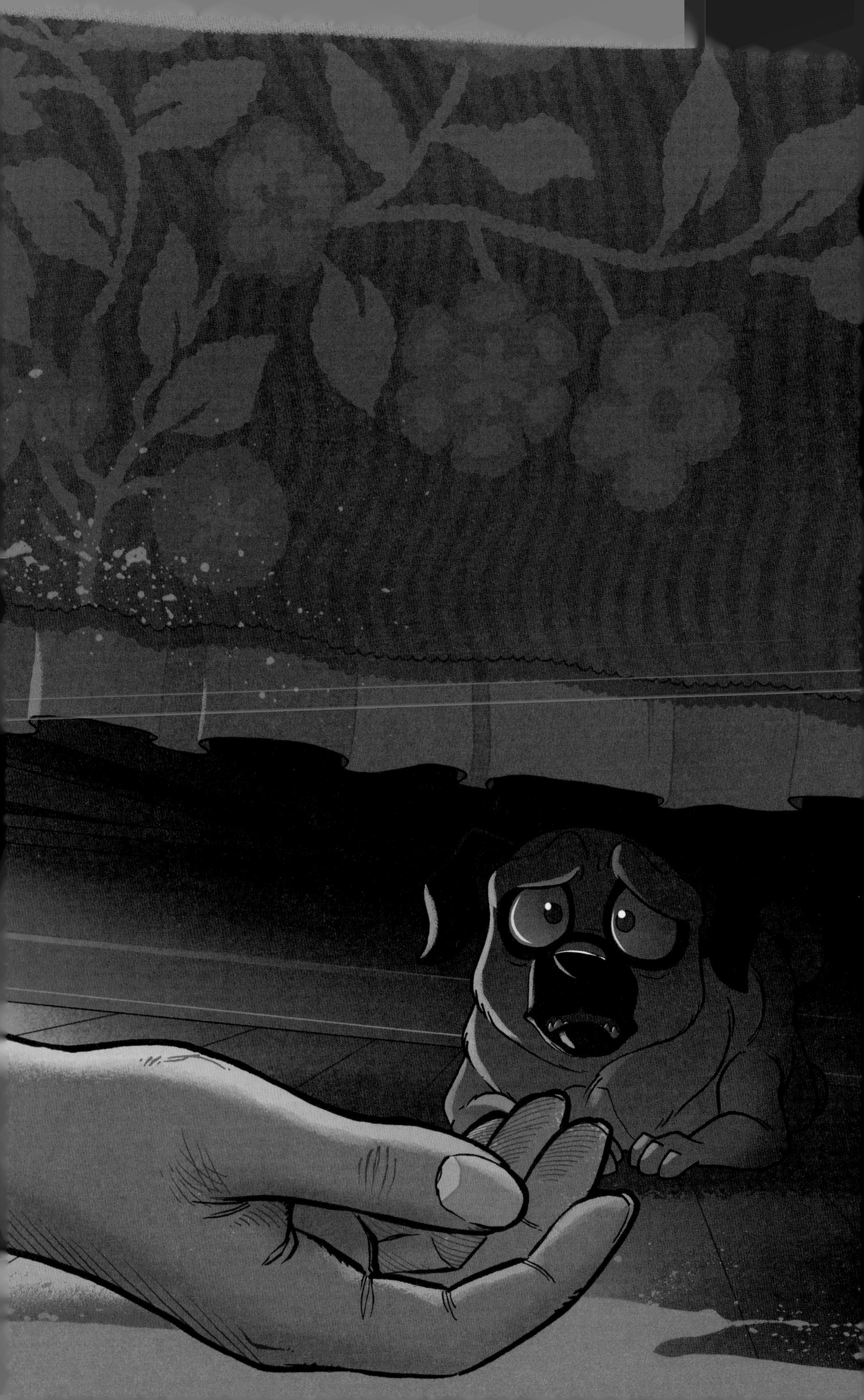

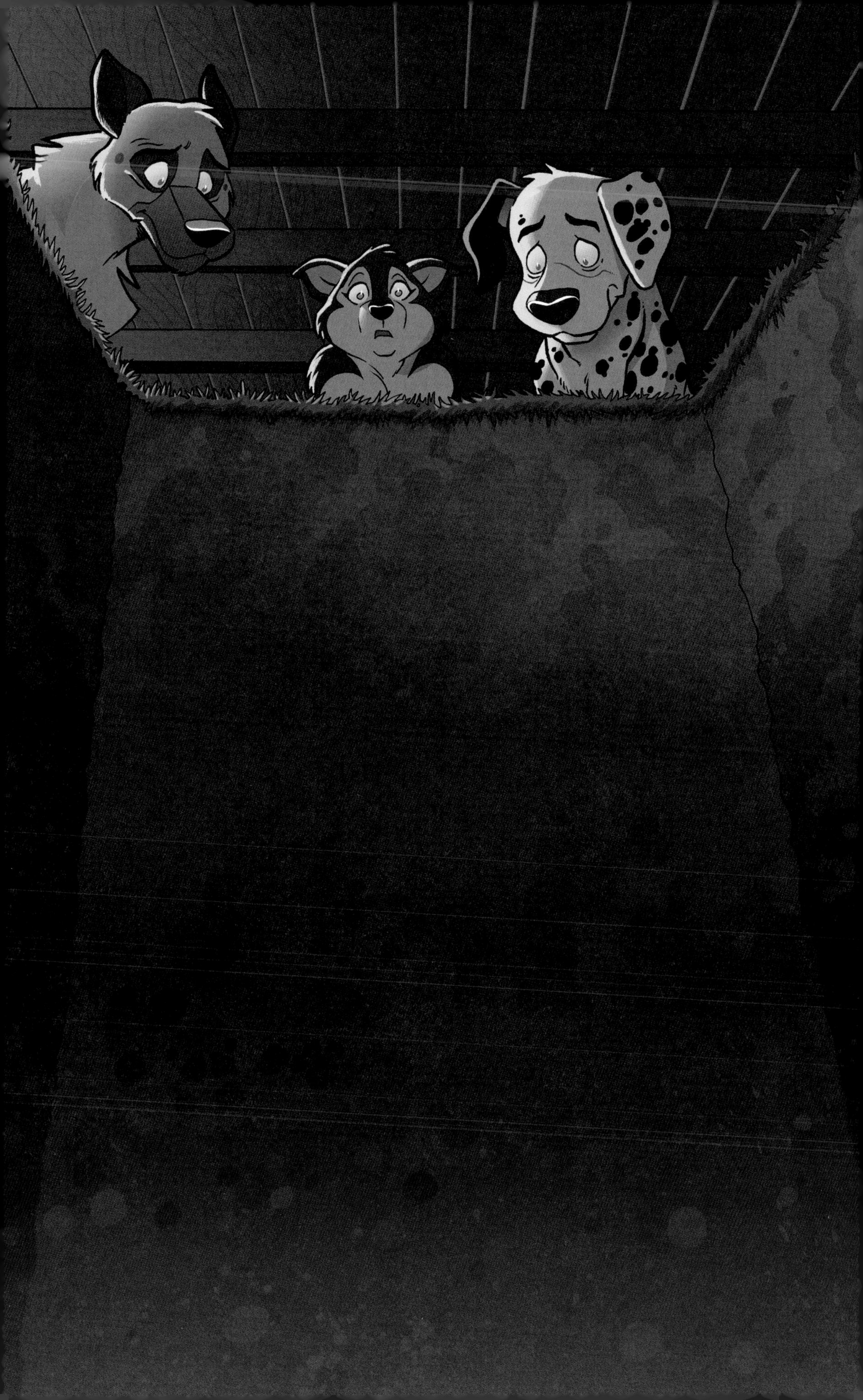

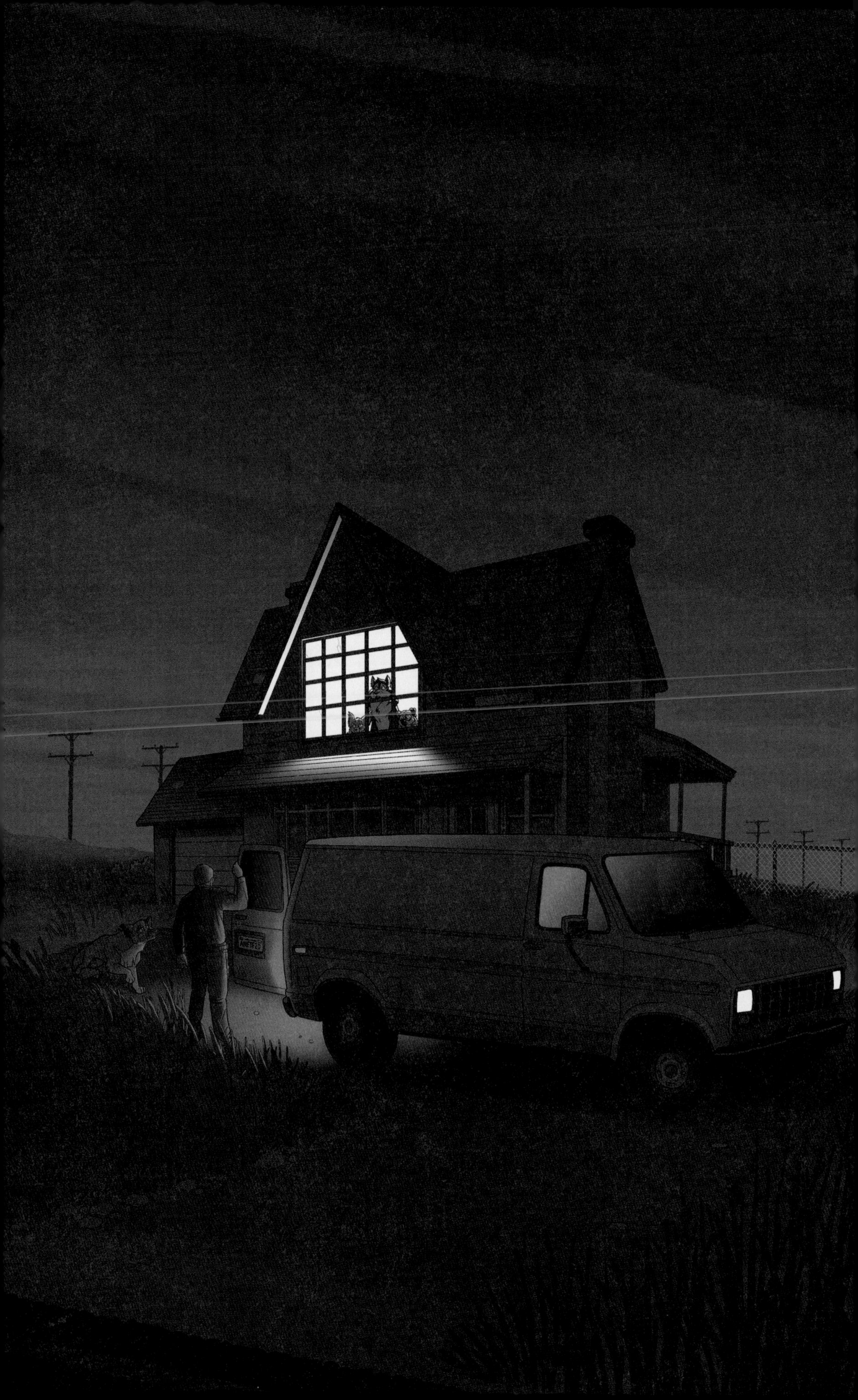

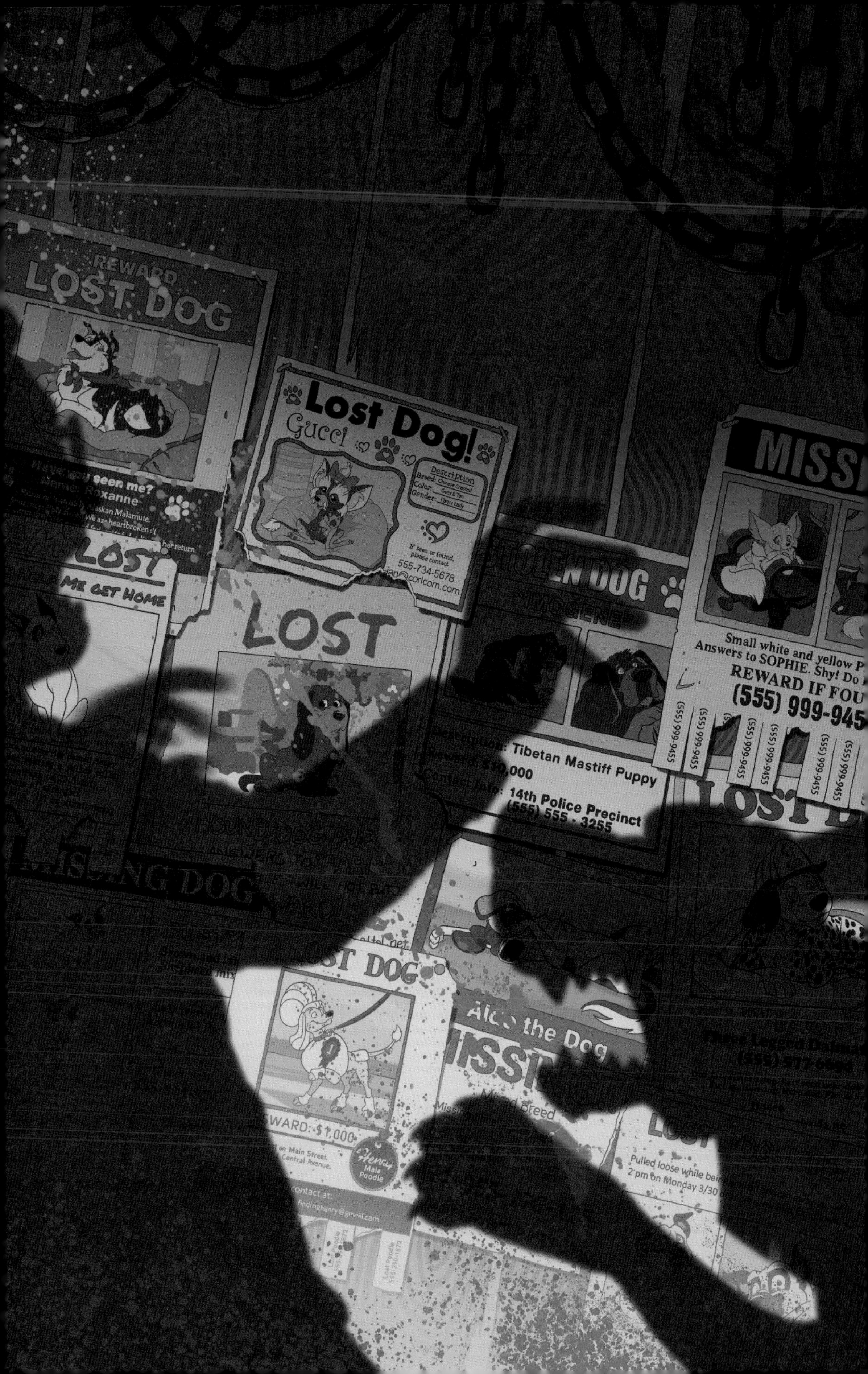
REWARD
LOST DOG
Lost Dog!
Gucci
Description
Breed: Chinese Crested
Color: Grey & Tan
Gender: Fancy Lady
If seen or found, please contact
555-734-5678
LOST
ME GET HOME
LOST
Tibetan Mastiff Puppy
14th Police Precinct
(555) 555 - 3255
Small white and yellow
Answers to SOPHIE. Shy!
REWARD IF FOU
(555) 999-945
(555) 999-9455
LOST DOG
REWARD: $1,000
Henry
Male Poodle
contact at:
findinghenry@gmail.com
Mixed Breed
2 pm on Monday 3/30

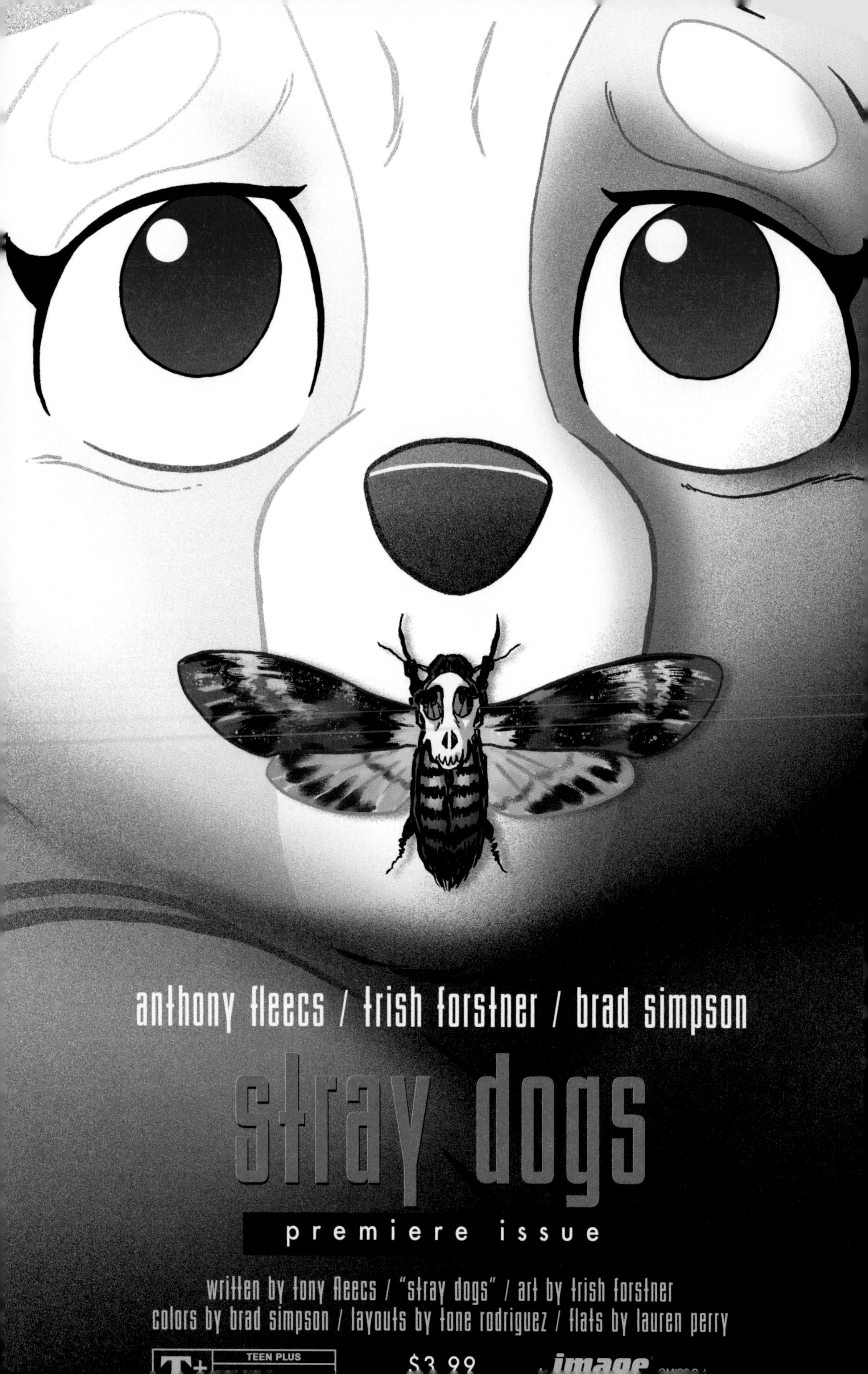
anthony fleecs / trish forstner / brad simpson
stray dogs
premiere issue
written by tony fleecs / "stray dogs" / art by trish forstner
colors by brad simpson / layouts by tone rodriguez / flats by lauren perry
T+ TEEN PLUS
$3.99

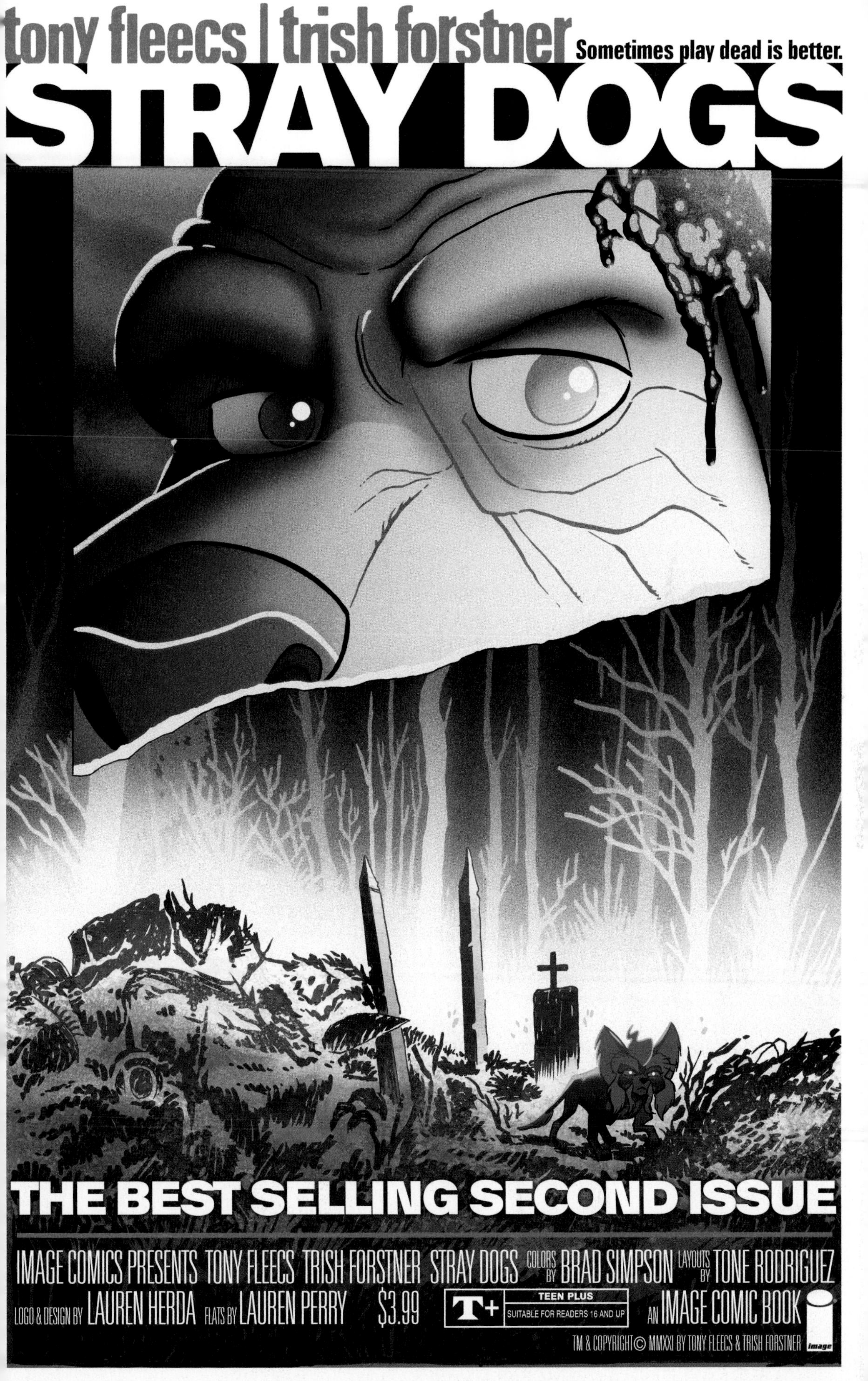

tony fleecs | trish forstner
Sometimes play dead is better.
STRAY DOGS
THE BEST SELLING SECOND ISSUE
IMAGE COMICS PRESENTS TONY FLEECS TRISH FORSTNER STRAY DOGS COLORS BY BRAD SIMPSON LAYOUTS BY TONE RODRIGUEZ
LOGO & DESIGN BY LAUREN HERDA FLATS BY LAUREN PERRY $3.99
T+ TEEN PLUS SUITABLE FOR READERS 16 AND UP
AN IMAGE COMIC BOOK
TM & COPYRIGHT© MMXXI BY TONY FLEECS & TRISH FORSTNER

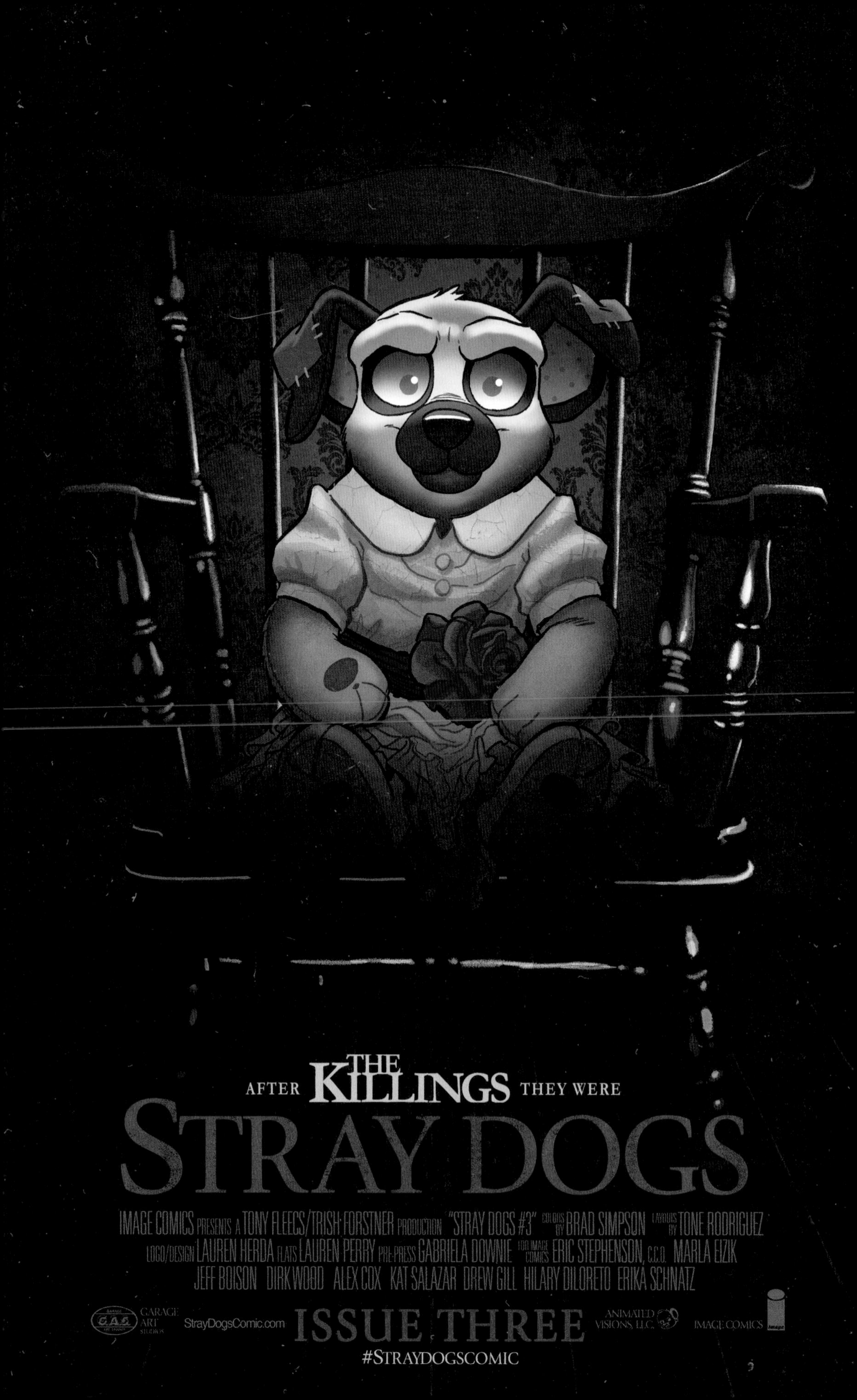
AFTER THE KILLINGS THEY WERE
STRAY DOGS
IMAGE COMICS PRESENTS A TONY FLEECS/TRISH FORSTNER PRODUCTION "STRAY DOGS #3" COLORS BY BRAD SIMPSON LAYOUTS BY TONE RODRIGUEZ
LOGO/DESIGN LAUREN HERDA FLATS LAUREN PERRY PRE-PRESS GABRIELA DOWNIE FOR IMAGE COMICS ERIC STEPHENSON, C.C.O. MARLA EIZIK
JEFF BOISON DIRK WOOD ALEX COX KAT SALAZAR DREW GILL HILARY DILORETO ERIKA SCHNATZ
GARAGE ART STUDIOS
StrayDogsComic.com
ISSUE THREE
ANIMATED VISIONS, LLC
IMAGE COMICS
#STRAYDOGSCOMIC

Something wicked has been unleashed.

IMAGE COMICS

presents

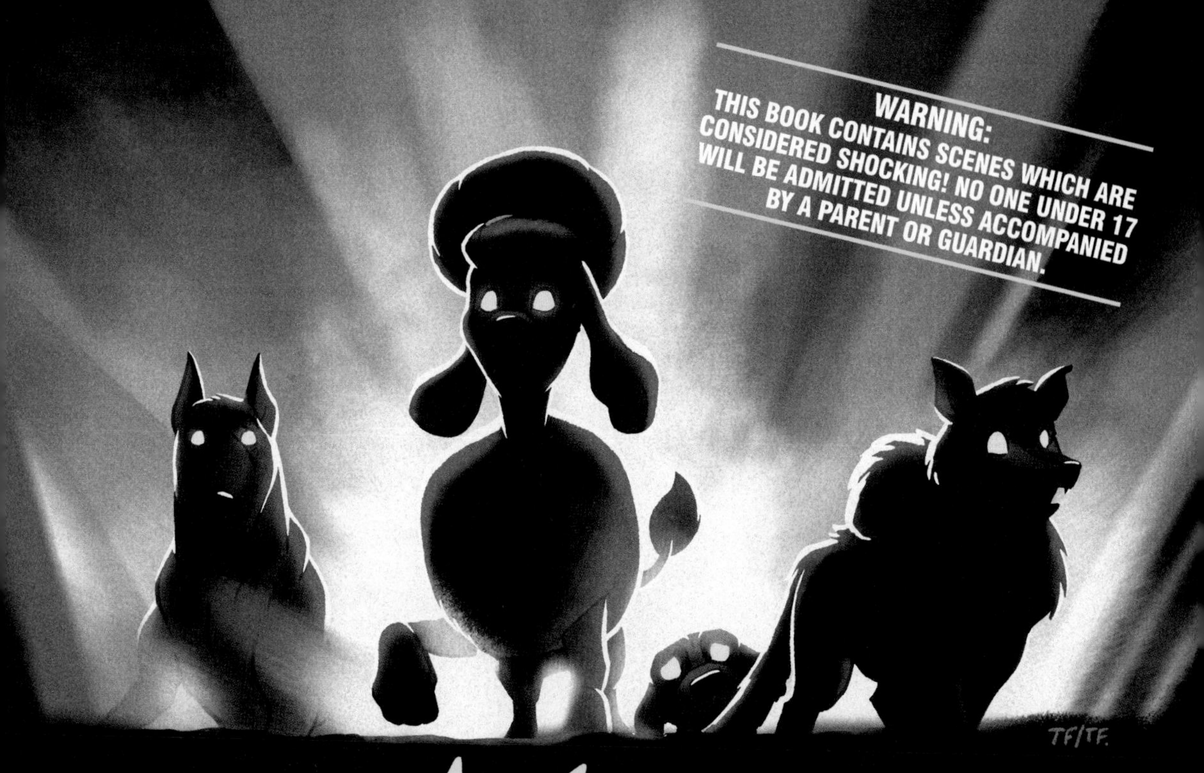
WARNING:
THIS BOOK CONTAINS SCENES WHICH ARE CONSIDERED SHOCKING! NO ONE UNDER 17 WILL BE ADMITTED UNLESS ACCOMPANIED BY A PARENT OR GUARDIAN.
TF/TF.

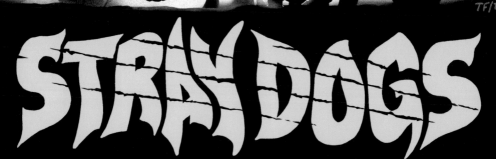

STRAY DOGS

"STRAY DOGS 4"

A Comic By **Fleecs & Forstner**

With:

Tone Rodriguez · Lauren Perry · Lauren Herda
Gabriela Downie

Colors By **BRAD SIMPSON** For **20 EYES STUDIO**

They were hunted...They were taken...
And in the Final Issue, no one will save them.
STRAY DOGS PART V
A 28 page nightmare of terror.
IMAGE COMICS PRESENTS STRAY DOGS #5 A TONY FLEECS/TRISH FORSTNER COMIC WITH BRAD SIMPSON TONE RODRIGUEZ LAUREN PERRY GABRIELA DOWNIE LAUREN HERDA
FOR IMAGE COMICS: ERIC STEPHENSON, C.C.O SHANNA MATUSZAK MARLA EIZIK NICOLE LAPALME LEANNA CAUNTER SUE KORPELA JEFF BOISON DIRK WOOD ALEX COX EMILIO BAUTISTA KAT SALAZAR HEATHER DOORNINK DREW GILL HILARY DILORETO TRICIA RAMOS ERIKA SCHNATZ DEANNA PHELPS
© MMXXI BY TONY FLEECS & TRISH FORSTNER
ALL RIGHTS RESERVED
AN IMAGE COMICS RELEASE
T+ TEEN PLUS
SUITABLE FOR READERS 16 AND UP

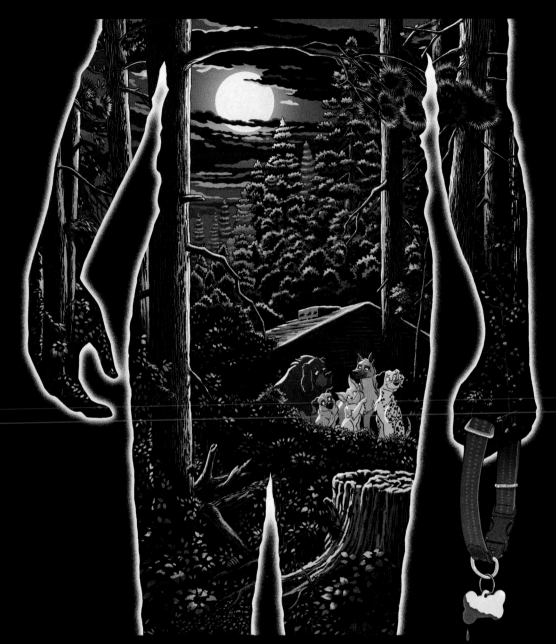

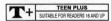

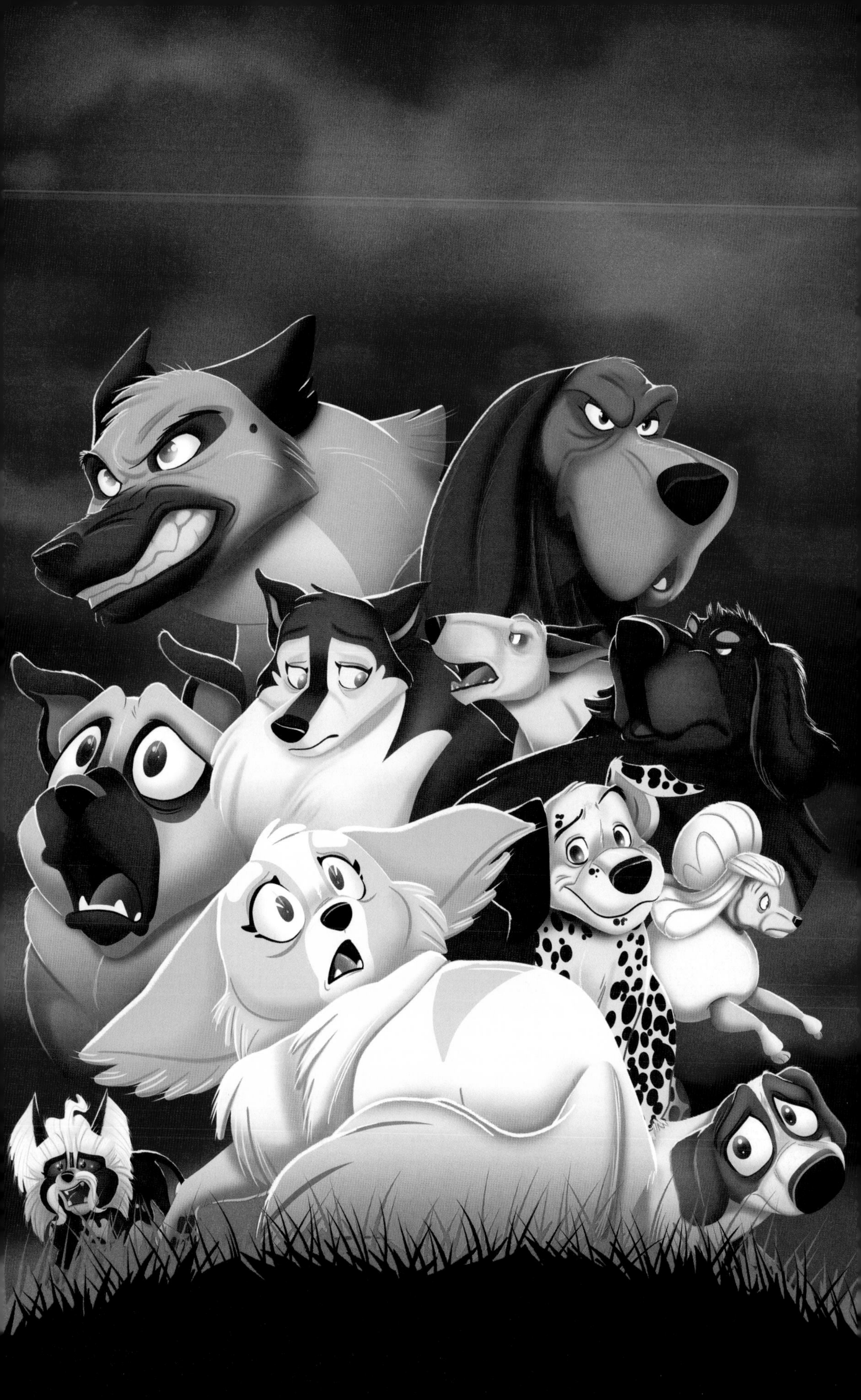

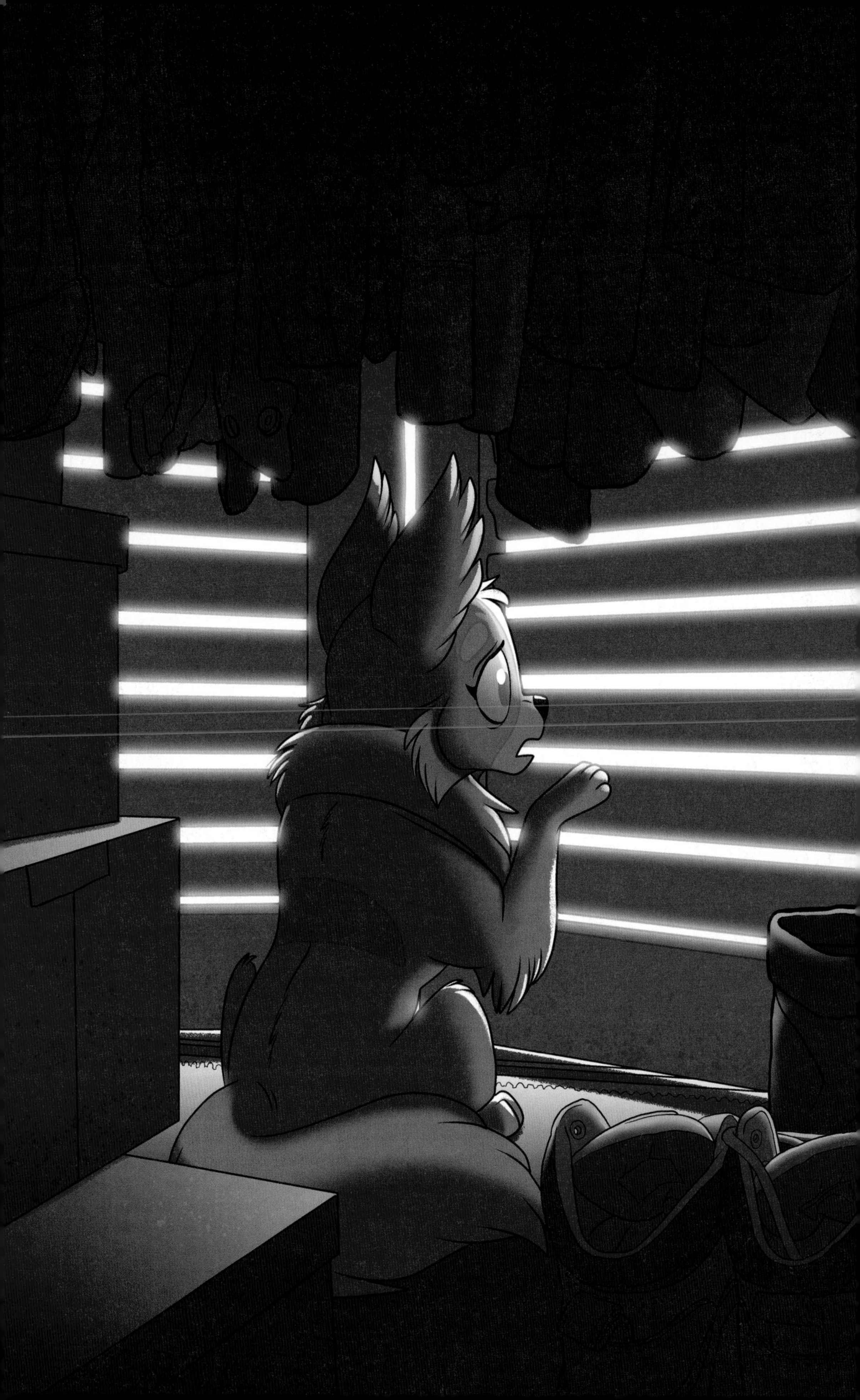

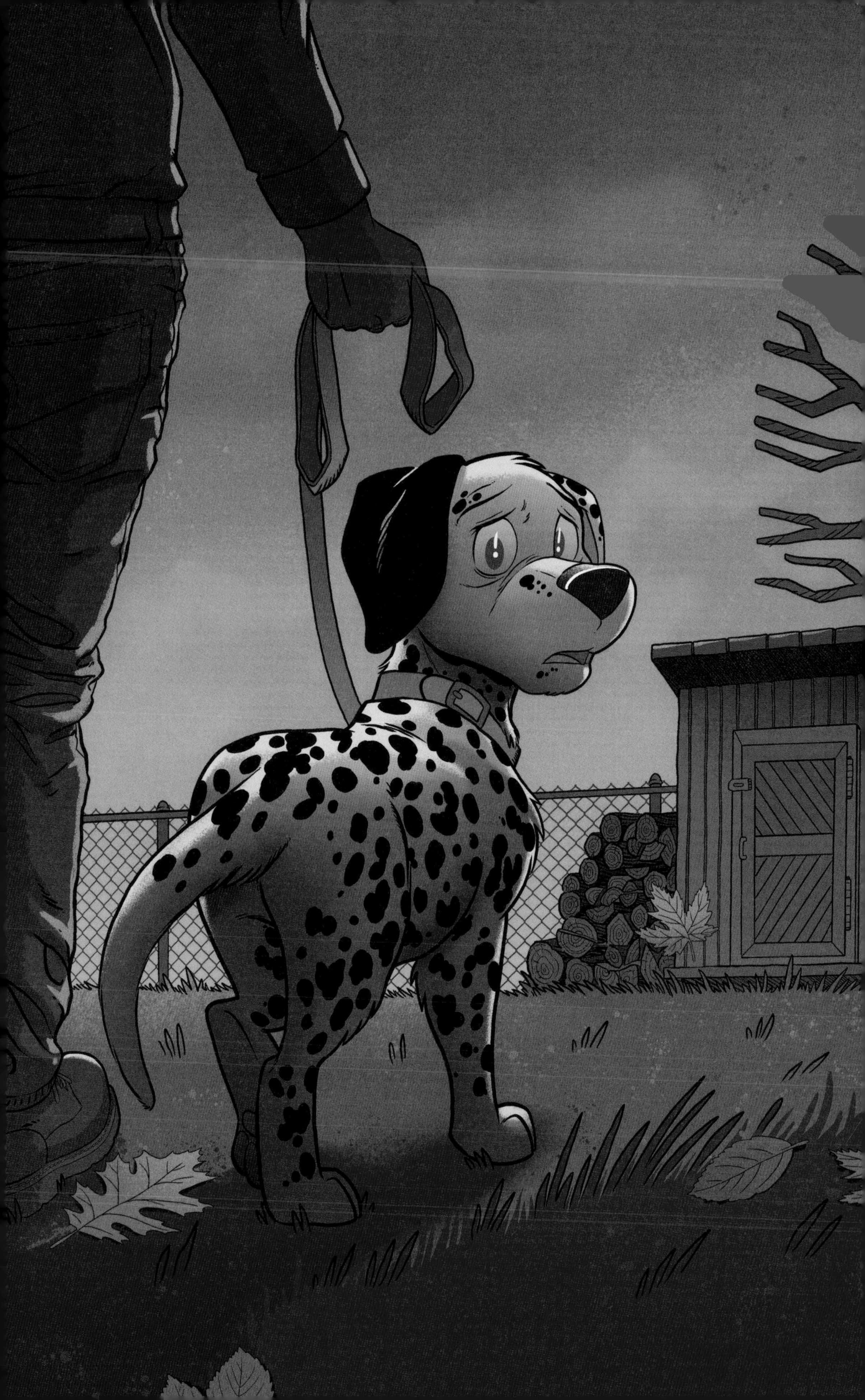

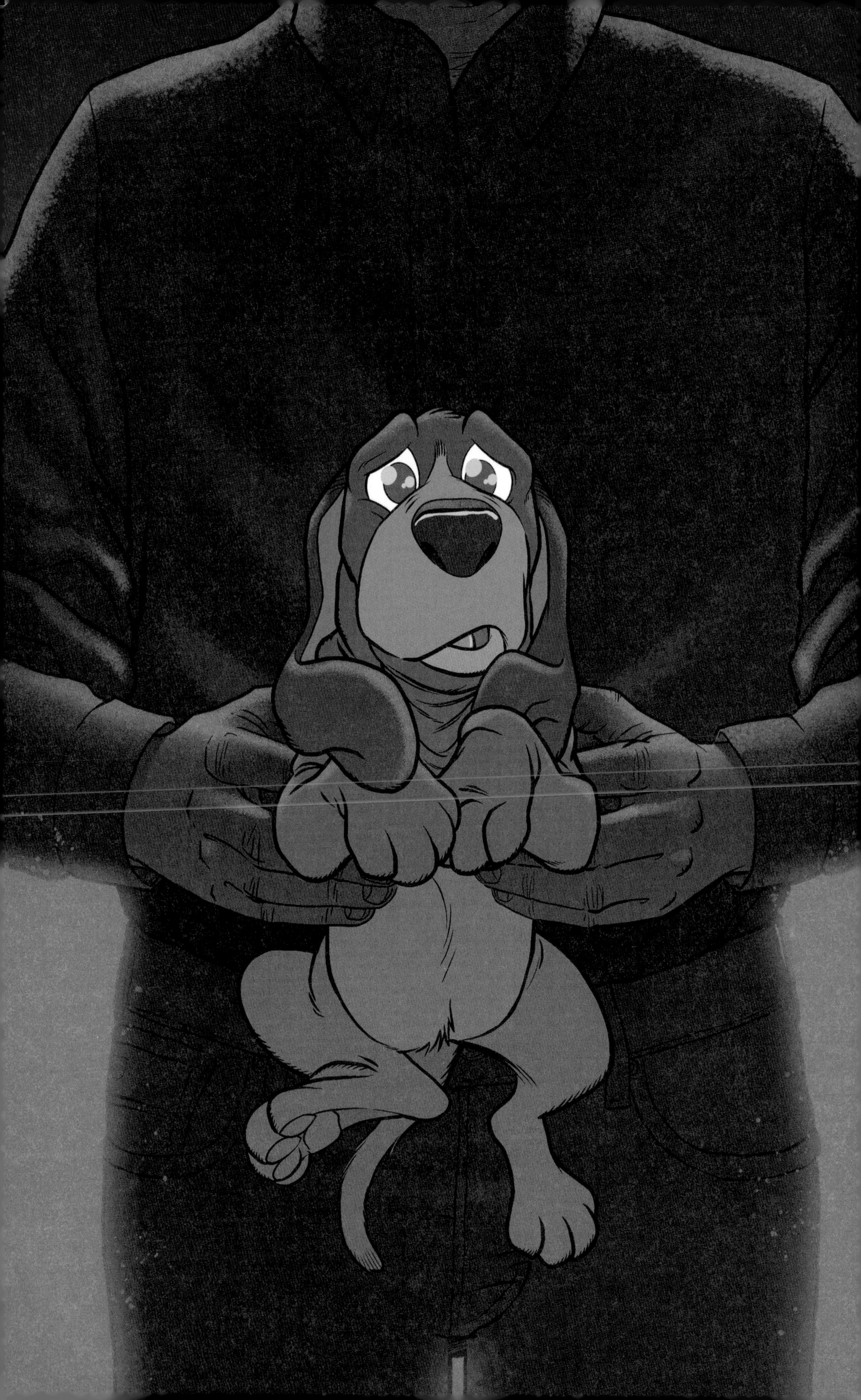

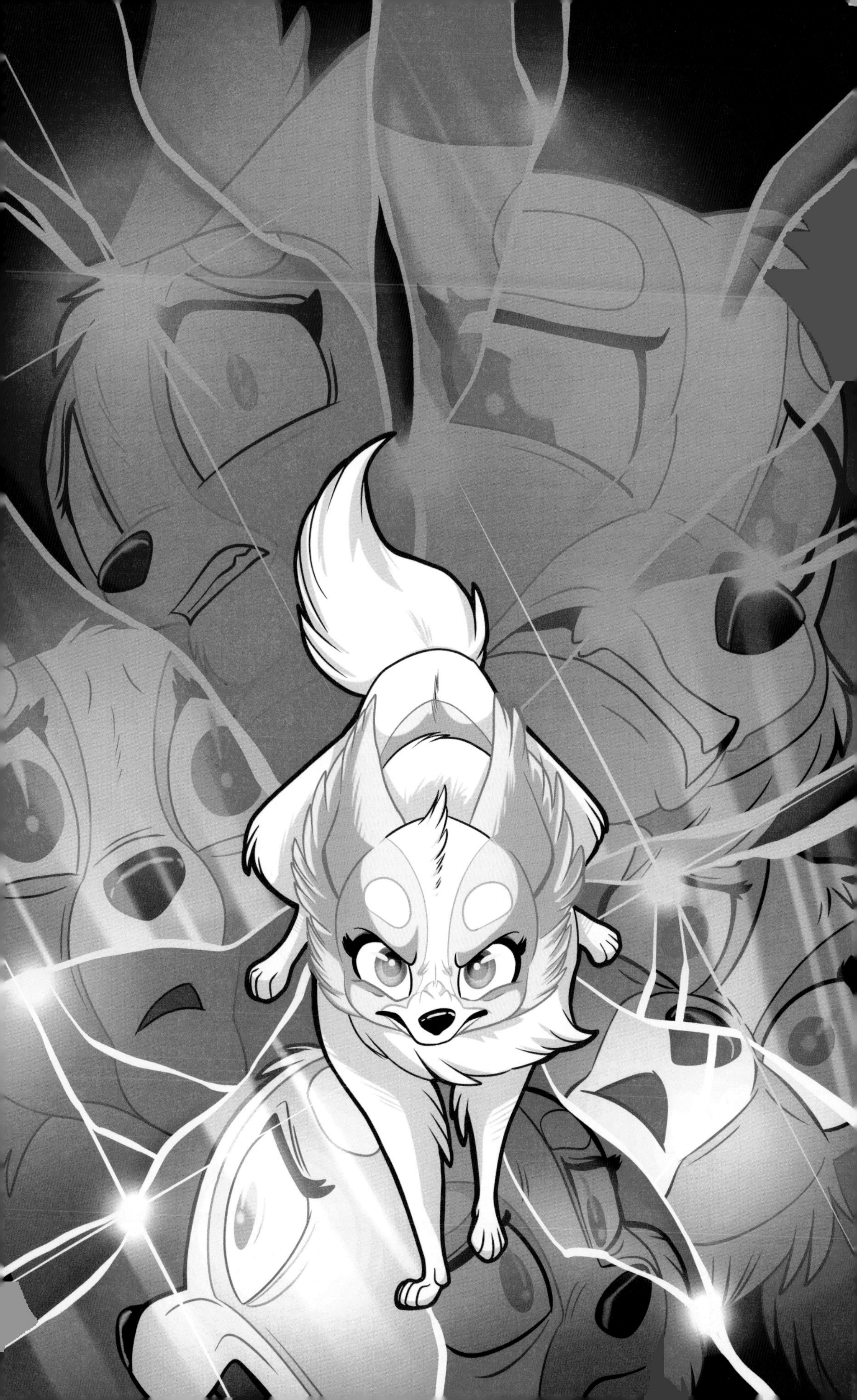

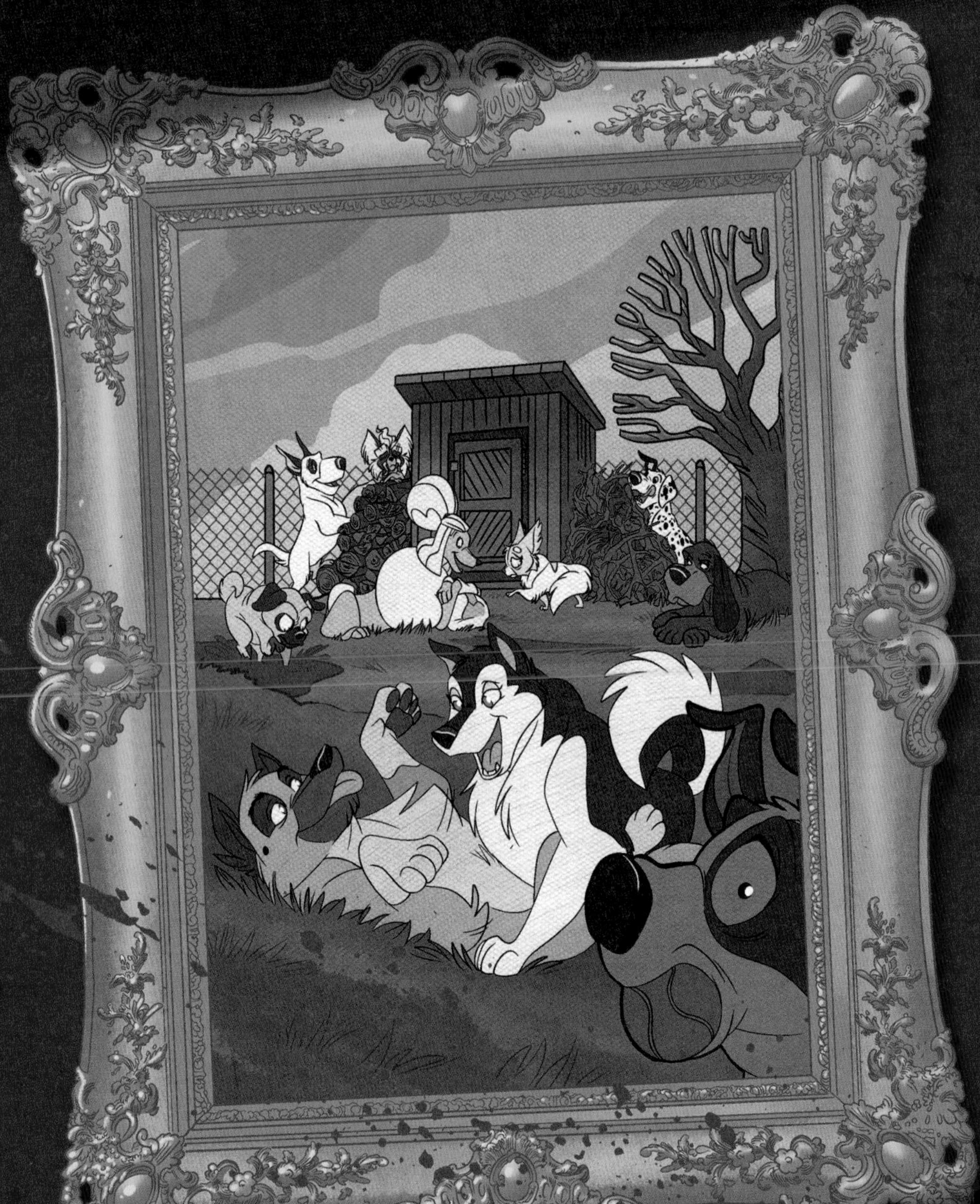

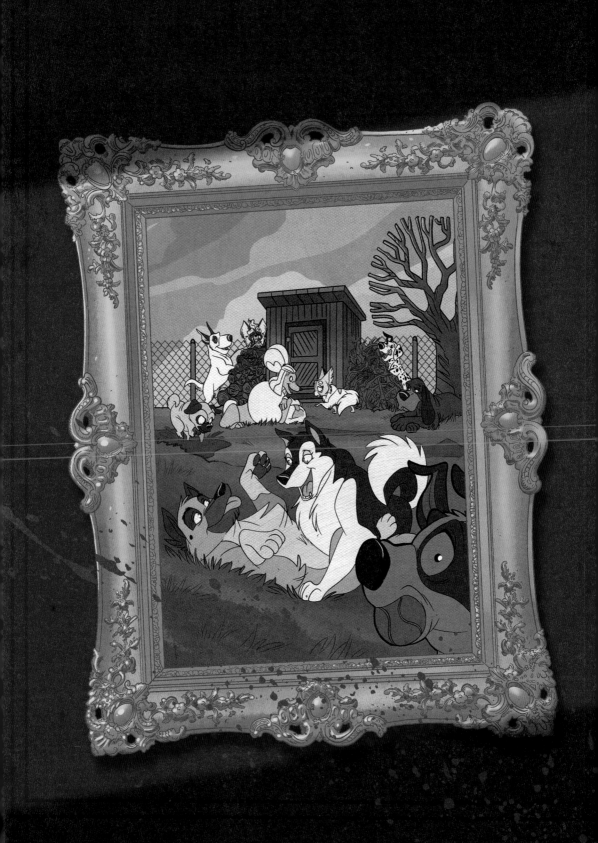

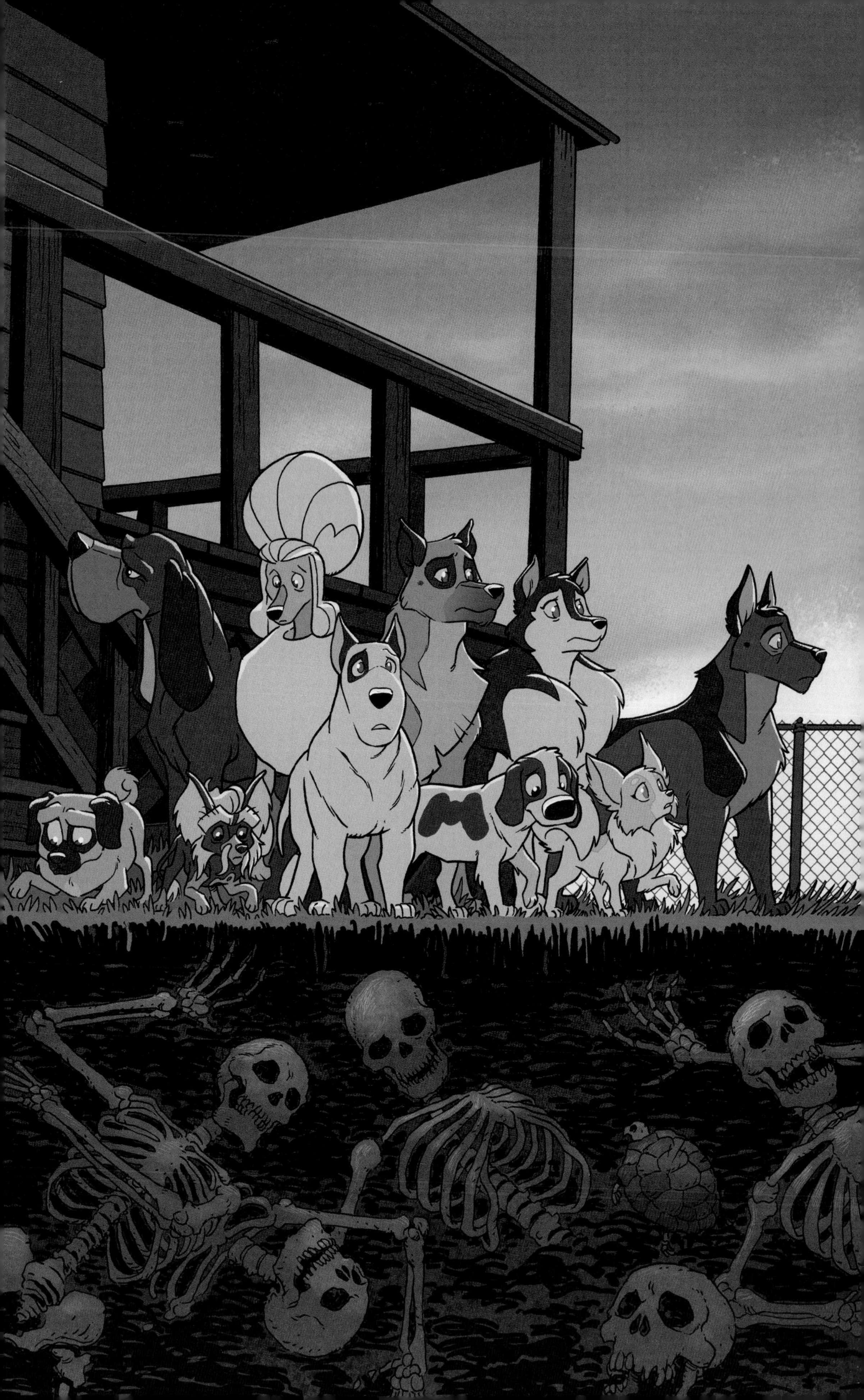

Creator Bios

TONY FLEECS is a prolific, critically acclaimed comic book creator. His licensed comic book work has sold hundreds of thousands of copies in the United States and has been translated and reprinted all over the world. Tony's creator-owned work includes IN MY LIFETIME (2006), JEFF STEINBERG: CHAMPION OF EARTH (2016), and the forthcoming TIME SHOPPER (2021). You've seen his art on some of your favorite titles like *Star Wars*, *Avengers*, *Spider-Man*, *TMNT*, *Transformers* and just a literal TON of *My Little Pony*.

TONYFLEECS.COM

TRISH FORSTNER is a relative newcomer to the comic industry but brings a lifetime of experience in creating fun, lovable characters. She's been drawing since she could hold a pencil. Trish loves classic animation and has drawn influence from many sources, particularly Classic 80s and 90s toons. You've seen her work most recently in IDW's *My Little Pony* comic series.

ANIMATEDVISIONS.COM